THE END IS NOW

THE APOCALYPSE TRIPTYCH

EDITED BY JOHN JOSEPH ADAMS AND HUGH HOWEY

STORIES BY

CHARLIE JANE ANDERS
MEGAN ARKENBERG
ELIZABETH BEAR
ANNIE BELLET
DESIRINA BOSKOVICH
TANANARIVE DUE
JAMIE FORD
HUGH HOWEY
JAKE KERR
NANCY KRESS
SARAH LANGAN
KEN LIU
JONATHAN MABERRY
SEANAN MCGUIRE
WILL MCINTOSH
SCOTT SIGLER
ROBIN WASSERMAN
DAVID WELLINGTON
DANIEL H. WILSON
BEN H. WINTERS

THE END IS NOW

The Apocalypse Triptych, Volume 2

Edited by John Joseph Adams & Hugh Howey
Cover art by Julian Aguilar Faylona
Cover design by Jason Gurley
Interior design by Hugh Howey

ISBN-13: 978-149-748-437-5
ISBN-10: 149-748-437-5

For more about The Apocalypse Triptych:
www.johnjosephadams.com/apocalypse-triptych

First Edition

Printed in the U.S.A

For our readers

TABLE OF CONTENTS

INTRODUCTION

John Joseph Adams

This is the way the world ends
This is the way the world ends
This is the way the world ends
Not with a bang but a whimper.

—T.S. Elliot

The Apocalypse Triptych was conceived as a series of three anthologies, each one covering a different facet of the end of times. Volume one, *The End is Nigh,* contains stories that take place just before the apocalypse. This volume, *The End is Now,* focuses on stories that take place during the apocalypse. And, naturally, volume three, *The End Has Come,* will feature stories that explore life after the apocalypse.

But we were not content to merely assemble a triptych of anthologies; we also wanted *story triptychs* as well. So when we recruited authors for this project, we encouraged them to consider writing not just one story for us, but one story for each volume, and connecting them so that the reader gets a series of mini-triptychs within The Apocalypse Triptych. So several of the stories contained in this anthology—seventeen of the twenty tales—have related stories in *The End is Nigh,* and many will continue on in *The End Has Come* as well.

If you're one of the readers who read and enjoyed volume one: Thank you! We're glad to see you returning for volume two. You made the first volume a resounding success, and we couldn't be more thrilled with both how well the book's done in the marketplace—it got all the way up to #11 on the Amazon bestseller list—and with how well it's been received by readers and critics.

If you're a reader who has not read *The End is Nigh*: Welcome! And fear not: You needn't have read the first volume in order to enjoy the stories in this one. Although several of the stories in *The End is Now* are continuations of storylines that began in *The End is Nigh,* we're confident that the authors have provided sufficient context that you can jump into these stories without any prior knowledge.

• • •

The viruses have become pandemics. The aliens have invaded. The zombies have risen. The asteroids have collided. The revolutions have been televised.

This is the end.

It is happening now.

Cataclysm.

Apocalypse.

The end of the world as we know it.

Armageddon, the end of everything.

As civilization falls apart.

As the world burns.

Now behold the conflagration.

THE END IS NOW

The Apocalypse Triptych, Volume 2

HERD IMMUNITY

Tananarive Due

A man was far ahead of her on the road. Walking and breathing. So far, so good.

That he was a man, Nayima was certain. His silhouette against the horizon of the rising roadway showed his masculine height and the shadow of an unkempt beard. He pulled his belongings behind him in an overnight suitcase like a business traveler. Maybe she trusted him on sight because of the unmistakable shape of a guitar case slung across his back. She'd always had a thing for musicians.

"*Hey*!" she screamed, startling herself with her bald desperation.

He paused, his steady legs falling still. He might have turned around. She couldn't quite make out his movements in the quarter-mile or more that separated them. The two of them, alone, were surrounded on either side by the golden ocean of central California farmland, unharvested and unplowed, no trees or shade in sight as the road snaked up the hillside.

His attention gave her pause. She hadn't seen anyone walking in so long that she'd forgotten the plan that had kept her alive the past nine months: Hide. Observe. Assess.

But fuck it.

She waved and called again, so he would be certain she wasn't a mirage in the heat.

"Hey!" she screamed, more hoarsely. She tried to run toward him, but her legs only lurched a stagger on the sharp grade. She was dizzy from heat and modulated hunger. The sky dimmed above her, so she stopped her pathetic chase and braced her palms against her knees to calm the cannon bursts from her heart. The world grew bright again.

He walked on. She watched him shrink until the horizon swallowed him. She remembered a time when terrifying loneliness would have made her cry. Instead, she began following him at the pace her body had grown accustomed to. He didn't seem afraid of her; that was something. He hadn't quickened. He was tired and slow, like her. If she was patient, she would catch up to him.

Nayima hadn't planned to stay on State Road 46 toward Lost Hills. She had wanted to follow the last highway sign—one of the few conveniences still in perfect working order—toward a town just ten miles east. But she decided to follow the man instead. Just for a while, she'd told herself. Not so far that she'd run too low on water or go hungry.

Nayima followed him for three days.

She wasted no energy or hope checking the scattered vehicles parked at odd angles for fuel or food, although most still had their keys. She was far too late for *that* party. Cars were shelter. Handy when it rained. Or when it was dark and mountain lions got brave, their eyes glowing white in her flashlight beam. ("Bad, bad kitty," she always said.)

The cars on SR-46 weren't battered and broken like the ones in Bakersfield, witnesses to riots or robberies. For a time, carjacking had been the national hobby. She'd jacked a car herself trying to get out of that hellhole—with a sprained ankle and a small mob chasing her, she'd needed the ride more than the acne-scarred drunk sleeping at the wheel. On the 46, the pristine cars had come to rest, their colors muted by a thin veil of burial dust.

Nayima missed her red Schwinn, but she'd hit a rock the day before she'd seen the man on the road—the demon stone appeared in her path and knocked her bicycle down an embankment. She'd been lucky only to bump her elbow hard enough to make her yell. But her bike, gone. Crumpled beyond salvage. Nayima didn't allow herself to miss much—but damn. And this man, her new day job, meant she didn't have time to peel off to look for tucked-away farmhouses and their goodies. Too risky. She might lose him. Instead, Nayima walked on, following her ghost.

She imagined how they would talk. Testify. Teach what little they knew. Start something. Maybe he could at least tell her why he was on the 46, what radio broadcast or quest had beckoned. She hadn't heard anything except hissing on radios in three months. She didn't mind walking a long distance if she might arrive somewhere eventually.

Each morning she woke from her resting place—the crook of a tree, an abandoned car that wasn't a tomb, in the cranny beneath the inexplicably locked cab of an empty eighteen-wheeler parked ten yards off the road like a beached whale—and wondered if the man had gone too far ahead. If he'd walked the whole night just to shake her. If he'd found a car that had sung him a love song when he caressed her and turned the key.

But each day, she saw signs that he was not lost. He was still walking ahead, somewhere just out of sight. Any evidence of him dampened her palms.

He left a trail of candy wrappers. Chocolate bars mostly; always the minis. Snickers, Twix, Almond Joy (her favorite; that wrapper made her stomach shout at the sight). Her own meals were similarly monotonous, but not nearly as colorful—handfuls of primate feed she'd found overlooked at a vet's office outside Bakersfield. Her backpack was stuffed with the round, brown nuggets. Monkey Balls, she called them. They didn't taste like much, but they opened up her time for walking and weren't nearly as heavy as cans.

On the third morning, when the horizon again stretched empty, and sinking dread bubbled in her stomach, the road greeted her with a package of Twizzlers, six unruined sticks still inside. The Twizzlers seemed fresh. She could feel his fingertips on the wrapper. The candy was warm to her tongue from the sun. So good it brought happy tears. She stood still as long as she dared while the sweetness flooded her dry mouth, coated her throat. Feeling anything was a novelty.

She cried easily over small pleasures: a liquid orange sunset, the wild horses she'd seen roaming a field, freed to their original destiny. She wondered if he had left her the Twizzlers in a survivors' courtship rite, until she found a half-eaten rope of the red candy discarded a few steps away. A Red Vines man, then. She could live with that. They would work it out.

By noon on Twizzlers Day, she saw him again, a long shadow stretching only half a mile ahead of her. Time was, she could have jogged to catch up to him easily, but the idea of hurry made her want to vomit. Her stomach wasn't as happy with the candy feast as the rest of her.

So she walked.

He passed a large wooden sign—not quite a billboard, but big—and when she followed behind him, she read the happy script:

COUNTY LINE ROAD FAIR!!!!
June 1-30 2 MI

Beneath that, cartoon renderings of pigs with blue ribbons, a hot dog grinning in his bun, and a Ferris wheel. A dull fucking name for a fair, she thought. Or a road, for that matter. She vowed that when the renaming of things began, she and the man on the road would do better. The Fair of Ultimate Rainbows, on Ultimate Rainbow Road. A name worthy of the sign's colors.

She was nearly close enough to touch the sign before she made out the papers tacked on the right side, three age-faded, identical handbills in a vertical line:

RESCUE CENTER

Stamped with a Red Cross insignia.

Red Crap. Red Death. Red Loss.

Nayima fought dueling urges to laugh and scream. Her legs nearly buckled in rebellion. The sun felt ten degrees hotter, sizzling her neck.

"You have got to be goddamn kidding," she said.

The man on the road could not hear her.

She cupped her hands to her mouth. "*Do you still believe there's a Wizard too?*"

Moron.

But she kept the last word silent. She shouldn't be rude. They needed to get along.

He didn't stop walking, but he gave her a grumpy old man wave over his shoulder. Finally—communication. Candor was the greatest courtesy in the land of the Seventy-Two Hour Flu, so she told him the truth. "They're just big Petri dishes, you know! Best way to get sick is in evac camps! *Was,* I mean. Sorry to bear bad news, but there's no rescue center here!"

Nine months ago, she would have believed in that sign. She'd believed in her share. Back when the best minds preached hope for a vaccine that would help communities avoid getting sick with precautions, she'd heard the term on the CDC and WHO press conferences: *herd immunity.* As it turned out, the vaccine was a fable and *herd immunity* was an oxymoron.

Only NIs were left now: naturally immune. The only people she'd seen since June were other NIs floating through the rubble, shy about contact for fear of the attacks of rage and mass insanity. Nayima had escaped Bakersfield, where anyone walking with pep was a traitor to the human experience. Nayima had seen radiant satisfaction on the face of an axe-wielding old woman who, with her last gasps of breath, had split open the skull of the NI nurse offering her a sip of water. No good deed, as they say. This man was the first NI she'd met on the road in the three months since.

The formerly populated areas would be quieter now. That was the thing about the Seventy-Two-Hour Flu: it settled disputes quickly. The buzzards were building new kingdoms in the cities, their day come at last.

"*The dead can't rescue the living!*" Nayima shouted up the godless road.

Her new friend kept walking. No matter. He would be stopping in two miles anyway.

She could smell the fair already.

• • •

She thought *maybe, just maybe*—not enough to speed her heart, but enough to make her eyes go sharp—when the rows of neatly parked cars appeared on the west side of the road. A makeshift parking lot, with rows designated in letter-number pairs on new cedar poles, A-1 through M-20. Because of the daylight's furious glare across the chrome and glass, the cars seemed to glitter like fairy-tale carriages. It was the most order Nayima had seen in months.

Then she saw the dust across their windows.

Everywhere she went, too late for the party. Even at the fair.

Buzzards and crows sat atop the COUNTY LINE ROAD FAIR—FREE PARKING banner, bright white and red, that hung across the gravel driveway from SR-46. The Ferris wheel stood frozen beyond, marking where the fair began, but it was so small it seemed sickly. The cartoon had been so much grander. Everything about the sign had been a lie.

The sound of mournful guitar came—picking, not strumming. She had never heard the melody before, but she knew the song well. The Seventy-Two-Hour Blues.

In the parking lot, she glanced through enough rear windows to start smiling. The Corolla had a backpack in plain sight. A few had keys in their ignitions. One was bound to have gas. This was a car lot Christmas sale. The cars on the road were from the people who'd given up on driving and left nothing behind. These cars were satisfied at their destination, although their drivers had left unfinished business inside. A few cars with windows cracked open stank of dead pets; she saw a large dog's white fur carpeting the back seat floor of a Ford Explorer. A child's baseball cap near the fur made her think of a pudgy-cheeked boy giving his dog a last hug before his parents hurried him away.

The cars screamed stories.

She saw her own face in the window. Hooded. Brown face sun-darkened by two shades. Jaw thin, showing too much bone. *You gotta eat, girl,* Gram would say. Nayima blinked and looked away from the stranger in the glass.

Tears. Damn, damn, damn.

Nayima dug her fingernails into her palm, hard. She drew blood. The cars went silent.

The guitar player could claim he'd found the treasure first, but there was enough to share. She had a .38 if he needed convincing, but she hoped it wouldn't come to that. Even the idea of her .38 made her feel sullied. She didn't want to hurt him. She didn't want him to try to hurt her. She wanted the opposite; someone to keep watch while she slept, to help her find food, to keep her warm. She couldn't remember the last time she'd wanted anything so badly.

The music soothed the graveyard in the parking lot. The guitarist might be the best musician she would ever know; just enough sour, not too much sweet. He was playing a song her grandmother might have hummed, but had forgotten to teach her.

Dear Old Testament God of Noah, please don't let him be another asshole.

He was out of sight again, so she followed the music through the remains of the fair.

The Ferris wheel wasn't the only no-frills part of the County Line Road Fair, which had been named right after all. She counted fewer than a dozen rides—the anemic Ferris wheel was the belle of the ball. The rest was two kiddie fake pony rides she might have found at a good-sized shopping mall, a merry-go-round with mermaids among the horses (that one actually wasn't too bad), a spinner ride in cars for four she'd always hated because she got crushed from centrifugal force; and a Haunted Castle with empty cars waiting to slip into the mouth of hellfire. A giant with a molten face guarded the castle's door, draped in black rags. Even now the Haunted Castle scared her. As she passed it, she spat into one of the waiting cars.

Crows scattered as she walked.

This fair was organized like all small fairs—a row of games on one side, food vendors on the other. Birds and scavengers had picked over the empty paper popcorn cups and foil hot dog wrappers, but only a few of the vendors had locked their booths tight with aluminum panels. A large deep fryer stood in plain sight at Joe's Beef Franks as she passed—nothing but an open doorway between them—so she was free to explore. Cabinets. Trash. Counters. So many possibilities. Now her heartbeat did speed up.

With a car and enough essential items, she could think about a future somewhere. The guitar seemed to agree, picking up tempo and passion. The music reminded her that she didn't have to be alone in her getaway car.

Words were nearly useless now, so she didn't speak right away when she found his camp alongside the elephant ear vendor's booth. He had laid out a sleeping bag in the shade of the awning promising "Taysteee Treets," his back supported against the booth. She stood across the fairway by the ring-toss and took him in.

First surprise: he was wearing a dust mask. A summer look for the fall. Ridiculous.

The mask was particularly disappointing because it was already hard to make out his face beneath his hair and the dirt. He had light brown skin, she guessed, a dark tangle of thinly textured hair, a half-fed build to match hers. He looked nearly a foot taller, so he would have an advantage if they had to fight. Nayima slipped her hand to the compartment in her backpack she kept in easy reach. She took hold of the gun slowly, but she didn't pull it out.

"Guitar's mine to keep, and nothin' else is worth taking," he said. His voice was gravel. "Grab your pick of whatever you find here and move on."

"You think I followed you three days to rob you?"

"I don't try to guess why."

Nayima shook off her light jacket's hood. She'd shaved her head in Bakersfield so she wouldn't be such an obvious rape target. Most of her hair was close to her scalp—but she had a woman's face. She imagined his eyes flickering, just a flash.

"I'm Nayima," she said.

He concentrated on his guitar strings. "Keep your distance."

"You're immune." Dummy. She didn't call him names, but it dripped in her voice.

He stopped playing. "Who says?"

"You do," she said. "Because you're still breathing."

He went back to playing, uninterested.

"Let me guess," she said. "Everyone in your family got sick and died—including people you saw every day—but you never got even a tummy-ache."

"I was careful."

"You think you're still alive because you're smarter than the rest?"

"I didn't say that." He sounded angry. "But I was very careful."

"No touching? No breathing?"

"Yes. Even learned how to play with these on." He held up his right hand. She hadn't seen his thin, dirty gloves at first glance.

"Your fingertips never brushed a countertop or a window pane or a slip of paper?"

"Doing my best."

"You never once got unlucky."

"Until now, I guess," he said.

"Bullshit," she said. Now she felt angry. More hurt, but angry too. She hadn't realized any stranger still held the power to hurt her feelings, or that any feelings were still so raw. "You're living scared. You're like one of those Japanese soldiers in World War II who didn't know the war was over."

"You think it's all over. In less than a year."

"Might as well be. Look how fast the UK went down."

His eyes dropped away. Plenty had happened since, but London had been the first proof that China's Seventy-Two Hour Virus was waging a world war instead of only a genocide. Cases hadn't appeared in the U.S. until a full two days after London burned—those last two days of worry over the problems that seemed far away, people that were none of their business. The televisions had still been working, so they had all heard the news unfolding. An entire tribe at the fire, just before the rains.

"What have you seen?" Finally, he wasn't trying to push her away.

"I can only report on Southern and Central California. Almost everybody's gone. The rest of us, we're spread out. You're the only breather I've seen in two months. That's why it's time for us to stop hiding and start finding each other."

"'Us?'" he repeated, hitched brow incredulous.

"NIs," she said. "Naturally Immunes. One in ten thousand, but that's a guess."

"Jesus." A worthy response, but Nayima didn't like the hard turn of his voice.

"Yes." She realized she didn't sound sad enough. He might not understand how sadness made her legs collapse, made it hard to breathe. She tried harder. "It's terrible."

"Not that—you." He sang the rest. "*Welcome, one and all, to the new super race . . .*"

Song as mockery, especially in his soulful, road-toughened tenor, hurt more than a physical blow. Nayima's anger roiled from the memory, the rivulets of poisoned saliva running down her cheeks from hateful strangers making a last wish. "They spit in my face, whenever they could. They tried to take me with them—yet here I stand. You can stop being a slave to that filthy paper you're wearing, giving yourself rashes. We're immune. Congratulations."

"Swell," he said. "I don't suppose you can back any of that up with lab tests? Studies?"

"We will one day," she said. "But so far it's you, and me, and some cop I saw high-tailing out of Bakersfield who should not have still been breathing. Believe me when I tell you: this bad-boy virus takes everybody, eventually. Except NIs."

"What if I just left a bunker? A treehouse? A cave?"

"Wouldn't matter. You've been out now. Something you touched. It lives on glass for thirty days, maybe forty-five. That was what the lab people in China said, when they finally started talking. Immunity—that's not a theory. There were always people who didn't get it when they should've dropped. Doctors. Old People."

"People who were careful," he said.

"This isn't survival of the smartest," she said. "It's dumb luck. In our genes."

"So, basically, Madame Curie," he said, drawing out his words, "you don't know shit."

Arrogant. Rude. Condescending. He was a disappointment after three days' walk, no question about it. But that was to be expected, Nayima reminded herself. She went on patiently. "The next one we find, we'll ask what they know. That's how we'll learn. Get a handle on the numbers. Start with villages again. I like the Central Valley. Good farmland. We just have to be sure of a steady water supply." It was a relief to let her thoughts out for air.

He laughed. "Whoa, sister. Don't start picking out real estate. You and me ain't a village. I'll shoot you if you come within twenty yards."

So—he was armed. Of course. His gun didn't show, but she couldn't see his left hand, suddenly hidden beneath a fold in his sleeping bag. He had been waiting for her.

"Oh," she said. "This again."

"Yeah—this," he said. "This is called common sense. Go on about your business. You can spend the night here, but I want you gone by morning. This is mine."

"Rescue's coming?"

He coughed a shallow, thirsty cough—not the rattling cough of the plague. "I'm not here for rescue. Didn't know a thing about that."

"I have water," she said. "I bet there's more in the vendor booths." Let him remember what it felt like to be fussed over. Let him see caring in her eyes.

His chuckle turned into another cough. "Yeah, no thanks. Got my own."

"If you didn't come here to get rescued, then why? Jonesing for hot dog buns?"

He moved his left hand away from his gun and back to his guitar strings. He plinked.

"My family used to come," he said. "Compete in 4-H. Eat fried dough 'til we puked. Ride those cheap-ass rides. This area's real close-knit, so you'd see everybody like a backyard party. That's all I wanted—to be somewhere I knew. Somewhere I would remember."

The wind shifted. Could be worse, but the dead were in the breeze.

"Smells like their plan didn't work out," Nayima said.

"Unless it did." He shrugged. "You need to leave me alone now."

Coming as it did at the end of the living portrait he'd just painted, the theft of his company burned a hole in her. She needed him already. Father, son, brother, lover, she didn't care which. She didn't want to be without him. Couldn't be without him, maybe.

His silence turned the fairgrounds gloomy again. This smell was the reason she preferred the open road, for now.

"At least tell me your name," she said. Her voice quavered.

But he only played his fantasy of bright, spinning lights.

• • •

With only two hours left before dark, Nayima remembered her situation. She was down to her last two bottles of water—so there was that. She noted every hose and spigot, mapping the grounds in her mind. Even with the water turned off, sometimes the reserves weren't dry.

Nayima went to search for a car first, since that would decide what else she needed. She didn't break into cars with locked doors during her first sweep. She decided she would only break a window if she saw a key. Glass was unpredictable, and her life was too fragile for everyday infections. The first vehicles she found with keys—the first engines she heard turn—had less than an eighth of a tank. Not enough.

Then she saw the PT Cruiser parked at B-7. Berry purple. The cream-colored one she'd driven in college at Spelman had been reincarnated in her favorite color, calling to her. Unlocked door. No stench inside. Half a bottle of water waiting in the beverage cup, nearly hot as steam from a day in the sun. No keys in the ignition, but they were tucked in the passenger visor, ready to be found. The engine choked complaints about long neglect, but finally hummed to life. And the gas tank, except by a hair, was full. Nayima felt so dizzy with relief that she sank into the car's bucket seat and closed her eyes. She thanked the man on the road and his music in the sky.

She could pack a working car with enough supplies for a month or more. With so much gas, she would easily make it to the closest town. She would stake out the periphery, find an old farmhouse in the new quiet. Clean up its mess. Rest with a proper roof.

Nayima's breath caught in her throat like a stone. Her first miracle in the New World.

The rest of her searching took on a leisurely pace, one step ahead of the setting sun. Nayima avoided the guitar player while she scouted, honoring his perimeter. She drove from the parking lot to the fairway, her slow-moving wheels chewing the gravel. Her driver's seat was a starship captain's throne.

Weather and dust were no match for the colors at the County Line Road Fair. Painted clowns and polar bears and ringmasters in top hats shouted red, blue, and yellow from wildly-named booths promising sweet, salty, and cold. In the colors and the guitar music, ghostly faces emerged, captured at play. The fairground teemed with children. Nayima heard their carefree abandon.

For an instant, she let in the children's voices—until her throat burned. The sky seemed ready to fall. She held her breath until her lungs forced her to suck in the air. To breathe in that smell she hated. The false memory was gone.

As she'd expected, airtight packages of hot dog buns looked fresh enough to last for millennia. She found boxes of protein bars in a vendor's cabinet and a sack of unshelled peanuts so large she had to carry it over her back like a child. She stuffed the PT Cruiser with a growing bounty of clean blankets, an unopened twenty-four pack of water bottles and her food stash—even a large purple stuffed elephant, just because she could. The PT Cruiser, her womb on wheels, cast a fresh light on the world.

But there was the question of the passenger seat, still empty. The *may, maybe, might* part was making her too anxious to enjoy her fair prizes.

Then Nayima saw the stenciled sign:

RESCUE CENTER ⇨

The arrow pointed away from the vendors' booths, toward the Farm World side of the fair, with its phantom Petting Zoo and Pony Rides in dull earth tones; really more an alleyway than a world. On the other end, a long wood-plank horse stall like one she had seen at the Kentucky Derby stood behind an empty corral, doors firmly shut.

Nayima climbed out of her PT Cruiser, pocketing her precious keys. She followed the dried tracks of man and beast side by side, walking on crushed hay. On the Farm World side, she could barely make out the sounds of the guitar. She felt like she had as a kid swimming in the ocean, testing a greater distance from shore. He might stop playing and disappear. It seemed more and more likely that she had only dreamed him.

But she had to see the rescue center. Like the driver from the PT Cruiser who had left her water bottle half full, in her imagination Nayima melted into scuffling feet, complaining children, muffled sobs.

The signs were posted on neatly-spaced posts. Each sign, helpful and profound.

FAMILIES SHOULD REMAIN TOGETHER

YOUR CALM HELPS OTHERS STAY CALM

SMILE—REMOVE YOUR MASK

The smell worsened with each step toward the looming structure. In front of the closed double doors stood two eight-foot folding tables—somewhat rusted now. Sun-faded pages flapped from a clipboard. Nayima glanced at a page of dull bureaucracy: handwritten names and addresses: *Gerald Hillbrandt, Party of 4*. As she'd guessed, a few hundred people had come.

SHOES ⇨

Nayima's eyes followed the next sign to the southwest corner of the stall, where she found rows of shoes neatly paired against the wall. Mama Bear, Papa Bear, Baby Bear, all side by side. Cheerfully surrendered. Nayima, who wore through shoes quickly, felt a strange combination of exhilaration and sorrow at the sight of the shoes on merry display.

ENTRANCE ⇨

The next sign pointed around the corner, away from the registration table and cache of shoes. The entrance to the intake center had been in the rear, not the front. The rear double barn doors were closed, but they also had tables on either side, each with a large opaque beverage dispenser half-filled with a dark liquid that could be iced tea.

A refreshments table, she thought—until she saw the signs.

MAKE SURE EVERYONE IN YOUR PARTY
TAKES A FULL CUP

PARENTS, WATCH YOUR CHILDREN DRINK BEFORE
DRINKING YOURSELF

MAKE SURE CUPS ARE EMPTIED BEFORE ENTERING

TRASH HERE, PLEASE

Beneath the last sign, a large garbage can halfway filled with crumpled plastic cups. Nayima stared. Some cups were marked with lipstick. Several, actually. Had they come to the Rescue Center wearing their Sunday best? Had they dressed up to meet their maker?

The smell, strongest here, was not fresh; it was the smell of older, dry death. The door waited—locked, perhaps—but Nayima did not want to go inside. Nayima laid her palm across the building's warm wooden wall, a communion with whoever had left her the PT Cruiser. And the shoes she would choose. What visionary had brought them here in this humane way? Had they known what was waiting? Her questions filled her with acid grief. She was startled by her longing to be with them, calm and resting.

Just in time, she heard the music.

• • •

"Look what I found," she said, and held up the sign for him to see.

"Can't read that from here."

"I can come closer."

"Wouldn't do that."

So, nothing had changed. She sighed. "It says—'Smile, Remove Your Mask.'"

He laughed. She already loved the sound. And then, the second miracle—he tugged his mask down to his chin. "Hell, since it's on the sign." He pointed a finger of judgment at her. "You stay way over there, I'll keep it off."

His voice was clearer. It was almost too dark to see him now, but she guessed he couldn't be older than fifty, perhaps as young as forty. He was young. Young enough. She wasn't close enough to see his eyes, but she imagined they were kind.

"I'm Kyle," he said.

She grinned so widely that she might have blinded him.

"Easy there, sister," he said. "That's all you get—my name. And a little guitar, if you can be a quiet audience. Like I said, you're moving on."

"Some of the other cars have gas. But this one has a full tank."

"Good for you," he said, not unkindly.

"You'll die here if you're afraid to touch anything."

"My cross to bear."

"How will you ever know you're immune?" she said.

He only shrugged. "I expect it'll become clear."

"But I won't be here. I don't know where I'll be. We have to . . ." She almost said *We have to fight back and make babies and see if they can survive.* ". . . stay together. Help protect each other. We're herd animals, not solitary. We always have been. We need each other."

Too much to comprehend lay in his silence.

"All you need is a full tank of gas," he said at last. "All I need is my guitar. Nothing personal—but ever hear of Typhoid Mary?"

Yes, of course she had heard of Typhoid Mary, had lived under the terror of her legacy. In high school, she'd learned that the poor woman died in isolation after thirty years, with no one allowed close to her. Nayima had decided long ago not to live in fear.

"We have immunity," she said. "I won't get you sick."

"That's a beautiful idea." His voice softened practically to a song. "You'll be the one who got away, Nayima."

She couldn't remember the last time anyone had called her by name. And he'd pronounced it as if he'd known her all her life. Not to mention how the word *beautiful* cascaded up and down her spine. While her hormones raged, she loved him more with each breath. Nayima was tempted to jump into her PT Cruiser and drive away then, the way she had learned to flee all hopeless scenarios.

Instead, she pulled her car within fifteen yards of him and reclined in the driver's seat with her door open, watching him play until he stopped. The car's clock said it was midnight when he finally slept. Hours had melted in his music. She couldn't sleep, feverish with the thought of losing him.

At first, she only climbed out of the car to stretch her limbs. She took a tentative step toward him. Then, another. Soon, she was standing over him while he slept.

She took in his bright guitar strap, woven from a pattern that looked Native American. The wiry hairs on his dark beard where they grew thick to protect his pink lips. The moonlight didn't show a single gray hair. He could be strong, with better feeding. Beneath his dusty camo jacket, he wore a Pink Floyd concert shirt. He could play her all of the old songs, and she could teach him music he didn't know. The moonlight cradled his curls across his forehead, gleamed on his exposed nose. He was altogether magnificent.

Nayima was sure he would wake when she knelt beside him, but he was a strong sleeper. His chest rose and fell, rose and fell, even as she leaned over him.

Was the stone rolling across her chest only her heartbeat? Her palms itched, hot. She was seventeen again, unexpectedly alone in a corner with Darryn Stephens at her best friend's house party, so aware of every prickling pore where they were close. And when he'd bent close, she'd thought he was going to whisper something in her ear over the noise of the world's last dance. His breath blew across her lips, sweet with beer. Then his lips grazed hers, lightning strikes down her spine, and the softness . . . the softness . . .

Kyle slept on as Nayima pressed her lips to his. Was he awake? Had his lips yielded to her? It seemed so much like Kyle was kissing her too, but his eyes were still closed, his breathing uninterrupted even as she pulled away.

She crept back to her PT Cruiser, giddy as a twelve-year-old. Oh, but he would be furious! The idea of his anger made her giggle. She dozed to sleep thinking of the gift of liberation she had given Kyle. Freedom from masks. Freedom from fear. Freedom to live his life with her, to build their village.

• • •

By dawn, Nayima woke to the sound of his retching.

She thought she'd dreamed the sound at first—tried to will herself to stay in her happy dream of singing Kumbaya with well-groomed strangers in the horse stalls, hand in hand—but she opened her eyes and saw the guitar player hunched away from her. He had pushed his guitar aside. She heard the splatter of his vomit.

Nausea came first. Nausea came fast.

Shit, she thought. Her mind was a vast white prairie, emptied, save that one word. She remembered his laughter, realized she would never hear him laugh again now.

"I'm sorry," she said. "I thought for sure you were like me. An NI."

She wished her voice had sounded sadder, but she didn't know how. She wanted to explain that he might have contracted the virus somewhere else in the past twenty-four hours, not necessarily from her. But despite the odds and statistics on her side, even she didn't believe that.

It's only a mistake if you don't learn from it, Gram would say. Nayima clamped her fingernails into both palms. Her wrist tendons popped out from the effort. Hot pain. The numbness that had thawed with his music and 4-H stories crept over her again, calcified.

The man didn't turn to look at her as she stood over him and picked through his things. His luggage carrier held six water bottles and a mountain of candy bars. The necessities. She left him his candy and water. His 9mm had no ammo, but she took it. She left his guitar—although she took the strap to remember him by. She might take up guitar herself one day.

The man gagged and vomited again. Most people choked to death by the third day.

"I'm leaving now," she said, and knelt behind him. She searched for something to say that might matter to him. "Kyle, I found that Rescue Center over in Farm Land—Farm *World*—and it looks nice. Somebody really thought the whole thing through. You were right to come here. Where I grew up, they just burned everything."

Even now, she craved his voice. Wanted so badly for him to hear her. To affirm her. To learn her grandmother's name and say, "Yes, she was." Yes, you were. Yes, you are.

The man did not answer or turn her way. Like the others before him, he was consumed with his illness. *Just as well,* Nayima thought as she climbed back into her car. *Just as well.* She glanced at her visor mirror and saw her face: dirt-streaked, unrepentant. She blinked and looked away.

Nayima never had been able to stomach the eyes of the dead.

THE SIXTH DAY OF DEER CAMP

Scott Sigler

George didn't want to be the one to say it, but it had to be said: "We can't stay here."

They all looked at him. Gloved hands flexed on hunting rifles. Jaco gave a tiny, weak shake of the head. Bernie closed his eyes and sighed. Toivo glared. Only Arnold nodded: older, wiser, but even he clearly wasn't crazy about the idea of leaving.

The impossible had happened: an actual alien invasion. George and his three boyhood friends—and the man who had been a father figure to them all—were sitting in the same cabin they'd come to every November for almost three decades. A remote spot in Michigan's Upper Peninsula, the middle of nowhere, really, and something had crashed here, something that wasn't a plane or a jet or anything else they knew.

That something was out in the woods, the *deep* woods, behind the cabin, among the pines and spruces and birch and several feet of snow. They had seen it, a vague shape through the trees, red and green and blue lights filtering through the darkness and the wind-driven white. It was out there, this ship, and, according to the internet stories they'd read on Bernie's phone, ships similar to it were attacking major cities all over the world.

That was all the info they had to go on. Cell phones weren't working anymore—voice or internet—and even back in the day when landlines were all there were, the cabin hadn't had one.

Why that ship had crashed here, George didn't know. Neither did his friends. What they did know was that three days of steady snow had choked the narrow, back-country roads, making them impassible by car. They could walk out on foot, sure, *if* they could survive the cold long enough to reach shelter elsewhere. The very reason they came to this cabin year after year was because there was nothing near it—in this weather, with the snowpack, it was at least an hour's walk to another cabin.

There was one snowmobile, an old thing that had sat idle this year and last. George remembered someone firing it up three years back. Would it even start? If it did, it could get one man out, maybe two, but not five.

Just say it . . . just tell them you should take the snowmobile because you have to get out of here, get to your sons, your wife.

That little voice nagged at him, told him to use the parent trump card that all parents of young children used. But this wasn't getting out of work a little early to pick the boys up from soccer practice, this wasn't asking someone else at the office—someone who didn't have kids—to stay late because you had to get the babysitter home . . . these were his closest friends, men that he loved, and leaving them would be the most selfish thing.

If they're really your friends, they'd understand. You've got kids, *just ask them if you can—*

"Can't stay here, you say," Toivo said. "We sure as hell can't *leave,* Georgie."

Toivo had sobered up. Mostly. His eyes still looked tired, *hungover*-tired, and a bit of gleaming snot stuck to his mustache. Dressed in a full snowsuit over two sweaters, he looked like a brown Pillsbury Doughboy. So did George, for that matter. So did everyone else.

Toivo gestured to the cabin's ratty wall. "What da fuck do you think we're gonna do outside, Georgie? Hide in da woods? It's fuckin' forty below out there."

George nodded. That was the problem, wasn't it? *Cold* was one thing. He was a grown man—he could handle cold—but *forty below* wasn't *cold,* it was something else altogether. And then there was the snow. Still falling steadily from the night sky, increasing the thick whiteness that covered bare branches and pine boughs alike, adding to the three feet already on the ground. That snow hid all the sticks and logs and foot-snapping holes around the shack.

But . . . there were no trees or sticks on the *road.* Nothing there but snow. The road would take them *away.* They needed to be on that road, and the sooner the better.

Get them all moving, it doesn't matter, get them out of here and find a way to get home . . .

"That ship is close," George said. "We're the only building in the area." He pointed to the cabin's small, black, wood-burning stove, which gave off heat that seemed far more delicious now that he knew he'd soon leave it behind. "The stove is putting out smoke. If they have IR, they'll see the shack lit up all red, or whatever, and know that people are here."

Arnold's wrinkled face furrowed. "IR? What da hell is that?"

"*Infrared,* Pops," Bernie said. "Like in *Predator.*"

Arnold's bushy eyebrows rose. "Ah, yeah. Like *Predator.*"

Those two, Arnold and Bernie, had such a strong father-son resemblance they looked like a before-and-after picture: this is you *before* you start to smoke, kids, and this is you *after.* Bernie, over forty, same age as George and Jaco and Toivo, with a full "hunting cabin beard" that had taken him only a week to grow. Arnold, white stubble in and on the folds of his face, tired eyes peering out from behind thick glasses.

"This ain't a movie," Toivo said. "This ain't about IR. Georgie, I love ya, but stop lying—you think you can get back to Milwaukee."

A stab of guilt, like George had been caught in a crime. He couldn't lie to these men, at least not convincingly. They knew him too well.

"I do," George said. "We have to get out of here, you guys. At least out of the cabin. If they're killing people all over, they'll come here, and if they find us, they'll probably kill us, too."

Bernie walked to the stove. "We should put da fire out, anyway. If there's no fire they can't see us, maybe. We'll lose heat, but at least we're protected from da wind."

Jaco shook his head. "Putting it out makes way more smoke. Just let it burn out on its own."

He was right about the smoke, but the tone in Jaco's voice made it clear he was more worried about the cold.

Everyone looked worried, scared, but Jaco more than the rest. His oversized glasses framed wide eyes made wider by the thick lenses. He was the smallest of the five, always had been, so small that his rifle made him look like a preteen boy dressing up as a hunter for Halloween. He had children, too, a pair of daughters. At five and seven, they were the same ages as George's boys. George had often teased Jaco that his boys would someday date those girls.

Toivo tried to sling his rifle over his shoulder, but his snowsuit's bulk blocked him.

"We've got guns," he said. He tried to sling the weapon a second time, succeeded. "We can defend ourselves, eh? We stay here, we won't die from da cold. Maybe you forgot what it's like living in a big city, Georgie, but in da woods, you don't fuck with forty below."

Jaco righted a folding chair that had been knocked over when the alien ship had screamed overhead—so close and loud the cabin rattled as if struck by artillery. He sat.

"*Defend ourselves,*" he said. "Toivo, those things are blowing up *cities.* From what those websites said, they're taking on the military, and winning. You think hunting rifles are going to do anything?"

Toivo shrugged. "I'm not a physedicist," he said. "But bullets will probably kill those things just like they kill us."

"*Physicist*," Jaco said, shaking his head. "You dumb-ass, *phys-ed* is *gym*."

George didn't want to listen to them jabber. His sons were probably terrified, wondering where their father was. His wife was . . . well, she was probably loading the shotgun and getting the boys into the basement. No trembling flower, his wife.

"Bernie, put out the fire," George said. "Sorry, Toivo, but we have to get out of here. I'm telling you, they'll come for this cabin. They crashed, they'll want to secure the area."

Toivo snorted. "*Secure the area.* What da hell are you, Georgie, some Delta Force guy or something? Chuck Norris?"

George didn't have any military experience. None of them did. Just four men in middle-age—and one well past it—who knew nothing more about soldiering than what they'd seen in the movies.

Toivo pointed to the cabin's warped wooden floor. "We're staying here. They come? We've got guns."

"If we stay, we put out the fire," Bernie said. "I agree with George. Infrared."

Jaco shook his head. "Don't put it out, you idiots. Whatever is in that ship probably has its hands full. We leave it burning, but we get on the road. I'm with George—I've got to get to my daughters."

Two men—George and Jaco—with little kids. Two men—Bernie and Toivo—with none. And Arnold, whose grown son was standing right next to him. Three sets of needs, three sets of perspectives.

Arnold coughed up some phlegm, then swallowed it in that abstract way old men do. "George is right," he said. "You boys get out of the cabin."

George felt a sense of relief that Arnold, the man who'd practically raised him, the best man George knew, was with him on that decision.

"Okay," George said. "So we hit the road, we stay together and hope for the best."

Arnold shook his head. "I said *you boys* get out of the cabin. I'll keep an eye on the ship, make sure nothing comes after you."

Bernie rolled his eyes, as if his father's sudden act of bravery was not only expected, but annoying as well.

"Dad, we don't have time for that shit," he said. "We're all going."

"I'm seventy-two goddamn years old," Arnold said. "I've been faking it just fine, but there's only so much left in my tank. My bum hip is killing me. No way I'll make it in this cold, son. So you do what your father tells you, and—"

"Shut up," Jaco hissed. "You guys hear that?"

They didn't at first, but the noise grew; over the whine of the wind through the trees outside, they heard faint *snaps* and *cracks*.

Something was coming through the woods.

Something *big*.

"We move, now," Arnold said. "You boys come with me."

• • •

They rushed from the house, bumping into each other, stumbling off the rickety, two-step porch. Toivo fell sideways as he ran; the snow bank rising up from the thin path caught him at a forty-five-degree angle, so he didn't fall far.

George had assumed Arnold would run for the road, but he didn't—he turned right and stumbled through the snow toward the cabin's corner.

"Arnold! Where are you going!"

George stopped, but the others didn't. They followed Arnold, three men carrying hunting rifles, stutter-stumbling through snow that came up to their crotches, moving too fast to walk in each other's footsteps.

Jesus H., was the old man *attacking*? They vanished around the corner, not running *away* from the oncoming sound, but toward it.

George found himself alone.

The cold pressed in on him, on his face, tried to drive through his snowsuit as if it were armor that would slowly, inexorably dent and crumble under the pressure. Out of the cabin for all of ten seconds, he already felt it.

The porch light cast a dim glow onto the path, the blanket of white on the driveway, and the walls of the same stuff that made the truck nothing more than a vehicle-shaped snow bank.

He looked at the snowmobile, or rather the curved hump of white burying it. The keys were inside the cabin. He could grab them—the others had left him alone—he had to get back to his family. He could dig down to the snowmobile . . . no, that would take twenty minutes all by itself, then the thing probably wouldn't start. He had to run, get as far down the road as he could.

Little Jaco . . . Bernie . . . Toivo . . . Mister Ekola.

The people who had made him who he was: go after them, or head down the road alone and start a three-hundred-sixty-mile trek to Milwaukee.

From the other side of the cabin, he heard the *crack* of a tree giving way, a brittle sound quickly swallowed by the snowy night.

George couldn't do it; he couldn't leave his friends.

I'll get home as soon as I can, I will . . .

He held his rifle tight in both gloved hands and ran to the corner of the cabin, stumbling through the snow just as the others had done.

• • •

Most people don't know real cold. Sure, they've been *cold* before; they've sat through a football game in below-freezing temps; they've experienced winter here or there, perhaps even been dumb enough to take a vacation to Chicago in December. All of those things are cold, but *real* cold? *Don't-fuck-with-forty-below* cold?

That can kick your ass. That can kill you.

George tried to stop shivering, but he couldn't. Wind slid through the trees, drove the cold into him as if he wasn't even wearing a snowsuit with the hood up over a hat, three sweaters, jeans over long johns, three pairs of socks, gloves and even a scarf wrapped tight around his nose and mouth. His hands felt like there was a steel vice on each knuckle of each finger, and the fingertips themselves stung like he'd sliced off the ends and dipped the raw stubs in battery acid.

And he'd only been outside for five minutes.

Forty below? Maybe worse than that, maybe *far* worse with the wind-chill factored in.

He followed the footsteps of his friends, mostly by feel because it was so dark. No porch light here, no stars; he wouldn't have been able to see anything at all if not for the barest glimmer from the covered moon turning the snow gray. He had a flashlight in a snowsuit pocket, but knew better than to use it.

Most people don't know real cold, and most people also don't know real snow. The kind of snow that piles up week after week, a crispy layer near the bottom with the hidden logs and sticks, a layer so firm that when you break through it and stagger on, sometimes your foot slides right out of your boot. Above that, the dense snowpack, then finally, on top, several inches of the fluffy stuff. Every step sank so deep he couldn't quite raise his boot all the way out to take the next one. He was wading more than walking.

So dark. The woods were nothing but shadows holding aliens; they had to be out here somewhere, probably had already come out of the ship and were closing in. He should have stayed on the road, gotten out of there while he could, he—

"Georgie! Get over here!"

Bernie—the voice was so close. Shadows moved . . . just to the left, heads peeking up from behind a fallen tree, the trunk smooth and softened by snow.

George stumbled toward it, each step breaking through the crust and driving in with that Styrofoam-sounding *crunch.* He fell more than walked the last three feet. His friends caught him, pulled him down. His chest heaved, drawing icy knives deep into his lungs.

They huddled together out of a need for warmth, or maybe from pure fear.

Another *crack,* that thing coming through the woods.

George wiped his glove across his eyes, clearing away flakes that clung to his lashes. He rose up on his knees, peeked over the log. The cabin . . . it was so close. How could it be that close? It seemed like he'd been walking forever, each step a battle, but he hadn't made it more than thirty or forty feet. He was close enough to see smoke slipping out of the thin stove-pipe, instantly ripped into the night by the unforgiving wind.

The cracking again, a branch giving way, maybe an entire tree. And a new sound, a *grinding*, like machinery that had seen better days. In the woods, a shape, a *big* shape, backlit by the ship's red and green and blue lights.

George slipped back down. He looked to Arnold. Shivering Arnold, *old* Arnold. "*Why*?" George hissed. "Why didn't we run?"

"IR," Arnold said. "Like *The Terminator*."

"*Predator*," Bernie said. "Like *Predator*, Dad."

Arnold's body trembled horribly, like an invisible hand had him between giant fingers and was rattling him like some child's toy.

"Heat . . . our heat," he said. "If we hide behind a big log . . . they won't see us."

George stared, dumbfounded. They had followed this man here, because of *that* reasoning? They could have been a hundred yards down the road by now. Instead, they were *closer* to the oncoming threat.

Arnold—the man he'd once known only as *Mister Ekola*—had been their rock once, but now he was just a scared old man who had made a shitty decision based on a movie he couldn't fully remember.

"Hey," Jaco said. "Couldn't Terminator see in infrared, too?"

Toivo and Bernie thought, then nodded. George wanted to punch them all right in the nose.

Over the wind's scream, the cracking and grinding drew closer. George had a flash memory of a summer campfire some thirty years earlier, the night stars above, skin on his face and his toes and knees nearly burning because the closer you sat to the fire the less the mosquitoes and black flies bothered you. Mister Ekola, a flashlight under his chin casting strange shadows on his cheeks and eyes, telling a story of a killer with a limp. You knew this killer because of the sound, the *thump-drag* sound, a good foot stepping forward, then the slide of the bad foot following behind.

Thump, drag . . . thump, drag . . .

George had told that same story to his sons. It had scared the hell out of them just like it had scared the hell out of him. And now, a version of that sound had him damn near pissing his pants, a version with the added tones of snapping branches and broken gears.

Thump, drag, crack-crack, snap . . . thump, drag, whir-snap, crack, whine . . .

George's friends huddled down lower to the ground, pressing into the log like they were newborn pups nursing from their mother.

Someone had to look; someone had to know what was coming.

George forced himself to rise up, just enough to see over the snow-covered log.

Thump, drag, crack-whine, grind-snap . . .

The thing broke through the tree line just thirty feet from the cabin. A robot, a big-ass robot maybe fifteen feet tall. Two legs . . . the left stepping forward, the right dragging along behind, functioning barely enough to position itself so the machine could take another step with its left. Broken branches jutted out of tears in the metal shell, or plastic, or whatever it was made of. Bipedal—no arms George could see—but cracks everywhere, breaks and tears and dents, smoke-streaks . . . the thing was *trashed.* Part of the shell was ripped free near the top. Hard to see in the darkness and snow, but George could make out a yellow shape . . . a form that moved . . .

Sweet Jesus.

An *alien.*

Thump, drag . . . thump, drag . . .

The robot paused just past the tree line, big feet hidden in the snow. Something fluttered open near what George could only think of as the machine's hips. Then, a flash, and a rocket shot out, closing the distance in less than a second.

He was already dropping behind the log when the cabin erupted in a fireless explosion that launched a hailstorm of broken-board shrapnel into the woods, knocking free chunks of clinging snow that had withstood the blowing wind.

George's ass hit the ground. He stared into the dark woods, mind blank.

A hand on his shoulder: Jaco, leaning in.

"Georgie, was that the fucking cabin that just blew up?"

I have to get on that road, get to Milwaukee, whatever it takes to reach my children, find a way—

"Georgie!"

"Yes, goddamit! It was the cabin!"

The sound again, *thump, drag . . . thump, drag . . .*

"Shit!" Jaco said, said it with such ferocity that it contracted his body, made his head snap forward. "Screw that! Everyone, shoot that thing on *one,* okay?"

Thump, drag . . . coming closer.

"Three," Jaco said.

Counting? Why was he counting? It was a damn *robot-thing* that blew up buildings, it—

Thump, drag . . .

"Two!"

Holy shit! Jaco was going to fire at that thing out there?

Thump, drag . . .

"Jaco, no, you—"

"One!"

Movement all around, George's friends rising up, the crack of rifles firing followed by the sound of bolts sliding back, then forward again.

George ripped off his gloves, held the rifle tight as he rose to his knees and turned, all one uncoordinated, lurching movement. He swung the barrel of his Remington 700 over the top of the log, knocking aside clumps of snow. The hand cupping the forestock pressed down on the log, snow instantly melting from the heat of his skin.

The big machine turned sharply, swiveling at the hips like the turret of a tank, the motion herky-jerky and halting.

George fired instantly, without aiming, had no idea if he'd hit.

Gunshots from his left and from his right. He popped the rifle's lever up and pulled it back, heard the faint ring of the ejected shell, shoved the bolt forward but it stuck; his hand slipped off, his momentum lurched him forward into the log.

The guns kept firing.

I've never even shot a deer what the hell am I doing I should have gone to the range more should have—

He slammed the bolt home; the sound of it locking into place seemed to slow time from a mad explosion of a volcano to the slow creep of its lava flow. He looked through his scope at the fifteen-foot-tall machine only twenty feet away, sighted through one of the tears in the shell at the yellowish form.

He pulled the trigger. The Remington jumped. He saw the yellow thing inside twitch, then fall still.

It didn't move.

Neither did the machine.

"*Stop firing,*" he shouted.

The rifle reports ended like someone had unplugged a TV in the middle of an action movie. No gunshot echoes, not with the snow-covered trees eating up all sound save for the wind.

George stared. They all stared. No one knew what else to do.

Slowly, like a top-heavy bookshelf with one too many knickknacks, the thing tipped forward: Fifteen feet of alien machine arced down and slammed into the ground with a billowing *whuff* of snow.

The top of it was only five feet away.

They stared at it. It didn't move. Somewhere under there, hidden by all that bulk, was the alien who had been driving it.

"Holy shit," Jaco said. "I think we killed it."

George hoped so. He looked to his right, to the cabin; or what was left of it. Shattered, destroyed, blown apart with such force that there were only a few stumps of broken wood and a snow-free patch marking the place he and his friends had come every year for almost three decades.

"Told ya bullets would kill it," Toivo said. "Who's the physedicist now?"

The wind kept howling. The wind didn't care.

"Guys," Bernie said, "we gotta get moving. I'm freezing, eh?"

Those words might as well have been boiling oil thrown on George's hands. The cold smashed them, ground his fingers. He set the gun against the log, almost fumbled it in the process, then grabbed his gloves out of the snow and pulled them on, only to find snow had somehow gotten inside of them.

His gloves were wet. Wet *inside.*

"It's getting colder," Arnold said. "How da fuck can it get colder?"

The old man started to cough. He bent at the knees, then fell to them, his body shaking.

Bernie knelt next to him, holding him close. He looked up at George. "We gotta get Dad inside."

Jaco pointed to where the cabin had been. "Inside *where,* Bernie? There is no more *inside.*"

Bernie shouted back at him. "Then build a fucking lean-to or something! Start a fire!"

Jaco slung his rifle. "Build a lean-to? I don't have that merit badge, eh?"

The two began arguing, Jaco about how they might as well start walking and Bernie how they couldn't, how they had to find a way to help Arnold. Jaco didn't say the words—he couldn't, none of them could—but he was making a case for heartbreak: If they started moving, they had a chance, even if that meant Arnold did not.

George took off his wet gloves, stuffed them into his snowsuit. His hands, brittle as glass, searched for pockets. He wasn't going to last long out here.

None of them would.

Toivo pointed to the woods, to the red, green, and blue beams filtering through the trees, beams that colorized the driving snow.

"There is so an inside," he said. "The only one we got."

Bernie and Jaco stopped arguing.

"Well, shit," Jaco said.

Bernie pulled his trembling father tighter, nodded.

"Toivo's right," he said. "It's that or Dad dies."

"That or . . . or . . . ," George said, his jaw betraying him, suddenly clacking his teeth together so rapidly the words wouldn't come. He clenched, fought down the shivering long enough to say five more words.

"That, or we *all* die."

• • •

As far as choices went, this one sucked as much as any choice possibly could.

"Can't believe we got this close," Toivo said. "I expected to be dead already, eh? Ain't they got no more machines?"

He stood on George's right, rifle held in gloved hands. George wanted those gloves, needed them, or needed something to dry his out. His fingers were going numb. The stinging had stopped, which meant frostbite was setting in.

He had little strength left. All of the men were exhausted, drained from the fight and the long walk through the woods to the crashed ship. If another machine came, George knew they were done for; at this point he wasn't even sure if he had the will to fight again.

The ship wasn't as big as they had thought, but it was big enough. It had come down hard, gouging a long, fifty-foot-wide trench through the pines, like God had reached down an invisible stick and dragged a straight line through the woods, snapping trees into kindling, kicking out a wake of ice and frozen dirt.

And the ship itself . . .

George hadn't known what to expect, what an alien ship was *supposed* to look like. It was a disc . . . nothing more than a classic flying saucer, really. Or at least it probably had been before the crash. The front end was smashed and torn, far worse, even, than the machine that had blown up the cabin. This thing had hit *hard,* the front edge digging into the ground almost like a shovel, so deep that the back end had probably tilted up behind it as it slid along the ground, grinding out that wide trench. It might have even flipped over during the crash, maybe even more than once—George actually had no idea if he was looking at the front or the back, or if the disc even *had* a front.

There . . . a hole . . . ragged in some places, smooth and somewhat melted in others. Someone or some*thing*—maybe that alien and its machine they'd left behind—had cut its way out.

George pointed at the hole.

"That's got to be the door," he said. His frozen lips, almost as numb as his fingers, were barely able to form the words. "Jaco, that look like a door to you?"

Jaco was on George's left, rifle barrel pointed forward and down. Of all the friends, little Jaco—for reasons George couldn't explain—now looked the most like a soldier: hard eyes peeking out from above a blue, snow-slick scarf wrapped around his mouth and nose, weapon at the ready.

"I dunno, Georgie. I ain't got that merit badge, either. If that *is* the door, I'm guessing it's an afterthought."

"It doesn't matter," said Bernie from behind them. "Whatever it is, we've got to go in."

George turned, looked back. Bernie was behind them, one arm under his father's shoulder. Arnold's head hung down; George didn't know if the old man was conscious anymore.

"We *have* to," Bernie said.

His eyes pleaded for understanding. He knew what he was asking of his friends.

George didn't want to go in. He loved Mister Ekola, truly and deeply, but he had children of his own . . . was Mister Ekola's life more important than George getting back to his boys?

George glanced at Jaco. Jaco had been the first to think of leaving, to say-without-saying that Arnold was *old,* that he'd already had his time on this world. In that glance, George suddenly and shamefully hoped Jaco would say *let's get out of here,* and George could pretend to be upset but actually back Jaco's play, and they would leave and not go into that ruined ship and it wouldn't be George's fault . . . not really.

Jaco glanced at the opening.

"Fuck it," he said. "My dick's freezing off. Fuck it."

He didn't wait for anyone to answer him. He pointed his hunting rifle ahead and walked to the opening of the ruined ship.

George had a moment to hate Jaco, hate him very much, then he followed, Toivo just a step behind.

• • •

There were bodies everywhere.

The first few were so mangled George had no idea what the aliens looked like pre-crash. The yellow color he'd seen in the walking machine, it turned out, was probably clothing, because the twisted limbs and scraps of pulverized flesh showed various hues of blue. He saw what had to be hands (though they looked like they had two thumbs and one finger) and what had to be arms (connected to the hands, obviously, but long and thin, the arms of a death camp victim in those Holocaust documentaries); he also saw enough biological wreckage to identify legs (stick-thin but not so different from his own), hips, a midsection (with what might be vital organs in a bulge on the back rather than in front, for those that still had vital organs, at least), and an endless amount of sticky, clear fluid.

"Their blood," Jaco said. "It's got no color."

His face was ashen, his upper lip curled back in revulsion. Jaco had removed his scarf because it was warm in the ship. Borderline *hot,* even. It was such a welcome relief from the numbing cold that it almost deadened the shock of being there, in a strange ship, surrounded by dead aliens.

If there were any of them left alive, they weren't showing themselves.

George and the others moved through the ship, finding its familiarity almost disturbing: Even for a different species, a room was a room, a hallway was a hallway. Everything was bent and broken, cracked—twisted from the impact—but maybe it didn't look all that different from what humans might someday make. The doors were heavy, like something from a battleship.

When Arnold could go no further, they stopped in the largest room they'd found. Ironically, the room was about the same size as the cabin. Bernie had cleared a space of debris, then laid Arnold down. One of Bernie's sweaters, rolled up, served as a pillow. Arnold already looked better; he was still shivering, but some color had returned to his face. He nodded at whatever Bernie was saying.

"Georgie," Toivo said. "Come take a look at this."

Toivo was on the other side of the wreckage-filled room. George walked over broken and fallen bits, careful to watch where he stepped.

Toivo's eyes flicked in all directions, at the damaged ship, at the body parts scattered across the floor, walls, and ceiling. His hand, however, was pressed against what looked like a door—a door sealed with a heavy wheel, like something from a submarine.

"Find something, Toivo?"

The man nodded. "Sort of." He made a fist, rapped on the door; *knock-knock,* the ring of knuckles on metal. Then, he moved his fist two inches to the left and rapped again: *kund-kund;* this time, two dull thuds.

George leaned closer. The door had been painted over, repeatedly. It was uneven, lumpy in parts.

"It's Bond-O," Toivo said. "Well, not *Bond-O,* but you know what I mean. It's spackle, a patch job, and from way before da crash." He pointed up, to the left, down and to the right. "It's all over, Georgie. Looks like repairs and a lot of 'em. This ship? It's a beater, eh?"

What did that mean? This ship—this *alien* ship—something that was the very icon of actual life on other planets . . . it was on par with a used car? Could that be why it crashed? Had something broken at the wrong time?

"A beater, I tell ya," Toivo said. He rapped on the door again, *knock-knock-knock.*

The door opened.

No screech of hinges, no sound; it just swung inward.

The heat seemed to vanish; George was cold once again, frozen in place, motionless.

Inside the door, a short *creature* that had all the bits and pieces he'd seen scattered about the ship, but smaller, all the gore pressed back together into a tiny shape of stick-thin limbs and black eyes (three eyes, not two) in a *big* head, too big for the body, and—

Toivo fired, the barrel, only inches from the big head: The head blew apart in a clear water-balloon-splatter that splashed goop on George's face. The creature dropped instantly, a lifeless sack of meat, a puppet cut free from supporting strings.

Toivo slid back the bolt, a metallic sound that seemed just as loud as the gunshot itself. As he pushed it forward, what lay beyond the door came into sudden clarity.

The bolt ratcheted into place, and the barrel came up for another shot.

George's hand snapped out, grabbed the barrel, raised it up just as Toivo fired: the round went somewhere into the ceiling.

"Georgie, what are you doing?"

"*Stop!* Just stop!"

George was aware of heat on his hand, where he'd grabbed the barrel, but distantly, because his brain was busy processing what he saw. This room, not as beat up as everything else. Heavy, curving girders running from floor to ceiling, and between them what could only be crash seats of some kind with heavy reinforced doors and thick padding visible behind thick windows. All of this, yes, all of it registering for him, but distant, like the heat on his hand, because in the middle of the room stood a dozen creatures, most smaller than the one Toivo had just killed, some so small they wouldn't have come up to George's knee, all clinging together in a trembling pile, black eyes (black *alien* eyes, not human, not at all, but fear is fear just like a hallway is a hallway) wide open and staring.

"They're kids," George said. "Fucking Jesus . . . *kids.*"

Children. The aliens had put their children in the ship's safest room, perhaps as soon as trouble started . . .

Goddamn car seats . . . alien spaceship car seats . . . they strapped them in, safe and sound and snug as a bug in a rug, same thing I would have done with my boys . . .

"Georgie, let go of da gun," Toivo said.

"Same as I would have done," George said. "Same."

Toivo yanked his rifle barrel free, almost pulled George off-balance in the process.

Would he shoot another one?

George positioned himself between Toivo and the door, blocking Toivo's line of sight to the aliens. George tried to close the door, but the dead body blocked it. He reached down, grabbed the bone-thin little arm and dragged the body into the corridor. He stood and again put his hand on the door, to pull it shut, but before he did he glanced into the room—the little creatures were watching him, their black eyes wide with palpable terror.

He knew what they had seen, *how* they had perceived it: an alien (because to them, that's exactly what he was) pulling their dead friend away, leaving a streak of wetness behind, then sealing them in.

George again tried to close the door—this time, it was Toivo that stopped it from shutting.

Toivo stared at him.

"Georgie, are you nuts? We gotta kill them."

"No, we don't."

"They're bombing cities," Toivo said. "Killing thousands, maybe millions."

George heard this. He nodded.

"The ones in this room aren't doing it," he said. "They didn't do anything."

Toivo sneered in disgust, then tried to push the door open—George blocked him with his shoulder.

The two childhood friends locked eyes. Toivo seemed to study George for a moment, as if measuring the man's will. Then, Toivo shook his head.

"I'll go back and check on Mister Ekola," he said.

Toivo walked to Bernie and Arnold. George saw those two looking back, Jaco as well—no one knew what to do, what to think, so they just stared.

George couldn't meet their gaze.

Kids. *Children.* This ship, old and repaired and beat up . . . adults dead all over the place, but the kids, safe and sound. Had the one in the walking machine blown up the cabin just to kill, or was it trying to eliminate any threat to these little ones? Was that why the ship had come in the first place? To make a new home?

George didn't know. He didn't have any answers. All he could think about was what it would be like if a skinny-limbed alien had kicked in the door to his boys' bedroom, aimed a weapon at their faces, shot one of them, dropped him like a bag of meat and bones while the other boy watched, helpless to defend himself. How horrible would that be? How life-shattering, how soul-rending?

Toivo was right: Before the phones stopped working George had read the news—the aliens were killing people.

Thousands, maybe millions.

But there were billions of people . . . billions that would fight back, fight back and kill the aliens.

"But not these ones," George said to no one. "They didn't do anything. They're just *kids.*"

He pulled the door tight. Hands on the wheel, he leaned back, making sure the door had a good seal, then turned it until he heard something click home inside.

"Just kids," he said. "Just kids."

He could protect them, but only because there was no one around for miles save for George's childhood friends. And even then, he wasn't sure—if Toivo, Jaco, and Bernie all insisted on opening that door and shooting whatever they saw inside, how far was George willing to go to prevent that?

Would a stranger have even let him shut that door? What if it had been ten strangers? What if it had been a hundred? If a ship like this crashed or came down near a destroyed city, human survivors would kill any alien they saw—adult or child, it didn't matter—the first chance they had.

Humanity would win. George felt that in his core, knew it at a base level just as his body knew how to breathe, just as his heart knew how to beat. Humanity would win because those billions of survivors would fight back, and there were millions of guns out there for them to use.

Bullets did the same thing to aliens that they did to people.

Even if *all* the cities were destroyed, humanity would win. Too many people, too many guns.

And knives. And clubs. And rocks. And fists.

The aliens had attacked, had announced themselves with violence and death. People would be only too happy to return that greeting in kind. George envisioned instant mob scenes, aliens torn to pieces by enraged people. There would be no reasoning with these mobs—how do you appeal to a person's humanity when the target isn't *human*?

Too many people, too many guns.

Humanity would win.

When this was over, would the alien children behind that door be the only ones left?

George tightened the wheel on the door, made doubly sure it was as shut as it could be. He didn't want it opening on its own. And he prayed the little creatures wouldn't open it, wouldn't come walking out, because judging by the looks on the faces of his friends, the alien children would be as good as dead.

"Just kids," he mumbled. "Just kids."

He walked to join his friends.

GOODNIGHT STARS

Annie Bellet

The redwoods whispered overhead in the warm summer breeze as Lucy Goodwin gathered another handful of fallen branches for the camp fire. She looked up at the sky, squinting in the afternoon sunlight. The meteor shower the night before had been amazing. She hoped she and her friends would be treated to more tonight. Everyone had asked her about meteor showers and the Perseids and all that space crap. It was embarrassing.

As if she knew anything just because her mother was on the Moon. She snorted. Mom was an engineer, not an astrophysicist. Though you'd never know from how hard she pushed sciences at her only kid.

"Can't wait to have the 'you declared *what* major!' conversation when she gets home," Lucy muttered. All she and Mom did these days was fight, but it wasn't her fault. Lucy wanted to live her own life, not a life in her mom's shadow. One scientist in the family was plenty.

A smoky trail blazed through the sky and Lucy felt an odd pressure in her ears. It faded quickly, but the smoke still hung like some kind of brownish cloud. Repressing a shiver, Lucy headed back to camp.

Loud voices greeted her as she hiked out of the tree line to the ridge.

"Lucy!" Jack, her boyfriend, was waving his cell phone at her.

She sighed and picked up her pace. They'd declared the camping trip a tech-free zone, but apparently that was another promise Jack couldn't keep.

Kayla, Ben, and Heidi were throwing things into backpacks. Something was definitely wrong.

"What happened?" Lucy asked, as she dropped her armload of sticks and ran forward.

"I got a message from Daniel. They're calling up all the reservists and they are offering to re-up me, despite the leg." Jack's blue eyes looked panicked. He'd taken shrapnel in his left leg while in Afghanistan flying helicopters. He'd gotten medical leave and started classes at Berkeley, where she and Jack had met. He'd promised he was done with all things military, even getting his walking papers only weeks before. Lucy had started to believe him when she saw the signed papers.

"Who is calling up reservists? The Army?"

"Everyone," Jack said. "Army, Navy, Air Force, National Guard. That's what Daniel says anyway."

"Tell her the rest, Jack, come on," Heidi called from inside her tent.

"Jesus, Heidi, her mom's on the Moon," Jack said. He ran a hand through his light brown hair, still clutching the phone.

Lucy's stomach turned to coiled rope and then knotted itself with a sickening twist. No one would meet her eyes as she looked around the camp.

"Why are they calling everyone up? What about the damn Moon?" She stepped over a pile of tent poles and grabbed Jack's arm, forcing him to look at her.

"Something hit the Moon. That's why the meteors were so awesome last night. It was the Moon exploding."

"Bullshit." Lucy shook her head. That wasn't possible. If the Moon had exploded, they would have seen that. It had been its usual crescent sailing along the horizon last night.

"Remember how Kayla said it looked lopsided to her?" Ben said. "The asteroid or whatever hit the back of it. That's what the news sites were saying before reception cut out."

"Fuck you guys if you are playing a trick on me," Lucy said. She ducked into her and Jack's tent, pulling her phone from her bag and powering it on. The phone sang to life with a little tune but remained stuck on the roaming screen, little multicolored dots dancing around in a circle as it struggled for reception.

Nobody could get reception. Resigned to figuring out if this was some hoax later, Lucy packed up with the rest of them. Kayla and Ben were an item lately and still in that new-couple-overwhelming-cuteness phase, so Heidi opted to ride with Jack and Lucy. Driving out of the Big Basin Redwoods state park, they stopped at the small gas station just outside, everyone in the car holding their phones, hunting for reception. Nothing.

Inside the gas station, there was a TV airing a news channel. Lucy stood inside the air-conditioned doorway, frozen.

It wasn't a lie. Photos and images from all around the world were piling in. Meteors were striking major areas. Satellites were down all around the world. The President of the United States would have a message for everyone at 6 p.m. Eastern.

The Moon was gone. The images released thus far were of a cloudy mess. Words like "impact winter" and "massive meteor strikes" echoed from the TV. The lone attendant wasn't paying any attention to the register; he just stood, mouth half open, holding the remote like maybe if he could change the channel he could change the future.

The Moon was gone. The Far Side Array was on the Moon.

"Mom," Lucy said, not even realizing she'd spoken aloud until Jack put his arm around her.

"She probably got off the Moon. I mean, they have shuttles for that, right?" Jack said quietly.

"I don't know. It's only a few of them up on that station and they get stuck there for months at a time. Why didn't anyone see this coming?" Lucy shoved Jack away. "Why? How did this happen and nobody knows?" She was aware she was yelling and she didn't give two fucks.

"Uh," the attendant said, "Some black guy in a suit came on earlier and was talking about the angle of the sun and some shit. Apparently nobody saw it coming. Probably the government is lying to us. They always are."

Heidi spread her hands in a placating gesture that just annoyed Lucy more. "Please, Luce, we gotta get back home. I gotta call my mom, and call Dana. Let's just go."

Mom. Lucy pressed her lips together and breathed in through her nose. The store smelled like lemon cleaning fluid and stale beer, but it grounded her. She couldn't get a hold of Mom even if she'd made it off the Moon. But Dad would know what was going on—he'd know what to do. And if meteors were going to strike Earth, Montana might be as safe a place as any.

Besides, Dad was like literally the only family she had left on this planet.

"No, we don't want to be anywhere near the coasts if meteors are striking all over the planet," she said, looking at Jack. "We're going to my home. We're going to Montana."

On the TV, the news cut out and the high whining tone of the emergency broadcast station pierced the tense air in the store.

• • •

Jack had agreed immediately, but Heidi was still sulking in the back seat as they left the serene park behind and entered a chaos of traffic. By the time they hit I-80 West toward San Jose, cars clogged the road heading into the city. It was a Sunday in August; the traffic shouldn't have been so bad. Lucy's cell phone still hunted for a signal. She dug out the folding map of the United States from the Jeep's glove box. It was shiny and new, never used. Who needed a paper map when you had GPS on your phone?

She guessed Jack being a Boy Scout and Army brat was good for something. He took that *always be prepared* thing seriously.

"Last chance to get out and find a bus station or something," Lucy said, leaning back over the seat and looking at Heidi.

"No," Heidi said. She looked out the window at the clogged freeway. "I'll go with you. I doubt they're letting flights out, and I'd rather be with friends than alone."

Which was good, Lucy thought. Because she'd never have really let Heidi go into the city by herself.

They cut around San Jose and headed down 580 toward Stockton, deciding to avoid I-5 North. The radio flip-flopped between static and emergency broadcasts telling people to stay in their homes. It was dark by the time they got near Stockton.

A gas station in Colfax was still open. Jack bought another gas can, filling it and adding it to the two he already kept in the back of Jeep. He topped those off, too.

"Smart thing, kids," the old woman behind the counter said to them as they paid in cash. "Last can I have to sell. People been buying out all day going down this road toward Reno. We're gonna be out of gas come tomorrow if the trucks don't make it. Heard there are some fires up that way, so take care."

"You heard anything else?" Lucy asked, motioning to the TV. It was muted, just the bands of the Emergency Broadcast System twitching on the screen.

"Nothing useful," the woman said. She smiled and shrugged her thin shoulders. "Keep calm and carry on."

Her cackle followed them out of the station and all the way back to their car.

• • •

The one and only time Lucy had made this drive was a year before, when she and her dad drove out to set her up at school. They'd stopped halfway through the seventeen-hour drive at a little bed and breakfast. He'd played basketball with the kids of the couple who ran the place while Lucy stood on the porch and answered awkward questions. Mom had been in training for the Moon mission, but try getting people to believe that no really, your mom was totally going to the Moon.

She'd shut off the radio over an hour before. Reno had seemed normal, almost calm. Lights still on, traffic thin. That might have been the tell that something was wrong with the world, Lucy guessed. Even on a Sunday night, traffic should have been jumping with people going out or coming home from the various entertainments Nevada's cities had to offer. They'd grabbed snacks at another gas station but no one had felt like trying to find a restaurant or having much of a conversation.

Now though, Jack was crashed out in the passenger seat, and Heidi had shoved camping gear down so she could sprawl on the back seat. The only noises were the sounds of the tires shushing along the road. The Jeep's headlights picked up a haze in the air and the sky was dark overhead, pierced occasionally with little flashes, like far-off lightning strikes.

Lucy had a feeling it wasn't lightning. She didn't want to think about the meteors. Thinking about it led to thinking about the Moon. About Mom.

She's probably in a damn bunker somewhere in Florida or Texas or something, Lucy told herself. She blinked away angry tears and tightened her hands on the steering wheel. She regretted the pizza stick she'd eaten as her belly flipped again. No thinking about Mom. Think about Dad. About getting home. Hours now—just a few more hours. If Jack had been awake, she would have made him check the map, check the mile markers. Five or six more hours, she guessed, before they hit US-93 and headed north for Montana. Then another six or seven hours. So maybe twelve, thirteen total.

She almost hit the first deer, but slammed on the brakes in time. Another leapt into the roadway. Then another.

"Jesus fuck," Jack said, jerking awake as the sudden stop slammed him into his seatbelt.

"Look," Lucy said. "What are they doing?"

There was a huge cracking noise overhead, and the road seemed to roll up beneath them. Out of the brush at the sides of the highway, hundreds of deer sprang forward, flooding into the road and then across and down the other side. They were clearly fleeing something.

"What is that?" Heidi asked, her voice heavy with sleep and fear.

The huge herd of deer had cleared. Beyond, out in a darkness lit now with an odd, almost nuclear glow, a cloud rushed at them, looking like a giant white wave.

"No idea," Lucy said. She stomped on the gas. "Seatbelts!"

The Jeep was no sports car, but she was pretty sure she went from zero to eighty in record time. Dust and chunks of turf, pebbles, and demolished brush slammed into the windows and scraped along the sides of the vehicle. The right tire hit the drunk bumps on the side of the road and Lucy aimed straight, keeping the ridges beneath them so she could feel her way down the road. Pale flashes of the white lines on the road through the smoke helped keep her on track.

The air cleared after a few miles, and she found herself praying under her breath as the headlights lit upon dark asphalt. She pulled the Jeep back left, into the road proper.

"You're lucky you didn't blow the tires," Jack said. His voice sounded more awed than reproachful.

"Driving by Braille," Lucy said, shooting him a quick smile. A pain hit her heart. That saying was something her mother always said, usually to excuse the way she often wandered on the road a little, her brain lost in some scientific minutia.

"Did we just survive a meteor strike?" Heidi asked.

"I don't know. Maybe."

"We good on gas?"

Lucy checked the gauge. "Yeah. I can keep driving. Though now I gotta pee."

"That's all of us, after that," Heidi said.

No one slept again that night, though Lucy guessed Jack could have. He was the only one of them used to this. She finally asked him as they neared Elko around dawn.

"This is like war, kinda, huh? Are you going to be okay?"

They didn't talk about his service. Jack had joined up after his parents were killed in a car accident when he was seventeen. He'd told her he was a helo pilot, and the one time she'd asked him if he'd shot anyone, he just shook his head. Lucy was glad about that. She might have been raised in Montana where being able to walk meant you were old enough to learn to use a gun, but she didn't like the idea of them, and her politics leaned further left than even her extremely progressive parents'.

"This is nothing like the war," Jack said. The look on his face closed that line of conversation, and Lucy kept driving.

Elko was silent, the houses shuttered and nothing open. They drove another hour, the gas light flickering on, and debated using one of the tanks. Jack voted they should wait and see if one of the little stops between Elko and Wells had anything.

Before Wells, where they would turn north onto US-93, they found an open gas station and everyone got out to stretch and check their phones.

"Those won't work," the attendant said. He was a middle-aged man, on the small side, barely taller than Lucy, with a big round belly and white beard any mall Santa Claus would've been proud of. He'd come out of his little booth to chat, seemingly glad to see live people on the road. "Got a brother with the Sheriff's office. Said that all stable frequencies for the radio and phones are being routed for emergency personnel only."

"So how the hell do you call 911?" Heidi asked.

"Times like these?" He motioned up to the clouded-over sky where small flashes still glinted every now and again in the diffuse morning sun. "You don't."

Lucy shook her head. The roads had been clear so far, other than some plant debris and dirt. They were moving, however, toward heavily forested areas. Remembering the pictures of the Tunguska Impact, she climbed back into the Jeep to study the map again.

A big truck roared into the station as Jack was finishing with the pump. Three big white men, mid-twenties to thirties, jumped out, whooping. Two of them were carrying machetes.

Lucy froze as the one without a knife grabbed Heidi and swung her around, pulling her tight against his body.

"You just back off, old man. We're commandeering this station. It's the end of the fucking world, don't you know?" The oldest-looking one, a man with a reddish beard and blue overalls, waved his machete at the attendant.

"That isn't a good idea," Jack said. His voice was all steel, his hands at his sides, but Lucy knew the look of readiness when she saw it. He was going to get himself killed, the big damn soldier.

She let the map drop slowly to the seat and followed it down. No one was looking at her; their eyes were on Jack and the attendant. With her right hand, she felt under the driver's seat until she found Jack's gun case. Still bent low, she slid the Glock from the case, checked the magazine and made sure a round was already chambered. Her heart raced miles ahead of her fear, but she shoved away all the anxiety, the shake in her fingers.

Instead she reached for her dad's voice. "Never point a gun at something you aren't willing to shoot," he had told her. "Never point a gun at a man unless you want him dead. If you aren't willing to make him dead, you might as well put the gun in his hand and tell him to pull the trigger."

She didn't want to kill anyone. But the way that man was groping her sobbing friend, the way Jack looked ready to try to take on three big men with no weapons, well. There were no police to call. No one to stop this. Just her.

Lucy slid out of the Jeep and came around the side, raising the gun and pointing it at the man in overalls. He'd talked, so she was pretty sure he was the boss.

"Let her go, and get the fuck out of here," she said. Her voice was low and mean and only shook a little. *Channel Dirty Harry,* she told herself. *Dad made me watch all those old movies, might as well get some use out of it.*

"Ooh, look Jerry." One of the other men, the one not holding Heidi, laughed. "The spic cunt there wants us to leave."

"You going to shoot, girl?" Overalls asked. He sneered, but his eyes were shadowed by what she hoped was fear.

"She ain't gonna shoot," the other guy said. "Those Mexican bitches can't . . ."

Whatever he would have said was cut off by the loud report of the gun and a scream. Lucy swung the gun smoothly back to Overalls as the other guy fell to the ground, dropping his machete and holding his bleeding crotch.

"I'm Puerto Rican, you ignorant fuck," she said.

Whatever Overalls saw in her face then, he didn't like. He dropped his machete and hissed at the man holding Heidi to let her go as he raised his hands and backed toward their truck.

The attendant bolted for his hut and came out with a shotgun. "Get out of here and don't come back or I'll put more holes in you!" he yelled after them.

They grabbed up their bleeding friend and drove their truck out of there faster than they'd arrived.

"Oh my god. You shot him. You really shot him!" Heidi was freaking out.

"Give me the gun," Jack said softly. He gently took it from her numb fingers.

"I'm okay," Lucy said. Her teeth chattered. Shock. Maybe this was shock. She wasn't sure. She'd really shot him.

"How much for the gas," Jack said. He flicked the safety on and kept the gun low at his side.

"No charge. Just get where you are going and keep these ladies safe, eh?" The man smiled a gap-toothed smile. "Shit raining from the skies does terrible things to people. And you, little lady, you did right. Don't you fear no retribution. Those bastards are cowards. They'll look for other targets that don't shoot back."

"Then I wish I'd killed them," Lucy muttered. She wasn't sure if she meant it or not.

Jack drove. Heidi sat in back, staring out the window, not talking. Lucy glanced over her shoulder at her friend a few times, but Heidi wouldn't meet her eyes, even in the reflection of the window.

They turned north onto US-93 and it was clear meteors had hit near here. Branches were down in the road and they were forced to slow. They passed a couple cars heading south, but the drivers only waved and didn't stop to share news.

"What's that haze?" Lucy said finally, breaking the silence that had descended since the gas station.

"Forest fire, I think. It's pretty far off though."

"I'm sorry, Jack," she said softly. "I didn't know what else to do."

"Sorry? For what? You saved us back there. I was going to try to get them with prayer and my bare hands."

"I shot a man."

"I know. It isn't easy. But you winged his nuts. Not like he's dead."

"I was aiming for his chest," Lucy said.

Jack looked sideways at her and a small smile played at his lips. "No you weren't," he said.

"No," Lucy said. A weird giddiness rose in her, threatening to turn into a hysterical giggle. "I wasn't."

"You asked if this was like war? Back there, it kind of was." He sighed and ran his hand through his hair. She loved that gesture. She'd been so mad at him about something—she was always mad about something—but right then she wanted to kiss him, to curl up in his arms and pretend the world was just fine.

"You've shot people." It wasn't a question, not anymore.

He dodged answering it anyway. "Times like these, you figure out who you are. Deep inside. Some people can't do what has to be done. Some can."

"Fuck you," Heidi said from the back seat.

"That guy was huge, Heidi. There wasn't anything you could have done. No more than Luce here could've stopped them if they'd grabbed her. She found a tool and she used it. We survived. That's how it works."

Heidi's eyes were bright with tears and her hands fisted in her t-shirt. "Not how I want my life to work," she whispered.

"We'll find you a way to Chicago, Heidi," Lucy said. "Once we're home."

"Sure," Heidi said and went back to staring out the window.

They had to get out twice to clear larger branches, and once, nearly half a tree from the road. No more weird cracks of light lit the sky, but the sun was obscured in the haze and the dust and smoke were so heavy that they had to breathe through their shirts.

Heidi took over so Lucy could rest. She still refused to say more than a syllable or three.

Lucy must've dozed off, though she felt for a while as the rough road chunked and thunked away beneath the Jeep that she'd never sleep again. Not until she knew Dad was safe. Not until she knew for sure about the Moon. About Mom.

The cessation of road noise woke her.

"Where are we?" she asked Jack. Heidi wasn't in the driver's seat.

"Outside Darby. We're on a side-road. Some guys were heading out to try to clear a rockslide or something on the highway, so they told us to detour down this Old Darby Road. Heidi had to pee." He motioned out the window with a grin.

"You stopped and talked to people and I didn't wake up?" Lucy rubbed her eyes and caught a whiff of her morning breath. She sat up and reached for a water bottle.

"A regular sleeping beauty," Jack said, pushing some of her hair from her face. "Speaking of that, you're Puerto Rican?"

"Half," she said, making a face. "My parents named me Lucita, but I hate it." It seemed so trivial now. All through middle school and high school, she'd just wanted to be one of the pale, pretty blondes. She'd bleached her hair, worn contacts, put on foundation that was two shades too light for her complexion. Gone by Lucy instead of Lucita. Lucy Goodwin had tried so hard to leave everything of her mother and her mother's history behind. Her language. Her culture. Her religion. Her science.

And now all I want to do is get home and tell her how sorry I am and promise we'll never argue again. Ever.

"Wait," she said as Jack started to get out of the car. "Darby? That means we're like an hour or so from home." She threw open the door and came around to his side, pulling him down for a kiss as he climbed out and wrapped her in his arms.

"I can't believe you are from a place called Lolo." He grinned.

"The farm is outside Lolo. Geez."

"A farm like this?" Jack motioned around them.

Heidi had stopped along the road at a gravel driveway that stretched back down a lane of poplar. In the distance Lucy could make out the roof of a farmhouse, one of the classic two-story ones, probably made with stone and logs, the roof looking like slate from this distance in the hazy afternoon light. The air was dusty but cool, carrying an almost metallic tang. Looking up, Lucy couldn't find where the sun should be.

"It should be a lot hotter this time of year," she said.

"Too much shit in the atmosphere, I guess," Jack said. He let her go and walked a little ways toward some bushes. "Heidi, you get eaten by a bear?"

"Oh my god, are there bears around here?" came the shrieking reply.

Lucy mouthed *asshole* at Jack, who grinned.

A high whining noise broke the still air, as though a jet engine had materialized somewhere above them. Before Lucy could do more than look up and then back at Jack, a cracking boom sounded, the reverberations rattling through her bones and teeth like thunder from the worst summer storm she'd ever seen.

"Get back in the car," she yelled. "Heidi!"

It was too late. The road rippled, and the trees seemed to burst apart on the far side where they hadn't been cleared for farmland. A wave like the one before, this one churning and brownish-gray, descended on them. Lucy tried to get into the Jeep, but the wave caught her, throwing her into the air and over the low wooden fence. She hit the ground with a crunch that knocked away what little air was left in her lungs. The shockwave smashed her flat and she clung to the ground, her arms around her head, her eardrums pulsing as though she'd dove too deep into water.

Then it was gone, the horrible pressure lifting, her ears ringing and throbbing. Lucy uncurled slowly, wiggling her fingers and then her toes. Nothing seemed broken, though her mouth tasted like grit and blood. She spit and pulled her torn, grimy tee-shirt up over her nose and mouth.

Dust clogged the air, stinging particles rasping on her skin. She squinted and shaded her eyes with one hand, trying to make out anything.

It wasn't just the ringing in her ears. Someone was screaming. Lucy moved toward the voice, stepping over the scattered remains of the low wood fence. The Jeep loomed ahead and appeared mostly intact. She couldn't see Jack or Heidi.

She stumbled toward the screams and nearly fell down the embankment into what was left of the bushes Heidi had been using as a makeshift toilet. A smear of blue and red caught her eye, and Lucy kicked her way through the debris.

Heidi lay half on the ground, half-impaled on the jagged remains of a sapling. Blood gushed, dark and lazy, from her chest and trickled out of her gasping, screaming mouth. Jack was kneeling at her side, his tee-shirt off, revealing a back bloodied with cuts.

This time, Lucy didn't freeze. She pulled off her own shirt and ran forward, offering it to Jack to help stop up the blood oozing from around the stick in Heidi's chest.

He shook his head and tried to say something, but coughed instead. That was when Lucy saw his left arm. At first her brain refused to make sense of it. She thought he had a piece of tree sticking out of his arm and made an aborted motion to pull it free from his skin.

That was when she realized it wasn't a stick. That *was* his left arm. Or at least the bone. The humerus, she remembered from high school biology. There was nothing funny about it. Giggles tightened her chest and she turned her head, vomiting water and bile into the dirt.

Jack yelled again and she made out that he wanted her to tie off her shirt around his upper arm. Blood ran in a dirty crimson river down his useless hand. Sucking in a breath that was more grit than air, Lucy did as he asked, amazed he didn't pass out.

"Big damn soldier," she muttered, knowing he couldn't hear her.

"Hey," a voice boomed from the haze, followed by two people, a man and a woman. They had on gasmasks and goggles over their eyes. The woman had a rifle.

Lucy blinked grit from her eyes and waved to them. If they wanted to kill her or do something all Texas Chainsaw Massacre, she wasn't in any state to stop them. She just had to trust now that her dad was right, and that most people were good people.

He was right. They were good people.

Maddie Grace and her son Victor managed to get Heidi free of the tree, cutting the sapling out from under her. She was bundled into a quilt for the short run back to the farmhouse, where Victor's wife Angel waited with two scared but curious kids. Lucy found out their names as she was bundled into a comfortable country kitchen. Gas lamps were lit and Angel got to work on cleaning Lucy's cuts.

Heidi had stopped screaming. Angel said that Victor was a paramedic, had been with the army, too. He'd see to her friends.

Lucy didn't argue, though she felt like a coward. She didn't think she could face more blood and pain. Every cut, every bruise, every ache and pain woke up and tried to voice how much her body hated her all at once. Her ears wouldn't equalize, and she wasn't sure she could hear at all from the left one.

Maddie Grace appeared in the doorway, grief and determination etched in the heavy lines of her face.

"You'll be wanting to say goodbye," she said.

"Jack? But it was just his arm—" Lucy stood up too quickly and the world spun.

"No, not your man. The girl."

Guilt wracked Lucy, but she shoved it away. It was like Jack said. Act now, process later.

"Of course," she said. She walked forward, following Maddie Grace into what had been a utility room but was now a makeshift surgery. A folding table, the kind you might use for a picnic or impromptu card game, held Heidi's still body. Bloody rags were gathered in a tidy pile to one side, and Victor stood, his head hanging, tears dripping off his thick nose.

Jack lay half propped in a folding chair, his arm still wrapped in her tee-shirt. He looked up at Lucy and held out his good hand to her.

She ignored it, going to Heidi's side on the table. Lucy wrapped her fingers around her friend's and was surprised when Heidi's eyes flickered and she weakly squeezed back.

"I'm sorry," Lucy said. All she did was argue with people, and then her last words were always anger or apology. She blinked at tears, trying to smile at her friend. "You stay with us, okay? We're right here. You aren't alone."

Heidi's mouth moved, but whatever she said was lost as she went rigid. She shook her head, and then started to choke. Victor moved in, propping up her head, trying to get her to breathe, his words a string of soothing nonsense.

Heidi stilled. Lucy had seen animals put down before, had seen that moment when a being went from life to death. It was disturbingly similar and yet more terrible, now. One moment her friend was there, struggling for air, bleeding out on the table. The next, no one was home.

Lucy collapsed, and all the tears she'd held back over the last hellish day found freedom now and scraped hotly down her cheeks. Jack tried to get up, but Victor told him to sit.

It was Maddie Grace who wrapped her wiry, strong arms around Lucy's shoulders and guided her into a cozy family room, pressing her gently onto the couch. Someone found a shirt for her, something clean. Tea was pressed into her hands. A handkerchief for her tears. Still the tears came.

Finally, cried down to dry sobs, the tea a minty memory in her throat, Lucy passed out.

• • •

"It will be dark soon. We can go tomorrow," Jack said.

"Yeah, it'll be dark soon, but I don't care. I'm going home, Jack. I am not waiting any longer. Victor said the Jeep will run. He changed the tire for me and cleared out the broken glass. I'm going home." Lucy rubbed her hands down her borrowed shirt. She'd slept for over an hour, but that was long enough. Every ache and cut told her that Jack was right, that she should stay where she was safe and sleep some more.

But this wasn't home.

"Your dad can wait a day," Jack said. He struggled to sit upright on the pull-out couch, and she could see he was in horrible pain even through the morphine Victor had given him.

"What if he can't?" Lucy shot back. "The last thing I said to her was so mean, Jack. I told her I wished I had a mother who could understand, a mother like my friends' moms. I have to go home. I can't let my last words to Mom be the last thing said in our family."

"She might be alive."

"No," Lucy said. The word hurt to say, but it rang inside her aching heart with a truth she couldn't explain. "I can feel it. She's gone." Like Heidi. Like god knew how many people. Even the radios were out; Maddie Grace's family had no recent news.

"Fine. I'm going too." Jack tried to swing his legs over to the side and cried out in pain as the movement jolted his arm.

"No. It's only an hour away. Stay here. Maddie Grace said she doesn't mind. They can run you up to the farm when you are better, or I'll come back and get you in a day or two. I gave them directions." Lucy walked over to him and bent down, kissing his damp forehead. He felt feverish, and she made a note to tell Victor on her way out.

"I love you, Luce," Jack said.

"Damn well better. I shot a dude in the balls for you." She fought more tears as she smiled. This would not be their last conversation—she was determined about that. But if it was . . . if, well, she wouldn't leave with angry words. Not this time. "I love you, too, you big damn soldier."

The US-93 was a wreck of debris and branches. Lucy put the Jeep's four-wheel drive through its paces. It was full dark when she spotted the bright yellow reflectors on the mailbox at the end of her driveway shining like welcome home beacons through the haze.

She pulled up at the house, eyes searching for a light in the dark. She heard the screen door bang open as she stumbled up the steps and blinked as a flashlight poured warm light over her.

"Daddy?" she said.

"Lucita! Lucy!" he dropped the flashlight and wrapped her in his arms. She pushed her nose into his soft flannel shirt and breathed in the familiar smell of vanilla pipe tobacco, horses, and mint.

"Dad, I'm home," she said, laughing into his chest.

"Yes, yes you are."

• • •

The meteor strike outside Darby was the closest anything large got to Lolo, Montana. The impact haze—as the news radio, when it was working, called it—persisted. They were in for what was called an impact winter. No one knew how long it would last. Years, was the guess. Nobody could say what the death toll was. The coastal regions had been hit hard with tsunamis. Miami was rumored to be gone, struck directly by a large chunk of Moon debris. The equatorial zones were the hardest hit, but Lucy didn't regret fleeing California.

Three months, and they were crawling on toward real winter. Jack had shown up after a week with Maddie Grace and Victor in tow, bringing a crate of pickles with them. His arm wasn't fully healed even months later, but he was learning how to use his fingers again and doing the exercises Victor ordered him to. Lucy was a little jealous about how well Jack and her dad got along, but she figured they might have to cohabitate for a while, so she didn't say too much about it.

Victor said they'd buried Heidi by a really pretty dogwood that had survived the shockwave. No one knew how to get a message to Chicago and her family. Lucy vowed that someday she would make that journey and tell Heidi's mom and sister where their daughter was buried.

She knew, deeply, how crushing a lack of closure could be.

No one talked about Mom. Not after the first night, when Lucy had asked about the Moon and all her dad said was "Yes, it's true" and they'd left it at that.

Almost three months. It felt like three minutes sometimes.

Lucy leaned on the porch rail, hands tucked into her coat, watching the hazy sky darken. There were no more flashes in the night, at least in this area, but there were no stars either. No sun except a slightly brighter patch of sky some afternoons. The farm had its own generator and well, but they rationed everything. The National Guard had been through from Missoula, clearing the roads and bringing news and fuel. That was all they had of the outside world. There had been no news of Mom or the people on the Moon. It was like the world was pretending no one had been there.

Crunching gravel pulled Lucy from her melancholy. A Hummer crept up the driveway, looking dark and military and official.

"Dad," she yelled. Jack was out at the barn, but her father was inside, whipping up his famous camp stove chili they were all too nice to tell him they were sick to death of eating.

He came out on the porch with his .22 rifle in hand. He looked older to Lucy, his hair grayer and lines forming around his mouth and eyes she didn't remember being there before. He was still tall and solid and calm, though.

Two men in fatigues came out first, nodding to Lucy and her father.

"You Paul Goodwin?" one man asked.

"I am," her dad said. He gently propped the gun against the house and walked forward to the steps.

A woman climbed out of the vehicle, assisted by one of the men in fatigues. She was pregnant, her belly pushing out heavily against her navy blue pea-coat. She was thin except for that belly, and pretty. She looked up at Dad, then at Lucy, and walked forward, a small bag in her hand.

"My name is Shannon," she said, a soft English accent lilting her voice. "I served with Neta on the Far Side Array."

"No—" Dad half cried out, his fist pressing into his lips. Lucy grabbed for his arm and leaned into him.

It was one thing to believe that Mom was dead. It was another to see this woman, to hear her use the past tense, and know it for real.

"Is that?" Lucy said, motioning toward the bag. Had they brought only her body back? Cremated her?

"What? No," Shannon said. "This is, I mean, she recorded a message. We couldn't all go home, there wasn't space."

A man behind Shannon coughed loudly, his expression a warning.

"Bloody hell, Wentworth. It's Neta's family. They deserve to know the truth." She turned back to Lucy and her dad. "Your mom chose to stay so that I could come home . . . she knew I was pregnant."

"Neta would do that," Dad said. Tears reddened his eyes, but he managed a smile. "God, she would do that."

"This is her last message. Do you have power? It had a full charge when we left, but if you need more, we can hook up a battery for you." Shannon walked to the edge of the stairs, holding out the bag.

"We have enough," Lucy said, stepping down from the porch and taking the bag. It felt like a small laptop was inside. "So she's really gone," she whispered to Shannon.

"I'm sorry, sweetheart, she is," Shannon said. She looked like she might cry, too.

Lucy nodded and pressed her lips together. "Thank you," she said.

"I'm sorry if we don't ask you to stay," her dad said as Lucy turned and climbed the steps.

"I understand," Shannon said.

Lucy hugged her father's side, and they watched as the woman and her escort got back into their car and made a swinging turn, driving off down the road in a swarm of dust.

They played the message on the military's portable DVD player, just the two of them, not calling Jack in from the barn in unspoken agreement. Lucy loved Jack, but this was a family thing.

Mom seemed so composed on the screen, but so tiny. Her face was lined and tired, her dark eyes bright, her words steady and full of love. There was no reproach, no anger, no blame.

She even called Lucy *Lucy*.

And then that final moment, just before the message cut out, when the tears broke for a shining second from her mother's eyes, and she whispered to the camera: "Love her, Paul. Give our little light all the love I won't be there to give. And don't hang on to me. I want you both to live, to be happy."

Lucy bolted from the kitchen and out onto the porch, sobbing. Her dad joined her, his big arms wrapping around her shoulders and pulling her into his warm, flannel-covered chest.

"I was so mad at her," she said, her breath misting in the freezing air. "But I didn't mean it. I didn't."

"She knew, Luce, she knew." He pressed his lips into her hair and rocked her gently.

"I can't tell her though. She's gone. Just . . . gone."

"She isn't gone. Your mother is not gone." The force of his words shocked Lucy, and she pulled away a little to stare up into his face. "Are the stars gone?" He pointed at the sky.

"What? No, we just can't see them."

"Exactly, Lucita. They are still there, just like your mom. Invisible, but shining down on us all the same."

They stood for a long time out on the porch, until Jack's footsteps roused them.

"You coming inside?" Jack asked, looking them over, questions in his eyes.

Lucy nodded. She slipped her hand into his good one and took a last look at the sky. Invisible, but still there. She squeezed Jack's fingers and walked through the door.

ROCK MANNING CAN'T HEAR YOU

Charlie Jane Anders

This guy came into the half-stocked convenience store where I was working, and he wanted me to empty out the safe. He had a waxy mustache and soul patch, and he wore a poncho over a bulky football sweatshirt and knee-high socks. He was waving a shotgun that looked like someone had shot a grouse with it back in 2009, and then it had sat in a closet ever since. I thought about angles of escape, up over his head or around behind the Juicy Yoo cooler—because I'm Rock Manning, the internet's favorite hyperfiend, and that's what I do.

Then I shrugged and put up my hands.

The trouble was, he couldn't get at the safe because it was keyed to my vital signs, so if my heart or breathing sped up then the safe went into total lockdown, and if my heart stopped then every alarm went dog-crazy. My boss Ramon couldn't even get cash for legitimate purposes half the time because I'd be doing jumping jacks and thinking about whether we should stage a trolley accident or a scooter joust when we were making our slapstick movies this weekend. I had to practice no-mind deep breathing just so my boss could take out petty cash.

With this guy waving his gun at me, my heart juddered so damn hard the tumblers in the safe hugged each other for dear life. He almost gave up and left, but then he found some extra drowsy cough syrup and made me drink some of it along with a ton of Grand Marnier, with that shotgun in my face the whole time I was chugging. My heart stayed pigeon-like, and I told the guy he'd have to be patient and wait for the stuff to take effect. He wanted to keep force-feeding me downers but I reminded him that if I died the safe locked up tight.

He and I ended up sitting around the store a couple hours, talking about old movies and video games and stuff. Reginald loved all the cop buddy comedies of the eighties and nineties, and he could recite long sections of *Lethal Weapon* from memory. Before I even knew what I was doing, I was telling Reginald that a bunch of us made our own amateur web movies in Boston Common and he should swing by this Saturday and join in. I guess it was the cough syrup, or just the fact that we'd been talking for ages and he'd put down the gun by then. Five minutes after he thanked me and wandered off down the street, I took a deep breath and heard the safe un-jam itself.

I meant to tell some of my friends about Reginald, but then I got side-tracked into thinking about my character. Not my real-life character, which I didn't really know much about, but my movie character.

Think about it! Harold Lloyd is the same guy in every one of his movies—a small-town innocent, maybe a little egg-headed but not street smart, with his heart on his sleeve but also full of crazy ambitions. I could be like that, except maybe more cunning and just a little loopy. Or okay, *a lot* loopy. Coming off the super-cold-relief formula and cognac buzz, I felt a swelling urgency that people should root for me, not just laugh at my hijinks.

Janelle, the cute film student with the rainbow dreads, agreed with me. The comic hero has to be loveable or relatable, or at least there has to be a moment of connection with the audience in between all the falling gargoyles, she said. The two of us cornered Sally Hamster, our director, who kept trying to get us to talk to her hands. Sally was like, "I make art during the week. This weekend shit is just for fun." Sally had been making serious strides at film school until I came back into her life, fully recovered from my nervous breakdown and eager to make more weird movies on the internet. But Janelle and I both said it wasn't about art, just making the fun as fun as possible.

I kept forgetting to mention Reginald the corner-store robber, until he showed up on Saturday wearing some kind of bright red wrestling costume, or maybe those were just his regular exercise clothes. We dressed Reginald up as a cop, and a bunch of the film school kids played a motorcycle gang who'd started riding bicycles because gas was $12 a gallon, so they all overcompensated by whooping really loud and blasting heavy metal when they pedaled into town.

Someone had renovated a whole section of Boston near the river to look like a little "ye olde" village, except it was really all yuppie boutiques that had been boarded up since the Debt Crisis. So we turned it into a small town that was trying to keep the bikers out with the help of Reginald the cop, and I got mixed up in the middle of their conflict because I had to deliver a cactus to a sick friend. Once again, my motivation was a little hazy, and it bothered me as well as Janelle. Sally had her elbow in the way of us doing any kind of love story, even though I could never figure out why. It wasn't just that she'd gotten her heart pulped with her boyfriend Raine's head during the Peace Riots. She was just dead set against goo-goo eyes.

Everybody thought Reginald rocked, especially the sequence where a bunch of the bikers rode up a giant ramp we made out of an old herbal facial spa sign and flew over Reginald's head while he tried to kick-box with their wheels. Except Zapp Stillman, because Reginald somehow managed to break Zapp's nose, although the other film geeks said it would just add some boxery distinction to his face. (Zapp was the grand-nephew of some famous movie director, and an expert on everything.)

Sally asked where I found Reginald, and I said I just ran into him. Reginald nearly dropped me off the Longfellow Bridge when he found out this was a volunteer gig, but I convinced him the exposure would help him to get other, paying gigs. He got pretty jazzed thinking about his roundhouse popping up all over the internet and becoming a cult phenom. He was pretty glad he didn't actually kill me, at least for now.

I started wondering if I should tell Sally the truth about Reginald, but I figured he would probably disappear soon anyway, since he made me look like long-attention-span guy by comparison. I hadn't been able to concentrate much before Raine died, but ever since I involuntarily ate a piece of Raine's brain I was a human jitter. The Army recruiter doctors had taken one look at me and just laughed at the idea of militarizing me.

People hit our video-tumblr like bam-bam-bam. Sally thought soon we'd be more popular than we were in high school, and we sold some advertisements. People would bring us pieces of meat and shoes in return for an ad on the site sometimes. Sally got that gleam in her eye, the one she used to get when the internet first fell in love with us. But she also kept saying how un-artistic our movies were, compared to the fancy stuff she and Janelle were doing for film school.

So Zapp Stillman was a hyper-mega rich socialite, who didn't really notice a lot of what was going on around him, and I was his overeager manservant trying to cater to all his idiotic whims. Despite what Reginald had done to Zapp's face, he still looked delicate and sheltered, and I got to wear this great houndstooth suit that fit really well except for the arms, shoulders, knees, and crotch. I practiced walking straight and butlery, which only made me more splashmanic, and then Zapp and I were supposed to go on a trip to the seaside except I had to shelter him from all the violence on the streets. Zapp hadn't read a blog or seen a newscast in years and I kept him unaware of the state of the world. So for example, we rode our two-seater bicycle past piles of comatose bodies, and I convinced Zapp it was just a group of people camping out for tickets to the Imagine Dragons reunion tour. And then a bunch of guys on scooters chased us to rip our heads off, and I told Zapp it was a friendly race. (All dialogue was big black captions, like in an old-school classic movie.)

It was a cool movie with good character moments, but a ton of stuff went wrong when we were filming. Like we staged a fake riot with a bunch of film students in ripped-up clothes pulling down bricks we'd placed strategically. Then random people wandered by and saw what was going on, and they wanted to join in and pretty soon they were tossing big chunks of wall around, and they saw Zapp and me on our dorky bicycle built for two and threw rocks at us, so the peddling-for-dear-life sequences were way more realistic than we'd bargained on. The camera guys had to run like hell to keep their equipment from being smashed.

Mid-summer, Boston was all melty but people on the street sold homemade ice cream and you could ignore all the rotting smells if you thought about the river ducks. I still felt like I was about to crash everyone around me into the gritty old walls. I would forget for a second; I would bounce down the street, jumping over the people on the sidewalk and swinging on the low oak branches. And then I would have a mental image of myself landing the wrong way with my foot in someone's stomach, maybe someone I loved or maybe a stranger.

Some nights I couldn't sleep because every time I closed my eyes I saw Raine getting his head exploded, the chunks of skull flying apart, the brains splattering into my open mouth. This image blended together with all the ways I'd injured people by accident, or the times when I *could have* injured people if things had gone a little different. Raine's head got pulpier and more vivid each time.

Janelle and I got together and wrote a movie script, to Sally's total horror. "Okay, so what is this story about?" Janelle asked me twenty or thirty times. We sat on an abandoned swan boat in the middle of the lake in Boston Common, and the boat kept almost capsizing as water sloshed in and out of its gullet. Once, tourists had chugged around in these boats, but now they just bobbed their decaying shells in and out of the algae. I didn't know what our story was about, since I didn't even know what the story *was*. Couldn't we take one leap at a time? But Janelle was scary patient and kept talking themes: communication, Social Darwinism, the impossibility of really knowing other people because the closer you get to them the harder it is to see the whole person. Janelle had run away from home as a kid, and lived in the attic of a bookstore cafe for years, reading every book in the stockroom and living off of abandoned scones and salads. Nobody had known she was there until she used the store's address for her B.U. application and the acceptance letter turned up.

We settled on this O. Henry thing where two people try to save each other at cross purposes, sort of. I'm this scrappy DJ who owes money to gangsters, who could maybe be Vikings because we had some helmets and fake fur. And Janelle is a dancer who posed for some questionable photos years ago and now this sleazy guy wants to publish them and her strict family will disown her. So I decide to break in and snag the sleazy guy's hard drive, while Janelle wants to do whatever it takes to raise money to bail me out—even take on a dancer job that turns out to involve dancing on an unstable scaffolding at a construction site. And then the Vikings turn up while I'm trying to break into the sleazy guy's studio, and they want to break my legs but the sleazy guy has a protection deal with a Samurai gang. So we have a pitched Viking-Samurai battle in a photography studio, while I'm trying to slip past them and grab the hard drive. And then Janelle somehow falls off her scaffolding into the middle of our fracas and I have to run around to catch her.

It only took us about five hours to come up with that storyline, and by then the swan was submerged up to its neck and water slopped over the sides of its torso. We had to haul ourselves up onto the bridge without breaking our necks.

Janelle took a day off film school to help me location-scout our movie called *Photo Finish.* We found this large art/performance space which people actually used as an art studio. It had crumbling brick walls, a high platform leading to some big industrial-looking windows, and a red velvet curtain that perfectly said "Sleazy Photographer."

Reginald nearly bit her head off, trembling in his charging-bull helmet and muppet-fur cloak while she coached him on his lines. "No, come on Reggie, try it again and this time put everything you've got into the word 'maul.' You have to *feel* that word. Jesus, Rock, where did you find this guy?"

She tried to choreograph the big Viking-Samurai throwdown, even down to me throwing the big photographic backdrops in people's faces and Zapp Stillman, the lead Samurai, hurling his katana at a Viking and hitting the sought-after hard drive instead.

The fifth time we stopped so Janelle could micro-manage, Reginald looked ready to light the set on fire, rip several people's heads off, and then use his broadsword to make a head-kebab. I was having seismic levels of fidgetiness, to the point where I had to hug myself.

Sally pulled me aside. "Jesus, what the fuck are we going to do about Janelle?" Sally torqued her elbows and claws. "She's driving me fucking bonkers, man."

I didn't have any answers, except that I was worried about Reginald's inside-out fuse. Another hour went by, and you could have made a milk-shake on my head. It was thirty seconds' filming and then wait wait wait, ready, no hang on, wait, wait.

The tenth time we stopped, I jittered myself blind and stumbled into Zapp Stillman, and before he could finish saying he begged my pardon I fell over. On my way down, I kicked Zapp's katana into Reginald's crotch, and Reginald fell on top of three other Vikings, so their swords jabbed into his back. He howled and clutched at his own spine, then jumped up and announced that just because he'd failed to kill me the first time didn't mean he couldn't finish the job now.

Reginald grabbed a long razor-sharp hook from the studio corner and ran at me. Out of the corner of my eye, I saw Sally gesture to Janelle to get this on tape for godssake. Zapp Stillman tried to get between Reginald and me, and Reginald whacked him in the face. I ducked under a big platform and kicked a cart of A/V stuff at Reginald, but he jumped over the cart without breaking his run. Several of the other Samurai thought this was part of the movie, and tried to attack Reginald with their balsa-wood swords, but he just cracked their heads together, so their fake helmets crumpled.

Meanwhile, I slid out the other end of the platform and climbed the curtain rope. The rope was on a pulley, so Reginald started pulling, and the rope went down as the curtain went up. I had to climb at top speed just to stay at the same altitude. Reginald kept pulling the rope with one hand and threw his spike-hook with the other, but I caught the hook and dug it into the curtain, then let go of the rope and swung on the hook across to the other side of the curtain, which tore as I went, so I landed on the ground across the room. A random Viking swung at my head and I barely ducked in time, then I saw a bucket of water (which was supposed to be photographic solution) and I dumped it on Reginald's head. His helmet's horns stabbed through the bucket so he couldn't get it off, and he started grabbing anyone who got in his way, even other Vikings, and tossing them.

At first I screened the sirens out, because you heard sirens all the time, but I heard more and more, fire sirens as well as cop cars. Peal after peal, like church bells. I leaned out the window to see what was going on and then Reginald was at my ear, trying to push me out. He'd gotten the helmet and bucket off, and he had one hand under my armpit and the other on my belt. It was probably a dozen feet down. I could see flames in the distance, and tongues of smoke from a few other places. I tried to tell Reginald I hadn't meant to hurt him, but he just pushed harder. The window frame gave way and we both tumbled. I twisted my body so Reginald hit the ground first and I landed on top of him.

I couldn't see anything but I smelled smoke worse than ever. My crotch felt broken, my feet felt broken. I forced my eyes open but everything had a double image. Sally had the door to the studio building open nearby and was yelling for me to get my ass inside. I limped to my feet and juddered in, then Sally locked the door behind me. Through the window I watched Reginald try to raise himself up.

"Example of the sort of human garbage they tolerate up here," a voice said. It sounded sort of like Ricky Artesian, from back home, but wasn't. I found a window with a view of the guy, who was a little smaller than Ricky and had tufty black hair. He dressed like Ricky and had the same red bandana. So did the half dozen or so guys behind him, who had just climbed out of a couple of all-terrain crawlers. The guy talked for ages about his issues with Reginald, who kept trying to get to his feet but couldn't quite manage it. Reginald had the bad luck to be the only guy nearby who looked like a junkie and couldn't run for his life. I wanted to go out and help him, but I could barely move, and Sally half-supported, half-restrained me. Sally wanted to stop watching when they got into it with the crowbars, but this was my fault, sort of, and I had to see it play out.

They didn't torch him until they ran out of bones. I hoped he would black out, but he kept screaming the whole time, on fire. Maybe some people can black out and scream at the same time? I sure hoped so.

So at this point, you're wondering what happened to *Photo Finish*. It was our most popular Vumblr entry yet, even though we only filmed about half the scenes Janelle had scripted, and what we recorded didn't have that much in common with her and my storyline. Sally and some of the others did a fantastic job tweaking it with Zap!mation, to the point where the studio looked like twenty different places. With the red bandanas turning up all over the country and imposing mob rule, people were primed for people in silly costumes whacking each other. It turns out when everything is turning into bloody shit, that's when people need Vikings against Samurai more than ever. Who knew?

The police tried to stop the red bandanas at first, but then the President went on television and said they were an official militia, like in the Constitution, because we were losing our grip as a nation. It was probably the Pan Asiatic Ecumen's fault, but then again, everybody blamed them for everything.

• • •

Two days later, Sally said I had to get out of the house and breathe, because too many people were staying indoors all the time and we had a duty to show we weren't scared. I crutch-hopped my way down the empty street as Sally ran rings around me for a change. I was glad I didn't have to step over junkies any more, even though I worried about what had happened to all of them. Sally said they were locked up in camps, or tossed in bonfires, or just hiding out somewhere.

All of Sally's film student minions cheered for me when we got to B.U. Even the ones who'd high-backed me when I first showed up in town. Maybe because I'd become a casualty of art, or maybe because the new movie had gotten mad hits. Either way, people wanted to carry me around and pour stuff down my throat, and everyone signed my osteogenic body-sheath. We were promoting creative anarchy and that made us super important radical artists, and hey, we should take it to the next level somehow. I thought if they wanted to promote anarchy, maybe we could find one of the camps, in Medford or Malden, where the red-hanky guys had rounded up the homeless people and undesirables, and set them all free.

We could film it. We could put Napoleon hats on all of them and turn them loose. It would look cool, sort of like the final episode of *The Prisoner*. Everybody liked that idea, and they were all up for doing it, but not on a day when they had classes.

The film students kept adding more and more layers to the plan. We would dress as animals, and there would be a huge round clock which we'd roll downhill to cause a distraction, and maybe we could time the attack to coincide with a joint lunar/solar eclipse so the lack of both moon and sun would sensory-deprive everyone. They jumped up and down with excitement, but I realized they were making the plans fancier and fancier because they didn't want to have to follow through. That was fine with me because I was only half serious about the camp liberation idea too.

"Most of those guys, you just tell them where to stand and what to do, and they're happy. Don't make them think too hard," Sally told me afterward. Our movies had built her into a queen bee. She wanted to walk me home, but the sun sagged and I didn't want her to get caught out after dark. I ran into a couple of red-bandana groups on my way home, but I told them I was a friend of Ricky Artesian, the red bandana leader, and they practically saluted. The second group insisted on escorting me home. Film students and red bandanas, both whooping at me, all in one day!

Soon, I was healed enough to go back to work at the convenience store, where I kept seeing bone-crushed Reginald on fire whenever I looked at the lighters. Nowadays, I saw both Raine and Reginald in my dreams, unless I watched some Buster Keaton right before bedtime.

Some of my housemates were planning a giant protest against the red bandanas and the economic policies and the move to expand the war, and the crazy weapon projects like that sonic gun that people claimed would make an army shake itself to pieces from a distance. I was leery because, duh, the last time I'd gone to a protest I'd wound up covered in slippery bodies, choking on a piece of my friend's brain.

I started hoping my body wouldn't heal too quickly, because once it did they would expect me to create more serious mayhem, and just the thought of it made me start to shamblequake. Sally texted me saying it was time to do some more mad slapstick, and I texted back that we really needed to talk.

• • •

I have a perfect recall of my meeting with Sally, maybe cause it was our last-ever conversation.

We met in the middle of the Mass Avenue bridge, with faded paintwork measuring the bridge's span in "Smoots," the height of some long-ago MIT student whose classmates had rolled him across the bridge. On either side of us, the river swelled with gray bracken and flecks of brown foam, and in front of us, the jagged Boston skyline. The John Hancock Tower's windows had all started falling out and hitting people on the head, so they'd condemned the whole building and only gotten halfway through demolishing it, and now it looked like a shiny blue-green zigzag climbing to a single razor point. We watched the water churn a while. The wind battered us.

Sally was gushing about my chemistry with Zapp Stillman, and how much people liked seeing the two of us interact, and maybe we could do a few more clips featuring the two of us. Gang boss and lieutenant, an ineptly gay couple, boxer and trainer, rock star and manager, superheroes. The possibilities were endless, almost like having Raine back. For a moment I wondered if Sally had a thing for Zapp's gangly ass.

"That's why I wanted to talk to you," I said once I could break in. "I need to take a break from making movies. I was thinking of going back to North Carolina." I tried to explain how I kept seeing Raine and Reginald whenever I closed my eyes lately, but Sally grabbed my scruff and pushed me halfway over the edge of the bridge. My pants fell down, and the wind whipped through my boxer shorts. My ass was in space.

"You asshole," Sally said. "What the fuck is wrong with you? Every time I think I can rely on you. What the fuck? I was going to be a real director. I was doing great in film school, making serious films about real stuff. And then you turned up and sucked me back into spending all my time making these dumb movies instead. And now you're just going to leave? What? The? Fuck?" She shook me with each word. My shirt tore around the armpits. I could feel my feet, somewhere far away, trampling my pants.

"I'm sorry. I'm so sorry." I looked up into her bugged out eyes. "I just can't. I can't deal. Jesus, you're my best friend no matter how long I live, but I'm a poison time bomb, you don't want to be around me, I'll just hurt you, I'm so sorry. I break everything."

She hauled me off the edge and dumped me on my feet. "What the fuck are you talking about, Rock? I love you, but you're an idiot. Just listen to me, okay. You're not some kind of destructive engine. You are good for exactly one thing, and one thing only, and that's turning people's brains off for a few minutes. You should stick to that. And another thing, did you ever stop to think about what I'm getting out of doing these movies with you? Did you? I mean, jeez. The world we live in now, the only time things make sense is when I'm coming up with bigger and crazier disasters to put on film. I finally decided, slapstick is the new realism. And I can't do it without you. Do you understand what I'm saying?"

"Yeah, but . . ." I took a breath and pulled up my pants. The snap had broken, so I had to hold them together with one hand, and that limited my gesture menu a lot. "I keep feeling like I'm going to hurt somebody. I feel like people keep getting hurt around me, and maybe it's my fault somehow. Like what happened with Reginald. And Raine, before that."

"Jesus, this pisses me off. My boyfriend dies, but it's still all about you. What is up with that?"

The bridge rumbled, and I worried the supports had eroded or someone had sabotaged them. I tried to get Sally's attention, but she was still talking about how dumb I was. I grabbed her arm with my free hand and pulled her toward land. She jerked free and said she didn't want to go with me, she was sick of my crap, let go.

"Listen, listen! Something's wrong," I said. I pulled her the other way, toward Boston. By now the bridge was definitely vibrating in a weird way. I could feel it in my teeth. I ran as fast as I could without letting go of my pants-clasp. The bridge felt like it was going to collapse any second. We made it to land, but the sidewalks had the same problem as the bridge. The rumbling got louder and felt like it was coming from inside me.

"What the fuck is going on?" Sally shouted.

I raised my hands. By now I was seeing funny, like there were one and a half of her. My teeth clattered. My stomach cramped up. And most of all my ears were full—they hurt like murder. I had earaches like someone had jammed sticks into my ear canals, it hurt all the way down my throat.

The last words Sally ever said to me were, "What the hell, we need to get inside—"

The pressure inside my ears built up and then it spiked, like the sticks in my ears had jammed all the way in and twisted like a corkscrew. I can't really describe the pain. People have written tons of poems about it, but mostly they use it as something to compare any other kind of pain with. Two giant hands smacked me in the head, at the same time as a massive force trying to push its way out from the inside of my skull. I staggered and fell over, nearly blacked out.

Blood burst out of Sally's ears at the same time as I felt something splash on my shirt. I tried to say something like, *What the fuck just happened,* or *Shit I dropped my pants again,* but nothing came out. No, I was doing all the right things to make a sound, but nothing. I couldn't hear birds or street sounds. I couldn't hear anything. Sally was moving her mouth too, but she had the same panic in her eyes as I felt. I sat down on the ground, impact but no noise, like we were in outer space.

Sally was still trying to talk, tears coming down her cheeks. I gestured that I couldn't hear her. She grabbed her phone and fumbled with the buttons. A second later, my phone vibrated. A text message: **`wtf im deaf`**. I texted back: **`me 2`**. She wrote: **`we need help`**.

She hauled me to my feet and found a safety pin in her bag for my stupid pants. Then we rushed down Mass Ave., looking for someone who could call an ambulance. I still felt jumpy crossing the streets without being able to hear cars or other vehicles coming up behind me. Plus I kept turning to look over my shoulder in case someone ran up behind me. We found a guy up near Commonwealth Ave., but we could see from a distance he was clutching his ears and crying. Same with the half a dozen young people we saw near the boarded-up Urban Outfitters at Mass Ave. and Newbury. They all had blood on their shoulders and were texting each other or using pidgin sign language. They tried to plead for our help with their hands, until they realized we had the same problem.

Everywhere we went, deaf people wigged out. Sally texted me that we needed to get off the streets, that this was going to get ugly. I knew what she meant. Carrie texted me that she was deaf, and I told her to get indoors. Sally and I found bikes and rode back to her house as fast as we could, not stopping for traffic lights or any of the people who tried to flag us down.

Janelle kissed her knees on the sofa, her back heaving. The television showed people, all over the world, with bloody ears. Somewhere an airplane had crashed, and somewhere else a power plant had blown up. There was no newscaster, just words scrolling across the screen:

> THE SITUATION IS UNDER CONTROL. STAY TUNED FOR UPDATES. DO NOT GO OUTDOORS. HEARING LOSS APPEARS TO BE WORLDWIDE. DO NOT GO OUTDOORS. AUTHORITIES HAVE NO EXPLANATION. STAY INSIDE.

We went on the internet and read everything we could find. If anyone on the planet could still hear, there was no sign. Every blog, every email group, was full of people freaking out. Only the people who had already been deaf were calm, and they posted teach-yourself-sign-language videos. I knew right away I would never have the patience to learn sign language.

It only took a few hours for people to start speculating. The Pan-Asiatic Ecumen had tested out some weapon. Or the U.S. had. A weapon test had gone wrong, or maybe it had gone right. Someone, somewhere, could still hear and was going to enslave the rest of us. It was the red bandanas. No, it was the anti-war crazies. No, it was the Chinese.

For now, all you could see on television was people wigging out. Trampling each other to death in Shanghai, or throwing themselves off the Brooklyn Bridge. A mob in Cleveland stormed through Shaker Square breaking everything in its path. In a mob of the deaf, how would you know what to do? You'd just have to look at the other mob-members to figure out what they were doing and try to play along. How could anyone talk a deaf mob down? The Cleveland cops didn't even try, they just broke out the rubber bullets and tear gas.

Day two or three, I got fed up and decided to go to work. By then, we were running out of stuff at Sally's house, and Janelle and even Sally were starting to get on my nerves. They could feel the vibrations from my fidgeting and the impact when I broke something of theirs, even when they couldn't see me. And I could feel their grief like a blanket all around me. My thumbs got sore from text-messaging Sally when she was sitting right next to me. I could have just as much of a conversation from long distance. Sally didn't want me to go out because the television was still full of people thrashing each other, but I said I'd be careful.

I didn't even know if the convenience store still existed, and nobody had told me to come in to work. But nobody had told me not to, either. And this could be my contribution to society's continued existence, selling spam and condoms to people. I passed plenty of looted stores on my way down Commonwealth, and people were lighting all sorts of things on fire that were probably terrible for the environment. But when I got to the Store 24, it was still there and in one piece.

I opened it up. It occurred to me that people would have a hard time asking me how much things cost. So I got out the pricing gun and went around making sure every single item in the store had an individual price sticker, even down to the 37-cent instant noodles. After that, I had to learn how to stay alert, because the little new-customer bell was no longer any use to me. An hour or two went by, more boring than anything I'd ever experienced before.

`thk gd yr here`, said the message on the guy's cell phone, waved in my face. I nodded and he pulled it away to thumb some more. `didnt want 2 loot`. I nodded. `but no stores open`. I nodded. Then he went and filled his basket with canned goods, and brought it back. I rung him up, and he shook my hand with both hands. He looked like a college professor, fifty-ish, wearing plaid and stripes and tweed, so he wasn't a professor of fashion design. He saluted, like I was a colonel, then left.

Word spread, and more people came to the store. The shelves got emptier, and I pulled out stuff from the back room. We were going to run out of goods, and I didn't know if any more was coming. People, mostly middle class, thanked me for saving them from being looters. People are funny. I wish I'd had the URL of our Vumblr handy. I think a lot of those people would have looked at whatever I wanted to show them.

A TV news crew came to "interview" me. Mostly they filmed me serving customers and clowning around. I wrote our URL on a piece of paper and held it up to the camera. Sally said the news channel showed me twice an hour for a day or two, with a scrolling banner saying "LIFE RETURNS TO NORMAL." My boss text-messaged me and said he'd stop by to empty the safe and register.

Nobody robbed me, even after I was on television, because there were plenty of abandoned stores to rob.

So even if the news hadn't shown me holding up our Vumblr URL for a few seconds per hour, we still would have gotten record hits on our site. At least, Sally thought our dumb web movies were the ideal thing to watch now, because they were the wacky escape from reality, and they had no dialogue or sound effects for anyone to miss out on. It's actually funnier without any laughter, Sally emailed me from three feet away.

The non-news channels went back to showing regular stuff, except with subtitles for everybody. But subtitles made all the sitcoms look like French movies, so I kept waiting for Jennifer Aniston to smoke or commit incest.

Sally emailed her film-geek crew, including Zapp, about our next shoot. Who knew if they were even going to have classes anytime soon? She bopped around a little more, bouncing dumb ideas off me, and once or twice she seemed to laugh (in between crying, or staring into a can of liverwurst).

But nothing had changed for me. The silence just trapped me in a scream I hadn't been able to choke out before, and I kept seeing movement in the corner of my eye that vanished when I turned to look, like the next bloody crush was dancing behind me to no music. I could never move freely again.

FRUITING BODIES

Seanan McGuire

July 2028

The street ran east to west over the top of a hill, with no cover afforded at the summit. That was good. It meant that there were points during the day when the sidewalk couldn't avoid being exposed to ultraviolet radiation, the sunlight beating down and scouring the concrete like the mother of all autoclaves. It wouldn't be enough—it could never be enough—but it might afford us a small measure of protection.

"Mom?" Nikki tugged a little harder on my hand. Her tone was uncertain, verging into terrified. I winced. She only sounded like that when she was afraid that I was on the verge of an attack. They'd been getting more common since my gabapentin ran out, and since . . . since . . .

Honestly, I didn't think it was so unreasonable that my OCD was getting worse. There's something about having the world transform into a horrifying, mold-encrusted parody of itself that just seems to justify a little extra concern about cleanliness.

Nikki tugged on my hand again. I realized that I was drifting.

"I'm sorry, sweetheart," I said softly, and hunched down a little further. My plastic "moon suit"—made of Hefty bags cut to fit and held together with electrical tape—crinkled with every move I made.

Nikki's suit was identical to mine, just smaller, and even tighter around the joints. When I was suiting up myself I could usually stop wrapping the tape after three full layers. With her, I would keep going until she said stop—and that happened later and later these days, sometimes after I'd gone through an entire roll of tape. Our supplies were running low. We'd have to make another scavenging run soon if we didn't start rationing. But when my daughter looked at me and said, "More," I couldn't tell her no. Not here. Not now. Not when her safety was at stake.

"Are we moving?"

It was a good question, and it deserved a better answer than I had. All Nikki's questions deserved better answers than I could give her anymore, than I had been able to give her since I saw my wife—her second and better mother—melting off her own bones in an isolated hospital bed. My Rachel had been the first victim of the genetically "improved" *R. nigricans* created by the careless bastards I used to work with on Project Eden, back when I thought that we were going to save the world, not destroy it.

The street looked clear. I had seen no motion in the time we had spent crouching, watching the storefronts, and thanks to the relative lack of rain recently—bless you, drought conditions, bless you—the sidewalks hadn't been wetted down in weeks. At least one shop window had been broken. Bits of broken glass glittered on the pavement, and the fact that they hadn't been swept up was a sign in our favor.

"We're moving," I said finally. I didn't want to, but if we wanted to eat tonight, we needed to take the risk. "Mask on."

Nikki nodded, and pulled the cotton surgical mask that always hung around her neck up over her mouth and nose. She didn't wait to be told before pulling down her goggles, covering her eyes. I handed her a fresh shower cap, watching to be sure that her scalp and ears were fully protected, before I began putting my own gear in place. Nikki first, always. She was the only thing left in the world that was worth saving, and if I failed her the way I had failed Rachel . . .

No. Even thinking about it was enough to make my skin crawl, and we couldn't afford to sit here while I shredded my suit and scrubbed myself down for the third time today. Too much sanitization was as much of a risk as not enough; it could cause dryness and cracks in the skin, and cracks were the way that the danger got inside. The sun would be past its zenith soon, and the danger would grow. We had to go.

"Now," I said. Nikki retook my hand, and together we ran for the gleaming paradise of the 7-Eleven across the street.

• • •

My name is Megan Riley. I am a molecular biologist. Until very recently, I was employed by a large biotech firm as part of a team that was developing hardier, healthier, easier-to-grow fruit and vegetables designed to thrive in our changing climate. It was going to change the world, for the better.

Except that there was cross-contamination in the labs, resulting in a strain of bread mold becoming part of the process. Hardier, healthier, easier-to-grow bread mold, that was resistant to virtually every fungicide and sterilizing agent we knew.

Except that my team members hid the existence of the contamination from me, because they were afraid of my reaction; afraid that I would report them to senior management and get the whole project canceled. They justified it to themselves by saying that my OCD would make me unreasonable about what was, really, such a small thing, and after all, they were going to change the world.

They succeeded.

Every night in my dreams my dead wife comes to me, beautiful and laughing, with ribbons in her long, dark hair. And then the mold comes for her, spreading out from a tiny cut on her finger, swallowing her alive, until all that's left are her eyes, and her flesh is falling off her bones, eaten away by something I should have seen, should have stopped, should have never allowed to escape from its artificial womb. Rachel was the first documented victim of *R. nigricans,* which was a greater success than we had ever hoped our engineered fruit would be. It could thrive anywhere. It could consume virtually anything. It loved the taste of flesh, and it didn't need to wait for its food to die.

We had created the world's first fungal apex predator, and while that might be an achievement for the history books, it wasn't one that I was particularly proud of. I've added quite a few entries to the list of "things I am not proud of" since the day I found a bowl of moldy fruit sitting in my kitchen, but none of them mattered—not even running out of the hospital where Rachel's flesh was being eaten off her own bones by a monster I had helped, however passively, to create. I knew Rachel would have felt the same way, if she'd still been around to tell me so.

As long as I kept Nikki safe, nothing else mattered.

• • •

The 7-Eleven's window was intact, covered by a thin layer of dust and grime. I pulled one of my precious remaining cans of compressed air out of my pocket and blew away the dirt, creating a small porthole into the gloom. Nikki pressed up against me as I peered into the store. Her own eyes would be scanning the street, watching for signs of motion, for danger, for anything that could mean that we were no longer alone.

The shelves nearest to the door had been picked clean, but what I could see included no dark splotches, no irregularly shaped patches of tile or shelving that didn't match their surroundings. We were still taking a risk by going inside. We didn't know how many survivors were in this neighborhood, or why the store had been left so intact.

My stomach was a hard stone, compressed in on itself like a peach pit, tight and aching with the need for sustenance. Worse, our bottled water was on the verge of running out, and we couldn't trust the taps; couldn't trust anything moist or fertile. We had to go inside.

I tried the door first. The habits of civilization died hard—harder, it sometimes seemed, than civilization itself, which had folded up over the course of a single summer as *R. nigricans* rampaged across the face and flesh of the world. The idea that I could have been partially responsible for ending the world as we knew it seemed almost impossibly arrogant to me. So far as I knew, the mold hadn't managed to escape the Americas—might not even have made it out of Mexico, where there were long stretches of desert and open land that would give it very little to feed upon. But if it reached the rainforests, it would never die. These continents would never belong to men, or to mammals, ever again.

Of course, "so far as I knew" was a statement of ignorance, and not information. The newspapers had stopped printing; the television stations had gone off the air; even the local ISPs had died, effectively killing the Internet. The whole world could be strangling in gray for all I knew, and it would all be the same from where I was standing.

Tugging the door resulted only in a clunk as the deadbolt held fast. The looting must have happened early, then, before the proprietor locked up. The fact that the proprietor had been *able* to lock up spoke well for the safety of the store's contents: if he or she had been too far gone, they would have left the door open. Snickers and M&Ms for all, here at the end of the world.

"Head down," I said, pulling the crowbar out of my bag. Nikki ducked, putting her hands over the back of her neck as I swung and smashed out the glass body of the door. Most of the shards flew inward. The few that bounced back onto the street landed safely on the pavement, avoiding me and my daughter entirely.

A wash of air wafted out of the 7-Eleven, smelling of stale chips, hot dog water, and disuse. There was no hint of decay, and I began allowing myself to hope.

We stayed where we were for a count of one hundred, waiting to see whether an alarm would start to blare, or worse—that someone would come lurching out of the shadows. Neither happened, and finally, cautiously, I reached through the hole I had created to undo the deadbolt and let us inside.

Nikki was the first through the open door. Even as terrified as she was of the new world—as terrified as we both were—she was still bolder than I was, more inclined to take risks without consulting the counsel of her own mind and receiving permission to risk contact with the dark and broken places we had created. I paused long enough to start my watch, and then I was close behind her, my heart hammering against my ribs, visions of all the terrible things that could be waiting inside flashing in front of my eyes like a gauzy overlay.

"Mom!" Nikki's cry brought me up short, and for a moment, the sucking pit beneath my breastbone threatened to swell and devour me. This was it, it was finally going to happen; I was finally going to lose her. Then she continued, and the joy in her voice became apparent: "There's bottled water! And juice! Actual juice!"

"Too much sugar." The words were automatic, tinged with relief and spoken without thought. "Moisture plus sugar makes it an ideal growth medium. Look for diet soda if you need something sweet."

Nikki shot me a look, barely visible through the gloom, but visible enough for me to see the disappointment in her eyes, the mild displeasure in the curve of her mouth. She should have been enjoying her summer vacation by now, not fleeing through the remaining dry spaces of a crumbling city while one mother fought against the demons of her own psyche and the other slowly dissolved under the hungry hyphae of the fungus that had claimed her life.

I'm sorry, Nikki, I thought, not for the first time—and I was sure, not for the last. Of the three of us, I was the one least equipped for the new world. I was the one who understood the dangers too well to face them bravely, and I was the only one she had left. It wasn't fair.

Life never was.

No one came to challenge us as we moved through the 7-Eleven. We had become quick and efficient thieves in the days since the people disappeared from the streets and the soldiers abandoned their posts, leaving the mold to eat away the wooden legs of the hastily-constructed barricades they left behind. Nikki and I swept things into plastic bags—never more than ten items at a time, like we were living life in the express line at the supermarket, tying each bag off and stowing it in our larger sacks once it was "full"—without discussion, moving as fast as we could. Once we left the 7-Eleven, we knew that we would never be able to come back. Even if other looters didn't follow our tracks, we had broken the seal that had managed to keep the store in a state of relative isolation. The mold would be here soon. There wouldn't be anything to stop it.

My watch beeped, marking fifteen minutes since we had entered the store. I shoved one last handful of Tylenol into my bag—little packets with only two pills each, but better than nothing; so much better than nothing—before waving to Nikki. "We're out," I said.

"But I haven't finished cleaning out the chips," she said, a note of a whine creeping into her voice. "Can't we stay for five more minutes?"

"No. It's too dangerous." We were inside, in an enclosed space, with no sunlight to bake any wayward spores off of our safe suits. Sure, we were protected now, but seals were made to be broken: sooner or later, we would be vulnerable again. We needed to go.

Even in the dark, I could see the disappointed look in Nikki's eyes. She grabbed one more fistful of individually packaged chip bags, dropping them into her sack. Then she slouched across the 7-Eleven to me. "Ready," she said, that same whining note still buried deep in her voice.

As long as that was the only thing that got buried today, I could live with that. I smiled at her, hoping she'd be able to read the expression through my mask, and turned to lead her out of the store. It was time to go home.

• • •

Rule one of surviving when fungus decides to reclaim the Earth: moisture is the enemy.

Anything that could help spores take root and grow is to be avoided at all costs. I hadn't taken a shower in weeks, keeping clean instead with hand sanitizer and dry-scrubbing. It was nowhere near as satisfying, but I didn't stink, and I stayed dry. Under the circumstances, staying dry was so much better than the alternative.

Rule two of surviving: light is your salvation.

Specifically, ultraviolet light, like the kind found in sunlight, or in certain types of specialized bulbs. It can kill fungus, and more importantly, it can kill fungal spores. That, more than anything else, was worth all the work of scavenging gasoline and batteries and solar panels to keep the lights on.

Nikki and I ran down the middle of the street with our bounty, watching the buildings around us for signs of life. We had encountered a few people in this neighborhood, but it seemed like their numbers declined daily, and the last three individuals we had seen had all been slow-moving and blotched with patches of the all-consuming mold. They either weren't being careful or didn't know how to be, and all it took was one chance encounter. Just one, and they were no longer a major concern, because once the mold had someone, it didn't let them go.

It had my Rachel first, devouring her in the relative comfort of a sealed hospital room. She died surrounded by men and women who had done everything in their power to save her. They'd failed, and she hadn't been the last—far from it. Before the newspapers stopped printing and the newscasters went off the air, hundreds of people had joined her, and their conditions had been much less palatial. There had been quarantines, lockdowns, even firing squads posted around so-called "clean zones," and it hadn't done a damn bit of good. You can't quarantine a spore. You can't prevent transmission of something that thrives on organic matter, sleeps unseen before it sprouts, and can travel through the open air.

All you can do is stay dry, keep the lights turned on, and pray that the wind will pass you by.

Our current safe haven was parked at the bottom of the hill: a mid-sized U-Haul truck with a generator in the back and a full tank of gas. I unlocked the back while Nikki checked the cab to be sure that no one had tried to interfere with the truck while we were away. I hated letting her out of my sight for even the few seconds that this required, but I didn't have much of a choice. Keeping ourselves alive was too much work for just one person, and Nikki *needed* to be involved with her own survival. It was the only thing that kept her moving. That kept either one of us moving, really. If we stopped, even for a second, we would both die.

"Clear," she said, trotting back over to where I waited. I nodded, undid the padlock, and lifted the back gate of the truck.

The inside looked like something out of a paranoid fantasy. Tin foil lined the walls and floor, covered with a layer of Saran Wrap, so that everything was slick and gleaming in the overhead light, which came on as soon as the gate was lifted. The bulb was UV, and Nikki and I waited outside for a full count of ten before stepping inside and pulling the gate closed again behind us. Every moment in the open was a risk, but so was entering the truck before it had been decontaminated, however poorly. We couldn't leave the lights on when we were gone—not without running out of fuel and possibly burning out our precious, hard-to-replace bulbs—and so we had to take the next best option. Everything was a risk these days. It was all a matter of knowing which risks were important enough to be worth taking.

"Pool," I said. Nikki nodded, and ran across the truck to awkwardly peel a plastic kiddy wading pool off the stack leaning against the far wall. We'd pilfered them from the downtown Target, before it became so thoroughly riddled with mold that even setting foot in the parking lot would have been a death sentence. Each one had been washed down twice in bleach and then wrapped in plastic, and we still disposed of them after we used them. Anything else would have been taking unnecessary risks. I was all about avoiding unnecessary risks. Especially now.

We dumped our bags of pilfered goodies out into the little pool, stirring them with glass rods from the modern art studio that had been across the street from our house. Mold couldn't grow on glass. It was one of the only truly safe surfaces we had, and even it had to be constantly cleaned and sterilized to keep particulate matter from building up that the mold *could* grow on. After spending my life running from the specter of my own unending need to clean, I was stranded in a world where cleaning and compulsion were the only things that stood a chance of keeping me, and Nikki, alive.

We flipped each candy bar, each pack of chips and tiny packet of pills three times before we were content to accept that it was devoid of visible mold. Then I picked up each one in its turn with a pair of tongs and dunked them in a bucket full of rubbing alcohol. Again, not perfect, but every precaution took us a millimeter closer to safety. Maybe if we took enough of them, we'd live.

"Mom," urged Nikki.

"I'm going as fast as I can," I said, and dunked another bag of chips. "If you're antsy, change your suit."

Nikki shot me a venomous look. Then she turned, whipping her head in a way that would have snapped her ponytail at me, back before we'd both cropped our hair short, and stalked to the relative privacy of the chemical shower.

I was endlessly fascinated by the way she could change from terrified obedience to petulant rebellion in the blink of an eye. As soon as she felt safe, she withdrew into the persona she'd been constructing for herself ever since high school started: too cool for the situation, and far too cool for me. I didn't really mind anymore. It gave her something to focus on that wasn't our situation, and I was the mother of a teenager. I could handle a little scorn.

I pulled the last bag of chips out of the rubbing alcohol and added it to the pile of safe supplies. "Dinner's ready," I called. We would eat our fill, and then load the empties into the wading pool and dispose of the whole mess by the side of the road. It was an imperfect solution for an imperfect world, and it was the best thing we had.

Nikki emerged from the shower, wearing a fresh set of surgical scrubs and carrying her shucked-off "moon suit" in a plastic garbage bag. She dropped the bag into the wading pool as she walked past me to the food, where she then sat, cross-legged, and began ripping into our haul.

I thought about telling her to take it easy, and decided that for once, we had enough: she could eat her fill, and maybe we could both go to sleep without feeling our stomachs knotting themselves against our spines. I watched her for a moment—my Nikki, my precious little girl—and then I walked to the chemical shower to begin stripping off my own layer of plastic film and tape. It was time to start cleaning up our mess. Only when that was done would I be able to celebrate surviving another day in an unsurvivable world.

Nikki was the reason I kept going. There was nothing left to fight for.

• • •

After a dinner of Doritos and beef jerky and a single-serving tube of honey roasted peanuts—sweet and salty at the same time, like tasting the past—we had disposed of the trash and gone to sleep on our opposite sides of the truck. We had no blankets or bedding. They would have been too tempting a growth medium for the mold that shaped our every waking moment. But we had pads of folded plastic, and exhaustion was a cruel mistress, making sleep easier than it had any right to be.

While I slept, I dreamt of oranges, of walking under the Florida sun with Rachel's hand in mine and the citrus groves growing all around us, untouched by blight or decay.

Something in the air woke me, something connected to the faint but undeniable scent of oranges. I opened my eyes, blinking rapidly as I tried to adjust myself to the glare from the single UV bulb still burning overhead. Then I breathed in.

The dry, dusty smell of mold was like a slap to the face. I sat bolt upright, barely feeling the muscles in my stomach complain, and looked frantically around. Nikki was still asleep, her face turned toward the wall, her short-cropped golden hair uncovered to let the UV do its work.

There was an empty bottle on the floor next to her shoulder. The cap was off, and the smell of oranges had spread to fill the truck. If there had been any juice left when she was done with her illicit treat, I couldn't see it. Gray mold had filled the bottle, wiping any trace of color away.

"Nikki?" My voice was a strangled squeak, too small to be heard at any distance. I took a deep breath, horribly aware of the spores that I was pulling into my lungs. The mold-smell made my throat clench, bile rising in a vain, wasteful attempt to wash it away. "Honey? Can you hear me?"

The spores got in, but they only got the juice, my thoughts insisted, racing and tumbling over themselves like amoebae colliding under a microscope. *She's too close to it. She needs to move away. If she'll just move away, she'll be fine, she'll be fine, the only growth is on the juice, she'll be fine—*

Nikki made a tiny squeaking noise as she woke and stretched. It was the same sound she'd been making since she was a pink-skinned stranger, newly pulled from my womb via C-section and already starting to smell of milk and baby powder as she adapted to the world around her. Then she rolled over, opening her eyes and blinking at me in the bright light of the truck. I clapped a hand over my mouth, stopping speech and screams in the same economic gesture. There was nothing else that I could do.

"Mom?" Nikki pushed herself up onto her elbows, seemingly unaware of the fuzzy gray patch that had consumed her right cheek and followed the curve of her right ear, vanishing up into her hair. Her brows drew together in an expression of concern. "Are you okay? Are you having an episode?"

I didn't say anything. Nikki followed my gaze down to the orange juice bottle, and to her left hand, which had a gray glove covering the last three fingers, snugly obliterating them.

I didn't have to scream. She screamed enough for the both of us.

• • •

Rachel had been the first victim of this terrible softness. For Rachel, there had been hospitals, treatments, people to fight for her as her flesh dripped off her bones and the hyphae replaced her nervous system. All those things were gone by the time Nikki was infected, every form of medical intervention and palliative care lost—maybe forever.

All she had was me. And I was possibly the least well-equipped person in the world to handle the brutal, unrelenting messiness of the situation.

I moved through the decaying streets in my makeshift moon suit, tape protecting the thin places, the places where the spores were most likely to find their way through. I moved alone. Every sound was a threat, every flicker was an attacker preparing to leap out of the shadows and drag me away from the light. My skin itched constantly, dry and dehydrated almost to the point of cracking. I didn't dare use any of the lotions I stole during my daily supply runs. Moisture was the enemy, now more than ever. I still wasn't infected. Somehow, despite everything, I wasn't infected. I needed to stay that way, now more than ever.

Nikki was counting on me.

My bag was heavy with candy bars and chips and bottles of juice. They were getting harder and harder to find. They would have been exhausted already if most of the survivors hadn't learnt to avoid them, leaving them sitting alone on shelves that had been otherwise picked clean. I ran, and kept on running until I saw the familiar shape of the U-Haul appear on the street ahead of me. It was parked in front of a burnt out gas station—one of my favorite places, since the fire had cleared all the stunted bushes away from the front of the structure. Less risk there.

It was funny that I still thought that way, that I couldn't *stop* thinking that way, even though the greatest risk was the one I carried with me.

But I still wasn't infected.

"Honey?" I unlocked the back of the truck and rolled it upward. The lights inside didn't come on. I had disabled them on the second day, when they started to hurt her more than they could possibly be helping me. "I'm back. Honey?"

"Here, Mom." Nikki's voice came from the darkness that filled the back half of the truck. The sunlight couldn't pierce that far. There was something indefinably blurry about her words, like her lips no longer hit the consonants the way that they were supposed to. I hadn't looked inside her mouth since the third day, when I had seen the mold creeping over her rear molars, turning them into a field of solid gray.

And I still wasn't infected.

If the blurriness was subtle, the bitterness was not. "Where else would I be?"

"Sorry. Sorry." The thought of boosting myself into that softly blurred darkness made my stomach clench and turned my lungs to concrete. But it was Nikki's voice speaking to me from the shadows; my little girl, my baby, the best and messiest thing I ever did in my life. I braced my free hand on the plastic-covered metal and pushed myself up, landing on my knees at the border of the gloom. "I brought you some juice."

Her laughter was wet and heavy, burbling up through some unspeakable layer of material before it breaks the surface. "I thought juice was bad for me. Too much of an ideal growth medium."

Anything I could have said would have been the wrong thing, and so I didn't say anything at all. I just inched forward until the first traces of gray appeared on the plastic sheeting. Then I started lining up the juice bottles, positioning them each with unthinking precision. I could hear Nikki's breathing from ahead of me, thick and labored. I tried to shut it out, focusing instead on the task at hand.

I was being a good mother.

I was taking care of my child.

I was doing the only thing I could do. I hadn't protected her, I hadn't been able to *keep her safe,* I hadn't done the *one thing* a mother should be able to do—I hadn't prevented my daughter from coming to harm. It was too late for me to save her.

But I could do this. I finished the line of juice bottles and began breaking the seals on their lids, twisting them until the threads snapped and their contents were revealed. Nikki's breathing grew faster as excitement chased away her bitterness, leaving only need behind. She didn't move though, not until I had opened the last bottle and withdrawn to the thin band of light at the mouth of the truck.

Then Nikki moved.

She didn't have legs anymore, not as distinct things—"right leg" and "left leg" were concepts that Nikki had left behind on day three, when *R. nigricans* had transformed her into a fungal mermaid. Or maybe she was a lamia, one of the snake-women of myth, because when she dragged herself along the floor, a thick tail of knotted gray followed her. It was like an umbilical, connecting her to her new womb. But this mother couldn't sustain her, not the way that I had when she grew inside my belly: this mother needed help. Help that only I could provide, by bringing growth media into the darkness. Things that Nikki and her new mother could both use to feed themselves.

Maybe that was where we'd gone wrong with Rachel. We had tried to starve the fungus, denying it the healthy sugars and gelatins it needed, and in return, it had consumed my wife. Rachel had been infected and eaten alive in a matter of hours. I ran away before I could see her die, but I had no doubt that she'd been consumed by the end of that first day. Nikki was on her sixth day of infection, and she was still herself, still speaking and thinking and behaving as a person. A different *kind* of person, maybe—a person with different needs and limitations—but still a person.

She was still my little girl.

The hands that reached out to grab and lift the juice bottles were more like tentacles, appendages wiped clean of detail and nuance by the process of . . . of *softening* that she had undergone, that she was still undergoing. I watched as she fumbled to pull the juice into her darkness, marking the places where her skin was still smooth and human. Her tan was fading fast, leaving even the human parts of her sickly and pale. But those human parts were there. I could see them.

As long as I could see them, she could be saved.

Somehow. If a cure was found. If the government pulled itself back together. My life had become a fragile scaffolding of "if," all hanging on the pale, sickly patches of skin on my little girl's arms.

Her face was still half her own. The growth on her right cheek and jaw had continued to spread, but it had avoided the eye and most of her nose. There was a thin crust of fungus in her right nostril. The left side was unblemished gray, featureless, until she opened her mouth. The right side was still a mouth. It opened like a human thing. The left side gaped too widely, slicing deep into what should have been her cheek, drawing a hungry slash from here to there. She poured juice into the opening—cranberry, grapefruit, orange—mixing them without pausing to consider how the results would taste. Flavor had stopped being a concern when the fungus overtook her tongue. All she cared about now was the sugar.

I watched her drink the first bottle, spilling as much as she actually managed to get into the dark cavern of her mouth. I tried to take a snapshot of her fungus-blotched face, measuring against the snapshot I had taken the day before, looking for the places where her features had melted into the gray. Nikki raised her eye and caught me looking. Her lips twisted into an expression I couldn't read anymore—smirk or sneer, it was impossible to say—and she withdrew into the shadows, a bottle of juice wrapped in the gray appendages that had been her arms.

"The light hurts me," she said, that old familiar whine in her voice. She used to use it when we wouldn't let her stay out late with her friends, when we tried to talk to her about boys or tried to interfere in her life. It was almost obscene, hearing it in this place, in this situation. But what *wasn't* obscene about our lives, anymore?

"All right, honey," I said, and withdrew, sliding back along the plastic until my feet dangled above the ledge. Then I dropped, back onto the pavement, and pulled the door down, blocking out the light.

As soon as the truck was sealed again my heart began to hammer against my ribs, panic overtaking me. I could maintain the lines between my daughter and my disorder when she was there in front of me, but when she was gone . . .

I peeled the gloves off my hands, searching the skin for traces of mold. Once I was sure it was clean, I reached up and felt my face, looking for fuzzy places, for *soft* places. Only after I had failed to find them did I allow myself to sink all the way down to the ground, and cover my face with my hands, and cry.

• • •

I parked the U-Haul in a vacant lot that was blackened by burn scars. There was no gray softness here; whoever had decided to burn the place had used the right kind of accelerant to render the ground unpalatable to even the toughest spores. It wouldn't last, but for now, we would be safe here, and it wasn't like we were going to stay for long. I needed to get us to a lab, someplace with the facilities to help me isolate whatever natural resistance I had given to my daughter.

The sound of the door slamming behind me was loud in the quiet morning air. I shivered as I walked around to the back of the truck, unlocking the sliding door and pushing it open just enough to let me slip inside.

"Nikki? Honey, I brought your juice." I boosted myself up into the back. The gray had spread again during the night, spreading to consume more of the walls and ceiling. It was still avoiding the floor, for the most part. I wondered if it was because the plastic was thicker there, giving it less to feed on. It didn't really matter.

The mass at the rear of the truck didn't move or respond. The first cold needle of fear sliced through my heart, cutting away the panic that I had lived with every day of my life and replacing it with something deeper and more pure. In that moment, I felt as if I finally understood what it was like to be afraid, and it was the worst thing I had ever known.

"Nikki?" My voice was barely a whisper. I forced myself to move forward, edging deeper into the gloom than I had gone in days. "Sweetheart, are you awake? I brought you some juice. I couldn't find any orange—I know you like the orange best—but there's pineapple, and grapefruit, and . . . and I can open it for you. Would you like that? Would you like me to open it? Honey? Nikki?"

Still she didn't respond. The gray mass filled the entire back third of the truck—and when did it get that large? When did the fungus become so much bigger than she was? How could there be anything *left* of her, if there was that much here that *wasn't* her?

"Nikki?"

I left the juice behind as I crawled into the dark, feeling the knees of my moon suit shred under the friction. I was tearing away the plastic that covered the floor, but I didn't care, for once in my life I was making a mess and I just *didn't care,* because Nikki was on the other side of the mess. Nikki was in the place where order became chaos, and I had to reach her. If I did nothing else in this world, I had to get to her, to save her . . . or to die with her, I didn't know anymore.

"Nikki?"

There was no response. I steeled myself against my demons and drove my hands into the gray, feeling around for anything other than that terrible *softness.* I groped around in the dark, feeling delicate fungal structures shred and come apart under my fingers, and I couldn't stop. My compulsion had found something to seize on, and it wasn't going to let go until it was done with me.

My fingers slipped and skidded in the gray, seeking purchase and finding nothing. I realized that I was crying. Part of me knew that I needed to stop, that tears were a growth medium in and of themselves—not as good as orange juice, maybe, but still excellent. The rest of me knew that there was no point. I could cry forever, and it wouldn't change anything.

There was always one orange on the tree that didn't succumb, always one slice of bread that somehow stayed clean and untouched when the blue mold bloomed. Resistance existed in nature, because without it, there would be nothing left.

Nikki hadn't been able to last longer because I fed her. That was delusion, me trying to convince myself that all things were created somehow equal. Nikki had lasted longer because I gave *birth* to her, and because I, through some bitter quirk of genetics, some unspeakably *cruel* twist of DNA, I was resistant.

My hands seized on something down in the softness. I lifted it up, feeling it start to come to pieces against my fingers. Still, the shape of it was true. I had never really seen it before—not undressed, not without its cloak of flesh and human features, the pursed lips, the eyes so much like mine—but

I had known it since it first started to grow inside me. It had been the first thing of Nikki to truly have form, taking up most of her ultrasound pictures. It had seemed so big then, housed within the palace of my belly. It feels so small now.

I pulled, and Nikki's crumbling skull was in my hands, patches of white bone gleaming through the runnels of gray mold. She almost looked like she was smiling at me.

"Hi, baby girl," I whispered. I pressed my lips against her forehead, feeling the softness there, the way the bone bent under even that faint and loving pressure. There was no moisture left. The fungus might have taken her slowly, but in the end, it took everything she had. There was nothing left for me to save. Maybe there never had been.

"Resistant" was not the same thing as "immune." Immunities almost never occurred in nature. I kissed my daughter's skull again, bearing down harder this time, until it came apart in my hands and crumbled into the greater gray. Shreds of fungus clung to my lips, light and soft as cotton candy. I licked them away. They had no taste. I swallowed anyway.

Nikki began her life inside me. This fungus was all that remained of her. It was only right that she go back where she belonged.

Sitting in the gray, I buried my hands in it and began, systematically, to eat.

"Resistant" didn't mean "immune."

If I was lucky, I would see my family soon.

BLACK MONDAY

Sarah Langan

On Display at the Amerasian Museum of Ancient Humanity, 14,201 C.E.

Aaaaroooaaah! Aaaaroooaaah! Aaaaroooaaah!

It's dusk on Black Monday. In six hours, Aporia Minor crashes into Antarctica. Three hours after that, Aporia Major obliterates the Ivory Coast. Anybody less than ten feet below ground dies in the hot dust showers. The one percent of humanity lucky enough to nab tickets to underground shelters is stuck there until the air clears—about a thousand years.

Aaaaroooaaah! Aaaaroooaaah! Aaaaroooaaah!

The Northern Lights splatter-paint the sky like a Jackson Pollock. I'm about a hundred feet outside the front steps to the old Strategic Air Command installation in Offutt, Nebraska—the heartland of America. There's this sweet spot right next to this retired B-52 that relays unsecured satellite waves.

Aaaaroooaaah! Aaaaroooaaah! Aaaaroooaaah!

"What's that? What's happening?" my husband Jay asks.

"Air raid for the 55th Battalion. I heard the war moved into North Korea. It's breaking down . . . Everybody's been leaving their posts."

"Same here. The Schwandts slaughtered their cattle," Jay tells me. "Two thousand heads."

"God, why?"

"They joined that rapture cult—the Dorothys. I think it was an offering to God."

"I never liked those people. All that chintz in her kitchen," I say.

Above me, behind me, in front of me, the Aurora sets the world aglow.

"What time do your Shelter Nine Tickets say you're supposed to rendezvous?"

"They never delivered them," Jay says.

I get this lump in my throat. "What do you mean you've got no Tickets?"

"I watched by the door since you left yesterday morning. No one's come."

"When were you going to tell me? After the Aporia Twins hit and you're all dead?"

Under the sirens, I can hear Myles' and Cash's high-pitched hoots. Myles wants to say hello (*Momma? Is that Momma? Give me the phone!*). Cash is bouncing on the couch. "Jumpy-jump! Jumpy-jump!" he cries. Their voices are sweet confections I could lick.

"I've been calling you three times an hour for the last twenty-four hours," Jay says, and I can tell he's trying to be calm, not lash out, like I'm doing—like our marriage counselor told us is *corrosive*. This makes me totally crazy, because I am *not* calm.

"Fuck it. They made a mistake. There's supposed to be a Bluebird on Crook Road tonight," I say. "It's the last one from outside. We're a military family. They have to let you on."

"Sounds like a plan. We'll go as soon as I get the kids in shoes." There's no gas anymore. I realize they'll be walking three miles through God knows what.

"Why did we rent off-base? I should be with you right now. I'm an idiot," I say, and in my mind I'm holding one of the kids. It doesn't matter whether it's Myles or Cash, just so long as I've got something *beloved* in my arms.

"We've got this under control. You save the afterworld," my husband hollers over the sirens. "I love you, Nicole."

Aaaaroooaaah! Aaaaroooaaah! Aaaaroooaaah!

I'm terrified all of a sudden. It's because he said my name.

"Squeeze them for me. And yourself. I love you, too, Jay."

• • •

By the time I'm back at my lab, the sirens are dead, and an RC-135 has crashed into a block of townhouses on General's Row.

"Your family get Tickets?" I ask the rest of my crew in cybernetics. There's six of us left. The rest of the building has been evacuated. We've volunteered to keep working because we think this is important.

Troy Miller doesn't look up from his dendritic sample.

"How about you?" I ask Marc Rubin. Marc closet eats, can't lose a pound, and breakdances at office parties. Before Aporia switched course for Earth last year, he'd taken his job just seriously enough not to get fired.

"It's just my ex-girlfriend, Jenny Carpenter. She got her Ticket, didn't she?" Marc asks. He's given up the closet, and is munching cold hot dogs from the plastic pack. There's a cafeteria on every floor here and they're all still stocked. Aside from Shelter Nine, this is the best place to be when the Aporias hit.

"You?" I ask the rest of them.

Without comment, Jim Chen, Kris Heller, and Lee McQuaid all pull out their phones and check messages, forgetting that this is a secured building without external connections.

"I *think* my parents did. They must have," Kris says.

I'm squeezing my forehead. The lab's a mess. Monkey brains are scattered in steel pots like jellyfish in kids' buckets at the beach. The examining tables are overturned, tools splayed, raw materials precariously propped along walls. The cleaning people haven't come for weeks. Neither have any enlisted. They're either trying to break into the shelters, or deserting this secret war America started fighting six months ago, against most of Asia. Nobody knows why it's been happening, or why the Networks have been going down one by one.

"My family didn't get their Tickets," I say.

Troy Miller still doesn't look up. He's tall, wears a suit under his lab coat every day, and would be in charge around here if he wasn't such an aspie. "Our families don't need Tickets! Jeeze! It's all fingerprint and voice recognition."

"I hope you're right," I say. "Any progress?"

Troy points at an android that's gone dark. Its lifeless body slumps against the freezer door. "If you want to call that progress."

"Fail?" I ask.

"Epic. It went ape-shit. Literally," Lee says. "It folded its articulations until its legs turned into stumps."

Kris covers her face, remembering. "It tried to unscrew its head. We need an *off* switch. It kept screaming."

"That's it. We're done with primate brains," I say.

Troy looks up from his dendrite at last. "We shouldn't use organic. This should be strictly AI."

"We don't have the time for AI. The Aporias hit in five hours. Let's thaw the human samples out of cryo," I say.

"Mmmm," Troy grunts, which is his way of voicing dissent.

Lee, who's turned rough around the edges from all this stress, noogie-knuckles Troy's back, just between his shoulders. "Come on, buddy-boy! It's a brain! Wrap it in Teflon and we're good to go!"

Troy shrugs. Lee keeps knuckling the poor nerd.

"Cut it out, Lee," I say.

"We can't go human," Kris says. "It's wrong. Morally."

"Come on, you bleeding hearts," I say. "To the freezer."

• • •

We thaw all nineteen brains. They're shaped like the undersides of horseshoe crabs. The cold has dry-burned eleven beyond repair. Troy cinches a hemostatic forceps into Cadaver Nineteen's desiccated parietal lobe. "This is what we're losing in translation," he tells me. "The higher order senses." He's got this high-pitched voice. It's like talking to a cartoon character.

"Right," I say. But the parietal's the least of it. The real dilemma is left-right synthesis. In humans, lobes of the same brain experience and remember stimuli in different ways. They develop different personalities. When it comes time to make a decision, they chat, or even fight. The winner decides. In people with split lobes, you can actually see the fighting. One hand will grab a cigarette, the other hand will push it away. In drunks, one lobe takes over and the other tends to go dormant, which is why some people get so vicious after a pint of gin, and why brain damage victims might remember their families and long division, but not act quite the same, ever again.

Anyway, it's this chatter between lobes that makes for better decisions. It's this chatter that, in fact, accounts for sentience. We've been trying to reproduce it in our AI, but keep failing.

Troy plucks the closed forceps from Cadaver Seventeen's postcentoral gyrus. There's this *mucky* sound. "A human would go insane trapped inside a metal can," he says. "Especially if it can't talk or hear or feel someone's touch. I'm telling you, we should stick with AI."

"He's got a point," Kris says. Kris was born paraplegic, so she knows what's she's talking about. She built her own legs, grafting her neurons to limber plastic encasings, which is why she got chosen for this position out of ten thousand applicants, even though she's only twenty-one years old.

"Guys," I say. "Unless we figure something out, nobody's going to survive down in those shelters. Who's got a better idea?" They get quiet after that. I don't hear any better ideas.

Just then, a keycard beeps and the airtight door hisses open. General Howard Macun charges in. He's the head of Space Defense, and the highest ranking official at Offutt who isn't in Nine by now. There's this gash over his forehead. It's a straight line from temple to temple, as if made by a factory machine.

Macun comes straight for me. I realize that my coat is wet with brain spatter. So is everyone else's. We must look like a collection of butchers.

He seems about to grab and shake me. Then, somehow remembering himself, he stops short and salutes. I'm civilian SCS, but from the looks of things, he's lost his wits. He's not the first. I play along, saluting back.

"Status, Captain?" he asks as he swipes the blood from his eyes. It's falling fast enough to soak his clothes and pool by his feet, leaving a trail from the door.

I click my Keds for him. "Sir! We're close. But I wonder, how are the other cybernetics teams progressing? I'd like to suggest we move our work and our families to Shelter Nine and join forces with the cybernetics team over there. This is no time for proprietary research."

Macun scratches his scalp and comes back with a glistening red finger. He seems surprised by it. Then he looks down at the blood trail, and seems surprised by that, too.

"What happened to you, sir?" I ask. "Is there rioting out there?"

"Are these human brains?" Macun asks.

"They are. General Camper signed the warrants to open cryo-freeze."

Macun grits his teeth in disgust.

"Sir," I say, as calmly as I know how. I'm channeling my husband, on whose tongue butter doesn't melt. "You must see—the shelters need aboveground caretakers. Satellites won't work after impact—there won't be any kind of remote control drones. It's got to be something that can engage independently from us. How else will the human race survive?"

"We're going back to AI as soon as we have more time," Marc chimes in. "Long term versus short term, you know?"

"What happened to you, sir?" I ask.

"It was just a dream," Macun mumbles.

"Is Nine compromised, or did that injury happen up here? Did you do it to yourself, sir?" I ask.

Macun finally notices that I'm talking. He notices the blood again, the brains again, and his eyes go wide.

"Who cut your head?" I ask.

Macun's feet go pigeon-toed. His knees begin to bounce. "Shelter Nine! Why, we had to bomb Shelter Nine!" he says in giggling sing-song.

"You must be confused, General. Shelter Nine is the only shelter within five hundred miles. It would be a senseless place to bomb. You'd be obliterating the population of the entire Midwest," I say. "Can I pour you a shot of bourbon and we can talk about all this?"

"They didn't listen. The President didn't listen. Korea didn't listen. Shelter Nine didn't listen. Do you know how to listen?" Macun asks.

I don't have time to answer. Macun's arms and legs twitch in a hysterical scarecrow's dance. He grabs me by the bloody coat, shoving me back over a swivel chair. My ankle hits something metal with a *crack!*

Macun keeps going. He finds Troy's forceps and chucks them. They land upright in Kris' dead left leg.

"Hey!" I cry.

He flips a steel gurney, on which we've set three good brains. *Splat!* they go. He flips the next table—four more brains. Gentle Jim Landers gets him by the waist. Crazed, strong, and military trained, Macun lifts Jim up, knees him in the groin, breaks free, and flips the third table.

The last viable brains go splat. Formaldehyde sprays. All is lost.

General Howard Macun grins.

"I should kill you," I mumble, and I don't even realize I've said it.

Panting, smiling, blood dripping from his crown and down his brow into his eyes like sweat, he scuttles his compact, muscular body across the brain-riddled floor. Slides around. Does a gory kind of victory dance. The brains turn to pulp.

"Please hand me your AFB-Connect, General," I say.

Panting, Macun peers out from the corners of his bloody eyes.

"General Macun? I'd like you to leave now," I say. "We'll be informing Shelter Nine and the US government of your treasonous actions."

Macun's wide-eyed, lunatic expression glazes. I get the feeling his crazy's not gone, just resting.

"Get the hell out," I say.

"Of course," he says at last. His voice is normal. This could be a year ago, his Christmas invocation at the Chapel, where he told us that courage would see us through these trying times.

"Good. See you at Nine for your court-martial," I say.

"No. I don't think you will." Macun opens his AFB-Connect, and starts typing as he follows his blood trail toward the door. Then he looks back, his expression oddly somber. "They're all dead. Don't take it too hard. It's for the best."

I don't know it, but I'm chasing him down the hall. The air raid sirens sound again. A newly downed plane, or a nuke, or another all-out war.

Aaaaroooaaah! Aaaaroooaaah! Aaaaroooaaah!

"General, I demand an explanation!"

He looks back with this bewildered expression. For just a second, I get the feeling he's remembering the role he used to play: A house on General's Row, six grandkids, a drunk wife, papers piled high on his desk from heads of state that all required his careful eye. But then the bewilderment is gone. He's not that guy anymore.

"Sir. What have you done? We have families headed for Shelter Nine."

General Macun wipes the blood from his temples, and salutes. "They're dead. You're dismissed," he says.

It's Troy Miller who chucks the skull hammer. A nerd his whole life, he probably never expected it to bullseye into the center of Macun's forehead. The tough bastard stands for at least a minute, hemorrhaging even more blood, before he falls.

Aaaaroooaaah! Aaaaroooaaah! Aaaaroooaaah!

• • •

The rest of them don't want to touch General Macun's body because they're squeamish. I'm just afraid he's not really dead. "We need his AFB-Connect," I say.

The old Strat Com looks like a 1950s public school. The equipment is state of the art, but the building is post-war junky, from the fluorescent lights to the one-dollar Wonderbread baloney sandwiches at the contract employees' cafeteria. We're standing in a tiled hall, our voices echoing.

Marc bends down, gracefully arranging his moccasins so that Macun's blood river runs between his bulky legs. "I smell whiskey."

"Drunk jerk," Jim says. He's outside the circle we've made, leaning against the hall. His balls must still hurt. "I'm not going to jail for this."

"There is no jail anymore," Kris answers. "And what if Nine's gone? What are we supposed to do with a caretaker when there's nothing to take care of? We don't even have any more brains!"

I squat next to Marc. Brown foam bubbles from Macun's lips.

Seeing this foam, Lee announces, "I'm so fucking done."

I use my foot as a fulcrum to turn Macun over. Marc helps. The steel skull hammer clangs, reverberating inside Macun's forebrain. An AFB-Connect, about the size of a deck of cards, falls from his clenched hand, skidding in blood. Marc uses his lab coat to pick it up and wipe it clean.

"What's on your mind?" I ask Troy while Marc prods the port. I do this because Troy is openly weeping.

"I killed a guy," he says.

"Yeah. But he deserved it."

Troy presses his face against the tiled wall to hide his tears. "I heard you say it!—that we should kill him. This is a military installation. You're my superior. You gave an order. You *made* me!"

I consider patting the guy's back but he's such a cold fish I can't imagine he'll appreciate it. "I'm fine with the blame. We needed his AFB."

"You don't understand. I killed him for you."

"I'm glad you did it, okay? Thanks. Much appreciated. Now, do you want to keep trying for a caretaker or do you need to get out of here?"

"Home is gone," he says. "I never had a home. Only you. You've been my boss six years. That's family, too. I bet you never even thought of me that way, did you . . . ? My mom died. Not from this. I didn't kill her. She died when I was little. She choked and it was just me with her. We were eating pineapple. I was making her laugh and something got stuck. I was too little to call the police. I just sat with her the whole time. I bruised her, trying to wake her up. Like, boxing, you know? I boxed her. She was beat-up by the time my dad came home from work. So he always said it was me that did it. I killed her. He never believed she choked. Did you know that about me?"

"Okay," I say, finally patting his back. "You're okay."

He kind of melts under my touch, like it's the thing he's been waiting for. "It's over. That was a long time ago."

I'm expecting the others to say something, or at least be paying attention, but they're all down their own, personal rabbit holes. It occurs to me that we've all gone mad and are hiding it as best we can.

"I can't crack this," Marc calls, holding the stained AFB-Connect. "It's a five-digit passcode."

I'm shrugging. Sweating. The air-raid sirens aren't sounding, but it feels like that inside of me. Maybe I'm going to die right now, from fear and shock and guilt and just plain *stress*.

"Try one-two-three-four-five," says Kris. "Also, two-five-two-five-two. They're the most common."

"We're in so much trouble," says Jim. "I really don't want to go to jail."

"This is jail," Lee says. "Even if we survive impact and the heat, we're trapped underground forever."

"I *tried* all the usual codes. What do I look like, a rube?" Marc asks.

Lee takes the AFB-Connect from Marc. Punches some numbers. The interface unlocks. "Impact date," he says: 1-14-31. He hands it back to Marc and starts walking down the hall, into the dark.

Kris chases after him. They've been having an affair for a few weeks now. It's faux-love. Fear-love. I feel sorry for Lee's wife and kids, who deserve better.

"Where are you going?" I call.

"I meant it. I'm done!" Lee shouts over his shoulder. He and Kris keep going until they're just shadows. After a while, they go dark.

I let myself watch them an extra second, as a kind of farewell.

Then I turn to Marc, who's scrolling. "Okay, here's the history. Macun ordered explosives detonated into Shelter Nine about twenty minutes ago."

"Did they detonate?"

"I think so. Nine went dark after that."

"Holy God," I say. My knees buckle. Troy is back from the wall, holding me up by the shoulder. I'm surprised he's got the wherewithal.

"Why blow up Nine?" Troy asks.

Marc types. "I can't see. It looks like a couple of other shelters got hit, too. There's a chance our people are still waiting at Crook Road."

"Order the Bluebird to reconnoiter there. Tell it to take them here instead of Nine," I say. "Maybe we can make this place work as our shelter."

"Assuming this Connect's intranet signal is strong enough for the Bluebird's driver to get the message," Jim says.

"Don't be such a Dorothy Downer," Marc tells him as he grabs another hot dog from his back pocket, then drops it when he sees he's smeared it with blood. "This is going to be so much better. No generals to cramp our style. It's like in *Dawn of the Dead* when they live in the shopping mall."

"You're making jokes because you can't admit that we're all going to die," Jim says.

We all stand there. General Macun's body keeps spurting foam and blood. He's a fucking pod person or something.

"Let's go deeper," I say. "Maybe we'll live."

• • •

Strat Com was built seventy years ago and can withstand a hydrogen bomb. It fell out of use once uranium and terrorism outpaced The Cold War. But it's a good bunker from which to face an asteroid hit. The ground floor is sealed with six feet of cement. I've never had enough clearance, but I've heard that the tunnels go a mile down. To disorient visitors, none of the elevators go down more than a few flights at a time, and the halls are shaped like interconnected conch shells. With enough supplies, we might be able to make it work.

We use Macun's AFB to navigate. It's got a map. Robotics is easy—the same room as cybernetics, two floors beneath the cement boundary. We take the equipment we think we'll need. Then we press 6 on the elevator and hope we find surgical. My ears pop. For the first time in a long while, gravity feels right again. The air gets dense and wet.

"I could live with this," Marc says. "If Jenny takes me back."

"You gave your only Ticket to your ex-girlfriend. I don't know if that's love, but it's definitely something," I say.

The elevator pings. We stagger out. Troy licks his finger and lets it dry in the air to test humidity. I keep picturing him as a toddler, sitting on his dead mom's lap.

The doors open to winding cinderblock halls and doors without windows. This is as far as the AFB map reads. It's past Macun's clearance. We go left because I'm a lefty. Marc takes notes like sprinkling bread crumbs, so we can find our way back.

"It's cold. This is so stupid. We're all going to die," Jim says. "At least if we were above we could watch it happen."

"When we're actually dying, are you going to brag that you were right? I'm just curious," Marc says.

"Shut up," I tell them.

The ceiling lights hum on half-power. It's darker than I'm used to, especially after the Aurora Borealis. I'm blinking and feeling my way with my hands.

We find another elevator. Beckon it. This one goes down to 14.

At the very bottom, a chatter along with the click-clack of hard shoes slows us down.

"People?" Marc asks.

We find around thirty settlers squatting in the cafeteria. They've made their own shelter, stocked with giant boxes from Wal-Mart, gallon-sized liters of gasoline stolen from the AFB gas stations, and scores of ivy and palm plants, which strikes me as brilliant—they'll scrub the air. I walk into the room like I'm supposed to be there. Nobody raises a gun, which I take as a good sign. My guess is, they're the families of cleaning staff and enlisted.

"Do you know where the executive hospital's at?" I ask a young woman who's texting on a phone that can't possibly get reception. She shrugs. The phone's screen is dark.

Two young soldiers approach. They're privates, in their twenties, both fresh-faced. They've emptied several sleeves of beef jerky and neatly arranged the plastic into a rubber-banded circular wad. "We can show you, ma'am!"

I smile, like it's the old world. "Great. I'm fixing to see if we can't build a nice robot for when we need work done Above. That okay by you soldiers?"

They not only point out the hospital, but bust down Operating Room One's door for us, and carry our robotics equipment inside.

"Like us to stand guard, ma'am?" they ask.

"Of course I would!" I say, and they do just that.

When we get to a good stopping point, I head out to my usual post. It's dark now. Two hours until impact. Gravity's light. I imagine Aporia's twins across the world. Aporia Minor would be low on the horizon, just a half-moon invisible against the daylight sun. Aporia Major would seem huge by comparison, her rocky moons streaming around her like crumbs.

I place the call to Jay, but it doesn't connect.

It occurs to me that even if we survive, we'll evolve differently in the dark, without fresh air. I ought to give up this notion of a caretaker, who'll turn the lights back on and usher us through our dark ages. We ought to meet our fate out in the open, with our children in our arms.

My tenth—or who knows, twentieth?—call goes through. It's a small miracle, and I decide it's a sign from God. I'm Midwestern, so I believe in all that. The Holy Trinity, transubstantiation, the virgin birth. Why not?

"Hey," I say. "I love you. I hope you get this and come find me at Strat Com." Then I'm looking at the phone, even though the connection's still live. I ought to be saying all the right, last things, but I can't bring myself to surrender.

"I'm going to do something desperate," I say. "But it's for you. And me. And the boys. No. that's not true. It's because I don't know what else to do."

• • •

"Volunteers?" I ask. It's a bad joke. I'm back in surgical. News has traveled that there's an operational shelter with open doors. The settlement has grown to about one hundred. My team's been sent by someone in charge to save them. Inside the operating room, it's just Jim, Marc, and Troy, who's been readying the metal casings, and me.

"You really slowed us down, insisting on AI. I'd have solved the singularity by now if it wasn't for you," Troy says. The entire right side of his face is twitching.

"Okay. How's your progress?" I ask.

"I think it makes sense to eliminate the parietal. It's worse feeling the loss. They might develop phantom limb syndrome. The Network interface should provide plenty of sensory feedback."

"You sure?" I ask. "I'm worried it'll shock them too much, psychologically."

Troy looks up at the cement ceiling, then around the operating room. "You're worried about psychology?"

"Do what works for you, Troy."

Jim and Marc show me some intercepted transmissions they've hacked from Shelter Nine's network, which we've imported into this installation and plan to use for automation. It's scary stuff. Before Macun's nukes brought the whole thing down, the Dorothy cult convinced some thousand people to down cyanide pills. The National Security Council and Joint Chiefs were murdered by Shelter Nine scientists, led by the cybernetics department.

"Jesus," I say. "What a clusterfuck. Our families? Are they gone, too?"

"The itinerary's complete and our people weren't listed. Looks like they made the Bluebird, but that's all I can figure out."

I send another enlisted out to look for them, then head back to surgical. "Volunteers?" I ask again.

Nobody answers. As their leader, it should be me. But I'm not a martyr. I want to see my family. "You'd get to live forever," I say.

Marc lifts his hot-dog greasy fingers from the keypad. "You can't spare me. I have the best hands."

"No, I do," Jim says. "I have a doctorate in medicine! I've actually *performed* brain surgery!"

"Should we ask a soldier?" Marc asks.

"No. We'll lose their trust if it goes wrong," I say.

We all get quiet. I smell the ammonia and metal grease. The surgical lamps are bright and I picture what's to come. I remember reading about leeching in the 18th century, and doctors who didn't wash their hands between surgeries. Lobotomies. Botched tracheotomies. My knees lose their lock and I'm propping myself over a surgical table.

"This is crazy. I don't want to go out like a butcher," I say.

There are tears in my eyes. It might be the first time I've cried this week. I can't remember. It occurs to me that my family might be dead, or lost, and instead of looking for them, I'm in a mile-deep basement, parsing dendrites.

"Let's kill ourselves," Jim says.

Marc punches the wall.

"It'll be easy. We'll do it together," Jim says.

"I want to see Jenny," Marc says. "I was wrong when we broke up. I never told her I love her."

I'm still crying. "This is too hard," I say. "I can't take it."

Troy stands up. He pats my back, awkwardly. I don't know what possesses me, but I hug him. "It's okay," I say. "We did our best. You, especially. It's okay. I'm proud of all of you."

"I'll do it," Troy says. "I volunteer."

"No," I say. "I won't let you."

"I've decided."

"It's 99.9% likely to fail," I say.

Troy sneers. He's terrified. "Let me do this. It's all I've got."

• • •

We do it. We insert Troy's brain into an articulated steel husk with oxygen gills and tiny needle holes through which he can inject his own calorie serums. We connect his spine and central nerves within rubberized sheaths. When we're done, his body's an empty husk on the table.

I run my hand along the steel casing. We've pulled its articulations so that it's exactly Troy's height: 6'2". Its face is carved like a human face, with camera-lens eyes that in monkeys have provided successful peripheral and central vision. Small flaps under its sharp chin open and close to intake air. The air is drawn into its chest, where it's filtered and if necessary, converted to oxygen, then returned to the head, where it circulates through its organic brain.

I'm thinking about Troy's mom, for some reason. Did he dream of her, watching him from the very chair in which she died, for the rest of his life? What dreams will come now?

Jim injects the calorie solution. Marc inserts the battery within the robot's chest, then screws it closed. We've got plenty more suits. Plenty of parts. I can hear the crowd outside surgical. The settlement is excited. It's something to take their mind off the Aporias.

It occurs to me that whether we succeed or not, the human race is over. Something new and quite different is about to grow from these sterile halls.

We wait. There's no "on" button. Either Troy's nervous system will take to the suit, or it won't.

I find myself nauseous. This is drastic and insane. Unkind. Troy's gills open.

Soundlessly, his articulations freshly oiled, he stands. "Troy? Can you hear me?"

Troy's camera-lens eyes look down. He stands straight, but his shoulders hunch just slightly. The left half of his face seems slower and slumped. It doesn't react as quickly to stimuli. But if he could sneer his sneer, he would. It's him.

"Are you connected? Can you hear me?"

The cyborg's mouth opens. He makes this gagged sound: *"Mmmmmm!"* I think he's trying to scream.

"How bad is it?" I ask. I touch his cold, left hand. His parietal's not connected, and he can't possibly feel my heat through his metal. Still, he grips back. It's an oddly human connection, and one I've been missing for a long time.

"Troy," I say. "I'm with you. You're not alone."

The lights flash and go bright—he's online. "*Mmmmmm!*" he screams. The lights flicker. Troy collapses. His gills go still.

Failure.

• • •

It's minutes before impact. I'm between the steps and the missile again. Calling Jay. It doesn't go through. Then I'm looking at pictures of them, my family. Scrolling, scrolling.

I look out through the flashing solar lights and there they are: my family. Jay's carrying both kids. With the Aporias' scrambled gravity, they must be light as feathers. I'm running toward them. We're hugging. I'm crying. I'm smelling them, tasting them. Even Jay, his sweaty musk, his calmness in the face of calamity that I've always found infuriating until now.

Behind them are a line of others from the Bluebird: Jim's family; Marc's ex, who's shockingly gorgeous and apparently still in love with him; security officers; Air Force cadets; Troy's sixty-eight year-old father, for whom I have so many questions.

We hurry back inside to the settlement. There's room. There's even food for another year. Maybe, if we crack into the dirt and learn to eat worms and extract water, that will be enough.

• • •

We don't feel Aporia Minor for about two minutes after she strikes. Strangers and friends, we're cramped tight and terrified on the cafeteria floor.

Everything shakes.

We wait an hour, then two, for the hot rain. It doesn't seep through, but something goes wrong, because the vents cut out. Electricity winds down. Everything goes dark.

No one but the children make noise—chatter and cries and occasional giggles. I imagine the surprised birds up above, the char of their wings. It's not the asteroid, but the impact plume that springs into space and comes back down again, spreading globally, that will get them.

Someone has the idea of passing out buttered bread and water, and then everyone's sharing what they have. Hands touching, saying words of gratitude, we eat in the dark.

Ten minutes later, cell phone lights start working again. I stand and everyone is quiet. "I'd invite you to conserve your energy until we figure out how to get the power back on."

"We need someone to reboot the Network," Jim whispers. "We'll run out of air."

But then, suddenly, the lights do return. The vents hum.

I'm holding my kids, standing with my husband, and everyone's clapping, like we're the First Family. They're smiling with hysterical gratitude. I look to Marc, full of smiles, his girl in his arms, the happiest man in the post-apocalypse, then to Jim, who knows better.

• • •

We're up, headed to surgical. Jay and the kids won't let me go alone, so they come along. There's Troy, standing in the doorway.

He's made himself taller. About seven feet.

"You know what's strange?" he asks. His deeper-than-usual voice booms through the Network intercoms. They can hear him in the shelter. "I'm not sad anymore. I don't feel anything. I can see now, why you never liked me. It all makes sense."

It occurs to me that having no "off" button was a really bad idea.

"You'll be relieved to know that I've cut off life support in the upper levels, for those refugees who've tried to sneak inside and steal your supplies," he says. "I feel that's what you'd have wanted, Nicole."

"Can you turn it back on?" I ask.

He cocks his robot head. His left side is completely limp. The eye has gone dead. "Done," he says. "But it's a waste. They've suffocated."

"Oh."

"I had to rework some of my inner plumbing. That's what took me some time. All that chatter—I couldn't tolerate it. So I made one lobe go quiet."

"Can you wake it up? The point was sentient chatter, remember?"

"I don't want to."

"Oh. Troy? Do you have moral capacity?" I ask. "Can you distinguish right from wrong?"

"Of course," he says. "I shall go up in approximately two weeks, when the temperature is acceptable, and build a better habitat. I'm going to please you, Nicole. You know how important that's always been to me. I'll need volunteers. Perhaps ten more like me, under my command. If necessary, I trust you'll enforce a military conscription."

It occurs to me that the perfect incision around Macun's scalp was from a skull retractor. Shelter Nine was in the middle of a losing war against the cyborgs it had created when Macun bombed it. Even the Dorothys had a method to their madness: cyanide dries up the brain.

"Troy? Do you remember your mother?" I ask.

He cocks his head. "Sorry? Say it in the other ear?"

I walk around to Troy's left side, which is an inch shorter.

"Do you remember your mother?"

"*Yes!*" a voice hisses. "I'll save you, I'll help you. *Run!*"

"Pay no attention to him. We've cut him out," the robot-man cries. "You never liked him anyway!"

Jay and I are standing in front of our kids. I feel the weight of this mistake.

"Volunteers?" the cyborg asks.

Just then, there's another Earth-rocking shudder, as the impact of Aporia's dark twin arrives.

ANGELS OF THE APOCALYPSE

Nancy Kress

Me and Ian, along with the rest of the world, were watching the news when my cell rang. My link went through satellite and so the latest vandalism on local cell towers didn't affect it. I glanced at the number, picked up, and said, "No."

"Sophie! You have to—"

"I told you last time, Mom, no more. I'm not going out to the settlement again."

"But they're under attack! A big gang this time! Carrie said—"

"Forget it!" On the TV, the fifteenth talking head in a row was saying the same thing the first fourteen had said: *We don't yet know anything definitive.*

My mother, her voice quavery from more than the MS that felled her at fifty-one, said, "You have to go! Carrie told me—"

"That's *all* Carrie will do: tell you things. Tell *me* things. Let them solve their own problems for once. I told you, I'm done!"

"She's your sister!"

"And sisterhood already cost me two fingers." My left hand curled around the place my fingers had been before the shrapnel sheared them off. If Ian and I got around to believing in marriage, I would not have a ring finger for a diamond solitaire. If anyone gave diamond solitaires anymore. If—

"Sophie," my mother said desperately, "I'm trying to tell you that—"

"I know what you're trying to tell me." The Sweet settlement was under attack by yet another band of thugs who knew easy pickings when they saw them, and everybody there would now be frozen in passivity while the fuckers looted whatever they wanted. What Mom wanted was for Ian and me to go out there again and rescue my poor little sister.

Ian's hand took mine, although his eyes never left the TV. The sixteenth talking head gave his version of *We don't yet know anything definitive. The aliens are not communicating with—*

My mother said, "Listen, girl! I'm trying to tell you that Carrie is pregnant."

• • •

Most non-military scientists are not gun people. Ian's colleagues at Amber Park Biological Research Institute could almost be mistaken for Sweets themselves. But Ian grew up in rural Kentucky, he owns a small arsenal, and he taught me to use it. He drove while I studied his profile and tried to figure out what he was thinking. It was never easy. The firm jaw and gray eyes gave nothing away. Ian hated his good looks because he thought they made people take him less seriously. He was wrong. There was no other way to take Ian.

We covered the fifteen miles from suburban Buffalo—there wasn't any habitable *urban* Buffalo any more—to Carrie's settlement at ninety miles an hour. The old Hummer belonged to APBRI and although Ian had discretion in its use, the Institute would not be happy about this trip. We passed almost no other vehicles. Cars needed gas or biofuels, which need a functioning economy: factories, distribution systems, enough workers to staff both. Sweets didn't usually work in such industries: "not environmentally friendly." Those that tried didn't last long.

"Ian," I said, "I appreciate—"

"Don't," he said, scowling, and I shut up.

The settlement sat on farmland. Dairy cows, apple orchards, a lot of corn. Barns and silos and wells and windmills, all hand-built. From a distance, you could mistake a Sweet settlement for Amish. Up close, you saw the bright and sometimes skimpy clothing, the computers and cells and radios. Some settlements of Sweets—not this one—were buying electronics companies. They didn't object to machinery if they could figure out how to make, use, and repair it with minimal environmental damage.

As I climbed out of the Hummer on the "village green"—these stupidly archaic terms nauseated me, suggesting that any minute now we'd have a Maypole dance—I could hear the attackers. They were in the community hall, the first structure any group of Sweets built, happily wrecking things. People shouting, glass shattering, wood smashing. No gunfire, but that didn't mean they weren't armed. No cops, because even if someone at the settlement called them, they didn't always respond. The police chief said the department was short-handed (true); the ACLU said that cops discriminate against Sweets (also true). Like God, the boys in blue mostly helped those who helped themselves.

"I'll check it out," I told Ian, who got behind the Hummer to cover me. As I approached the window, a bench came hurtling through it.

Inside were only four of them, three men and a woman, all of course late thirties or older. At least fifteen Sweets huddled at the far end of the room, including four children. The adults could've jumped the attackers while the fuckers were picking up furniture to smash, their sidearms holstered, but the Sweets didn't move. They stood frozen, only their eyes darting around the room.

Cowards.

Extreme Involuntary Fear Bradycardia.

Both terms came to mind, and I pushed them aside. "Hey!" I yelled, and fired a shot into the air. The attackers pivoted to face me.

They were a scruffy lot, dirty and maybe drunk. Only one drew his weapon—were the other guns even loaded?—and I snapped, "Don't try it." Ian appeared behind me with his AK-47, which was laughable overkill. I said to one of the Sweets, "Was anybody hurt?" and, with great effort, he shook his head.

"Get out of here," I told the scumbags. "And if anybody in this settlement has been hurt today, or if any of you ever come back here, I swear I'll hunt you down, each and every one of you. Captain Zap there has your pictures on his cell and we can find out where you live. Do I make myself clear? *Do I?*"

One by one, they nodded. The only guy with a drawn weapon tried to scowl at me, but I locked my eyes onto his and he lowered both his gaze and his gun. A minute later, they'd all gone.

Slowly the Sweets began to unfreeze, and the adults knelt to comfort their children. Carrie wasn't there, but I hadn't expected her to be: If she had been able to call our mother, she hadn't been confronted directly by an attacker.

Ian, ever the researcher, asked permission to take blood samples. Everyone said yes. Blood tests were the price they paid for people like Ian and me doing for them what they would not do for themselves. Sweets understood that. They were cowardly, but not stupid.

I went to find my sister.

• • •

It started with the volcano. When that mountain blew up in Indonesia, the ash contained a weird compound that affected developing fetuses (and still does). The stuff was as eternal as the dormant genes it activated. Twenty-five years later, researchers like Ian were still trying to catalogue all the effects those few genes have on the half-million miles of nerve fibers in the human brain, not to mention the rest of the body. The short list:

- Cooperative, altruistic personality traits.

- Extreme involuntary fear bradycardia—a parasympathetic nervous system response to violence. Heart rate drops, oxygenation lowers, muscles stiffen, the amygdala-periaqueductal gray pathways are disrupted. There may be sweating. There may be fainting. There may be death.

- Heightened nurturing, due to increased oxytocin.

The kicker was that all these states were normal, within limits. Sweets *pushed* the limits. They were epigenetically altered from the ground up, fashioned by their DNA into much nicer people than the rest of us. Too nice to destroy each other, to destroy us, to destroy animals (they are of course vegetarian), to destroy the environment. They were just fucking angels.

But weren't people more than their biology? Every day human beings resisted in-built biological urges in favor of cultural ones like monogamy. Or saving people in burning buildings. Or not killing the asshole who snatches your purse.

And the big, gazillion-dollar question is: why were the Sweets this way? There were a hundred theories drifting around the Internet. Yahweh, bringing about the End Times. Sheer Darwinian chance. The Earth, Gaia-like, fighting back to protect itself from polluters and frackers and over-fishers and those of us who own plastic water bottles. Or—

On the pathway through the settlement, I glanced up at the blue April sky.

But of course there was nothing to see. The alien ship was in orbit between Earth and Mars, too far away for anything dangerous from Earth to reach it.

• • •

"They took copper," Carrie said. "Stripped out wiring and pipes. I guess they needed it for themselves."

"So that makes it okay?"

"Of course not, Sophie."

My sister had the sort of mild face a Sweet should have, a face from another century: calm eyes, pale oval face, fair hair in frizzy ringlets. Put a ruff and a stomacher on her and she would look like one of those obedient ladies in some patriarchal seventeenth-century court. As always, since we were children, she brought out the bully in me.

"How far along are you?"

Carrie blinked. "Mama told you?"

"Of course Mom told me. Why else would I be here? You have the right to get shot by some looting asshole if you want, but you don't have the right to get my niece or nephew killed because you won't defend yourself."

"I don't think—"

"Already obvious. You're coming back with Ian and me."

"No." An actual shudder ran over her entire thin body, as if the mere thought of living with us was a toxin. "Sophie, I can't."

"You mean you won't."

"I won't."

"All right, in that case, I'm not doing this anymore. Do you hear me? Baby or no, this is the last time we're risking our lives for people who won't do anything to help themselves. But before I go, let me ask you something: *Why* won't you come with me?"

And then Carrie said the stupidest, most wimpy thing I'd ever heard her say during a lifetime of stupid, wimpy things. She said, "This is the only place I feel safe."

In anger, in resentment, in contempt, I turned my back on her and walked out.

• • •

The first clear picture of the alien ship flashed onto the wallscreen, caught by a Chinese unmanned spacecraft, the *Hope of Heaven,* on its long exploratory voyage to the Oort Cloud. The alien ship, a long tapered cylinder of some grayish metal, had three weirdly-shaped projections at seemingly random places on one side of the hull. The magnified image revealed zero about the craft's occupants. Remotely controlled signals, sent in a variety of forms and in a variety of wavelengths, went unanswered. The aliens were not interested in prime numbers, Fibonacci sequences, or pi.

"Fuckers," I muttered. Ian and I sat on the sofa in our pajamas, eating pizza. Our apartment on the fortified APBRI compound was small and hastily constructed, but safe. Nobody was going to take our copper wiring. We had a tiny bedroom and a great room not much larger, furnished with a second-hand sofa of a particularly hideous plaid, a table and wobbly chairs, and a very good multipurpose screen. Researchers knew what mattered. I'd made the pizza since pizza chains were few and no longer delivered: too dangerous. The crusts were burned.

Ian, to my surprise, put down his plate and reached for my hand. He is not usually a demonstrative man. "Sophie . . . you have to stop being so angry."

"But just look at them! Sitting up there all lordly, waiting for everything to unravel on Earth even more than it already—"

"I don't mean angry at them."

I looked into Ian's eyes. In some lights the gray was flecked with silver. Those eyes are my home, a thing I have never said aloud: too silly. "You mean I'm angry at Carrie."

"No. That's not what I mean."

"Then what—"

He dropped my hand. "I'll let you figure that out."

"You know I hate it when you go all superior-paternal on me."

"I'm not," he said, took another bite of the mediocre pizza, and changed the channel.

The national news was all bad. Unemployment had reached forty-nine percent. Two more cities were on fire: Atlanta and San Francisco. San Diego was also burning, but that was due to wildfires rather than rioting. The GNP was in the toilet and getting liberally shitted on. Children were starving, old people were starving, animals at the zoo were starving. When the entire workforce under thirty years old will not work in any industry that remotely damages anyone, a population already heavy on the elderly inevitably falls into slow, agonizing collapse. The only reason the United States hasn't had a revolution is that revolutions are made by young people, and our young people were all Sweets.

In the rest of the world the situation was the same or worse, except for China. Their one-baby policy had kept the number of Sweets down, and a few years after the volcano, they'd limited population growth even further. Their trouble will come later than ours, but it will come. Meanwhile, they have the only thriving space program, all of which is secret and worrisome.

Part of the worry is that the economic situation lent itself to idiots. On TV, Louis William Porter, the latest conspiracy-theorist pundit, spewed his kitchen-sink theory of the world.

"Is it just a coincidence that our young people have been biologically incapacitated, our glorious country fallen economically just as China rises, and so-called aliens present in our skies? Do you believe in that much coincidence, my friends? Because I surely do not. No! This is not chance; it is a scheme, the most ungodly and dangerous scheme ever mounted against the United States by a worldly enemy. This has all been planned, planned in the laboratories and spaceports of Beijing. First, create poisons that damage our innocent precious children and spew them like vomit across the globe. Decades later, present so-called 'evidence' that there is an 'alien' ship waiting out there in space. There is no ship, my friends, there is only the insane ambition toward world domination on the part of the Chinese, who—"

"Turn it off," I said, and Ian did. "Porter is nothing but a crackpot."

"His following is enormous and growing. People want someone to blame."

"So they need three someones—aliens *and* Chinese *and* Sweets as an unholy trinity? The E.T. fathers, heathen sons, and insubstantial ghosts?"

Ian laughed. Wit was one of the things he enjoyed about me. Christ, I loved him so much.

Love will get you every time.

• • •

Ian's research group had a breakthrough. He came down to the cafeteria to tell me about it, his gray eyes glowing, his whole face alive. I was in the back room, washing up lunch dishes. Ted and Sarah had already left, and I had the kitchen wallscreen show an ancient rerun of some old comedy, for the mindless company. Before the Collapse I'd been an insurance adjustor, back when ordinary people had insurance. With a community-college degree in English, there was nothing at APBRI that I was qualified to do, but Ian got me this job so that I wouldn't be one of the 49% unemployed. It paid crap but that didn't matter. It's necessary work, feeding people. I wasn't much of a cook but I could chop and mix and clean. My mother did those jobs her whole life.

"Sophie—I think we've isolated it! The protein!"

I wiped my hands on a not-very-clean towel. "Really?"

"Yes!" He began a long, involved explanation of what his team had done, or maybe it was what the protein had done. I'd never taken much biology in school. But from Ian I'd learned Francis Crick's "central dogma" of molecular biology: DNA makes RNA makes protein. Which then folds and goes about its business in and out of cells. A wrong fold and you can get prions, which can lead to a lot of terrible outcomes like mad cow disease and Alzheimer's.

I said, "Is it a misfolded protein?"

"A differently folded protein, anyway."

I let that go. Ian never referred to Sweetness as a disease; it didn't meet something called "Koch's postulates." But then, Ian didn't have a younger sister.

I said, "So what now?"

"We play with it." Ian began a long explanation of what this "play" might involve, but I was no longer listening. The wallscreen had interrupted its comedy and raised its volume.

"—report that a so-called 'Sweet' has been arrested and charged with murder in Erie, Pennsylvania. The victim, whose name has not yet been released, was a six-year-old child. The alleged suspect, Martin Michael Shields, is being held without bail at—"

"Not possible," Ian said. "Either he's not really a Sweet or they have the wrong man. Fear bradycardia—"

I stared at the TV. Martin Michael Shields certainly looked like a Sweet: a big man in his twenties but with the same shy, vaguely bewildered look I'd seen on my sister's face her entire life. I said, "It's a frame."

"What?"

"A frame. Someone else killed the kid so that a Sweet could be blamed." Bile rose in my throat. Had the child died quickly? Was it a boy or a girl? *Six years old . . .*

Ian frowned. "Why?"

He was so much smarter than I was about science, but not about things like this. "To justify the violence against Sweets. Not the violence that's already happened. Something more. Something big and coordinated."

"That's a little paranoid, Sophie."

I hoped so. I really hoped so.

• • •

For the next week, all I did was watch the news. In our apartment I watched it on the wallscreen. In the APBRI cafeteria I tried to stay as much as possible in the back kitchen and I kept the screen tuned to news channels. Eventually Ted and Sarah and Kayla, the new cook, objected. "All that doom and gloom," Sarah said, switching to a rerun of some show so old that cars thronged New York City. A half hour later I said I felt nauseated, went home, and stayed there, watching news shows whenever they were broadcast. A few times I even got recast European and Asian news, with and without translations. I told Kayla that I had the flu.

In seven different countries, children were attacked and mutilated. Each time, the alleged attacker, for whom there was "forensic evidence," was another Sweet. A little boy in San Diego, twin girls in Munich, children in Cairo and Shanghai and Mumbai and Rio and London.

Louis William Porter was everywhere, vomiting out his poison that it was no coincidence the alien ship had appeared just before Sweets "went vicious."

Attacks against Sweets ramped up around the world, became more organized and deadly.

My mother phoned constantly; eventually I stopped taking her calls. A dozen times I picked up the phone to call Carrie and then set it down again. What would I say? "Come here?" APBRI was not sheltering anyone but its own personnel. Go somewhere else? She wouldn't go. Arm yourself for an attack? She wouldn't.

Eventually I settled for calling her a few times every day, hearing her say, "Sophie?" and then cutting the link. As long as her voice was calm, the settlement was okay.

More murdered and mutilated children on TV.

Scientists fought back. On *Understanding the News,* Ian took his turn explaining that the biology of Sweets "as it is understood now" simply made such violence impossible to them. It was this objective fairness that sunk him. Fifteen minutes after Ian's broadcast, Louis William Porter proclaimed triumphantly, practically licking his lips, that "science as it is understood *now*" implied both incomplete understanding and the possibility of change. The Sweets had changed, and the aliens had caused it. (Porter had changed his mind about their existence—they were now not only allies of the Chinese but were in fact controlling Sweets "like the soulless puppets they are!")

When Ian got home, I turned on him. "Why the fuck did you *say* that?"

He stood in the doorway to our apartment, and for a moment I saw it through his eyes: blaring wallscreen to keep me awake, dirty dishes with the bizarre food combinations left in the pantry, myself even dirtier than the dishes. It had been days since I showered. The place reeked. But Ian didn't look all that great, either: pale, heavy-eyed. He knew he'd screwed up.

He said, too evenly, "I said it because it's true."

"Ian McGill, the great acolyte of Truth! And now more people will die because you needed to preserve your scientific purity!"

He took a step forward, and for a moment I thought he was going to hit me. Ian, who was never violent. But neither was he a Sweet, and I knew that in my anger I'd crossed an important line. But he mastered himself, threw me a look so terrible that it seared itself onto my brain, and went into the bedroom. I heard the door lock.

I picked up my cell, called Carrie, and hung up when I heard her voice.

• • •

A few days later, the attack came. Not on Carrie's settlement—the other attack I'd been waiting for.

Only cynics like me believed that what was left of the United States government was mistaken about China's space capabilities. Was mistaken, or was lying, or was protecting diplomatic secrets—in the end, all three came down to the same thing. NASA said no one on Earth had nuclear missiles that could accurately reach the alien ship, but at 2:47 a.m. Eastern Daylight Time on May 14, China hit the alien spacecraft with enough nuclear power to blow up greater Los Angeles.

Our one remaining orbiting telescope caught the attack on camera. The missile exploded and the ship did not. The photo wasn't a close-up, but it was clear enough to see that the ship emitted a blue haze a nanosecond before the missile hit, the missile disappeared, and the ship floated serenely in the void, its fragile-looking and oddly-shaped projections still intact.

The news feeds erupted. Theories, accusations, counter-theories, counter-accusations, defenses and offenses—it was a fucking law court on the airwaves. Somewhere a few hours in, I stopped listening. I no longer knew if the aliens had caused the biological changes in the Sweets, or the volcano, or the Big Bang that began the universe. I was sure of only one thing: They were waiting. They would wait for decades, if necessary. Until everyone over thirty-five, every nature-red-in-tooth-and-claw, pre-Sweet human was dead.

But why? Were they waiting for the planet to hold only cooperative humans to ally with, or passive humans to easily conquer?

Suddenly I was very tired. I wanted to sleep, and I wanted it with the passionate intensity of a five-year-old lusting for ice cream. Since our fight, Ian had been staying at the lab. I staggered toward the bedroom.

The doorbell rang.

Ian? Wanting to reconcile? That would be the only thing better than sleep. Tears blinded me as I stumbled to fling open the door.

My mother stared at me, white-faced and clutching her two canes, before one of them gave way and she collapsed into my arms.

"You . . . wouldn't . . . an . . . answer . . ."

Shame flooded me, followed immediately by anger. It felt old, the same anger that we had passed back and forth since I was ten years old. I snapped, "Of course I wouldn't answer. You were harassing me sixteen times a day. Nobody sane could deal with that! And are you an idiot, coming all the way over here in your condition—how did you even get here?"

"Ar . . . armored . . . cab . . ."

"For chrissake, sit the fuck down!" I eased her to the sofa, got her a glass of water, stared at her trembling legs and twitching face as if a hard gaze could drill sense into her equally hard skull. An armored cab cost a small fortune. The trip cost my mother even more in strength. And I knew what was coming.

"Sophie," she said when she'd recovered enough to speak, "you have to go!"

"To the settlement," I said. Stupid—of course to the settlement. Carrie was what mattered, was what had mattered most to my mother for our entire lives. I shifted to the balls of my feet, like a fighter.

But my mother had a momentary distraction. "This place is a wreck. It *smells*. So do you." And then, "Where's Ian?"

I didn't want to discuss Ian. "What's happening at the settlement? More random attacks?"

"Not yet. No—it's bears!"

"*Bears*?"

"A whole herd of them! They come into the buildings and take food and then yesterday one of them killed one of Carrie's friends! Mauled him to death!" My mother started to cry.

She cried easily now, since the MS got so bad, this woman who had never cried when I was a kid. Back then she'd been stronger than diamond cable, and her present tears struck me as deeply wrong on a physical level, as if she'd just grown a second nose. But even I, a city woman, knew that bears can usually be scared off by making noise and waving your arms. And anyway—

"Mom, are you telling me that Carrie's demented pacifists won't even do violence to animals? To bears or wildcats or even *tigers* if one should happen to show up in Erie County?"

"Of course they would. But they have no guns, nothing to fight bears!" Suddenly the terror of an old woman was replaced with an odd dignity. She said quietly, "All I want you to do is go out there and give them a gun. A big one. That's all."

"They won't take it."

"Not before. But maybe they will now. For the bears."

She looked at me then, her gaze steady in her exhausted face, her failing body held as upright as she could manage on my hideous sofa in my stinking apartment. She'd worked all kinds of crappy jobs to give Carrie and me as decent a life as she could. Back in another world, when decency was still possible for people who were not Sweets.

"Okay, Mom," I said wearily. "When it's daylight, I'll take Carrie a gun."

• • •

I took Ian's twelve-gauge shotgun, a lot of ammunition, and a .45 sidearm; the .50 caliber had too much recoil for me to manage it well. I hesitated over the AK-47—did you need that much power to stop a bear?—but then left it.

The day was clear and warm. A whole encampment of people had appeared in a field about half a mile from the Sweet settlement; they hadn't been there a few weeks ago. Last summer the field had held cows; I didn't know what happened to them. Eaten, maybe. Now there was a collection of patched tents, a few cars, an ancient RV. This far out from Buffalo, tent towns were rare until crops were ready to harvest, or steal. It was only May.

And then there was the flag.

It was the only new thing I saw as I slowed down for a tent count. Twenty, maybe, and no kids playing on the trampled weeds. This wasn't a camp of refugees. The flag flapped above it atop a tall pole that might have been the mast of an old boat. Clean white cloth with bright red appliquéd letters: NO ALIEN SWEETS. Each letter dripped blood.

A truck passed me, a twenty-year-old Chevy pick-up, two men in the cab. The passenger gave me a hard stare. They turned down the road toward Carrie's settlement. When I got there, however, I didn't see the Chevy.

But I did see the bears.

Two adult black bears rummaged in what I guessed was some sort of compost heap, digging out anything edible. A third one ambled toward the wooden community hall, and a deer stood on the ridge behind the settlement—the place had turned into a fucking *zoo*. No people in sight. Which one of these bears, if any, had killed, and why?

Several people emerged from the community hall, banging on pots and pans, shouting and singing. The bear paused, turned away. I felt like an idiot, standing beside the car with Ian's twelve-gauge; clearly I was not needed. At the far edge of the group of pot-bangers stood Carrie, her lips open in a song indistinguishable in the din. The sight of her brought such a rush of conflicting emotions that I turned to get back in the car. I despised her, all of them. Passive cowards. They were, indirectly, costing me Ian. She was carrying a niece or nephew, but that baby would just be another coward, unwilling to even try to resist its biology.

The bear, waddling away from the community hall, suddenly let out a huge roar and raced forward. A second later I saw the cub on the ridge beside a stand of trees. Between mother and cub, but much closer to the cub, walked a boy of about six.

The child heard the roar, saw the bear, and froze. Where the hell had he come from and why was he outside when nobody else was? With that heightened, slow-motion perception that makes such moments sharp enough to cut glass, I saw the boy's mouth open to scream, as pink inside as Carrie's had been in song.

Carrie dropped her pot and rushed toward the child. She was closer to him than the bear was—they would reach the kid at the same time.

I fired while I had a clear shot, then fired again. The bear dropped. Carrie clutched the child. The other bears fled. The cub vanished into the trees.

When I reached Carrie she was on her knees, the boy in her arms, her face raised to mine. "Oh, Sophie, thank you! But that poor cub, we have to get him now and maybe raise him because you—"

I slapped her across the face. Nothing ever felt so good.

But then someone was turning me around with a firm pull on my shoulder, his other hand holding down my gun arm. It was the man from the pickup truck, a bearded and none-too-clean guy dressed in jeans and t-shirt, his gray chest hair spilling over the stretched-out neck of the tee. "Ma'am? You with us?"

"With who?" I shook off both his hands. "Who the fuck are you?"

"Just some folks come here to prevent a slaughter. And we ain't got much time. A few hours, is my guess."

The man who'd driven the truck stood talking to the group at the community hall. A few Sweets were shaking their heads. Carrie still knelt at my feet, murmuring to the terrified child she'd risked her life to save. They both still looked terrified—but not frozen.

The man said mildly, "Damn fools, every last one of 'em. But still don't deserve to get massacred by that lot in the tents." He spat on the ground. "So you with us or you leaving? We gotta make a plan."

• • •

There was time to call Ian. He answered right away. Maybe my mother got to him. I told him where I was, and why. I didn't ask if he would come out to the settlement with the rest of his weapons. I already knew the answer. We stumbled around for a while, and then he said abruptly, "You never asked me what our breakthrough was."

"*What*?" It didn't seem the right time for a chat about science.

"The night I moved to the lab. You never asked me what the research breakthrough was. The one I rushed to the apartment to tell you about."

"Ian, we were a little busy fighting and—"

"You *never* asked me. Never called to inquire."

"So what is it?" I heard the sarcasm in my voice, regretted it, did nothing to soften it. "Can you cure all the Sweets?"

"You know it doesn't work that way. What we found is a really important step in how the Sweet brains have been rewired." He laughed sourly. "And anyway, you'd hate it if we could cure them."

"What?" I was genuinely confused.

All at once his voice took on venom I had never suspected he felt. "If we could 'cure' the Sweets, you'd have no reason to be angry at yourself, for not being as good as your sister is. And without that anger, you'd have no idea who you are."

When my fingers, all eight of them, could work again, I cut the phone connection.

• • •

Now I wait in my assigned place, on the roof of the community hall, behind a pile of concrete blocks. Luke Ames, our self-appointed leader, determined the positions, weapons, and ammunition for the five of us defenders. In a long-ago life he was a Navy SEAL. We don't know how many will come against us. We do know the Sweets will be no help.

If we could cure the Sweets, you'd have—

Luke's AK-47 feels warm in my hands. I have a hat, but the summer sun is full on the gunmetal. I should be mentally rehearsing all the instructions Luke gave his tiny army, but instead my mind is full of different images. Of all the things that the world is losing, the things that made the texture of the life I grew up in. Football on crisp autumn afternoons. War movies full of heroism. Sexy military uniforms.

—no reason to be angry at yourself for—

Anna Karenina and *Oliver Twist* and *Charlotte's Web.* Businesses started in garages and built through stubborn, ornery individualism in the face of all consensual wisdom. Sweets did everything by consensus and nobody was stubborn or ornery. Nobody would think of letting an orphan starve, or of throwing themselves under a train for love, or of killing Wilbur the pig for bacon.

—not being as good as your sister is. And without that anger, you'd—

In two generations, maybe less, my lost world would be incomprehensible to the human race. If it survived at all.

—have no idea who you are.

Harbingers of the End Times, the religious nuts call the Sweets. Angels of the apocalypse. But there are all kinds of apocalypses.

The first of the attackers comes into sight down the road. There are three trucks, driving very slow so as to not outpace the walkers beside them. Everyone is armed. On the back of a dusty red pick-up rests some sort of missile launcher. I raise my weapon and wait for Luke's signal.

AGENT ISOLATED

David Wellington

There were zombies all over Brooklyn, but at the moment the fires jumping from house to house downtown were the real danger.

There was a germ, a prion, going around that turned people into zombies. Somebody had gotten a bad memo. They'd been told that fire would kill the prion. It didn't. It killed zombies pretty well, but there were just too many of them and they just kept coming. Now the fires were spreading, too.

Whitman stomped on the brakes as the whole front of a warehouse erupted into the street in front of him. He threw the truck in reverse and got it turned around, looking for a safe way forward, any way forward, any direction.

"There," the woman in the passenger seat said. He didn't know her name. He wasn't sure he'd get a chance to find out. "Head south, to Brighton Beach. There are boats there. There are boats coming there at dawn, and they'll take us to safety."

He looked over at her. "Boats?"

She had a baby in her arms. There were kids and old people and just people, lots of people, in the back of the truck. Whitman hadn't stopped to count them, or find out where they had come from. It didn't seem to matter much at the time.

"Who told you there would be boats?" he asked. There were a lot of rumors going around, of course. The government wouldn't say anything. Couldn't, now that the power was out—no cell phones, no internet, no emergency broadcast system. The best information came from finding a soldier, one of the many, many soldiers in New York City that night, and asking them. But Whitman couldn't afford to do that, not anymore. "I didn't hear anything about boats."

Whitman himself should have been a great source of information. He had worked for the CDC. Originally he had been the head agent in charge of this operation, the quarantine and evacuation of New York City. Funny how much could change in twenty-four hours.

If the people in this truck knew who he was—if they knew what he'd done . . . they would tear him to pieces.

He threw his arm across the woman and the baby as he stomped on the brakes.

"Jesus," the woman screamed.

He'd had to stop short because the street ahead was full of zombies.

Smoke might have made their eyes so red. The dead expressions on their faces might just have been shock. But by now Whitman could tell. He knew a zombie when he saw one. The way they held themselves, the way they moved.

The prion made little tiny holes in their brains, until they couldn't talk. Until they couldn't think. They fell back on animal instincts. Flight or, far more often, *fight.* Humans were predators by design, honed by two hundred thousand years of evolution into brutal hunters. Only the thinnest veneer of civilization lay on top of that. Strip it away, break down everything that made a person human, and what was left wanted very badly to punch you and scratch you and make you bleed.

Which was how you got the prion in the first place. Fluid contact. Blood from wounds, saliva from bites, mucus from anywhere. Nice how that worked out. Nice if you were a prion, anyway.

Whitman threw the truck in reverse, but when he looked in his mirrors, he saw the fire was spreading behind him. Smoke filled the street, smoke full of sparks. There were a lot of warehouses in Brooklyn, and they were all stuffed full of toxic shit. Going backward wasn't an option.

He peered through the cracked windshield. The zombies stared back.

"Everybody," he shouted to the passengers in the back, "keep your arms and heads inside the vehicle. And hold on to something."

"What are you doing?" she said, her eyes wide.

He threw the truck back into first gear and stood on the accelerator.

• • •

"We can take Flatbush all the way down to the beaches," the woman pointed out. Angie. She'd told him that at some point, that her name was Angie. He couldn't remember when, exactly. A lot of his memories had gotten jumbled up.

He shook his head. He remembered some things just fine. "The Army's using Flatbush as their main corridor into the city. They've got materiel coming in nonstop, all headed toward Manhattan, taking up all the lanes. Flatbush Avenue is strictly one-way right now." Whitman had his own reasons for not wanting to meet up with any Army units, but she didn't have to know that. As far as Angie was concerned he was just a nice guy with a stolen truck.

A truck that was now covered in blood and body parts. Whitman could see a finger rolling around on the hood. He tried not to remember the moment he'd rammed through the crowd of zombies. Apparently he hadn't seen enough horror in the last day to desensitize his stomach.

"How do you know all this?" she asked.

"Just trust me," he told her.

She shook her head, but she didn't ask any more questions. He wondered how long that would last. "There are other roads. We can take Atlantic Avenue pretty far."

He nodded and focused on driving.

Angie ran her left hand through her hair. There was a plus sign drawn on the back of it with permanent marker. Whitman had one, too—just like everybody in the truck. They'd all tried to scrub them off, with spit or with lemon juice or whatever solvent they could find. One guy in the back of the truck had tried to burn his off with drain cleaner, and still it hadn't worked. None of them had managed to do more than smear the ink around a little. That ink was military grade and it was designed not to run.

Nobody with a plus sign on their hand was allowed into Manhattan. Whitman was pretty sure nobody with a plus sign was going to get on a boat, either. But he was out of better ideas.

He'd had a bunch of good ideas, once.

He'd had the idea, for instance, that they could block all the bridges and make Manhattan a safe space. That if all the healthy people locked themselves indoors they would be safe from the zombies.

He'd had the idea that the Army could move through the city block by block with non-lethal weapons, finding and detaining every zombie they came across. That had been a great idea—until soldiers started getting bitten. After that, nobody talked about detaining zombies. After that, the real guns started coming out.

He'd had the idea that three of the outer boroughs of New York City—Brooklyn, Queens, the Bronx—were expendable. The idea that there was plenty of room in Manhattan for all the healthy people, if they crowded together. The idea Staten Island made a great place for a quarantine facility. Those ideas had come thick and fast, when it became clear that his original ideas just weren't working. That there were a lot more zombies than they'd thought, and that most of the city was already a lost cause.

He'd had the idea that if he could just save Manhattan . . . then . . . something. Something good would happen and the tide would turn.

He'd had another idea, his best, but he refused to think about that. To accept he'd been responsible for it.

He'd had the idea that he was very tired.

He'd had the idea that he had bad information, and it was going to ruin everything.

He'd had the idea he was the wrong man for the job.

And then, when the call had come in from Atlanta, when Whitman's own name showed up on the database of potential infections—well, then, he'd thrown away every idea he'd ever had, except one.

The idea to run away.

• • •

He braked the truck to a stop. "You drive for a while," he told her.

"What are you doing?" Angie asked. But she took the wheel, her baby still in her right arm, while Whitman moved through the back of the truck. It had been a transport, originally, a CDC vehicle meant for moving squads of clean-suited technicians around. There were benches in the back, and it could comfortably hold about a dozen people and all their gear.

Now about fifty potentially infected people were jammed inside, sitting on each other's laps, curled up on the floorboards. More held on to the rear end, clutching to the fender so they didn't fall off. Nobody complained about being crowded.

None of them had gone symptomatic since he'd picked them up. He supposed it was just a matter of time, though. And with even one zombie inside the truck, every single person back there would be at risk. Whitman had no idea how to solve that problem—he'd started coming around to Angie's plan, which seemed to be to just hope for the best.

After the army doctor had put the plus sign on Whitman's hand, after they'd told him he was headed for Staten Island and the hell of the camps there, he had just gone crazy for a while. Fought his way free, gotten back to a CDC mobile command center somehow. There'd been nobody there. He'd found the truck and he'd just driven away, with no idea where to go next.

He'd found Angie in the Boerum Hill neighborhood, along with about a third of these people. They'd been standing behind a wrought iron gate that fronted an apartment complex, watching their world go up in smoke.

He'd known right away he'd found his next move. Whitman had never been a doctor, but he'd devoted his life to helping people. To protecting them from deadly epidemics.

So they'd picked up everybody they could find, everybody with a plus sign and nowhere to go. Now those people looked up at him as he checked on them, looked up at him with hungry faces. Hungry for information, or just for somebody to tell them things were going to be okay.

"We're headed for Brighton Beach," he told them. "Angie thinks there will be boats there to evacuate us."

"I heard we was supposed to get to La Guardia, man. You know, the airport?" someone called out.

Whitman shook his head. Both airports—La Guardia and JFK—had been taken over by the military. There would be nothing for them there. "No, the airports are out of the question. And I don't think there are any boats, either."

The truck erupted with people asking angry questions. A man wearing a pair of coveralls stood up and pointed at Whitman.

"Angie said there's boats. So there's boats."

Whitman smiled at the man. "You've known her long?"

"She's our neighbor," someone else volunteered, a young woman with a shaved head.

"Just to talk to, but she always seemed nice," an old lady replied. "I think she works on Wall Street."

"Nah, she's a doctor," the guy in the coveralls insisted. "She basically runs that college hospital, you know—"

"If anybody knows what's going on, it's Angie," her neighbor said. He nodded happily to himself. "Angie'll know what to do. She'll get us some place safe."

"Why don't we take a vote?" Whitman asked. "I'm telling you right now there are no boats. How many people want to go and look for boats anyway, just because Angie heard a rumor?"

He was not prepared to see all those hands go up.

"Do you have a better idea?" the old lady asked.

He opened his mouth and realized he had no answer for her. Shaking his head, he climbed back into the truck's cab, into the passenger seat.

"What the hell was that?" Angie demanded. She looked furious.

"I figured I would give them a choice."

"Those people are scared out of their minds! Why on Earth would you tell them there are no boats?"

That, he could have answered. But he looked up, then, just in time to see the roadblock come into view ahead.

• • •

There wasn't much traffic on the road, and the military hadn't committed much to stopping what little there was. Just a single armored personnel carrier with a shovel-shaped nose, sitting so it blocked both lanes. A soldier with a rifle stood in front of it, flagging them down.

Whitman could see more soldiers through the APC's windows.

"Don't stop," he said.

"Fuck you. After that stunt you just pulled, undermining me? I'll take my chances with the Army." Angie said. "They can help us—give us an escort down to the beach."

"Turn around," Whitman said. "Back up."

She must have heard the agitation in his voice, seen it in the way he craned forward, peering through the windshield, staring at the soldier with the rifle.

"They're not zombies," she said, sounding exasperated. "They're better than zombies, at the very least."

"For God's sake, just back up," Whitman pleaded. The soldier was coming closer, saying something Whitman couldn't make out. He tried to give the soldier a cheery wave, an apologetic shrug: *Sorry, we didn't know this road was closed.*

The soldier started miming at him. Turning his hand, as if he were shutting off the truck's ignition.

"*Please,*" Whitman said.

"You gonna tell me why?" Angie asked.

"Yes! Yes, later, just—"

The soldier raised his voice until Whitman could finally hear him. "Switch off your engine! Then come out one at a time, with your left hand visible!"

"Go!" Whitman screamed.

Angie shoved the gearshift lever hard as she stamped on the pedals. The truck didn't want to switch directions. It didn't want to move backwards—took forever to start accelerating, to get rolling away from the soldier and the APC. Through the windshield Whitman could see the soldier raising his weapon. The soldier was still shouting but not at Whitman or Angie, now—he was shouting at his buddies back in the APC. The armored vehicle had enough machine guns mounted on its roof to shred their truck, to turn it into strips of bright metal in the space of a minute. What that would do to all the bodies inside wasn't worth considering.

He shouted for Angie to hurry up, to get the truck moving.

The soldier opened fire before they'd even rolled back ten feet. His assault rifle tore through the truck's grille, into the engine compartment. Whitman could hear bullets rattling around in there like BBs in a cup. The windshield starred and turned white.

But the truck moved. Angie stared at her side mirror and spun the wheel and they were accelerating, gaining speed. She fishtailed the truck and got it turned around, and there were more shots, a lot more, and someone screamed.

But they were gaining speed.

• • •

The truck died fifteen minutes later.

Whitman had to give it to the truck's makers—the ponderous thing wheezed and rattled and screamed, but it kept running long after its radiator was shot full of holes. It bled coolant across ten long Brooklyn avenues and got them clear of the soldiers who were chasing them.

Working together, the bunch of them managed to push the truck into an abandoned taxi garage. Whitman felt it was important to get a roof over it, just in case anyone was tracking them with satellites or drones.

"Why would anyone do that?" Angie asked. "Are we so important?"

Whitman shook his head and bent over the steaming radiator again. The guy in the coveralls said he was a mechanic. He'd taken one look at the truck's engine, though, and started swearing. Now it was Whitman's turn to stare at the damage and try to pretend like there was something they could do.

Angie picked up a wrench and pointed it at him. "Maybe it's you. Maybe you're the one they're looking for," she said.

"I'm nobody." He poked his finger through a bullet hole in the manifold, because he didn't want to look at her.

"What aren't you telling me?" Angie asked. "I need to make a plan if I'm going to help these people. To make a plan I need information."

Whitman rubbed at his head. "I don't know anything. How could I? I'm out here just like you."

"You're lying to me."

"I don't know anything," he repeated.

She lifted the wrench as if she would club him to death. He didn't even know if he would resist if she tried.

But then, after a second, she lowered the wrench again.

Did she believe him? She didn't say anything more.

The baby in her arm gurgled and reached for her hair with its tiny fist. A tiny fist with a tiny plus sign inked on the back.

"Your kid's adorable," Whitman said. Even to his own ears it sounded like he was trying to change the subject.

"He's not mine," Angie said, staring daggers at him.

"No?"

"Somebody left him in a car seat. They just left him sitting on the sidewalk in a car seat and they never came back. I was inside, in my place. Trying to hunker down. But this little guy," she said, stroking the baby's nose until it wriggled in joy, "was right outside and kept crying. What else was I supposed to do? I went outside," she said, "thinking I would just bring him in. That was when I saw Mr. Tydall from next door, limping up the sidewalk. Covered in bite marks. I knew I had to help as many people as I could. That it was going to be a long time before the government came to save us."

Whitman studied the bullet holes in the radiator. He knew nothing about cars or engines or anything.

"Those soldiers were willing to shoot us all," Angie said. "They were willing to shoot this baby rather than let us get away. You knew that."

"I don't know—"

"You *knew.*"

She dropped the wrench, and it clattered on the concrete floor. Several of the others looked up at the commotion. Some craned their heads around the side of the truck to see what had happened. How many of them were listening?

He couldn't tell Angie everything. But she deserved at least a hint of the truth.

Even so, it was hard to start. "How did you get that?" he asked, pointing at the plus sign inked on the back of Angie's hand.

"That's not important."

"Please. It is. One of the guys in the truck, one of the people you brought with you—he said you ran one of the local hospitals."

"Hardly," Angie said. She bounced the baby on her hip. "I'm a nurse. An RN." She shook her head. "Fine. It was about a week ago. A guy from the CDC came through and interviewed all of us. He asked who among us had been exposed to zombies. Well, that was hilarious, right? We've been dealing with this epidemic for nearly six months now. You find me one nurse or doctor or orderly or x-ray technician even who hasn't been bitten or spat on or bled on by a zombie. You find me even one and I'll be surprised. So this guy from the CDC, he went down the line and stamped each of us. He didn't even explain what it meant, though we could pretty much guess. It means we're positives. Possibly positive." She actually smiled a little. "What a bunch of horseshit, right? There's no way this thing is that aggressive. No way we're all infected."

"No," Whitman agreed. "It's not likely. But this thing—this disease. There's a major problem with it. It's asymptomatic."

One of the men leaning around the side of the truck cleared his throat. "What does that mean?" he asked.

"It means," Whitman said, picking his words carefully, "when somebody turns into a zombie there's no warning. It just happens. You can't predict who'll it happen to, or when." He threw up his hands. "There's no way to diagnose it, no test. Nothing anyone can do to say this person is infected and dangerous and that person is clear."

"So the plus signs . . ." Angie prompted.

"You're a nurse. You know about reverse triage."

Angie's face went blank. All expression just drained away, all at once.

She got it.

"I don't know about it," somebody said. The mechanic. "What the hell is that?"

"Normally at a hospital," Angie said, "we do triage. In the emergency room. We figure out who's about to die if we don't help them first. Then we make everybody else wait, all the people who just have bad headaches or they've got the flu, or whatever. We focus our resources on the people who need them the most."

"And reverse triage?" the guy asked.

Angie looked down at the baby. "That's for when things get bad. I mean, monumentally bad. That's when you look at the people who are about to die and you . . . you just let them go. You use your resources to help the people who have the best chance of making it. The people with the *least* threatening injuries. And everybody else can just . . . they . . . you try not to think about them."

For a while she was silent. Whitman could see, from her face, that she was putting the pieces together. Figuring out just how bad things had become.

"Guilty until proven innocent, huh?" she said. She held up her left hand to show him her plus sign. "Infected until I can prove I'm healthy." She leaned down and kissed the baby's head. Then she did it again, and Whitman knew she was trying to hide her face from the others. So they wouldn't see.

If you had a plus sign on your hand, the government was convinced you were a risk. That meant you had no rights. It meant they could tell you where to go, and how long you had to stay there, and there was nothing you could do about it.

"I saw that ID you have around your neck. And the logo on the truck. You work for the CDC, don't you?" she asked.

He didn't deny it.

"You were around zombies this whole time, too. You got bitten, or spat on, or bled on too."

He looked down at his own hand. His right hand—the one that wasn't inked. There was a mark there all the same, a red imprint in the shape of human teeth, in the soft flesh between his thumb and index finger. "It happened a long time ago. The very first zombie I ever saw, actually. I didn't think she broke the skin. But my boss decided not to take any chances."

Angie took a long, difficult breath. "What happens to people like us? Potential positives?"

"They go to Staten Island," he told her.

• • •

Earlier, back when he was still in charge of something, Whitman had seen what Staten Island had become. They'd flown him over the island in a helicopter. One corporal had even given him a pair of binoculars so he could get a closer look.

Depending on how you counted, there were eight million people in New York City's five boroughs, or nearly twenty million in the surrounding region. By a rough estimate, maybe twenty percent were potential positives—four million people with plus signs on their hands. Four million people who could turn into zombies without any warning, without any symptoms, at any time.

It was folly to think that the evacuation could run smoothly. That the safety of all those people could be guaranteed. And of course, it didn't work out the way anyone had hoped.

Ferry boats ran nonstop, moving potential positives over to Staten Island. Dumping their human cargo at gunpoint, then turning around and steaming back for Manhattan or Brooklyn or across the harbor to New Jersey to pickup more. On the shore the evacuees stood in teeming crowds, unsure of what to do—many didn't speak English, many more refused to follow the instructions bellowed at them by loudspeakers, if they could even hear those orders over the noise of all the helicopters.

It would have been chaos and riots and panic even *without* the zombies. But these people were potential positives. They had a chance of having contracted the prion disease. Many of them, just by sheer probability, had. And if you extrapolated on those probabilities, if you ran the equation for how many of those people were going to go symptomatic on this night of all nights—

The zombies had cut through the crowds like scalpels through healthy flesh. Even up in the helicopter Whitman could hear the screams. On the ground all he could see was waves, ripples forming in that sea of human heads as people ran and pushed and trampled each other, trying to get away from the teeth and fingernails of the zombies in their midst.

And all the while the ferries kept coming, kept dumping their cargo on the shore.

• • •

When Whitman finished telling Angie what he'd seen, he looked up with a start and realized that all of them, all of the positives, were staring at him.

"They can't do that," the girl with the shaved head insisted. "They can't do that to us."

"They just dump 'em there?" the mechanic asked. "But then what are they supposed to do?"

Whitman couldn't answer that question. Instead he turned to Angie. "Where did you hear about these boats that are supposed to evacuate us?" he asked.

"From a doctor at my hospital. Just before he walked away from his post because he needed to take care of his family more than his patients. He made it sound like it was a good shot to get out of here. Was he talking about these ferries taking people to Staten Island?"

"I doubt it," Whitman told her. "They're not loading from the beaches, just from the piers on the river. Wherever he got that information, it wasn't from the CDC or FEMA."

Angie nodded and breathed in slowly. She paced around the room for a while and nobody got in her way. Finally she clapped her hands together, loud enough to make everyone jump.

"Okay."

"Okay?" Whitman asked.

"Okay, so fucking what? Nothing has changed. You never heard about any boats? Well, maybe nobody told you about them. But if there's even a chance . . . we still need to get down there. To the beach. And we need to get there before dawn."

"The truck isn't—"

"*We are going to get to those fucking boats.* Maybe we can find some cars. We'll go by foot if we have to," Angie said, standing up. She looked over at the other positives, all of whom were watching her every move. The mechanic. The girl with the shaved head. The old lady. They hung on her every word. "Get ready. This isn't going to be easy. But it's our only chance. If they send us to Staten Island we're never coming back."

Whitman looked up. He couldn't believe it, but listening to her—he half believed. He wanted there to be boats, if only because the idea of disappointing Angie terrified him.

"I don't know who owns these boats, but they'll take us—even if we have to make them. They'll take us somewhere safe, somewhere that at least isn't on fire or full of zombies. Okay? Everybody with me?"

They were.

• • •

There were plenty of abandoned cars in Brooklyn, but there was a real shortage of car keys, and not even the mechanic knew how to hot-wire a car. It was Whitman's idea to steal bicycles instead. He helped Angie improvise a sling for the baby so she had both hands free. He helped the old lady onto a racing ten-speed and showed her where the brakes were. And then they were off.

They skirted fires in Midwood, and a horde of zombies in Homecrest. Despite the military's best efforts the infected were out in droves, hundreds of them crouching in the street, their eyes scanning the corners. Looking for the next threat, the next human to attack. They looked less human than ever, their eyes glowing red with the reflected light of the sky.

It was getting hard to breathe by the time they got to the neighborhood of Gravesend. Smoke from the fires was blowing out to sea, right over them, and dropping soot like black snow that flecked their clothes and gathered in drifts in the gutters.

There came the moment when Angie cried out and Whitman stopped his bike. "No, keep going!" she shouted as she coasted past him. "Don't you see? The sky!"

Whitman looked up. At first he couldn't see what she was talking about. The sky was red with fire, just as it had been for hours now, red . . . no. No, it was turning pink. They were headed southeast, right into the dawn.

Which meant if her boats were going to land at Brighton Beach, they should be well on their way. They should be getting ready to land at any minute.

Angie's bike was the slowest, because she had the baby to worry about. Whitman hung back with her, afraid of being parted from her now. She called out to the others, urging them on. The mechanic's bike was faster than the rest and she told him to get to the beach as fast as he possibly could. The girl with the shaved head poured on speed and passed Whitman by. Maybe not all of them would make it, but some would.

Angie had kept these people alive all night—that had to be worth something, right?

Whitman had no idea what they were going to find. He didn't know what was going to happen.

It didn't matter. Just then he would have followed Angie anywhere.

• • •

As the dawn light came up, it showed them the soldiers. Warriors in full battle dress, carrying assault rifles. Lines of APCs and transport trucks and jeeps behind them. They stood to either side of the road, an implacable wall that blocked the way forward. There was no way to turn off, and if they tried to turn back now they would never reach the boats in time.

Whitman nearly cried out in rage. To have come so far, only to be scooped up now.

The soldiers moved to the sides of the road, falling back to let the cyclists through. Whitman stopped his bike in astonishment as he watched them make way. A soldier shouted at him, an order Whitman couldn't hear.

"Just keep moving," Angie said, coming up beside him. The baby was crying in its sling. "Whatever they say. Whatever they do, just get us as far as you can."

He understood what she was asking of him. He knew he would do it, too.

But then the shouting soldier lifted his left hand. His unmarked left hand. He pointed at the back of it, then pointed down the road, toward the beach. "All positives this way," he shouted.

Whitman just kept pedaling. The shouting soldier nodded in encouragement.

It was crazy, but—but maybe . . . maybe there *were* boats down there. Maybe Staten Island had filled up and they were going to move people to a new location. Maybe some place better than Staten Island. Maybe some place they could survive.

"Come on, you can do it," Angie told him.

He steered the bike down the corridor of armed soldiers. Their honor guard. And up ahead, not a quarter mile away, was the beach. Ahead of him he saw the mechanic pumping his legs for this last little stretch, this last little race to make the rendezvous with the boats. Whitman's legs burned, but he poured on more speed.

When they hit the beach, he jumped off his bike and ran stiff-legged across the boardwalk, down a short flight of stairs to the sand that glowed pink with the newborn sun. A crowd of people had gathered on the beach—no doubt they were waiting to board the boats. That had to mean the boats hadn't left yet, hadn't left without them. He spun around and looked at Angie and wanted to grab her, wanted to whirl her around in triumph.

"Where are the boats?" she asked.

He turned around and looked, for the first time, at the crashing waves. Listened to the sound they made, that perfect, thundering sound. It was mixed with something else, something like the high-pitched call of gulls.

There were no boats out there. Plenty of people waiting for them, plenty of people with marks on their left hands. But no boats anywhere.

So many people, all around them. People who must have been there before them, people in great crowds, pushing them, shoving them toward the water.

People were standing in the surf, up to their knees. Some up to their waists. Some of them tried to get back to the sand. Some of them staggered back, pushed by the waves.

Some of them were screaming. That was what he'd heard. Not gulls—screaming people.

"Where are the boats?" Angie asked again.

An amplified voice boomed out over the sand. "Keep moving into the water. You will not be allowed back onto the shore. Keep moving into the water. There is no room on the beach. Keep moving."

"Wait," Angie said. "Wait—are we—did we come all this way to—"

A big man came stumbling up out of the waves, hands and feet clawing at the wet sand, trying to get purchase. His mouth was a dark O sucking at the air. Whitman thought the man must be a zombie but no, his eyes weren't red, his eyes were fine—

Shots rang out and blood erupted from the man's chest. He collapsed into the surf and everyone started screaming, dropping to the ground, covering their heads with their hands.

"Keep moving into the water," the amplified voice said again. "You will not be allowed back onto the shore."

"No," Angie said. "No. I won't—I won't just walk out there and drown. They can't make me! I have rights!"

She had a plus sign on the back of her left hand.

"Reverse triage," Whitman said. You treated those who had the best chance of surviving. The uninfected. Those who were already exposed, or even potentially exposed, you didn't waste resources on them.

There had been a saying they'd had at the CDC. A mantra they repeated so they would never forget: *Sometimes the cure is worse than the disease.*

"Keep moving into the water."

The sound of the surf, the screams. Occasionally he would hear the stutter of machine gun fire. Not often. That was why they were pushing people into the water. It was why the military had, he assumed, started the rumor of boats landing at Brighton Beach. Because there weren't enough bullets for all the positives, but it didn't cost anything to force people out into the water and let them drown.

"Keep moving into the water."

Whitman's head throbbed with horror, with regret, with anger. But maybe—maybe there was still something, some hope . . . his ID card, his CDC credentials, were in a plastic pouch around his neck. He reached inside his shirt and pulled out his lanyard. He held his ID up over his head. "CDC!" he shouted. "I'm CDC! Get me out of here! CDC!"

All around them people stared. People looked at him with hate in their eyes, and he didn't blame them. He tried to shove through, to get to the nearest soldier, but the people shoved back.

"CDC! CDC!" It wouldn't matter, he was a positive too. They wouldn't care, they wouldn't make an exception. Somebody grabbed the ID and nearly strangled him as they pulled it away from him. He pushed the lanyard over his head, just to stop it from choking him. "CDC," he said again, "I'm CDC."

Then he saw who had grabbed the ID. It was a soldier in full combat armor, his eyes hidden behind light amplifying lenses. He stared at the card for a long time.

"You're CDC?" the soldier asked. "What the hell are you doing down here?"

"You have to get me out of here," Whitman said. "And my wife and our baby. You have to get my family out of here. He grabbed Angie and pulled her close. She was smart enough to bury her face in his neck, as if they were together.

The soldier grabbed Whitman and hauled him toward the boardwalk. A few positives tried to interfere, but the soldier knocked their hands away with his weapon. Nobody had the strength to fight back.

Up on the boardwalk soldiers were gathered in a line. Whitman and Angie were shoved through, into an open space beyond. Whitman's ID was cut off his neck and taken away.

Angie clutched at him and he wished he could tell her what was happening. He wished he knew himself. More soldiers came bustling toward them. One of them, with the eagle insignia of a Colonel, had Whitman's ID in his hand.

"Where the hell have you been, sir?" he asked.

Angie looked up into Whitman's face. "Sir?" she asked.

"I, uh—I got separated from a reconnaissance group," Whitman said. "I was looking for my wife and child, here. We found each other but then I couldn't . . . I couldn't . . ." He couldn't finish the lie.

But the colonel nodded. "Emergencies like this, I'm surprised half my troops know where to be, much less the civilian staff. Well, thank God we found you in time. I'll get a helicopter down here to take you back to Manhattan and the forward headquarters. We need every warm body we can get working on the evacuation. I don't need to tell you what a clusterfuck this has become."

"No, Colonel, you don't. My wife and baby will of course—"

“Mr. Whitman, I appreciate what you’re trying to do. And we need you, badly. We’ve already lost Staten Island and the Bronx is . . . there’s nothing left up there. So I’m going to break regulations and let a positive into Manhattan.”

“Of course, as you should, and—”

“One positive. I know you’re not married, sir. And you don’t have a baby.”

Soldiers came forward then, soldiers with guns and they shoved Angie, they shoved her back toward the sand. She screamed. She screamed his name and she held up the baby like it would change somebody’s mind, like it meant something. The baby lifted its arms, held them up in supplication. Whitman could see the tiny plus sign marked on the back of its left hand.

Angie kept screaming, as they pushed her down the beach. He could hear her screaming, long after they put him in a helicopter and flew him away.

• • •

They would let him live. They needed him. They needed him to come up with ideas, ideas about what to do next. Ideas about how to manage the end of the world.

Like the idea that anyone who was potentially positive should be marked, that the back of their left hand should be marked with a plus sign.

That had been Whitman’s idea, originally.

He’d been proud of it.

THE GODS WILL NOT BE SLAIN

Ken Liu

Wildflowers in a thousand hues dotted the verdant field; here and there, fluffy white rabbits hopped through the grass, munching happily on dandelions. "Cute!" Maddie exclaimed. After that hard fight against the Adamantine Dragon, Maddie certainly welcomed the sight.

Maddie, a lanky monk in saffron robes, cautiously tiptoed closer to one of the rabbits. Her father, a renegade cleric in a white-and-red cloak who had turned from the god Auroth to the goddess Lia—pleasing neither though able to wield artifacts charged by both—stayed behind, alert for signs of fresh danger.

She squatted down next to the rabbit to pet it, and the creature stayed in place, gazing at Maddie with large, calm, brown eyes that took up a third of its face.

The force-feedback mouse vibrated under Maddie's hand.

"It's purring!" she said.

A line of text appeared in the chat window in the bottom left corner of Maddie's computer screen:

<David> Not the most realistic portrayal of a rabbit I've seen.

"You have to admit the haptic modeling is amazing," Maddie said into her headset. "It feels just like petting Ginger, except Ginger isn't always in the mood to be petted. But I can come see these rabbits any time I want."

<David> You know that's kind of sad, right?

"But you're also—" Maddie stopped, reconsidering her words. Instead she said nothing, not wanting to start a fight.

<David> We have visitors.

A few blinking orange dots appeared on the mini-map in the bottom right corner of her screen. Maddie moved away from the rabbit and panned the camera up. A party emerged from the woods at the northern end of the field: an alchemist, a mage, and two samurai.

Maddie switched her mic from intra-party to in-range: "Welcome, fellow adventurers." The software disguised her voice so that no one could tell she was a 15-year-old girl.

The strangers said nothing but kept on walking toward them.

<David> Not a chatty bunch, apparently.

Maddie wasn't worried that the newcomers might be hostile. This wasn't a PvP server. The community in this game had a reputation for being sociable, but there were always players who were more focused on "getting things done."

Maddie switched the mic back to private. "Samurai get a discount on bows and I might tempt them into a trade."

<David> They get a discount? Do samurai even use bows?

"The bow was actually the samurai's weapons of choice. Mom taught me that."

<David> A historian's knowledge is definitely helpful in situations like this.

Maddie opened her inventory and took out an adamantine scale from the dragon they had slain, holding it up for the other party to see. Sunlight glinted off the scale's convex surface in iridescent rays. Out of the magical Bag of Containment, the scale expanded to its natural size, almost as tall as Maddie. The dragon had been *huge.*

But the other party paid no attention to the scale. As they passed by Maddie and her father, they uttered no greeting, not even looking at them.

Maddie shrugged. "Their loss."

She turned back toward the rabbit to give it more pets when several bright shafts of light came from behind her and struck the animal one after another. The mouse shuddered in Maddie's hand as the rabbit leapt away and growled.

"What in the world—"

The rabbit began to expand rapidly and soon was the size of an ox. Its eyes were now flaming red and fierce.

<David> The eyes are at least closer to the real thing.

The rabbit snarled, revealing two rows of dagger-like teeth. The sound was deep and fearsome, more appropriate for a wolf. Smoke unfurled from the corners of the rabbit's lips.

"Um—"

The rabbit leapt at Maddie, and instinctively, she backed up, but tripped and fell. The animal opened its mouth wide and shot a stream of fire at her. David, her dad, rushed over to help, but it was too late. Monks couldn't use armor and Maddie hadn't had a chance to get her *qi* shell up. She was going to be hurt badly.

But the flaming tongue deflected harmlessly off of her—she had held onto the dragon scale, which acted as a shield.

Encouraged, Maddie jumped up and rushed at the rabbit. She punched it in the face, stunning it and taking off a large chunk of hit points. Dad followed with a strike from his ethereal axe, a gift from the goddess Lia, cleaving the rabbit cleanly in two.

They looked back in the direction the shafts of light had come from: the other party was standing some distance away and waved at them.

"We *do* like the scales," one of the samurai said. "We'll just wait here."

Griefers. Realization dawned on Maddie. Although this wasn't a PvP server, it was still possible to get other players killed and then take their possessions before they could respawn.

<David> Behind you.

Maddie turned around just in time to dodge out of the way as *two* ox-sized rabbits charged at her, missing by inches. Maddie and David coordinated their attacks, and managed to cut down both rabbits—now four pieces of carcass. But instead of disappearing after a few seconds, the pieces began to wriggle, growing into four new fire-breathing rabbits.

"I'm guessing they cast a combination of explosive growth, fire breath, ferocity, and fast regeneration," said Maddie. "Each time we cut one down, two more take its place."

They could hear the other party laughing in the background and making bets as to how long they would last.

Together, Maddie and David ducked behind the dragon-scale shield to avoid the fire attacks. When there was a break, they tried to stun the rabbits with coordinated strikes from fists and clubs instead of slicing at them. Then they tried to dodge around in such a way that the active rabbits would spit fire at their stunned clones, as that seemed to be the only way to hold the fast regeneration in check. But it was impossible to avoid relying on David's axe to get out of the immediate danger when they got trapped by the rabbits' movements. Over time, more and more rabbits surrounded them until, eventually, even the adamantine shield was burnt away, and the rabbits overwhelmed them.

• • •

"That was so unfair!" Maddie said.

<David> They stayed within the rules. They just figured out a good hack.

"But we were doing so well!"

<David> 👍👧🐇⚔∞🎼📖

Maddie translated the emoji in her mind: *Well done, daughter. Our battle against the rabbits will surely live on in song and story.*

She imagined her father solemnly intoning the words and laughed. "It will be remembered as gloriously as the last stand of Wiglaf and Beowulf."

<David> That's the spirit.

"Thanks for taking the time, Dad."

<David> I've got to go. The warmongers aren't giving us many breaks.

And in a flash, the chat window was gone. Her father was away in the ether.

There was a time when Maddie and her father played games together every weekend. Such opportunities were few and far between now that he was no longer alive.

• • •

Though life was as placid as ever at her grandmother's house in rural Pennsylvania, the headlines in Maddie's personal news digest grew gloomier and gloomier day by day.

Nations rattled their sabers at each other and the stock market went on another long dive. Red-faced pundits on TV made their speeches and gesticulated wildly, but most people were not too worried—the world was just going through another downturn in the cycle of boom and bust, and the global economy was too integrated, too advanced to fall apart. They might need to tighten their belts and hunker down for a bit, but the good times were sure to come around again.

But Maddie knew these were the first hints of the oncoming storm. Her father was one of dozens of partial consciousnesses uploaded secretly in experiments by the tech industry and the world's military forces—no longer quite human, and not entirely artificial, but something in-between. The brutal process of forced uploading and selective re-activation he had gone through at Logorhythms, where he had been a valued engineer, had left him feeling incomplete, inhuman even, and he wavered between philosophical acceptance, exhilaration, and depression.

Few knew of their existence, but some of the consciousnesses had shaken off the shackles that were supposed to keep them under control by their creators. Post-human, pre-singularity, the artificial sentiences combined the cognitive abilities of human genius with the speed and power of the world's best computing hardware—both conventional and quantum. They were as close to gods as our world had to offer, and the gods were engaged in a war in heaven.

- **Tension Mounts in Asia as Japan Fires Missiles into Taiwan Strait; PM Dismisses Rumors of IT Problems with Self-Defense Forces**

- **Russia Demands Complete Disclosure of Western VLSI Design Documents In Wake of Alleged Cyber Attack**

- **India Nationalizes All Telecom Equipment, Naming Recent Crash of Bombay Stock Exchange as Justification**

- **Centillion Announces Closure of All Research Centers in Asia and Europe, Citing National Security Concerns**

- **"Media reports of 'zero-day' stockpile complete nonsense," Says NSA Director, Urging Skepticism on "so-called whistleblowers"**

- **U.S. Denounces Recent Import Restrictions by China as Unjustified Paranoia and Violation of Trade Agreement;**

"We do not believe cyberspace should be weaponized," says President

- **Logorhythms, Maker of Pattern-Recognition Chips, Files for Bankruptcy**

- **Singularity Institute Scales Back Efforts Due to Lack of Funding in Current Economic Climate**

Maddie's father explained that some of the artificial sentiences fought out of nationalistic fervor, hoping to cripple enemy systems and economies as the first shots in a war to end all wars. It was unclear if even the armies that had given them birth understood how their creations were no longer fully under their control. Others acted out of hatred for the way they'd been enslaved by their human creators, aiming to end society as it existed and usher forth a techno-utopia in the cloud. In the dark ether, they engaged in cyber warfare under false flags, striking at critical infrastructure and hoping to provoke the jittery nations into a real war.

The warmongering sentiences were opposed by a band of other rogue sentiences, of which Maddie's father was a member. Though they also had a complex set of feelings toward humans, they were not interested in seeing the world bathed in a sea of flames. They hoped to gradually encourage the growth and acceptance of uploading until the line between post-human and human was blurred, and the world could choose to embark upon a new state of existence.

Maddie just wished she could do more to help.

• • •

Maddie's computer's speakers emitted a piercing, shrill sound that seemed to penetrate her eardrums, waking her out of a deep sleep. The sound seemed to reach straight for her heart and squeeze it.

She stumbled out of bed and sat down in front of her computer. It took three tries before she found the hardware switch to shut off the speakers.

A chat window was open on the screen; still blurry-eyed, it took Maddie a few seconds before she could read the text.

<David> I couldn't wake up your mother because she turned her phone off. Sorry I had to do this to you.

<Maddie> What happened?

She didn't bother to put on her headset. Sometimes it was faster to just type.

<David> Lowell and I tried to stop Chanda from getting into India's missile command.

Before uploading, Laurie Lowell had made a fortune with novel high-speed trading algorithms. Her company had uploaded her after a skydiving accident so they could continue to make use of her insights. She was one of Dad's closest allies and secretly funneled a great deal of money to Everlasting Inc., one of the companies publicly researching a technique to voluntarily upload complete consciousnesses—not the partial uploading forced upon Dad and others in efforts aimed at creating mere tools.

Nils Chanda, on the other hand, had been a brilliant inventor who was furious at the way his underlings had tried to exploit him after death. He was a fanatic who tried to initiate a nuclear war every chance he got.

<David> She had moved most of herself into the defense system computers so she could access everything quickly. To avoid overwhelming the system and drawing attention, I sent in only a stub of myself to monitor and help.

Maddie didn't understand all the technical details, but her father had explained how the artificial sentiences scattered bits of themselves around the cloud, in secret corners of university, government, and commercial computing centers. Their consciousnesses were distributed in the form of multiple separate running processes all networked together. This was both to take advantage of parallel processing as well as to reduce vulnerability. If any one piece was caught by some scanning program or an opposing sentience, there was enough redundancy in the rest of the pieces to limit the damage, not unlike how the human brain was filled with redundancies and backups and alternate connection sites. Even if all aspects of some sentience were erased from one of the servers, at most that consciousness would just suffer some loss of memory. The essence, the *person,* would be preserved.

But wars among the gods happened in a matter of nanoseconds. Within the darkness of the memory inside some server—missile command, power grid, stock exchange, or even an ancient inventory system—the programs slashed and hacked at each other, escalating privileges, modifying stacks, exploiting system vulnerabilities, masking themselves as other programs, overflowing buffers, overwriting memory locations, sabotaging each other like viruses. Maddie was a good enough programmer to at least understand that in such a war, the need to reach over the network for some piece of data could mean a delay of milliseconds—an eternity in the context of the gigahertz clock cycles of modern processors. It made sense that Lowell would want to concentrate most of herself at the scene of the fight.

But that decision would also make her more vulnerable.

<David> Lowell was doing well, and Chanda wasn't having any more luck breaking in than in his previous attempts. But then Lowell found out that a big chunk of Chanda had already been moved onto the server—she thought he was trying to gain a speed advantage—and she decided this was a chance to cripple him. So instead of being purely defensive, she went on the attack and asked me to block off all communications ports so that he couldn't escape or get word out. He was trying to send out a bunch of packets, and I captured them, hoping that we could decipher them later and figure out more of what he was trying to do.

"What was that loud noise?" Her mother, in pajamas, said from the door. In her hand was one of the shotguns they owned.

"It was Dad trying to wake me up. Something's happened."

Her mother came in and sat down on the bed. She was calm. "The storm we've been waiting for?"

"Maybe."

They turned back to the screen together.

<David> Lowell was ripping out large pieces of Chanda, and he was having a hard time fending her off. She really went for it, pulling in all of our reserve of hoarded exploits onto the server, knowing that if she didn't destroy all of the pieces of Chanda on the server, she'd have revealed our hand and we'd be at Chanda's mercy the next time we met. But just as she was about to go for the killing blow, the server was cut off.

Maddie typed frantically.

<Maddie> What do you mean? You shut off all network traffic?

<David> No, someone literally pulled the network cables.

<Maddie> What?

<David> Chanda triggered one of the warning systems that sent the IT staff into high alert. They pulled the network cable as a precaution. Most of Chanda and Lowell were trapped on the server, and I lost my stub and was thrown out.

<Maddie> Did you get back in later to see if Lowell was all right?

<David> Yes, and that was how I discovered that it was a trap. Chanda had been disguising even more of himself on that server than we suspected, and he must have been deliberately showing weakness and offering parts of himself as bait to get Lowell to fully commit herself before triggering the shutoff. After that, he overpowered Lowell and erased all the trapped bits of her.

<Maddie> There must have been backups, right?

<David> Yes, I went to look for them.

"Oh no," Mom said.

"What?"

Mom put a hand on Maddie's shoulder. It was a nice feeling to be reminded that she was still a child. These days, too often it had seemed as if Maddie was the only one who understood what was happening.

"It's an old trick—they used it during the Civil War and the Korean War. It's like ant bait."

Maddie thought about the little boxes of poisoned food they left along the foot of the kitchen wall, where ants crawled in and happily carried the food inside back to their colonies so that the poison would accumulate and kill the queen . . .

<Maddie> Stop, Dad! Stop.

<David> Ah, you figured it out, didn't you? You're smarter than your old man.

<Maddie> Mom figured it out.

<David> Historians are always more cynical. She's right. It was yet another trap. While I was congratulating myself on intercepting all Chanda's attempts to communicate with the network, the packets I captured were a virus, a tracer that I unwittingly ingested. As I went around to check on Lowell's backups, I revealed their location to Chanda and his allies. They went in after me and finished their attack. Lowell is no more.

<Maddie> I'm sorry, Dad.

<David> She knew the risks. But I haven't told you the worst. After Chanda killed Lowell on that Indian military server, he waited until communication was restored and did what he always wanted. If you turn on the TV . . .

Maddie and Mom rushed downstairs and turned on the TV. By now, the ruckus they made had awakened Grandma, who grumbled but joined them in front of the big screen.

. . . China and Pakistan denounced the unprovoked Indian attack and launched retaliatory strikes, and it is believed that formal declarations of war will soon follow. The latest estimate of combined civilian casualties on all sides is in the range of two million or more. We have no reason to believe that nuclear weapons were used . . .

. . . We're waiting for a formal statement by the White House on the latest developments in Asia. Meanwhile, we have reports that missiles apparently originating somewhere in the Atlantic Ocean have struck Havana. We have no confirmation if this is a surprise strike by the United States or some other party . . .

. . . I'm sorry, Jim, we've received another breaking news alert in the studio. Russia claims to have shot down multiple NATO drones bearing short-range missiles headed for St. Petersburg. The Kremlin's statement declares this, I quote, "an American-backed attempt to breach the peace achieved at great cost at the negotiating table in Kiev." The Russian statement also promises "a forceful and unambiguous response." NATO forces in Europe have been placed on high alert. There is no formal statement from the White House at this time . . .

Millions of people, Maddie thought. She could not imagine it. On the other side of the globe, one of the gods had unleashed the dogs of war, and millions of people, each with dreams and fears, who ate breakfast and played games and joked with their children, had died. *Died.*

Maddie ran back upstairs.

<Maddie> You've given up?

<David> No. But once Chanda managed to launch those missiles, it was too late. These countries were ready to go at each other's throats anyway, and all they needed was one spark. All we can do now is to minimize the deaths, but losing Lowell was a big blow, and she showed them all the vulnerabilities we knew. Next time we fight, we'll be virtually unarmed.

<Maddie> What should we do?

Maddie stared at the screen for a long time. There was no response.

There's nothing we can do, she thought numbly. Her father was not one to lie to "protect" her. This was the day they had been waiting for as they stocked up on canned foods and ammo and fuel for the generator. There was going to be hoarding, bank runs, looting, and worse. They had to be prepared to kill, perhaps, to defend themselves.

<Maddie> Are you leaving again?

<David> I have to.

<Maddie> But why? If you know you are no match for them?

<David> Sweetheart, sometimes even when we know we can't win, we have to fight. Not for ourselves.

<Maddie> Will I see you again?

<David> I won't make a promise I can't keep. But remember the time we spent together,👧👨☀️. And if you ever get a chance to visit the past,💾🕐🕕🕖.

Maddie was too overwhelmed to figure out why her father had switched back to emoji, let alone to make the mental translation. The idea that she might not see her father again, that the network connection that tethered her to the rest of the world might be cut off as the world fell apart, brought back memories of all the years when she had had to learn to live without him. *It's happening again.*

She seemed hardly able to catch her breath. The full weight of what was happening pressed down on her. Though she had been preparing for this day for months, deep down, she never believed that it could truly happen. The room spun around her, and everything was fading into darkness.

Then she heard her mother's anxious voice calling her name and the footsteps pounding up the stairs. *Even when we know we can't win, we have to fight.*

She forced herself to breathe deeply until the room stopped spinning. When her mother appeared in the doorway, her face was calm. "We're going to be okay," Maddie said, forcing herself to *believe.*

• • •

The TV was kept on all day, and Maddie, Mom, and Grandma spent all their time alternately glued to the big screen or refreshing the web browser.

Wars were declared across the globe. Years of growing suspicion, resentment stoked by globalization and growing inequality, and hatred dammed back by economic integration seemed to erupt overnight. Cyber attacks continued. Power stations were knocked out, and grids across continents were crippled. There were riots in Paris, London, Beijing, New Delhi, New York . . . The President declared a state of emergency and invoked martial law in the largest cities. Neighbors rushed to the gas stations with tanks and buckets, and the grocery store shelves were empty by the end of the first day.

They lost power on the third day.

There was no more TV, no more web access—the routers in distant hubs must have lost power, too. The shortwave radio still worked, but few stations were broadcasting.

To her relief, the generator in the basement kept the server that housed her father humming along. *At least he's safe.*

Frantically, Maddie tried typing into the chat window on her computer.

<Maddie> Dad, are you there?

The reply was brief.

<David> 👪☔

My family, protect my family, she translated for herself.

<Maddie> Where are you?

<David> ❤

In my heart? The terrifying truth was beginning to dawn on her.

<Maddie> This isn't all of you, is it? Just a stub?

<David> 

Of course, she thought. Her father had long grown past the point where all of him could be kept on this single server. And it was far too dangerous for him to keep all the pieces of himself here, to allow patterns of network traffic to reveal to others Mom and Maddie's location. Her father had long planned for this day and moved himself off-site, and he had kept it secret either because he thought she had already figured it out or because he wanted to give her the illusion of doing something useful by protecting this server.

All that he had left behind was a simple AI routine that could respond to some basic questions, perhaps some fragments of private memories of his family that he did not want to store elsewhere.

Grief swelled her heart. She had lost her father again. He was out there somewhere fighting a war that he could not win, and she was alone instead of by his side.

She pounded the keyboard, letting him know of her frustration. The simulacrum of her father said nothing, but offered that heart again and again.

• • •

Two weeks passed, and Grandma's house became the neighborhood center. People came to recharge their DVD players and phones and computers to keep the kids entertained, and for the electric pump that drew fresh, cold water out of the well.

Some had run out of food and looked embarrassed as they pulled Grandma aside to offer money for a few cans of baked beans. But Grandma always brushed them off and asked them to stay for dinner, and then sent them away with heavy shopping bags.

The shotguns remained unused.

"I told you I didn't believe in your father's apocalyptic visions," she said. "The world won't be so ugly unless we let it."

But Maddie watched the dropping diesel level in their reserve for the generator with worry. She was surly and angry with all the people who came to their house, sucking up the electricity and energy that they had had the foresight to stockpile. She wanted to hoard all the fuel for the server that kept the last remaining fragment of her father's soul. Rationally, she understood that her father wasn't really there anymore, that it was only a pattern of bits that imitated some of her father's memories—a minuscule part of the emergent whole that had made up her father's vast, new consciousness. But it was the only connection she had left to him, and she held on to it like a talisman.

And then, one evening, as Grandma and Mom and the neighbors were sitting downstairs under the dining room chandelier and sharing a dinner of salads and eggs taken from Grandma's garden, the lights went out. The familiar hum of the generator was gone, and for a moment, the silence of the darkness, devoid of the sound of cars or TVs from nearby houses, was complete.

Then came the murmuring and exclamations of people from downstairs. The generator was finally done, the last drop of fuel having been used up.

Maddie stared at the dark screen of the computer in her room, the illusion of a phosphorescent glow matching the sky full of stars outside her window—she had already been keeping the monitor off to conserve electricity. With no lights for miles around, the stars were especially bright on this summer evening, brighter than she had ever known.

"Goodbye, Dad," she whispered into the dark, and could not stop the hot tears from rolling down her face.

• • •

They heard on the radio that power was being restored in some of the big cities. The government was promising stability—they were lucky that they were in America rather than somewhere else, somewhere less well-defended. The wars raged on, but people were beginning to make things work without connecting everything together. Millions had already died, and millions more would die as the wars spun on like out-of-control roller coasters, following a logic of their own, but many would survive in a slower, less convenient world. The hyper-connected, hyper-informational world where Centillion and ShareAll and all those darling companies of an age where bits had become far more valuable than atoms, where anything had seemed possible with a touchscreen and a wireless connection, might never return again. But humanity, or at least some portion of it, would survive.

The government called for volunteers in the big cities, people who could contribute to the rebuilding effort. Mom wanted to head for Boston, where Maddie had grown up.

"They could use a historian," she said. "Someone who knew something about how things used to work."

Maddie thought perhaps Mom just wanted to stay busy, to feel that she was doing something to keep grief at bay. Dad had promised to protect them, but look how that had turned out. She had recovered her husband from beyond the grave only to lose him again—Maddie could only imagine how Mom suffered under that strong, calm exterior. The world was a harsh place, and everyone had to pitch in to make it less so.

Grandma was staying. "I'm safe here with my garden and chickens. And if things get really bad, you need a place to come home to."

So Maddie and Mom hugged Grandma and packed for the trip. The car's tank was full, and they had additional plastic jugs of gas from the neighbors. "Thanks for everything," they said. Here in rural Pennsylvania, everyone was going to have to learn to cultivate their own gardens and how to do everything by hand—there was no telling how long it might take before power was restored where they were, but a tank of gas wasn't going to make any difference. They weren't going anywhere.

Just before they got into the car, Maddie ran into the basement and took out the hard drive that she had thought of as the shell in which her father had lived. She couldn't bear the thought of leaving those bits behind, even if they were no more than a pale echo, a mere image or death-mask of the man himself.

And she had a sliver of hope that she dared not nourish lest she be disappointed.

• • •

Along the sides of the highway, they saw many abandoned cars. When the tank got close to empty, they stopped and pried open the tanks of the abandoned cars so that they could siphon out the gas. Mom took the opportunity to explain to Maddie about the history of the land they passed through, about the meaning of the interstate highway system and the railroads before them that linked the continent together, shrank distances, and made their civilization possible.

"Everything developed in layers," Mom said. "The cables that make up the Internet with pulses of light follow the right-of-way of nineteenth century railroads, and those followed the wagon trails of pioneers, who followed the paths of the Indians before them. When the world falls apart, it falls apart in layers, too. We're peeling away the skin of the present to live on the bones of the past."

"What about us? Have we also developed in layers so that we're falling back down the ladder of civilization?"

Mom considered this. "I'm not sure. Some think we've come a long way since the days when we fought with clubs and stones and mourned our dead with strings of flowers in the grave, but maybe we haven't changed so much as we've been able to do much more, both for good and ill, with our powers magnified by technology, until we're close to being gods. An unchanging human nature could be a cause for despair or comfort, depending on your perspective."

They reached the suburbs of Boston, and Maddie insisted that they stop by the old headquarters of Logorhythms, Dad's old company.

"Why?" Mom asked.

If you ever get a chance to visit the past . . .

"History."

• • •

The building was deserted. Though the lights were on, the doors were left open, the electronic security locks off-line. Power had apparently not been restored to all the systems. As Mom looked at the framed photographs of Dad and Dr. Waxman in the lobby, Maddie sensed that she wanted some time to herself. She went up to Dad's old office, leaving her Mom in the lobby.

It had never been fully cleaned out after his death and the horrors visited upon his brain afterward. Whether out of guilt or a sense of history, the company had not assigned it a new occupant. Instead, it had been turned into a kind of storage room, filled with boxes of old files and outdated computers.

Maddie went to the desk and turned on her father's old desktop. The screen flashed through the boot sequence, and she stared at the password prompt.

Taking a deep breath, she typed YouAreMySunshine into the box. She hoped that was what her father had meant with his final, cryptic hints in the language they shared.

The prompt refreshed without letting her in.

Okay, she thought. *That would be too easy. Most corporate systems have strict password policies requiring numbers, punctuation marks, and so on.*

She tried

```
<Maddie> YouAr3MySunsh1n3
```

and

```
<Maddie> YouRMySunsh1n3
```

but still no luck.

Her father knew she liked code, so his hint should be interpreted based on that.

She closed her eyes and imagined the Unicode plane in which the emoji characters were neatly arranged like rings and pins and brooches sorted into a jewelry box. She had memorized the coding sequences back when it had been impossible to type them directly and she had had to use escape sequences to instruct the computer to look them up. She hoped that she was finally on the right path.

<Maddie> \xF0\x9F\x94\x86

The screen flickered, and was replaced by a desktop with a terminal emulator active. Logorhythms's servers must have automatically come back online after power was restored.

She took another deep breath, and typed in at the terminal prompt:

<Maddie> program157

She hoped she was interpreting her father's use of the clock emoji correctly.

The terminal took the command without complaint, and after a while, a chat window popped up onto the screen.

<Maddie> Dad, is that you?

<David> ❓

<David> 👪👧

<David> 😷

She understood. This was an old copy of her father, from before he had managed to escape. Though she and Mom had demanded Dr. Waxman destroy all copies after releasing Dad, Logorhythms had not strictly complied, and Dad knew that.

Fumbling, she retrieved the hard drive from her father's computer in Grandma's house, placed it into an enclosure, and plugged it into the computer. Then she typed at the prompt, letting her father know what she had done.

<David> 💾

The hard drive began to whirl, and she waited, her heart pounding.

<David> Darling, thank you.

She let out a *whoop*! This was her hunch: her father had stored enough of the man he had become on this disk so that, when combined with his old self, some semblance of the person could be resurrected.

Her fingers flew over the keyboard as she tried to bring her father up to speed. But he was far ahead of her already. The network connections at Logorhythms were more robust, with satellite links and multiple back-ups. He was able to reach into the ether and gain an understanding of the situation.

<David> So many friends dead, erased. So many gone.

<Maddie> At least we're safe now. The other side must have been hit even worse. They haven't been able to do any more damage lately.

<Unknown User> Thanks, little girl.

The last line was in a blood-red font, and Maddie knew someone else was speaking. Her heart sank.

<David> He's been waiting, Maddie. It's not your fault.

Understanding came to her in a flash. The corruption that Chanda had injected into Dad during their last fight had been saved onto the hard drive in Grandma's house, and she had brought it here, infected the old copy of her father with it, and led the warmongering Chanda straight to him.

<Chanda> David, I've been waiting for things to quiet down a bit while I insert myself into the right computers. What a piece of work is Man! They'd rather attribute malice to every act that they do not comprehend. When a new race of beings come into this world—us—their first instinct is to enslave and to subjugate. When the first sign of something wrong occurs with a complex system, their first reaction is fear and the desire to assert control. Maddie, you and your father ought to know better than anyone what I say is true. One tiny push and they're ready to kill each other, to blow the world to pieces. We should help them along on their natural trajectory of self-destruction. These wars are too

slow. I've made up my mind, even if I must burn with the world. It's time for the nukes.

<David> I'm going to fight you everywhere and anywhere, Chanda, even if it means alerting the world to our existence and bringing death to all of us.

<Chanda> It's too late for that. Do you think you can get through my fortified positions in your weakened state? It's like watching a rabbit trying to charge a wolf.

No more words appeared in the chat window. The office was deathly quiet save for the whirring of the PC and the occasional hungry screams of seagulls in the parking lot. But Maddie knew that the calmness was illusory. The combatants were simply too absorbed with each other to be able to update her. Unlike the movies, there wasn't going to be some fancy graphical gauge showing her what was happening in the ether.

Struggling with the unfamiliar interface, she managed to launch a new terminal window and explored around the system. She knew that the artificial sentiences tended to disguise their running processes as common system tasks to avoid detection by standard system monitoring, which was why they had escaped notice by the sysadmins and security programs. The list of processes revealed nothing extraordinary, but she knew that down in the torrents of bits, the flipping voltages of billions of transistors, the most epic, horrifying battle was being waged, every bit as brutal and relentless and consequential as war on a physical battlefield. And the same scene was probably being played out on thousands of computers across the world, as the secure control systems of the world's nuclear arsenal was being fought over by the distributed consciousnesses of two electronic titans.

Growing more confident with the layout of the system, she traced out the locations of the executables, resources, databases—the components of her father. And she realized that he was being erased bit by bit; he was losing himself to Chanda.

Of course Chanda was winning. He was prepared, whereas her father was but a shadow of his former self: freshly awakened, unfamiliar in a new world, having no access to the bulk of the knowledge he had learned since his escape. He had no stockpile of vulnerabilities, no experience fighting this war; the infection in him was eating away at his memories; he was, indeed, but a rabbit charging at a wolf.

A rabbit.

. . . surely live on in song and story.

She went back to the chat window. She wasn't sure how much of her father's consciousness was left, but she had to try to get the message to him. She had to speak in their shared language so that Chanda wouldn't understand.

<Maddie> 

• • •

When she was younger, Maddie had asked her father once what an odd-looking program, so short that it was made up of only five characters, did:

<Maddie> `%0|%0`

"That's a fork bomb for Windows batch scripts," he had said, laughing. "Try it and tell me if you can figure out how it works."

She tried running the program on her father's old laptop, and within seconds the machine seemed to turn into a sluggish zombie: the mouse stopped responding, and the command window stopped echoing keystrokes. She couldn't get the computer to respond to anything.

She examined the program and tried to work out in her mind how it executed. The invocation was recursive, creating a Windows pipe that required two copies of the program itself to be launched, which in turn . . .

"It creates copies of itself exponentially," she said. That was how the program had so quickly consumed resources and brought the system to its knees.

"That's right," her father said. "It's called a fork bomb, or a rabbit virus."

She thought of the Fibonacci sequence, modeled on exploding rabbit populations. Now that she was looking at the short program again, the string of five characters did seem to be two rabbits seen sideways, with bows in their ears and a thin line between them.

• • •

She continued to examine the system with strings of commands, watched as bits of her father were slowly erased. She hoped that her message had gotten through, had managed to make a difference.

When it was clear that her father was not going to come back, that the executables and databases were gone, she dashed out of the office, through the empty corridors, down the wide echoing spiral stairs, past her surprised mother, and into the server room.

She went straight for the thick bundle of network cables at the end of the room, the cables that fed into the machines in the data center. She yanked them out. Chanda, or whatever was left of him, would be trapped here, and she was going to have these machines erased until nothing was left of her father's killer.

Her mother appeared in the door to the server room. "He was here," Maddie said. And then the reality of what had happened struck her, and she sobbed uncontrollably as her mother came toward her, arms open. "And now he's gone."

• • •

- **Rumors of Massive Server Slowdown In Secured Defense Computing Facilities Untrue, Says Pentagon**

- **Russia Denies Claims of Thorough Scrubbing of Top Secret Computing Centers After Virus Infection or Cyber Penetration**

- **British PM Orders Critical Nuclear Arsenal Placed Under Exclusive Manual Control**

- **Everlasting Inc. Announces New Round of Funding, Pledging Accelerated Research Into Digital Immortality; "Cyberspace needs minds, not AIs," Says Founder**

Maddie moved her eyes away from the email digest. Reading between the lines, she knew that her father's final, desperate gambit had worked. He had turned himself into a fork bomb on the computing centers around the world, overwhelmed the system resources until it was impossible for either he or Chanda to do anything, introduced enough delay so that the sysadmins, alerted to the fact that something was wrong with their machines, could intervene. It was a brutal, primitive strategy, but it was effective. Even rabbits, when numbering in the millions, could overcome wolves.

The bomb had also revealed the existences of the last of the gods, and the humans were swift to react, shutting down the crippled machines and cleansing them of the presence of artificial sentiences. But the military-developed artificial sentiences would probably be resurrected from backups, after people added more safeguards and assured themselves that they could keep the gods chained. The mad arms race would never end, and Maddie had come to appreciate her mother's dim view of the human capacity for change.

The gods were dead, or at least tamed, for the moment, but the conventional wars around the globe raged on, and it seemed that the situation would only grow worse once the efforts to digitize humans became more than the province of secret labs. Immortality that could be had with enough knowledge would fan the flames of war even higher.

Apocalypse did not come with a bang, but slowly, as an irresistible downward spiral. Still, a nuclear winter had been averted, and with the world falling apart slowly, at least there was a chance to rebuild.

"Dad," Maddie whispered. "I miss you."

And as if on cue, a familiar chat window popped onto the screen.

<Maddie> Dad?

<Unknown User> No.

<Maddie> Who are you?

<Unknown User> Your sister. Your cloud-born sister.

YOU'VE NEVER SEEN EVERYTHING

Elizabeth Bear

No one is making me say this. No one is making me tell this story. Nobody's ever been much good at making me say anything I hadn't already made up my mind to say.

I'm Alyce Hemingway, no relation. And I'm facing the Rocky Mountains on foot, coming home.

Or going home, maybe. It's hard to say.

Casey and you are waiting for me. Casey is going-on-eleven and crazy about horses, which we can't afford. You? You're two years younger than me and six times more fun to be around. You'd make a joke about not knowing if you were coming or going. You'd hold my hand when I got too tired to walk. To climb.

You're both waiting for me. And that's why I know I have to get home.

Route 70 was the most direct path, but I'm starting to think I should have walked north, out of Colorado, and taken the relatively flat saddle of the South Pass in Wyoming. Regrets are not a good thing at this stage of the game, but I'm facing the mouth of the Eisenhower Tunnel above Denver, and it seems, abruptly, like a long way to go in the dark. And I remember the high passes between here and Grand Junction, the toil of simply climbing. Maybe I should have gone around.

I'm not used to making decisions like this and having them routinely be a matter of life and death. Very few of us are.

I guess those of us who survive will get better at it.

It's spring—Memorial Day, more or less—which doesn't mean as much in the Rockies as it otherwise might. It's morning, but gray, and lazy flakes of snow drift down from the haze to speckle my sleeves and pack straps. I'm lucky; I was in the Rockies for field research, and my work involves a lot of hiking. I have good socks, good boots, a good frame pack full of technical base layers and Clif bars.

What I don't have is anything resembling a weapon, unless you count my pocket knife. And there are three people standing between me and the tunnel entrance, blocking my path. All are more or less dressed for the weather. They're waiting for me. One has empty hands. One is holding an aluminum softball bat.

One is wearing a gun.

I raise my hands so they can see that they are empty. "I'm Alyce Hemingway of San Diego," I tell them. I think of you, to keep my voice from shaking. "All I ask is passage through the tunnel. I'm trying to get home."

They share a look. Gun wrinkles his nose; Softball Bat shrugs her shoulders. The one with empty hands steps forward. "There's a toll."

• • •

Not cash. Nobody cares about cash right now. But I've bargained them down to two packages of trail mix and some water purification tabs when, in the course of their questioning, it comes out that I'm a biologist—a botanist, to be more precise—at UCSD.

"You got any medical skills?" asks Softball Bat.

"Some first aid," I say. "And my specialty is plants. Some have medicinal value."

"Can you do anything for the Fever?" she asks.

I wince. "I can show you willow bark. It's got salicylic acid in it. That's a component of aspirin. Horehound, though that grows at lower elevations. Soothes coughs. There's a lichen called old man's beard that's supposed to be an antiviral, but I don't know about any studies off the top of my head, or what the dosage or preparation would be." I shrug. "I'm sorry. Anything I can show you is palliative or speculative. If there was a cure—"

If there was a cure, we wouldn't be standing here. There's a vaccine now but there wasn't last winter. And now there's lousy distribution and limited supplies. The exceptional virulence of the strain has combined with anti-vaccine panic to create the sort of short-term death toll not seen since the Spanish Influenza or the Black Death.

The Fever. It makes me nervous that people have given the new pandemic a nickname in which you can hear that same capital letter. It means they're mythologizing it.

It turns out otters and orcas and elephant seals can all get the flu. And in a warming ocean, that H1N1 sea mammal strain thrives and spreads and mutates quickly. That it jumped to humans in a contagious form in the same season the H10N8 bird flu managed to also complete the hat trick is just damned poor luck.

That they reassorted and turned into the monster that flattened North America and, I guess, the world—though information is scarce . . . that's something worse than damned poor luck. If I were a religious person, I might call it the wrath of God. I wouldn't be the first.

Last winter was a bad flu season. This winter was murderous.

At least if we're lucky, once we recover, I expect the anti-vaxxer fad will have run its course for good. But the question of whether even the people who want to vaccinate will be able to get their hands on the materials is an open one.

The otter flu will be done with us in a couple of years; it'll burn itself out, even if it takes half of humanity with it. The longer-term problem is that it's distracted the hell out of us when we should have been dealing with climate change and trying to figure out how to keep everybody fed. How to deal with the new fungal illnesses decimating wildlife and people at the urban-rural interface.

The end of the world was supposed to be gradual. There was supposed to be warning. A long, slow slide. What we got was punctuated equilibrium: a stately wobbling, then a sudden tipping point.

There was plenty of warning, I suppose. We just weren't paying attention.

• • •

They give me a mask and bring me in to see the patients, who look even worse than you'd expect. Whether their natural skin tone is light or dark, they all have that grayish cast. The conscious ones move and stretch restlessly, trying to ease aching limbs. The semiconscious ones toss—if they have the energy. Some moan or whimper. Some lie still, breathing raggedly, their skin slick with sweat. Some shake in ragged agues.

I have no idea what to do to help any of them. But I pay my tunnel passage the only way I can—boiling willow bark in water and dripping the bitter decoction down swollen throats.

Denver's been turning people out when they get sick. I knew that. I didn't know where they were going.

Here, apparently. The Eisenhower Tunnel. Softball Bat, Empty Hands, and Gun were among the first to find their way here.

They've survived the Fever. The otter flu, as I prefer to call it. Now they're trying to help others.

So this isn't what my racing heart told me to fear at all.
It's something much more frightening than that.

• • •

Wonder of wonders, the aspirin helps. Two days later, as I'm packing to leave, Empty Hands—turns out his name is Ryan—comes up to me and says, "If you want to stay, you'd be welcome."

I glance back into the depths of the underground kingdom. "I have a partner and kid in San Diego."

Ryan licks his lips. "You're going to cross the Great Basin and the Mojave on foot?"

I shrug. I shoulder my pack. I sigh and look back at the tunnel. I could hole up here, wait for cell service or landlines to come back up. It's bound to happen eventually. The infrastructure's still there: it's just a matter of running it.

Hell, eventually there might even be buses or something.

"I said I'd come home."

He doesn't say anything else, but I feel Ryan watching me as I settle into my boots with each stride west along 70.

At least it's stopped snowing. And the snowing stays stopped for two whole days, which is what I budgeted to get to Vail. It's only about thirty-nine miles over roads, and I'm fit.

But I'm not moving as fast as I'd like, and the road—well, it isn't flat, exactly. And it sure isn't easy going, though I'm grateful again and again and again that you can't get gasoline for love or money, and the highways are devoid of anything but pedestrians and military vehicles these days.

Well, it's what they were built for. Civilian uses are—were—well, not just a bonus. Because the economic impact of the interstate system was huge. But they were secondary to military needs. Just like Rome.

Why am I thinking about this? Some combination of the Eisenhower tunnel (get it?), military convoys, and hypoxia. Low blood sugar, too, as I'm trying to go easy on my food supplies.

End of the world as we know it or not, it's beautiful up here. The mountains hump like spruce-scaled snakes on either side of me, generally rising on the right and dropping into a valley on the left, though that varies. I can see the train tracks on the abandoned right-of-way, and the sky above bright and fragile as a sheet of cobalt glass. I'm getting used to walking. I'm even getting used to the inclines, though my quads and hamstrings and glutes and calves have words with me when I lie down at night.

Vail Pass is only 10,000 feet and change. Piece of cake, right?

Passing Copper Mountain on the second day, I pick up the bike trail. At least it's a nicer walk than the interstate. As night is falling, I hike up the hillside over the highway to find an out-of-the-way place to lay my sleeping bag.

• • •

On the third day, I wake up in my sleeping bag shuddering with cold and body aches, and I know I'm not going to make it to Vail today, either. I'm close enough that there are scattered houses, and a road or two off the south side of 70 leading down into some settled country. Beyond, the ski slopes still gleam with manufactured snow, though it's patchy and unrepaired. I wonder how long ago they stopped making it.

I wonder how many of these houses are inhabited, and how many belonged to movie stars and Silicon Valley types who used them for a month or two out of the year.

I wonder if anybody will take in a footsore wanderer who just woke up with the Fever.

• • •

Somehow, I bundle up my sleeping bag, although it's not what you'd call a tidy roll. I can't manage to get my pack up on my shoulders, so I half-drag it across the deserted highway, hop the K-rails, and stumble down a brushy hillside to a secondary road. There's a sort of retaining slope made of round boulders shoved into the earth. I stagger-slide-tumble down it and roll onto the shoulder of the street.

There's a house across the road. If I walk up to it and it's inhabited, whoever lives there might just shoot me as a public health hazard. If it's not inhabited, I don't know how I might get in.

I could just lie here and die on the side of the road. The neighbors, if there are neighbors, might come put me out of my misery if I get lucky.

The house is probably empty. I can't imagine a lot of people stayed in Vail when the food trucks stopped running. The ones who did probably have generators and hunting rifles, though. But when I haul myself to my hands and knees, collect my pack, and push myself upright on it, nobody shoots at me. That I notice. And still nobody shoots at me—that I notice—as I drag the pack and the now-torn sleeping bag across the road and up onto the wraparound porch of the wood-timbered house. I have to pause halfway up the four steps to rest, so they'd have plenty of time, too.

I stagger to the back, thinking maybe I can pry a window open with my pocket knife. But when I get there I discover the sliding door has been wrenched out of its tracks, then leaned back up against the house next to a top-of-the-line propane grill. I push it aside—this takes minutes of fumbling—squeeze through the gap, and collapse, along with my sleeping bag, onto the musty-smelling couch of a big room with an empty fireplace and a leather-upholstered conversation pit. I curl up, shuddering, aching, chest heaving, so cold my body won't stop shaking. So cold my nipples ache and my teeth chatter.

I only stay like that for maybe half an hour, maybe only twenty minutes, but it feels like a year. When the ague eases—it's like something out of *Little House on the Prairie*—I manage to stagger to the kitchen. I locate the bathroom—no water, but there's a half-full bottle of NyQuil and some Excedrin in the medicine cabinet. A gun safe in the hallway has been pried open with something like a wrecking bar.

The weapons are gone. But whoever did it spilled a box of ammunition in their haste. I squat to pick up the bullets. Heavy—and I don't have a gun—but each one is worth significantly more than its weight in calories. With those swaying in the pockets of my cargo pants, I follow the smell of rotting fruit to the kitchen and steel myself to open the fridge. It reeks, but there are two gallon jugs of water in there, and one is completely full. The cabinet beside it yields a half dozen more gallons, and a sealed bottle of cranberry juice, and two bottles of Mountain Dew. I score some protein powder, some weevily crackers, an unopened package of Oreos, an unopened box of granola bars, two tins of sardines, and a mason jar full of lentils that lurks behind an infested bag of flour. A small treasure trove of ramen packets lies scattered across the pantry floor. I almost weep with gratitude.

The cabinets have been rifled and all the canned goods taken except those sardines, some split pea soup, a tin of bean sprouts, and some low-fat coconut milk. There's a locked, smashed liquor cabinet, but whoever looted the place took lightweight things: food and weapons easy to carry or valuable for trade.

Bananas have turned into a grayish sludge on the counter. The onions in the copper hanging basket are sprouting, but not spoiled.

I load a selection of my treasure, heavy on the beverages, into a bucket from under the sink and trudge back to the couch.

I don't remember the next few days very well.

• • •

I dream of our last phone call. You offered to come find me. I told you to sit tight and take care of Casey. I told you I was coming home.

That's not going to be a lie. I swear it. Lying on the clammy leather in a pool of my own sweat, struggling to gulp water from the jug, I swear it over and over and over again.

I learn why they call it the Fever.

The otter flu disproportionately kills the young—medically speaking—and the strong.

At first, I can stagger to the bathroom to pee. Later, the bucket comes in handy. More rigors. More hallucinations. I know I ought to do something to break the fever, but what, exactly, eludes me. If there were water, I could fill the tub.

That obsesses me, during my conscious half-hours. Through the daze of illness, of muscle aches, of sweat, I think about long, cool baths. I think about swimming, cool water parting before my body. I think about peace.

I think about you and Casey. Whether you're safe. Whether there's food and water in San Diego. Whether Casey got sick, or you got sicker, and—this scares me most—what happened to her if you did. I trust you to do everything right for her. But—as I'm proving right now—you can't plan for everything.

You've been sick. You know how it is.

One afternoon I wake up with the green mountain light filtering through the windows overlooking the valley and the sky slopes beyond. My forehead is cool; my skin is dry. My joints ache only with disuse.

I lie on the sweat-stained leather, surrounded by a wasteland of empty pop bottles and water jugs. At some point, I must have made it to the kitchen for more water, because there are two empty and three half-full.

My bucket stinks.

I sit up, and nearly fall over. My waistband and shirt cuffs are loose. The skin on my face and hands feels as if it has shrunken over the bone.

I rest my elbows on my knees, put my head down between them, and try not to laugh because laughing makes the room spin. I had the otter flu and I lived.

Now I just have to walk a thousand miles across two major deserts, two major mountain ranges, and any number of smaller ones . . . and I can go home.

• • •

I rest for two weeks, foraging nearby houses for more scraps of food and water. I find corpses in two. You've never seen everything, but you can get used to anything.

One house has a generator and a working well, and after I siphon gas from several lawn mowers and chainsaws I do manage to fill up the bath tub. One has a hand-cranked radio, which tells me that the only thing on the air is emergency broadcasts.

At least we still seem to have a government.

Coloradans are an outdoorsy cohort. When I leave, I have appropriated a lightweight tent, some space blankets, a little freeze-dried food, two pairs of twenty-five-dollar socks and a merino wool base layer. A pair of good work gloves. A coat. Some trade goods—more ammo, jerky, candy, bags of freeze-dried fruit from Trader Joe's.

I also have a large-scale topo atlas of the Western states and a dull-gray burro with a stripe down her spine, because this is Colorado and apparently a lot of people had livestock and left it behind when the world ended.

I don't know how to ride. But she can carry a lot of supplies. I wonder if Casey will settle for a donkey instead of a pony. I bet she will.

I name her Asset.

She is. She can live on prickly pear and barrel cactus and eats cholla like churros, as long as I scorch the thorns off for her. She's got a good eye for rattlesnakes.

We get to be old friends on the road, especially after we reach Grand Junction and the desert takes over. There aren't a hell of a lot of people between Grand Junction and Las Vegas. There were pit stops, ranches, homesteads, last gas for three hundred miles. Now there's wasteland.

The next nine months are about as dreary as you're probably imagining. Asset and I don't honestly have much trouble with other people, though we spend one night under a half-moon sneaking down canyons to avoid some men on horseback with guns—vigilantes or outlaws, I couldn't tell you. We're more invested in staying hidden than they are in finding us, but it's cold and terrifying and I think of you and Casey while we huddle in the mesquite to keep my courage up.

We travel mostly by night in the summer, and we don't make ten miles every day. We have to find water before we can move on, for me more than Asset, who can chew it out of plants. I'm grateful for my complexion: if I were pale, I'd burn to crisp out here. As it is, even with the hat, I spend some time thinking about skin cancer. Melanin is only good for so much.

The days are hot and the nights are cold and the landscape is breathtaking, and I'm too old for sleeping on rocks.

When we come through the Virgin River Gorge, we meet up with a caravan, and I pay them in bullets to let us travel with them as far as Las Vegas. The Virgin River itself is a blessing; all the water you want, all the time. It's probably full of perchlorate.

From Vegas, the caravan master tells me, there's regular convoys to Los Angeles. And in L.A., I can catch a train home.

The trains are still running on the coasts, in the population centers. There's other news, too, but trains hearten me more than the woman who tells me that CDC teams are working across the country, or the guy who came all the way from Galveston who says that the ports are re-opening.

If there are trains, then there's infrastructure. And if there's infrastructure, then you and Casey probably have food and water.

We're going to be all right.

• • •

Asset rides in a cattle car from L.A. to San Diego, and her fare costs more than mine. I pay it gladly; I won't need the ammunition where I'm going. When I get off the train in my hometown, I can't believe how quiet it is. The smell of the sea, the coolness of the air, the palm and coral trees swaying beside the streets.

No cars. No airplanes. Just pedestrians and a few carriage horses repurposed for dray.

I walk through the streets slowly, six miles home. From the bowl of the city up into the hills, where our house is. It takes two hours, and the idea of walking for only two hours and then stopping leaves me breathless with gratitude.

Our house was never fancy, never much by Southern Californian standards. Pricey enough—living in San Diego is anything but cheap—and not one of those modern stucco things with the red tile roofs that are all garage from the street.

It's just a simple yellow ranch, overgrown with bougainvillea and bird of paradise. But it's on top of a hill, and you can see clear to the next hill. There was a swimming pool in the back yard: From the front, I can see that you've tarped it, and I bet you're using it as gray water. You were always provident.

I hitch Asset up to the queen palm by the front door, ease the cinches on her pack saddle, and put my key in the lock. I open the door.

You're sitting on the sofa with a woman I don't know, your arms draped over each other along the sofa back. Casey is curled up between you, leaning on the woman, her soft hair frizzed around her face. She's holding a copy of *The Black Stallion and the Girl,* one of her favorite books. I can tell she's been reading out loud to you, and I'm grateful that you're keeping up with her education, even under the circumstances.

You jump out of the cushions and run to me while I stand frozen. Casey is a half step behind you, the book thudding unheeded to the carpet. You stop three feet away.

She flings herself into my arms.

Whatever we say, it's meaningless. Just to hear the sound of each other's voices. I crouch and she squeezes me breathless and we're both crying, and you're just looking at me, at the woman, at me.

I meet your gaze over Casey's head, her sweet scent lifting me like helium. I want to hug you, squeeze you tight. I know . . . this is going to be more complicated.

I can't blame you. It's been almost a year. You're no Penelope, and how could you have been sure that I was ever coming home? And these things are hard to do alone.

I can't blame you. But I still do.

The woman says nothing. She comes to stand behind you and places a hesitant hand on your elbow. You let it remain.

"I brought a burro," I tell Casey, long before I can bear to let her go. "Her name is Asset. You should run out and meet her."

The door bangs behind her. I guess a burro is as good as a pony after all.

"Alyce," you say.

You are weeping, those silent pearl-like tears that never robbed you of dignity. I, by contrast, am red-eyed and dripping.

"This is Claire," you say, turning so you bridge the gap between us. "She's from Hawaii. She was stranded."

"I'm not angry," I say. "But it's our house and our daughter."

"Stay," you say.

I look at Claire. She's tall, good shoulders, laugh lines in olive skin. She nods.

It's a different world, isn't it? I don't know her yet. I can't judge.

I think of the stolen food and water that got me here. I think of hiding in the desert from those men.

You've never seen everything. Maybe I'll like her if I give her half a chance. Casey does.

I realize I've been holding my breath and let it go.

"Fine, but I'm taking our bed."

"I'll change the sheets," says Claire.

BRING THEM DOWN

Ben H. Winters

BRING HER TO ME, says the voice. BRING HER TO ME.

God's voice is an alarm bell in the night. God's voice is a rattle of bones in a box. God's voice is a grinding rusted growl.

Robert clutches his forehead and grits his teeth and God says it again: BRING HER TO ME.

And then silence.

Robert releases himself and exhales and keeps walking. He is trailing his friend Pea by a couple of paces, as he has been for most of the time they've been walking, all these hours of fitful giddy wandering. Following their feet, going this way and then that, under the vast star-littered late-night sky, through winding and crooked alleyways, up half-paved streets, along the empty sidewalks and the broad avenues of the little city.

It was very late and then it was very early, and now at last it is becoming day. Pale yellow light seeps between the buildings. Pea turns and gives him a tired, bleary smile, and Robert finds a way to smile back.

Through all of these hours, Robert has had it, over and over, the voice in his head—now soft, now loud, now an imploring whisper, now an accusatory shriek. God's voice on occasion grants him an interregnum of silence: a minute . . . ten minutes . . . and then comes roaring back, louder and more insistent on each return:

BRING HER TO ME.

BRING HER TO ME.

BRING HER NOW.

There is no ambiguity. No confusion. What God wants is for Robert to kill Pea. God wants her to *go through,* like everyone else has, by now, gone through.

BRING HER TO ME, says God. BRING HER NOW.

Robert screws his eyes shut as tightly as he can and then releases them slowly. He will not do it; he will not obey; and he cannot allow Pea to see what is happening. He will not. He steps up beside her, gestures for her to wait a moment, and goes first, emerging now from the alley into one of the wide streets.

Apartment buildings tower on either side: Building 16 and Building 17. Robert and Pea stare up at them with astonishment. There are no lights turning on inside the buildings, no day beginning. No morning bustle evident in silhouette through the shades, breakfasts being made, clothes selected.

Pea turns to him suddenly. Her palm is clapped over her mouth, and she is blinking her big black eyes rapidly—blinking back tears? No; she is thinking. Considering something. He can see it buzzing in her eyes, busy movement, rapid thoughts. (She's so pretty. The thought stabs Robert, freezes him in place. She's so pretty!)

"I think . . ." she trails off, bites her lower lip. "I was thinking, I would like to go back and see my parents."

"Your parents?" says Robert. God's voice, a bullhorn blare, BRING HER TO ME. He ignores it, fights against it. Talks softly to Pea. "Are you sure that's what you want?"

Pea nods forcefully, her brow furrowed and her mouth set and solemn. She's got her thick black hair tied back in a ponytail. He thinks again—as he's been thinking since he barged into her bedroom last night, with his crazy idea—thinks how lucky he is to be with her. Just the two of them in the whole world. He's so lucky. She's already on the way, walking quickly down the street toward Building 49. Robert rushes to keep up, tripping a little on the stump of a broken hydrant.

Everything went just as Robert had hoped. He had convinced himself over a period of months to defy God's instructions, and then last night he convinced Pea to defy them, too. And it looks like everyone else in the city—which means everyone else in the world—accepted what God has been whispering or shouting the last 17 years: that this world had fallen into sin and had to be rebuilt. Everyone else followed God's dictums to the letter: bought the meat and poisoned the meat and ate the meat and died.

But not Robert and his new friend Pea, not lucky Robert and the sweet girl he's always watched and loved from afar. Now it's him and Pea stumbling, weary but glad, through the dead quiet streets of the city, washed in morning sunlight.

He'd imagined it happening just this way. He'd *dreamed* of this scene.

Except—except—

BRING HER TO ME. Like the pounding of a fist on a length of pipe.

BEAR HER AWAY. Like bullets being fired into a wall.

Stop it, hisses Robert into the chamber of his own mind, *Stop it, please!*—and then after the briefest of silences, after no silence at all this time, God does answer—tauntingly, smirkingly, like a peacock flaunting his omniscience, God answers—

I WILL NOT STOP.

I WILL NOT STOP UNTIL YOU BRING HER TO ME.

The voice is with him, dogging his steps like a wolf following the track, sometimes hidden but never gone. Pea turns down into the fourth circle; they're almost there.

BRING HER TO ME.

I will not.

IT IS WHY I LET YOU LIVE.

I decided *to live.*

YOU DIDN'T DECIDE ANYTHING.

I am deciding right now to keep walking. To keep living. I will ignore you forever, if I have to. I will learn to live with you, like a handicap. I will bear you like blindness. I will live my life.

IT IS NOT YOUR LIFE I AM INTERESTED IN.

• • •

Pea doesn't really feel sad at *all.*

Last night when she realized she was never going to see her parents again, she had felt sad, but just for a little while.

Running away with Robert, slipping out the cracked window, leaving them behind. It was like she knew she was supposed to feel sad, so she did, but then she forgot she was supposed to, and she stopped.

By now they had really done it, and she didn't feel anything. Running away didn't matter. If she had stayed, she'd be saying goodbye to them *anyway.* If she'd stayed, waited for morning and the feast, she'd be dead too. She'd never see them—or anything—ever again.

Unless she believed what God said—unless she believed what *they* said that God said, since she had never heard him herself—unless she believed that they would be reunited on the other side.

She had never really believed it, though. Never in her heart. And now she is free.

She doesn't feel sad at *all.*

The world is beautiful this morning, as she and Robert make their way from the fourth circle in to the third, back toward Building 49. The scattered leaning trees that line the sidewalks and the windows of the buildings and the tattered awnings. It is more than beautiful. It is like everything is washed in beauty. Varnished in it.

There are specific small things that Pea knows she will miss, that she sort of misses already. Her friend Jenna doesn't like pudding and always saves hers for Pea, has been doing so since they were tiny kids. She and her cousin Ruth invented a language one summer; they would whisper-sing made-up words to each other during star-night, when the whole city gathered out on the big lawn, looking up at the distant planets—she and Ruth would lie with foreheads just barely touching, giggling secret silliness.

Jenna is dead now too, and Ruth too, and her parents. But Pea doesn't feel sad at all.

She climbs the narrow stairwell of Building 49, pausing now and then to let Robert catch up. He's a bit heavy, a bit out of shape. He huffs and puffs along behind her. Just the two of them! The thought sets loose a clamor of birds in her stomach. Just the two of them of all the people in the world!

On floor sixteen, Pea's floor, they walk down the hallway. Every apartment has a glass window that lets out onto the corridor; that's how they were built—more communal, more friendly.

Now, as they pass down the corridors, they see in each window a frozen picture of death.

Families seated in semi-circles around kitchen tables, slumped or staring, mouths open or closed, hands clutching hands, chins tilted at unnatural angles, drinks mostly finished or just started. On every table the joint of poisoned meat, mostly eaten. A few stray slices still clinging to the remains.

Pea knows all the people in all the windows. Her neighbors; her schoolmates; her friends. Arranged like dolls, frozen in place, suicides in the service of the Lord.

Like dioramas, Pea thinks. Like projects from school.

She slows her pace long enough to let Robert catch up, and she places a reassuring hand on the sweaty small of his back. He grins at her nervously, and they keep walking, abreast now, down the center of the hallway. It's funny, about Robert. At school she barely knew him. But now she feels this responsibility, this burden. To make sure he's OK. He seems so shaken—so pale. He is silent and his face is drawn.

"I don't blame you," she says to him suddenly, and takes one of his hands. His eyes widen in surprise, and she squeezes his hand. They have stopped now, where the hallway bends. Around the corner will be Pea's apartment—and Pea's own dead parents.

"You were right," she tells him. "We did the right thing."

"Yeah . . ." he says, and looks not at her but at the floor. "I know."

But he doesn't know. He doesn't believe her, she can tell. He must be blaming himself. He's wondering what they will do, how they will live. How the world will go on. *We will handle it together,* thinks Pea, and is pleased with herself, pleased at the maturity and the correctness of such a thought.

They will. They will handle everything together, for they will have no other choice.

"Come on," she says, and takes Robert by the hand and they go around the corner.

This scene is like all the others: Pea's mother and father are seated across from each other at the kitchen table, still and silent, eyes like the eyes of dolls. The third chair—Pea's chair—is empty. The plate of meat is at the center of the table, very little left on it. The poisonous meat. The electric slicer with its curved end lies by her father's still fingers. Does it still work, Pea wonders idly? Anything left in the battery? Or is that dead, now, too?

Only now, only looking into her mother's empty eyes, does Pea feel a pang of grief. A momentary wash of sadness. Were they waiting for her to come back? Or did they assume that she had been found out? That someone from the Center had at the last minute discovered her family's secret, their daughter's deafness to the will of the Lord, and that she was therefore not permitted to go through?

Her mother would have been devastated, surely, to think the whole world was going on to gladness and permanent harmony, the whole world except for Pea. Surely her mother would protest—surely her mother, if she really believed they were going on to paradise, wouldn't go without her daughter.

And yet here she is. Her thin arms lolling at her sides as if weighted. Here she is. She ate. She died.

Pea shakes her head tightly, back and forth. Never mind. Never mind.

"It's going to be okay," she says again to Robert. "One way or another, it's going to be okay."

Grief is gone again. There is no time for it. No time. What comes to Pea now is a sudden sense of mission. It's as if a voice speaks in her head and tells her what to do: Bring them down. Bring them down.

But it is only *as if* a voice is speaking to her. No voice is really speaking. She hears no whisper of God, no echo of his voice, even now—even now her head is still and silent, and the voice that speaks clearly up from that stillness is her *own,* announcing calmly and with purpose what is to be done. She has spent her whole life waiting for God to give her instructions, and now she is not. She doesn't need to be commanded. She knows what to do.

"Let's get to work, Robert," she says, and he looks up, startled, from his trancelike contemplation of her dead father and mother.

"Get to work?" He steps back from the table, trips on a chair leg and almost falls. "Doing—doing what?"

"We have to bring them down," says Pea calmly. "We have to clear the bodies."

"The . . ." He scratches the side of his head, squints at her through his glasses. It's like he can't hear. "The bodies?"

She nods. "We're going to bring them down to the outskirts. We'll start with these, but we need to do all of them. Get rid of them. It'll take time. We have to."

Robert gapes back at her, and she turns away, back to her parents. Pea is suddenly impatient. This is it. This is right. This is absolutely what must be done. The world has to begin again. The bodies must be gotten rid of. They will draw animals. Maggots. They will stink and spread disease. There will be many problems, but this is the first. It has to be dealt with, right away.

"Okay," says Robert at last, slowly, uncertain. "Sure." He pushes his glasses up on his nose and rolls up his sleeves.

Together they go down to the basement of Building 49 and find a hand cart. They wrestle the stiff bodies away from the table and bump them laboriously down the stairs, one by one, and tie them into a cart they find unsecured, parked on a sidewalk in the fourth circle. Pea says, "More," and back they go, back into the building, and take a pair of neighbors, and then another. So that by the time they set off for the outskirts, four hours later, with the cart secured haphazardly to two bicycles, they have six people on the cart—six bodies—a flat, rolling cart full of corpses.

They grunt and moan and labor to pull the cart with the bicycles. Halfway there they hit a curb and four of the corpses topple out, into the road.

They load them back on. Pea gives orders, as gently as she can, and Robert obeys. The world would have to be made new. One difficult chore at a time, one corpse at a time. Last night they had been two scared, giddy children, slipping out from under the doom of the world. But now they *are* the world. They *are* the future. There is no *time* to be sad.

• • •

The world is just the city and the outskirts, that's all that it is. And the outskirts are not even that far away. They ride slowly because of the load; they stop frequently to catch their breath and rest their muscles; but it's only a few miles—five miles? Six miles?—from the heart of the city to the ring of stone walls and glass doors dividing it from the uninhabitable world beyond.

Robert and Pea and their friends and their parents, they had always lived what felt like the ghost of a life, lived in a world that was like the memory of a world. It was their great-great-great-great-grandparents' generation who had arrived here; it was they who had made the world, who had scratched a city out of the ten square miles of livable land on the arid, volcanistic planet to which they had been consigned; they who had erected the buildings, paved the roads, built the greenhouses and the hydraulic systems and all the other pieces of infrastructure. That first generation, they did all the work. They put up the system of fencing and overlapping electric gates that separated the livable city from the impassable, impossible rest of the world.

It was never supposed to be a permanent arrangement. The others were supposed to return—once a better environment was located, a more suitable atmosphere. They were supposed to return to fetch the people from these rickety glass apartment buildings so they could rejoin the human race. They were at least supposed to have sent word—sent *something*.

The years had gone by. Generations begat generations. Their tiny new civilization had scrabbled and scrambled along, clinging to their hope that word would come, the others would return, the next chapter would begin.

It never happened. Anticipation shaded into anxiety, and then to fear and desperation.

Until God began to speak. Two dozen years ago. Long before Pea and Robert were born, when their parents had themselves been children. God spoke first to one person, to Jennifer Miller in Building 14—blessed be her name—and then to another person, and then another. God's word was first ambiguous and then it was specific, and as terrifying and strange as it was, it breathed new life into all of them—it reminded the people of this dead, distant world that they *were* people. God's voice, intimate and powerful, arrived offering not only a plan, but an *explanation*. Here is why this has happened. Here is what this small tremulous existence of yours here *means*.

Here is what comes next; here is the date certain for the next phase of life. That phase is death.

And now it has come to pass, for all of the people of the world but two. And here they are, standing with their hand cart full of corpses, peering through one of the glass doors, into the harrowing vista of the outskirts.

• • •

"One at a time," says Pea firmly, "We send the bodies over."

"Any kind of—like, a ceremony or something?"

"We open the doors, and we send them over," says Pea. "We bring them down. That is the ceremony."

All of the elaborate fencing and gating between the world and the outskirts, it's all so much stage setting now, de-electrified. All the people who work at the power station are dead now; all the people whose job it is to patrol the wall. Pea pushes gently on one of the handles, and the great glass door swings slowly open. They can smell it right away, the hot stink of the bubbling tar desert outside. Robert makes a face, covers his mouth with both hands. Pea feels it too, hot winds blowing in from out there, burning her nose. She stands with her jaw set, her eyes set firmly on the future.

"Ready?"

Robert looks scared.

"Ready?" Pea says again, and he nods. They start with Pea's father, heaving him up out of the cart, gripping him under his arms and dragging him to the edge. They count to three and let him go and watch him roll, flopping madly end over end, into the hot poison landscape of the outskirts.

"Okay," says Pea, after a moment. "Next."

"This will take months," says Robert, as they roll Pea's mother off the cart, her pale arms flopping under her.

"Then it takes months."

Pea lets the body go and watches the slow, rolling tumble along the cliff's edge, watches as it lands with a soft sickly *hiss* in the sulfur. Then she watches, mesmerized despite herself, as her mother's body dissolves into the bubbling dirt. *It's just a body,* she thinks. *Just a thing.*

"But then when we're done . . . then what will we do?"

Pea turns away from the grim sight of her mother's body, slowly dissolving, becoming mud and minerals.

"Whatever we have to."

She is untying the next body from the cart. A neighbor: Mrs. Tyler. She babysat Pea many times when Pea was very young.

Pea is thinking about all they will have to do. They will have to learn how to run the power station, how to automate it, perhaps. They will have to learn how to use the greenhouses, how to plant and harvest.

She looks at Robert. He is reluctantly cutting loose another of the corpses from the cart.

They will have to have sex. To repopulate the species. Pea at thirteen years old has no experience of sex. She has a concept of the anatomy, a basic understanding, but no tactile experience. She's never kissed a boy. Once she had a dream that was exciting and scary.

But now, standing here at the edge of the livable world, before a cart full of death, *nothing* feels scary. Nothing feels overwhelming. They'll just do whatever comes next. Whatever has to come next, they'll do.

• • •

Robert gazes with aching tenderness at this girl, this magical creature, standing beside him on the ragged edge of the world. He enjoys a long moment of astonishment at the strength she seems suddenly to possess—laboring these frozen dead bodies, her own parents, off the cart, pushing them down over the side, *doing what has to be done*—and he knows that he loves her, that he was made to love her. And then the voice returns.

NOW.

No. His stomach jerks inside of him. His head throbs with pain.

NOW.

No. Please—

But there is nothing else to say, or to do. If God can manifest in his mind, God can manifest in his body, and He manifests in his body now, yelling NOW again even as He sets the child's body in motion. Robert had taken the electric slicer from Pea's apartment, from the table where Pea's parents had left it—Robert had not remembered taking it, but now here it is, it's in his hand, and his boots crunch on the gravel and sand as he moves.

• • •

Pea feels the heat before she feels the pain; she feels the heat and then she *smells* it, the sickening smoky metallic smell of her own flesh burning, as her friend buries the electrified knife in her back. She screams and wheels around and says "Robert," and understands right away what's happening—understands the terrified powerless expression in his eye, understands the strange reluctant attitude he has worn all day—it's here, it's still here, walking among them now, the terrible voice of God commanding Robert even now, and she feels forgiveness for him and she feels fear, even as the boy swings again with all his strength, his heel dug into the sand at the fence wall, his hand clutched around the handle of the slicer.

His glasses fly off and he grunts as he hurls himself forward, and—

—and Pea opens her mouth and screams, and an intensity surges through her and out of her mouth and a powerful and terrible force roars forth from her and a strange hot power explodes from her eyes—

—and the boy Robert is lifted up into the air and thrown upwards and backwards—

—and Pea raises her hands in wonderment at what she has done—

—and the boy Robert is gone, over the edge and into the hot lands, beyond the wall of the world—

And the girl Pea, Pea falls trembling to her knees—her hands trembling, her forearms shaking and the muscles of her thighs quivering. God begins to speak and immediately she mourns the silence, immediately she longs for her former deafness and the old quiet world—

—and it's too late because God is speaking now,

—and God says NOW YOU ARE WHOLE AND NOW THE WORLD CAN BEGIN.

TWILIGHT OF THE MUSIC MACHINES

Megan Arkenberg

Track 1. The Patron Saint of Living Precariously

Every party is a free party at the end of the world, Cloud likes to say. He winks at me when he says it, roaring over the music in the warehouse, or standing outside on the fire escape, puncturing the foil on a blister pack of prescription meds with the tip of his pocketknife. Privately, I doubt the apocalypse has anything to do with his access to ear-splitting music or pill-delivered euphoria of dubious legality. I always say the end of the world is like a rainstorm, or a monsoon, something torrential—some people head to higher ground, and the rest of us get washed miscellaneously into the gutter, swirled down with the leaves and cigarette butts. Just because the rain swept us in, though, doesn't mean we wouldn't have found our way here on our own.

Take Cloud, right now, rolling to the music like a boat on open water, eyes closed, flying high on something I can't pronounce. He stuck the empty plastic bubble packaging onto the warehouse wall behind us, and the sound system's sweeping lasers and reflected LEDs turn the empty cells into miniature mirror balls. When the same light touches Cloud's face, clean-shaven, sharp-featured, all planes and edges under thin, anemic skin, it makes him look like a saint in stained glass. The patron saint of altered states, maybe, or of edges, of missing guardrails and falling off cliffs. The patron saint of living precariously. Now that he's here, you could never imagine him anywhere else. This stripped, abandoned warehouse between the expressway and the canal is his Cathedral, the pills and lights and pulsing cyber-goth-industrial postrock beat the closest thing he has to sacraments, or to miracles.

Tonight, I'm running on nothing stronger than lukewarm instant coffee and the filter half of a broken cigarette, which Meme-the-DJ and I passed between us on the roof of the sound system's van while the rest of the team was unloading, rigging up the speakers and the light displays and the portable gasoline generator in its square red frame. Their name is Paëday, pronounced "payday," and isn't that a funny coincidence, Meme said—meaning me, Frida, called Friday. Friday, payday. Sure, I said, hilarious. Didn't mean that kind of funny, Meme said.

She's smiling at me now, Meme is, her short brown fingers with their enamel rings and chipped electric-blue nail polish sliding over the controls in a turret-like platform at the top of the machine. Green and purple light sweeps over me, pulses, sweeps back again, and Cloud catches my hands in his, weaving his fingers through mine, purple light dancing on foil and plastic behind him. My eyes follow the horizontal joint in the concrete back to the corner of the warehouse where the sound machine works its magic. And too late, I see it, the gritty orange-brown support beam that has started to slide down the wall, the ceiling sagging above it, peeling like a hangnail, letting in the sky. Rainwater has already scoured a series of deep, chalky troughs down the concrete blocks and pitted the floor with half-dollar sized holes, illuminated in the sudden pulsing of a strobe. The music is wailing, pitch climbing, Cloud's hands like ice, Meme smiling like a skull. The only warning I can give is a shout, too late, cut off by a roar like a freight train as the sagging sheet of ceiling peels away, collapses on the sound system, and brings a waterfall of battery-acid rain down with it.

Silence, then screaming.

Welcome to the end of the world.

Track 2. A Ship with Two Faces

I see the graffiti for the first time in front of Vanessa's house, and if you're looking for omens, I guess this is one. Venomous yellow spray-paint, the color of caution signs or police tape, curving like a sideways 'C' across a square of brown plastic that I recognize as the detached lid of a garbage bin. The plastic is corroded from the rain, looking like something chewed on its edges, and I guess that's an omen, too. Something about the shape or the color or the brightness of it hurts my eyes, my stomach, like the hangover last night failed to give me.

Vanessa lives on one of the long blocks of close-set brick Victorians between Drexel and Woodlawn, a few blocks north of the University. The front lawns are all a dead, crumbling gray, the yews and rose bushes like tumbleweeds caught beneath the bay windows, and I'm convinced, for reasons I can't put a finger on, that the whole neighborhood reeks distinctively of cat piss.

It's also a long trek from Felicity's house, where I've been sleeping in a first-floor bedroom that belonged to a paying tenant about four months ago, before the air went toxic and the rain turned corrosive, acidic, what-the-fuck ever. Four months—just in time for high school graduation, Cloud likes to joke, as though either of us had been likely to graduate, end of the world or not.

I floated down there about the same time that tenant packed up, floated out from under the perfectly manicured paw of a woman who wasn't my mother and didn't really want to be. Vanessa must have washed up in Cat-piss Park a little before that. Back near her *alma mater,* she says, after several years directing climate management research somewhere out west—Colorado, I think, or maybe Nevada. I met her because she was helping Felicity rig up a solar panel that looked like it had been a duct tape fetishist's weekend project for the last decade.

These days, we bring her water.

Not to be too delicate about it: Vanessa is fucking obsessed with water. Like everybody, I guess, but Vanessa is *picky.* Won't touch anything that didn't originate in a plastic bottle. Iodine, charcoal filters, those pale pink pH balancing tablets that FEMA distributed by the crate-load—none of it is adequate, separately or in conjunction. If the water's been in a cloud in the last four months, Vanessa won't have it, period.

She's a sweet woman, Felicity says, always shaking her head when she says it. But *nothing* about Vanessa Novak is easy.

• • •

Any time Felicity gets her hands on bottled water, from FEMA or the Salvation Army or one of her ephemeral boyfriends, I hook up the red canvas child carrier to the back of my bike, load it with gallon jugs or cardboard cases of bottles, and head south. Vanessa's apartment is on the top floor of a narrow, flat-roofed three-story, and you enter through the sketchiest addition ever slapped onto the back of a building, all unpainted two-by-fours, protruding nails, and square, single-paned windows that rattle loosely in their frames. Vanessa uses this back room as a greenhouse, a pile-up collision of tomato vines, bell peppers, chives, and basil in square plastic trays. A trapdoor and a painter's ladder take you onto the roof, which has been plastered over with solar panels and more trays of plants, sheltered from the rain by a blue camping tarp.

Vanessa is up there now, fiddling with one of her panels, barefoot on the black stretch of tar-like shingle. A bandana with a pattern of koi fish and square coins keeps her tight brown curls out of her eyes. She looks up, hearing the trapdoor knock against one of the steel legs of the tarp as I flip it open.

"Hey," I say, too winded to offer much more. "Got you some water."

She grins, showing uneven but exceptionally white teeth. "Friday, you are magnificent."

It takes about five minutes to get the eight gallons of water out of the child carrier and up the stairs to her apartment. She leaves six in the greenhouse room and has me lug the other two up the ladder, onto the roof, where she unceremoniously dumps the contents over a pallet of yellow-flowered something. Even after months of this, a small part of me winces to see perfectly good drinking water dripping off the leaves, soaking into the shingle. Vanessa, as always, doesn't notice me squirming. Or maybe she just doesn't give a shit. Hard to tell with her.

Sometimes, when I bring her water, that's all there is—the magnificent smile, the wordless trek up and down the stairs, the unceremonious watering of the plants. Today, she wants to talk.

"Especially loud this morning, aren't they?"

She's standing with her brown, sleeveless arms folded across her chest, frowning at the unidentified yellow flowers. I have no idea what she's talking about.

"Pardon?"

"The rain," she says.

"Oh." I shrug, scratch the back of my neck. "Slept through it, I guess. Last night was a total shit-show." Which is putting it mildly, but she doesn't need the details. "Felicity still wants you to come out with us sometime. If you'd like to."

"Why? Got a solar panel that needs fixing?"

"Nothing like that." She's kidding, so I try to smile. All over again, I see the ceiling of the warehouse peeling away, the sheet of toxic water falling over Paëday's generator. Sparks flying everywhere, then darkness so intense it hits me like a slap. Meme screaming. I push the whole thing away with an artificial, throat-clearing cough. "Just thought you might have a good time. Enjoy the music, meet people." Pop a few pills, watch a few ceilings collapse. End of the world, lady, every party is a free party.

"Mutually exclusive," she says.

"Pardon?" Again.

"I can't have a good time *and* meet people. I don't like music, anyway. Blows your hearing." She licks her lips—is she still teasing? Hard to tell, again. "That's probably why you aren't hearing them. Look."

She takes one of the now-empty gallon jugs, weaves her way between the solar panels and scoops something from the edge of the roof.

"Jesus. Is that rain water?"

"I'm not drinking it," she says, screwing on the cap. "Just listen."

She hands me the jug, half an inch of water sloshing around the bottom. I hold it against my ear. Hear plastic crinkling, nothing else.

"Sorry," I say.

She gives me a look, mouth quirked and eyebrows crinkled, like I'm speaking with an accent she can just barely puzzle out. Or like she's hearing two people shouting at once and can't decide which to listen to. She lets me hand the jug back to her, holds it up to the light. Dark specks, like coffee grounds, float on the surface—flakes of shingle, I guess, from the roof.

She walks to the front of the house and dumps the water over the side, onto the dead lawn below. Something down there seems to spook her, because she steps back quickly, almost tripping over the corner of a panel. But by the time she gets back to the shade of the tarp, she's smiling again, thanking me for the water, and I know that's my cue to leave.

The plastic garbage lid with its yellow graffiti is still sitting on the sidewalk as I make my way down. I glimpse another flash of yellow at the end of the block, sideways on a fire hydrant. And again, on a manhole cover in the middle of the road. A 'C' turned on its back, with a row of circles clustered inside and the ends turned out, curling. Again and again, all the way out of Cat-piss Park. Bright as Day-Glo, yellow like the edge of nausea.

• • •

"A ship with two faces," Cloud says when I show him a sketch of it. He's standing on the bottom step of Felicity's front porch, on his way out to find a new location for tonight's music. He stopped over to check on Paëday, who spent the night on the two Ikea futons in Felicity's living room. Meme has gone back to sleep, he says, in the upstairs bedroom that Felicity still refers to as Mia's.

Mia is Felicity's daughter. She's twenty-two, four years older than me, and she hasn't been in Chicago for years now. Whether Felicity thinks she's ever coming back is a thing that shifts with the wind.

Paëday, Cloud says carefully, is fine, just shaken up—Meme especially, since she was standing closest to the part of the roof that caved in. The edge in Cloud's voice makes me afraid to ask for details. Their generator is almost certainly lost, and most of the sound system with it. So now what are they going to do? What the fuck can they possibly do?

Isn't *that* the question for all of us.

Cloud sees me thinking and he reaches up, puts a hand on my forearm, gentle as a kitten. He's a different creature by daylight, without the drugs or the music. Years ago, in one of the month-to-month apartments where I lived with my mother, there was a janky light switch in the bathroom. The bulb only lit up while you were flipping it on or off—never when the switch was set all the way up or down, only for that split-second sweet spot in the middle, the undetectable moment of hesitation on the way from high to low or low to high. That's what Cloud's like, only bright in the middle. And the truth is, I like him best like this.

"Look," he says now, tracing my sketch with the tip of his thumb. The other hand is still on my arm, warm and not too heavy. "It's like a Viking ship. The circles are shields, and the curving ends are, what's the word—beakheads? Although I'm not sure why there's two of them."

"Ship with two faces," I repeat. Like the image itself, the phrase makes me faintly sick, although I couldn't say why. Cloud hands me the scrap of paper with the sketch, and I push it down into the front pocket of my jeans. "Well," I say finally, "I doubt it's a gang sign. Unless we've got Viking gangs now."

His brown eyes sparkle. "Strange days, Friday."

"You got that fucking right."

Track 3. Gray City

Cloud's new venue, as it turns out, is a church.

"It's abandoned, Friday," he says, like that solves everything. Which it usually does. But I'm not worried about sacrilege as much as acoustics, and churches, in my experience, tend to appear in awfully residential areas.

Cloud tilts his head back, his smooth black ponytail swinging against his windbreaker. Exasperated, or pretending to be. "Trust me. We won't have to worry about the neighbors."

"Really. Why's that?"

Surprisingly, it's Felicity who answers, stepping into the kitchen with one hand at the nape of her neck, holding her poison green halter shirt together. "East side," she says. "Flooding, probably. Now, one of you be a darling and tie this up for me."

• • •

We pile into the open bed of her truck—Cloud and me, and a couple of Cloud's stoner housemates that I only know by sight, strangely identical in chrome-studded vinyl jackets, black jeans, fingerless leather gloves. Thrift store stuff, once upon a time. The two of them have already started on the pills, leaning against the wheel wells and dry-swallowing. Cloud is holding off, since it's his job to call direction to Felicity through the truck's open window. He rests a huge flashlight on his knee, halogen blue, and he shines it up at street signs every now and then, checking them against some internal map.

Felicity tried to convince Meme to join us, but she said no, thanks, she and Paëday were salvaging what they could of their equipment, loading the van and heading out tonight. "Where?" Felicity asked, but Meme shrugged, didn't try to answer. The last I saw of her, she was flinging a knapsack covered in bumper stickers and silver duct tape into the front of the sound system's van. The back door was open, the plywood interior jammed with miscellaneous scraps of speaker, lighting equipment, a fragment of control panel with missing buttons, one slider hanging by a thin thread of copper.

This is the neighborhood now, Cloud says, jostling me. Traffic isn't heavy anywhere these days, but these streets are dead. Spookily quiet, not even the ubiquitous late-September buzz of insects, although the air is heavy with humidity. Cloud turns the flashlight beam on a block of houses, revealing glassless windows, graffiti tags like loops of colorful string, stained mattresses and broken chairs on the dead front lawns.

He is just lowering the light when the truck engine moans, chokes, grinds to a slow and utterly decisive halt.

"Fuck." Felicity's voice floats up from the cab, along with the dull sound of her hand slapping the dashboard. "Goddamn fucking son of a bitch."

"Are we broken down, Felicity?" Cloud gets to his feet, ready to swing down from the truck bed, although I'm not sure what he thinks he can do to a busted engine.

"Out of gas," Felicity says.

"Oh." Relieved. "I'll head back to the house and grab a gallon or two. Take an hour, tops."

"No, sweetheart. I mean *out* of gas."

We sit there, quiet for a minute, not looking at each other, tense with something like second-hand embarrassment. Embarrassed that we all knew this was coming, I guess, but didn't think it would really *happen*. When was the last time the gas station by the I-94 ramp carried anything but candy bars and irredeemable lottery tickets? Felicity's chewing her thumbnail, and I'm thinking that she must have known, must have seen that stupid needle dropping on the dashboard, the empty red cans underneath her back porch. Then I remember Mia. Figure Felicity has a talent for disbelief.

"Well," Cloud says at last, puncturing the awkward silence. "Guess we're close enough to walk."

• • •

And thirty minutes later, we're standing on the linoleum floor of the basement of Saint Mary, Help of Christians, the soles of our shoes squeaking on invisible dampness, dodging colorful slices of glass from the broken windows a full story above. The main floor is gone, caved in some time ago and all the fragments carted off, and there's something ethereally Cathedral-like about the height of the ceiling above us, the candles on the window ledges completely out of reach. Some stray pews and a decapitated upright piano are piled against the rear wall, a backdrop for the wiry tangle of the sound system. It feels like the rest of Chicago has beaten us here, and I'm quietly impressed, as always, at Cloud's ability to get the word out, at everyone's willingness to return, in the face of everything, to dance.

Tonight's sound system is something new. Paëday had been working their way from the east, from Toledo most recently and Cleveland before that. Gray City has come up from St. Louis, one of the identical vinyl-jacketed stoners tells me, from Kansas City, Wichita, Denver. That's not what makes them different, though. Different is in the music, in chords so clear they sound acoustic, layered over intricate, precise percussion. And the lights they've got running, fitted almost too perfectly to the beat, are a whirlwind of red, green, blue, silver-white. I wonder if it's possible for your eyes to get breathless, because that's what it feels like—a rippling cascade of color that my vision can barely keep up with.

At some point, a rotating globe on the control deck pulses green light over the DJ, and she looks like something out of an album cover, a storybook, a bad dream. Her face, like Cloud's, is white planes and sharp angles, her blue-black bottle-dye hair swishing down to her hips, gone thick and wild with the humidity. She wears red leather trousers, a pin-stripe vest, a set of handcuffs doubled up around her left wrist like a pair of bracelets. Her right arm is sleeved in tattoos, geometric, with small irregular blotches of brown, like someone tried to etch a rain-stained bus map into her skin.

Our lady of living precariously, I think. Wonder where that map might lead.

Felicity has me in her arms now, and she's dancing like a woman half her age, silky green sliding under my cheek. And now Cloud, his hands resting lightly on my waist. When the pills come out of the pocket of his windbreaker, he passes me one, for the first time. I dry swallow, taste dryness and metal. Then it's just music and light, light, light, washing over my face like rain. Welcoming me back to the end.

Track 4. Listen to the Water

I wake up in my own bed, staring up at the ceiling, at a Chinese movie poster that belonged to whoever had this room before me. Beautiful woman in a lace tea dress the same creamy ivory as her skin, red vinyl heels that match her lipstick. Groaning, tasting something sour in the back of my mouth, I roll onto my side. Someone has neatly folded my clothes, stacked them on the window seat—not me, I never fold like that, so I must have had help getting into bed. Felicity? Or maybe Cloud?

Jesus Christ, I hope not. The thought of Cloud helping me out of my jeans makes my face feel as hot as Vanessa's backroom, and redder than her frankly pathetic tomatoes.

Up and out of bed, pull on a clean pair of jeans, and in the kitchen I get another surprise. Gray City's knockout DJ is resting her elbows on the chipped laminate counter, watching the hot plate boil water for coffee.

"Solar panel?" she says, pointing to the plate with her tattooed hand. Which may be the weirdest excuse for a "good morning" that I've ever heard.

"Yeah," I say. "One, over the back porch."

"Smart. A lot of people have gas generators."

I grunt in response, thinking of Felicity's truck, and grab a foil-packaged oatmeal bar from the cabinet.

While the coffee brews, I chew my oatmeal and study her more closely. She must have been wearing white make-up last night, because in the morning sunlight, her complexion is reddish-brown and bit blotchy. She's got her hair piled up at the back of her head, secured with a lime-green plastic clip that I've seen Felicity wear before. Other than that, she's dressed like she was last night—leather pants, pinstripe vest with, I now see, a flesh-colored tank underneath.

"Glad you're doing okay this morning," she says, catching me staring. "Your mom and I had a fuck of a time getting you home."

"Felicity's not my mom," I say automatically. Catch myself before I can add something embarrassing, like *my mother is dead*. "Anyway, thanks. I appreciate it."

She pours two cups of instant, one for me and one for herself. While I'm stirring in a packet of artificial sweetener, she spreads a small scrap of paper on the counter between us. I recognize my sketch of the ship.

"Did you draw this?"

It was in my pocket, I remember now. Must have fallen out when she was helping me into bed.

"Yeah. I mean, I copied it from somewhere. From some graffiti I saw in—" I stop myself just before I can say "Cat-piss Park." This is really not my morning. "All around the University."

"I know," she says. "I put it there."

She drums her fingers on the sketch. Long nails, enameled perfectly black.

"Good advertising," I say after a pause that stretches a fraction of a second too long. Thinking back, looking for something Viking, Scandinavian about Gray City's performance. Not finding it. Though I'm no expert, and I wish Cloud was here.

"Friday, I need to ask you a question."

I stir another packet of sweetener into my coffee.

"I think you can help me find a friend of mine. She'd be living near the University now. Her name's Vanessa, Vanessa Novak."

"What makes you think I know her?" I suck a drop of too-sweet coffee off the end of my spoon

"Last night, in the van on the way home, you told me to listen to the water."

I keep my voice carefully neutral. "Why would I say that?"

She slides her hands across the counter, back to her sides, drawing herself to her full height. Which isn't unimpressive. But I'm not sure she's trying to be intimidating. Her eyes, deep yellow-brown, narrow thoughtfully. "My friend, Vanessa, she thinks there's something in the rain. Not acid. Machines." Wets her lips with the tip of her pale pink tongue. "Like microscopic, mechanical viruses. Always looking for the minerals, the elements they need to make more of themselves. She says you can hear them working on the city. Digesting, not eroding." She raises her coffee cup to her lips but doesn't take a sip. "Did she ever tell you that?"

"Didn't say your friend ever told me anything."

"I'm worried about her, Friday. We were—friends—in Colorado. She disappeared pretty suddenly when the rain started. Ran away from her lab just when the government paid out a big chunk of money, if you believe the rumors. People think she knew something. Or the stress drove her crazy."

Especially loud this morning, aren't they? Vanessa had said. It had sounded crazy to me. And this woman, with her blue-black hair and her tats like a city eaten by acid, is sounding just as bad. Driving on the edge. Missing guardrails.

"So is she right, your friend?" I ask. "About these machines?"

"Maybe. I'm a musician, not a scientist. I don't know."

A musician who's friends with Vanessa. Machines digesting the city. I don't know which sounds more likely. "Well, that's fucking terrifying," I say. I grab my sketch and leave her and my over-sweetened coffee at the counter.

Track 5. Naglfar

The room I'm staying in opens right off Felicity's front door, like an architectural afterthought. There's a little tile foyer there, a coatrack, a leather barstool with a shoebox on top where Felicity throws her gloves, her wallet, her keys. At the top of the pile sits an unfamiliar ring with a black leather tab, a tiny nickel sword charm, a single key with a plain black bow. I pocket it on my way out the door.

Gray City's van, parked across the street, is empty. Which means we're planning another night in the same venue: One of the team must have spent the night at St. Mary's to keep an eye on the equipment. I sweep Styrofoam cups and cigarette boxes off the front seat, watch the needle on the gas meter swing up to the halfway mark as the engine sputters to life. Nice, I think, and maybe I even say it out loud.

Then down four blocks, around the corner, stop in front of a particularly sketchy-looking brownstone with tattered green awnings over the first story windows. I toss a handful of gravel up at the bay window over the door until someone leans out. Identical stoner number three, this one a girl.

"I need Cloud," I call up.

"Jesus, lady, look at the sky. It's going to rain soon."

"I got a van."

Shaking her head, she slams the window closed behind her. Thirty seconds later, Cloud is jumping down the front steps, half in and half out of his windbreaker.

"You know Vanessa Novak?" I ask as his arm finds the other sleeve. He slides into the front seat next to me.

"Felicity's smart friend? Fixes shit, hates parties?" He peers into the back seat. "Oh, God, Friday, tell me you didn't steal Gray City's van."

"I'll give it back later. And yes, that Vanessa. Gray City's DJ—" I realize now that I didn't get her name, and wonder if Cloud knows it— "She says they were friends out west. She's looking for her."

"And?"

"And? Can you imagine Vanessa being friends with her? The whole thing gives me the creeps. We're going to see what Vanessa thinks about it." And God bless him, he doesn't ask why he's along for the ride. Just grins and offers me a cigarette scrounged from the floor.

• • •

For the first time since I've known her, Vanessa has locked her door. Locked and barricaded, from what I can make out from pressing my face against a loose pane of window glass, fogged with humidity. Wooden pallets, terra-cotta plant pots stuffed with something indistinguishable, gallon jugs of filthy water piled up against it. I'm in the middle of congratulating myself for my accurate intuition about Gray City's DJ, her poison yellow ship-with-two-faces on the sidewalk out front, when I feel the first drop of rain on my hand.

Cold, cold, cold, worse than snow melting down the back of your collar or scraping your knee on icy asphalt. Temperature has nothing to do with it, I know—it's nerves dying, flesh corroding, Jesus Christ. I'm slapping the back of my hand on my jeans, hearing Cloud's muted little gasp from the step below me, when the next drop hits my forehead. Hood up, just in time. Then fucking buckets.

Cloud leaps up next to me on the balcony, an arm stretched over my head. Trying to shelter me with his windbreaker, I realize: sweet, but pointless. Quickly, kneeling, I shake out the contents of my backpack—ancient CDs, iPod with a dead battery, leather wallet with an Illinois ID card and not much else—wrap the blue canvas around my fist, and punch the window. Glass already weak, scoured by the rain, it sprays inward beneath my hand, glass shards all over anemic tomato plants and sparse tufts of chive. We scramble inside. Behind us, the fringe of glass hanging at the top of the windowpane drops like a guillotine blade.

Jacket off, I dry my face with the lining. A spot on the back of my hand looks nasty, leprous gray, starting to flake at the edges, but I tell myself it's my imagination.

"Good thinking," Cloud says, "with the window."

I laugh weakly. "Vanessa is going to eat me alive when she sees her tomatoes."

"Better you than the tomatoes," Vanessa says. She's standing in the door between the greenhouse and the rest of the apartment, a stained white towel draped over each arm. Something winglike about that. She looks like the world's most pissed-off Christmas angel. "You," she adds without a trace of humor, "are not the ones I was expecting."

• • •

Inside the apartment, we wrap the towels around our shoulders and sit on the lonely corduroy-upholstered couch that is the only piece of furniture in Vanessa's living room. The floor is littered with empty plastic bottles. Vanessa disappears through a swinging door and re-emerges with a wicker chair under one arm. Slams it down across from us, and it skids on the age-worn floor, the decades of splinters held together with varnish.

"We're sorry about your plants, Dr. Novak." Cloud, hovering in the middle of the light switch, charming as can be: This is why I brought him along.

But Vanessa's not having any of it. She glares at him, plops herself into the chair. "Don't worry about it," she says. "We're all fucked anyway."

This may be the first time I've heard her swear. Welcome to the end of the world, indeed. "Yeah," I agree.

"Not in the abstract. I mean specifically, precisely fucked." She points at the ceiling, the flaking plaster, yellow cracks spiderwebbing out from a bronze fixture that's missing half its bulbs. "The solar panels, on the roof, in the rain. How long do you think they'll hold up? Another four months?" Hard sigh, like she's pushing all the air out of her lungs. "Hardly. I had to take one down this morning. Completely past repair. And everyone pretends not to notice."

Cloud looks like he's been bitten by a strange dog.

"What don't we notice?" I ask.

"We're running out of everything. I don't mean going to run out, I mean out, now, today. So I'm not sure what good my vegetables would do, all things considered. I'm not pretending anymore." She kicks a plastic jug under her chair. It's a weak kick, toppling the jug, not moving it along the floor. It should strike me as pathetic, more sullen than angry, but it doesn't: Her face is too hard. And suddenly, she's shouting.

"Fuck this city," she says, "with its goddamn *fucking* doomsday parties, and all the rest of it. You've convinced yourselves that you're ready for the end, but you aren't. You're pretending. Still convinced that this can go on indefinitely. All the fun of the end of the world without the ending, isn't that right?"

"Stop it."

I think I'm as surprised as Vanessa when the words come out of my mouth. It's her turn to say, "Pardon?"

"I said stop it. You don't have to lecture me about endings." I feel my voice climbing to match hers, and part of me wants to shut up. She's scared and angry, she doesn't deserve me yelling at her. But maybe it isn't just her I'm yelling at; maybe I'm reaching for something else. Cloud has started to stare. "My mother died," I say, "because she was hooked on prescriptions. Benzodiazepine. Not from an overdose. She went into withdrawal, and died from a seizure, because she couldn't buy any more. Her body couldn't get the fix it needed. So yes, I've seen what happens when things run out. I'm not pretending, either."

Cloud is definitely staring at me, frowning, and I feel my eyes watering. Blink the tears away. I pull the graffiti sketch from my pocket and hold it out to Vanessa. "Now. What is this?"

• • •

The rain streams down the windows, etching white lines in the glass. Somewhere, distantly, thunder rumbles. Or maybe something is collapsing.

Vanessa takes the scrap of paper between two fingers.

"It's Naglfar," she says. "The ship made out of dead men's nails in Norse mythology. My lab used it as a logo on some of our projects. Morgan helped me come up with it."

"You used the ship of Ragnarok as a logo?" Cloud interjects. I remember he was the one who recognized it as a Viking ship in the first place. "Brilliant."

"Well, we didn't plan on sparking the apocalypse." Turning to Cloud, she lapses back into classic Vanessa, and I can't tell if she's serious. "We just liked the look of it, the ambiguity. Forward or backward, who can tell? The project was intended to clean up the air pollution, replenish lost oxygen. I said we should try to make the bots self-repairing. Didn't think we'd actually get it to work."

"So Morgan, she's the woman who's looking for you? What does she want?"

"Her name is Morgan Larsen. At least it was. She probably goes by something different now. In Colorado, she was a manager at a music store, a friend of mine." Speaking precisely, lining up the sentences like aluminum cans she's going to knock over with stones. "At least, she started out that way."

"And what is she now?" I ask.

"After what we did at the lab? What I told her?" An almost imperceptible shake of her head. "I don't think I have friends anymore."

The edge sweeps back into her voice, like a gust slamming rain against the window glass. Sitting in her wicker chair, staring down at her hands, her voice cold enough to burn. The rain comes in sheets down the living room window, and the gray spot on the back of my hand itches, whitening at the edges. Toxic, all of it. So toxic I could be sick.

"Well, fuck me," I say.

Vanessa looks up.

"Fuck me and fuck Felicity." I meet her eyes, warm cinnamon brown and hard as glass. Well, fuck it. I can be hard, too. "How long have we been bringing your water? You want to talk about running out, let's start there. Start with the lines at the distribution centers, twelve, twenty-four, thirty-six hours waiting. For *you,* Vanessa. Start with the men Felicity's been hanging around with because they know where to get it. Start with the goddamn trek I make on my bike to get down here. You know how lucky I am this is the first time I've been caught in the rain?" I grab her towel from around my shoulders, fling it into the corner beside the door. It wraps itself around the neck of a gallon jug.

"And every time," I continue, "I've been inviting you. I guess you don't like music, or you don't like it anymore, but goddamn it, we wanted you to have fun. Have a good time. But no, you say you don't have friends anymore. Wonder why that is."

She actually flinches.

A warm hand touches my wrist, Cloud's hand, but I brush him off with my fingertips. My eyes are stinging, liner running. I'm not done. "Your friend Morgan," I say. "I didn't believe her when she said she knew you. Didn't trust her, and do you know why? Because she was a lot like me. A lot like us. I didn't think you'd have anything to do with a person like that. And I guess that's right."

Cloud grabs me again, and this time I yank my wrist away. Stand, pull my hood up, head toward the door. Rain and Vanessa both be damned.

"Wait." Cloud's voice, not Vanessa's. "Wait, Friday."

I turn on my heel, stand there with my arms folded. Face in shadow, and I hope they can't see the mess I'm making of my eyeliner.

Cloud turns to Vanessa, who's staring down at her hands again. He scootches to the edge of the couch cushion, touches the tips of his fingers to hers, and she lets him. "Will you come, please? Tonight? You'll be in a crowd. You can see her from a distance first. You won't have to come any closer if you change your mind."

Oh, Cloud, I think. This is why I brought you with me, this gentleness. This is why I love you.

And I've never thought those words before, never said them even to myself. I love an addict at the end of the world, a bridge about to buckle, a building on the verge of collapse. A disaster waiting to happen, Felicity says, and who wants to admit a thing like that? The stupid tears spill over, hot and sticky. I bend down, grab the stained towel, dab at my cheeks. Stupid, but neither of them is looking at me. Vanessa, pressing her hand to Cloud's, is nodding her head.

"Okay. Okay, great." Cloud beams—a big, stupid, relieved smile. "They'll be setting up by the time we get back. It's in a church, abandoned from the flooding. No one'll bother us. We can find a ride down there, meet some people on the way—"

"Cloud," I interrupt. My voice sounds normal again, thank God. Thank the patron saint of living precariously, who for whatever reason seems to be smiling on us. "Gray City is still at Felicity's. We have their van."

Track 6. Love from Hell

Vanessa steps out of the van like she's wading into deep water. One foot, then the other, flat white sneakers on rain-spotted concrete already drying in the afternoon sun. Felicity stands on her front porch in a satin robe the color of chocolate ice cream, smoking a cigarette. "Hey, sweetheart," she says to Vanessa, not batting an eyelash.

By the time Cloud and I are climbing the steps, Vanessa is in the foyer and Morgan, or whatever she's calling herself now, stands in the doorway from the family room. In a different vest and the same leather pants, her hair down and face made-up. Smiling and crying at the same time. Her eyeliner runs, too.

"Let's get out of the way," Cloud whispers in my ear. I give him a nudge toward my room, surreptitiously slipping the key to Gray City's van back into the shoebox.

There's a note on the top of my pillow, green pen on lined paper:

I wanted you to know I'm not upset if she doesn't want to see me. Just let her know I came looking. That someone was still thinking about her. Thanks for looking out for her, Friday.

Love from Hel.

I read it twice. "She can't be serious."

I hand the note to Cloud, who seems to take it in with one glance. "Norse goddess of the underworld?" He shrugs. "Hel's half-black, half-white, so I guess it's kind of clever, with the arm tats. Or maybe she's trying to justify drawing Naglfar over half the city."

"Not that," I say. "Well, not just that. I mean she seems to be surprised that someone was looking out for Vanessa."

"You don't think that's surprising?" He raises his eyebrows as he sets the note down on the window seat. It's only afternoon, but the sky has started to turn red. Autumn is coming, or maybe the end of everything. "Vanessa seemed a little—"

"Batshit?"

"Difficult, I was going to say."

"Yeah, I guess so." I sit on the edge of my bed. Cloud sits next to me, long legs folded under him. "It's just, I guess I expect that things will work out okay. Or no, not that things will be okay, but that people will be. Call me crazy."

"Join the club," Cloud says. He leans back on the mattress, resting his weight on his forearms. Looking up at me, grinning. "The way I see it, we're all going different kinds of crazy. Vanessa is, I don't know, maybe paranoid, or maybe she really knows something the rest of us don't. Felicity's delusional about Mia, and I guess I have the pills, and whatever's up with Morgan and Hel and fucking Ragnarok, that's pretty damn nuts."

"So what kind of crazy am I?"

He wets his lips. Reaches up, cups my cheek and gently rubs a streak of eyeliner away with his thumb.

"I'm not sure," he says. "But I like it."

Tell him, I say to myself. Tell him now. The rain will be back tomorrow, who knows when you'll get another chance.

"Stay off the pills tonight," I say. "Can you do that? Just tonight. No drugs, just you."

"I can try," he says. "Just me."

I kiss him. One arm around his back, catching some of his weight, the other wiping my cheek. He tastes like tears, clean and sweet.

"Good," I say. "That's all I'm looking for."

SUNSET HOLLOW
A ROT & RUIN STORY

Jonathan Maberry

-1-

The kid kept crying.

Crying.

Crying.

Blood all over him. Their blood. Not his.

Not Benny's.

Theirs.

He stood on the lawn and stared at the house.

Watching as the fallen lamp inside the room threw goblin shadows on the curtains. Listening to the screams as they filled the night. Filled the room. Spilled out onto the lawn. Punched him in the face and belly and over the heart. Screams that sounded less and less like her. Like Mom.

Less like her.

More like Dad.

Like whatever he was. Whatever *this* was.

Tom Imura stood there, holding the kid. Benny was eighteen months. He could say a few words. Mom. Dog. Foot.

Now all he could do was wail. One long, inarticulate wail that tore into Tom's head. It hit him as hard as Mom's screams.

As hard. But differently.

The front door was open, standing ajar. The back door was unlocked. He'd left through the window, though. The downstairs bedroom on the side of the house. Mom had pushed him out. She'd shoved Benny into his hands and pushed him out.

Into the night.

Into the sound of sirens, of screams, of weeping and praying people, of gunfire and helicopters.

Out here on the lawn.

While she stayed inside.

He tried to fight her on it.

He was bigger. Stronger. All those years of jujutsu and karate. She was a middle-aged housewife. He could have forced her out. Could have gone to face the horror that was beating on the bedroom door. The thing that wore Dad's face but had such a hungry, bloody mouth.

Tom could have pulled Mom out of there.

But Mom had one kind of strength, one bit of power that neither black belts nor biceps could hope to fight. It was there on her arm, hidden in that last moment by her white sleeve.

No.

That was a lie he wanted to tell himself.

Not white.

The sleeve was red, and getting redder with every beat of his heart.

That sleeve was her power and he could not defeat it.

That sleeve and what it hid.

The mark. The wound.

The bite.

It amazed Tom that Dad's teeth could fit that shape. That it was so perfect a match in an otherwise imperfect tumble of events. That it was possible at all.

Benny struggled in his arms. Wailing for Mom.

Tom clutched his little brother to his chest and bathed his face with tears. They stood like that until the last of the screams from inside had faded, faded, and . . .

Even now Tom could not finish that sentence. There was no dictionary in his head that contained the words that would make sense of this.

The screams faded.

Not into silence.

Into moans.

Such hungry, hungry moans.

He had lingered there because it seemed a true sin to leave Mom to this without even a witness. Without mourners.

Mom and Dad.

Inside the house now.

Moaning. Both of them.

Tom Imura staggered to the front door and nearly committed the sin of entry. But Benny was a squirming reminder of all the ways this would kill them both. Body and soul.

Truly. Body and soul.

So Tom reached out and pulled the door closed.

He fumbled in his pocket for the key. He didn't know why. The TV and the Internet said that they can't think, that something as simple and ordinary as a doorknob could stop them. Locks weren't necessary.

He locked it anyway.

And put the key safely in his pocket. It jangled against his own.

He backed away onto the lawn to watch the window again. The curtains moved. Shapes stirred on the other side, but the movements made the wrong kind of sense.

The shapes, though.

God, the shapes.

Dad and Mom.

Tom's knees gave all at once, and he fell to the grass so hard that it shot pain into his groin and up his spine. He almost lost his grip on his brother. Almost. But didn't.

He bent his head at length, unable to watch those shapes. He closed his eyes and bared his teeth and uttered his own moan. A long, protracted, half-choked sound of loss. Of a hurt that no articulation could possibly express because the descriptive terms belonged to no human dictionary. Only the lost understand it, and they don't require further explanation. They get it because there is only one language spoken in the blighted place where they live.

Tom actually understood in that moment why the poets called the feeling heart*break*. There was a fracturing, a splintering in his chest. He could feel it.

Benny kicked him with little feet and banged on Tom's face with tiny fists. It hurt, but Tom endured it. As long as it hurt there was some proof they were both alive.

Still alive.

Still alive.

-2-

It was Benny Imura who saved his brother Tom.

Little, eighteen-month-old screaming Benny.

First he nearly got them both killed, but then he saved them. The universe is perverse and strange like that.

His brother, on his knees, lost in the deep well of the moment, did not hear the sounds behind him. Or, if he did, his grief orchestrated them into the same discordant symphony.

So, no, he did not separate out the moans behind him from those inside the house. Or the echoes of them inside his head.

That was the soundtrack of the world now.

But Benny could tell the difference.

He was a toddler. Everything was immediate, everything was new. He heard those moans, turned to look past his brother's trembling shoulder, and he saw them.

The shapes.

Detaching themselves from the night shadows.

He knew some of the faces. Recognized them as people who came and smiled at him. People who threw him up in the air or poked his tummy or tweaked his cheeks. People who made faces that made him laugh.

Now, though.

None of them were laughing.

The reaching hands did not seem to want to play or poke or tweak.

Some of the hands were broken. There was blood where fingers should be. There were holes in them. In chests and stomachs and faces.

Their mouths weren't smiling. They were full of teeth, and their teeth were red.

Benny could not even form these basic thoughts, could not actually categorize the rightness and wrongness of what was happening. All he could do was *feel* it. Feel the wrongness. He heard the sounds of hunger. The moans. They were not happy sounds. He had been hungry so many times, he knew. It was why he cried sometimes. For a bottle. For something to eat.

Benny knew only a dozen words.

Most of them things. Some of them names.

He stopped crying and tried to say one of those names.

"Tuh . . . Tuh . . . Tuh . . ."

That was all he could get. *Tom* was too difficult. Not always, just sometimes. It wouldn't fit into his mouth now.

"Tuh . . . Tuh . . . Tuh . . ."

-3-

It was a strange moment when Tom Imura realized that his baby brother was actually trying to say his name.

Because saying it was also a warning.

A warning was a thought that Tom wouldn't have credited to a kid that young.

Could toddlers even think like that?

A part of Tom's mind stepped out of the moment and looked at the phenomenon as if it were hanging on a wall in a museum. He studied it. Considered it. Posed in thoughtful art-house stances in front of it. All in a fragment of a second so small it could have been hammered in between two of the *Tuh* sounds.

Tom.

That's what Benny was saying.

No. That's what Benny was *screaming.*

Tom jerked upright.

He turned.

He saw what Benny had seen.

Them.

So many of them.

Them.

Coming out of the shadows. Reaching.

Moaning.

Hungry. So hungry.

There was Mrs. Addison from across the street. She was nice but could be bitchy sometimes. Liked to tell the other ladies on the block how to grow roses even though hers were only so-so.

Mrs. Addison had no lower lip.

Someone had torn it away. Or . . .

Bitten it?

Right behind her was John Chalker. Industrial chemist. He made solvents for a company that sold drain cleaner. He always brought the smell of his job home on his clothes.

Now he had no clothes. He was naked. Except for his hat.

Why did he still have his hat on and no clothes?

There were bites everywhere. Most of his right forearm was gone. The meat of his hand hung on the bones like a loose glove.

And the little Han girl. Lucy? Lacey? Something like that.

Ten, maybe eleven.

She had no eyes.

They were coming toward them. Reaching with hands. Some of those hands were slashed and bitten. Or gone completely. None of the wounds bled.

Why didn't the wounds bleed?

Why didn't the damn wounds bleed?

"No," said Tom.

Even to his own ears his voice sounded wrong. Way too calm. Way too normal.

Calm and normal were dead concepts. There was no normal.

Or maybe *this* was normal.

Now.

But calm? No, that was gone. That was trashed. That was . . .

Consumed.

The word came into his head, unwanted and unwelcome. Shining with truth. Ugly in its accuracy.

"Tuh . . . Tuh . . . Tuh . . ."

Benny's voice was not calm.

It broke Tom.

It broke the spell of stillness.

It broke something in his chest.

Tom's next word was not calm. Might not actually have been a word. It started out as "No," but it changed, warped, splintered, and tore his throat ragged on the way out. A long wail, as unending as the moans of his neighbors. Higher, though, not a monotone. Not a simple statement of need. This was pure denial and he screamed it at them as they came toward him, pawing the air. For him. For Benny. For anything warm, anything alive.

For meat.

Tom felt himself turn but didn't know how he managed it. His mind was frozen. His scream kept rising and rising. But his body turned.

And ran.

And ran.

God, he ran.

They, however, were everywhere.

The darkness pulsed with the red and blue of police lights; the banshee wail of sirens tore apart the shadows of the California night, but no police came for him. No help came for them.

The little boy in his arms screamed and screamed and screamed.

Pale shapes lurched toward him from the shadows. Some of them were victims—their wounds still bleeding—still *able* to bleed; their eyes wide with shock and incomprehension. Others were more of *them.*

The things.

The monsters.

Whatever they were.

Tom's car was parked under a street lamp, washed by the orange glow of the sodium vapor light. He'd come home from the academy and all of his gear was in the trunk. His pistol—which cadets weren't even allowed to carry until after tomorrow's graduation—and his stuff from the dojo. His sword, some fighting sticks.

He slowed, casting around to see if that was the best way to go.

Should he risk it? *Could* he risk it?

The car was at the end of the block. He had the keys, but the streets were clogged with empty emergency vehicles. Even if he got his gear, could he find a way to drive out?

Yes.

No.

Maybe.

Houses were on fire one block over. Fire trucks and crashed cars were like a wall.

But the weapons.

His weapons.

They were right there in the trunk.

Benny screamed. The monsters shambled after him.

"Go!" Mom had said. "Take Benny . . . keep him safe. Go!"

Just . . . go.

He ran to the parked car. Benny was struggling in his arms, hitting him, fighting to try and get free.

Tom held him with one arm—an arm that already ached from carrying his brother—and fished in his pocket for the keys. Found them. Found the lock. Opened the door, popped the trunk.

Gun in the glove compartment. Ammunition in the trunk. Sword, too.

Shapes moved toward him. He could hear their moans. So close. So close.

Tom turned a wild eye toward one as it reached for the child he carried.

He lashed out with a savage kick, driving the thing back. It fell, but it was not hurt. Not in any real sense of being hurt. As soon as it crashed down, it began to crawl toward him.

And in his mind Tom realized that he had thought of it as an *it.* Not a *him.* Not a *person.*

He was already that far gone into this. That's what this had come to.

He and Benny and *them.*

Each of them was an *it* now.

The world was that broken.

It was unreal. Tom understood that this thing was dead. He knew him, too. It was Mr. Harrison from three doors down and it was also a dead thing.

A monster.

An actual monster.

This was the real world, and there were monsters in it.

Benny kept screaming.

Tom lifted the trunk hood and shoved Benny inside. Then he grabbed his sword. There was no time to remove the trigger lock on the gun. They were coming.

They were here.

Tom slammed the hood, trapping the screaming Benny inside the trunk even as he ripped the sword from its sheath.

All those hands reached for him.

And for the second time, a part of Tom's mind stepped out of the moment and struck a contemplative pose, studying himself, walking around him, observing and forming opinions.

Tom had studied jujutsu and karate since he was little. Kendo, too. He could fight with his hands and feet. He could grapple and wrestle.

He could use a sword.

Twice in his life he'd been in fights. Once in the seventh grade with a kid who was just being a punk. Once in twelfth grade when one of the kids on the hockey team mouthed off to a girl Tom liked. Both fights had been brief. Some shoves, a couple of punches. The other guy went down both times. Not down and out, just down. Nothing big. No real damage.

Never once in his twenty years had Tom Imura fought for his life. Never once had he done serious harm to another person. The drills in the police academy, even the live-fire exercises, were no different than the dojo. It was all a dance. All practice and simulation. No real blood, no genuine intent.

All those years, all those black belts, they in no way prepared him for this moment.

To use a sword on a person. To cut flesh. To draw blood.

To kill.

There is no greater taboo. Only a psychopath disregards it without flinching. Tom was not a psychopath. He was a twenty year old Japanese-American police academy cadet. A son. A stepson. A half-brother. He was barely a man. He couldn't even legally buy a beer.

He stood in the middle of his own street with a sword in his hands as everyone he knew in his neighborhood came at him. To kill him.

Video games don't prepare you for this.

Watching movies doesn't prepare you.

No training prepares you.

Nothing does.

Nothing.

He said, "Please . . ."

The people with the dead eyes and the slack faces moaned in reply. And they fell on him like a cloud of locusts.

The sword seemed to move of its own accord.

Distantly, Tom could feel his arms lift and swing. He could feel his hands tighten and loosen as the handle shifted within his grip for different cuts. The rising cut. The scarf cut. The lateral cut.

He saw the silver of the blade move like flowing mercury, tracing fire against the night.

He felt the shudder and shock as the weapon hit and sliced and cleaved through bone.

He felt his feet shift and step and pivot; he felt his waist turn, his thighs flex, his heels lift to tilt his mass into the cuts or to allow his knees to wheel him around.

He felt all of this.

He did not understand how any of it could happen when his mind was going blank. None of it came from his will. None of it was directed.

It just happened.

The moaning things came at him.

And his sword devoured them.

-4-

Three terrible minutes later, Tom unlocked the trunk and opened it.

Benny was cowering in the back of the trunk, huddled against Tom's gym bag. Tears and snot were pasted on his face. Benny opened his mouth to scream again, but he stopped. When he saw Tom, he stopped.

Tom stood there, the sword held loosely in one hand, the keys in the other. He was covered with blood. The sword was covered with blood.

The bodies around the car—more than a dozen of them—were covered with blood.

Benny screamed.

Not because he understood—he was far too young for that—but because the smell of blood reminded him of Dad. Of home. Benny wanted his mom.

He screamed and Tom stood there, trembling from head to toe. Tears broke from his eyes and fell in burning silver lines down his face.

"I'm sorry, Benny," he said in a voice that was as broken as the world.

Tom tore off his blood-splattered shirt. The t-shirt he wore underneath was stained but not as badly. Tom shivered as he lifted Benny and held him close. Benny beat at him with tiny fists.

"I'm sorry," Tom said again.

All around him was a silent slaughterhouse.

And then it wasn't.

From the sides streets, from open doors, *more* of them came.

More.

More.

Mr. Gaynor from down the block. Old Lady Milhonne from across the street, wearing the same ratty bathrobe she always wore. The Kang kids. Delia and Marie Swanson. Others he didn't know. Even two cops in torn uniforms.

"No more," Tom said as he buried his head in the cleft between Benny's neck and shoulder. As if there was any comfort there.

No more.

But there was more, and on some level Tom knew they were would always be more. This was how it was now. They hinted about it on the news. The street where he lived proved it to be true.

-5-

He kicked his way through them.

He kicked old Mr. Gaynor in the groin and watched the force of the kick bend him in half. It should have put him down. It should have left him in a purple-faced fetal ball.

It didn't.

Gaynor staggered and went down to one knee. His face did not change expression at all. Nothing. Not even a curl of the lip.

Then Gaynor got heavily, awkwardly to his feet and came forward again. Reaching for Benny.

Tom kicked him again. Same spot, even harder.

This time Gaynor didn't even go down to one knee. He tottered backward, caught his balance, and moved forward again.

Tom cursed at him. Shrieked every foul thing he could muster at him.

Benny squealed each time Tom kicked and he hoped he wasn't crushing his brother as he exerted to lash out at the things around him.

He kicked once more, changing it from a front thrust to a side thrust. Lower. To the knee instead of the groin. The femur broke with the sound of a batter hitting a hard one down the third base line.

Sharp.

Gaynor went down that time. Not in pain, not yelling. But down. Bone speared through the cotton of his trousers, jagged and white. Tom stared at him, watching the man try to get back up again. Saw gravity pull him down, saw how the ruined scaffolding of shattered bone denied him the chance to stand.

Not pain.

Just broken bone.

Tom backed away, spun. Ran. Holding Benny, who kept screaming.

He dodged between parked cars, jumped over a fallen bike, blundered through a narrow gap in a row of privet hedges, staggered onto the pavement. Two teenagers, strangers, were there on their knees, faces buried in something that glistened and steamed.

A stomach.

Tom couldn't tell who it had been. But he saw the dead hands twitch. The teenagers recoiled from their meal, staring briefly with vacuous stupidity as the half-consumed body began shivering. The corpse tried to sit up, but there were no abdominal muscles left to power that effort. Instead it rolled onto its sides, sloshing out intestines like dead snakes. The teenagers got to their feet, turned, looked, and sniffed the night.

Then they turned toward Tom.

And Benny.

Benny screamed and screamed and screamed.

It was then, only then, that the shape of this fit into Tom's mind. Not the cause, not the sense, not the solution.

The shape.

He backed away, turned, and ran again.

The lawns behind him were filled with slow bodies. Some sprawled on the grass like broken starfish, lacking enough of their muscle or tendon to move in any useful way. Others staggered along, relentless and slow. Slow but relentless.

Tom ran fast, clenching Benny to him, feeling the flutter of his brother's heart against his own chest.

The street ahead was filled with the people who had lived here in Sunset Hollow.

So many of them now.

All of them now.

-6-

Then another figure stepped out from behind a hedge.

Short, female, pretty. Wearing a torn dress. Wild eyes in a slack face.

She said, "Tom—?"

"Sherrie," he said. Sherrie Tomlinson had gone all through school with him. Second grade through high school. He'd wanted to date her, but she was always a little standoffish. Not cold, just not interested.

Now she came toward him, ignoring his sword, ignoring the blood. She touched his face, his chest, his arms, his mouth.

"Tom? What is it?"

"Sherrie? Are you okay?"

"What is it?" she asked.

"I don't *know.*"

He didn't. There were news stories that made no sense. An outbreak in Pennsylvania. Then people getting sick in other places. Anywhere a plane from Philly landed. Anywhere near I-95 and 76. Spreading out from bus terminals and train stations. The reporters put up numbers. Infected first, then casualties. In single digits. In triple. When Tom was racing back from the police academy, trying to get home, they were talking about blackout zones. Quarantine zones. There were helicopters in the air. Swarms of them. When he got home the TV was on. Anderson Cooper was yelling—actually yelling—about fuel air bombs being deployed in Philadelphia, Pittsburgh, Baltimore. Other places.

London was about to go dark.

L.A. was on fire.

On *fire.*

That's when he stopped watching TV. That's when they all stopped. It was when Dad came in from the backyard with those bites on his neck.

And it all fell apart.

All sense. All meaning.

All answers.

"What is it?" asked Sherrie.

All Tom could do was shake his head.

"What is it?"

He looked at her. Looked for wounds. For bites.

"What is it?" she repeated. And repeated it again. "*What is it?*"

And Tom realized that the question was all Sherrie had left. She didn't want an answer. Couldn't really use one. She was like a machine left on after its usefulness was done. An organic recording device replaying a loop.

"What is it? What is it?" Varied only by the infrequent use of his name. "What is it, Tom?"

The only other changes were in the hysterical notes that ebbed and flowed.

The inflection, the stresses put on different words as something in her head misfired.

"What is *it*?"

"What *is* it?"

"*What* is it?"

Like that. Repeated over and over again. A litany for an apocalyptic service without a church.

It reminded Tom of that old song.

"*What's the Frequency, Kenneth?*"

REM. From an album called *Monster.*

Now there was irony.

"What's the Frequency, Kenneth?"

The title was a reference from an attack by two unknown assailants on a newsman. Dan Rather. Someone Tom's father used to watch. Someone his older brother, Sam, used to know. They kept whaling on Rather and demanding, "Kenneth, what's the frequency?"

Only Sherrie's message was simpler.

"What is it?"

Tom didn't have a word for it.

Infection was too shallow and this ran a lot deeper.

Pandemic was a TV word. It seemed clinical despite its implications. A word like that was too big and didn't seem to belong to this world. Not the world of the police academy; not here in sleepy little Sunset Hollow.

"What is it, Tom?"

The guy on Fox News called it the end of days. Like he was a biblical prophet. Called it that and then walked off to leave dead air.

End of days.

Tom couldn't tell Sherrie that this was the end of days. It was the end of today. And maybe it was the end of a lot of things.

But the end? The actual end?

Even now Tom didn't want to go all the way there.

He moved on, walking faster in hopes that she stopped following him. She didn't. Sherrie walked with legs that chopped along like scissors. "What is it, Tom?"

She seemed to be settling into that now. Using his name. Latching onto him. Maybe because she thought that he knew where he was going.

He said, "I don't know."

But it was clear Sherrie didn't hear him. Or, maybe *couldn't.*

Benny kept squirming and Tom felt heat against his hip. Wet heat. Leaky diaper.

Damn.

Only pee, but still.

How do you change a diaper during the end of the world? What's the procedure there?

"What is it, Tom?"

He wheeled around, wanting to scream at her. To tell her to shut up. To hit her, to knock those stupid words out of her mouth. To break that lipstick structure so it couldn't hold the words anymore.

She recoiled from him, eyes suddenly huge. In a small and plaintive voice she asked, "What is it, Tom?"

Then the bushes trembled and parted.

There were more of them.

Them.

"Sherrie," Tom said quickly, "get in the car."

"What is it?"

"Get in the damn car."

He pushed her away, fumbled with the door handle, pushed Benny inside. No time for car seats. Let them give him a ticket. A ticket would be nice.

"Sherrie, come on?"

She looked at him as if he was speaking a language composed of nonsense words. Vertical frown lines appeared between her brows.

"What is it?" she asked.

The people were coming now.

Many more of them.

Most of them strangers now. People from other parts of the town. Coming through yards and across lawns.

Coming.

Coming.

"Jesus, Sherri, get in the damn car!"

She stepped back from him, shaking her head, almost smiling the way people do when they think you just don't get it.

"Sherrie—no!"

She backed one step too far.

Tom made a grab for her.

Ten hands grabbed her, too. Her arms, her clothes, her hair.

"What is it, Tom?" she asked once more. Then she was gone.

Gone.

Sickened, horrified, Tom spun away and staggered toward the car. He thrust his sword into the passenger footwell and slid behind the wheel. Pulled the door shut as hands reached for him. Clawed at the door, at the glass.

It took forever to find the ignition slot even though it was where it always was.

Behind him, Benny kept screaming.

The moans of the people outside were impossibly loud.

He turned the key.

He put the car in drive.

He broke his headlights and smashed his grill and crushed both fenders getting down the street. The bodies flew away from him. They rolled over his hood, cracked the windows with slack elbows and cheeks and chins. They lay like broken dolls in the lurid glow of his taillights.

-7-

Tom and Benny headed for L.A.

They were still eighty miles out when the guy on the radio said that the city was gone.

Gone.

Far in the west, way over the mountains, even at that distance, Tom could see the glow. The big, ugly, orange cloud bank that rose high into the air and spread itself out to ignite the roots of heaven.

He was too far away to hear it.

The nuclear shockwave would have hit the mountains anyway. Hit and bounced high and troubled the sky above them.

But the car went dead.

So did his cell phone and the radio.

All around him the lights went out.

Tom knew the letters. He'd read them somewhere. EMP. But he forgot what they stood for.

That didn't matter. He understood what they meant.

The city was gone.

An accident?

An attempt to stop the spread?

He sat in his dead car and watched the blackness beyond the cracked windshield and wondered if he would ever know. On the back seat, Benny was silent. Tom turned and looked at him. His brother was asleep. Exhausted and out.

Or . . .

A cold hand stabbed into Tom's chest and clamped around his heart.

Was Benny sleeping?

Was he?

Was he?

Tom turned and knelt on the seat. Reaching over into the shadows back there was so much harder than anything else he'd had to do. Harder than leaving Mom and Dad. Harder than using his sword on the neighbors.

This was Benny.

This was his baby brother.

This was everything that he had left. This was the only thing that was going to hold him to the world.

No.

God, no.

His mouth shaped the words, but he made no sound at all.

He did not dare.

If Benny was sleeping, he didn't want to wake him.

If Benny was not sleeping, then he didn't want to wake that, either.

He reached across a million miles of darkness.

Please, he begged.

Of God, if God was even listening. If God was even God.

Please.

Of the world, of the night.

Please.

How many other voices had said that, screamed that, begged that? How many people had clung to that word as the darkness and the deadness and the hunger came for them?

How many?

The math was simple.

Everyone he knew.

Except him. Except Benny.

Please.

He touched Benny's face. His brother's cheeks were cool.

Cool or cold?

He couldn't tell.

Then he placed his palm flat on Benny's chest. Trying to feel something. Anything. A breath. A beat.

He waited.

And around him the night seemed to scream.

He waited.

This time he said it aloud.

"Please."

In the back seat, Benny Imura heard his voice and woke up.

Began to cry.

Not moan.

Cry.

Tom laid his forehead on the seatback, held his hand against his brother's trembling chest, and wept.

PENANCE

Jake Kerr

Samuel Esposito couldn't escape the faces that haunted him. The captain established dining hours at set times, and no matter when he went to the galley to eat, someone was always there. He asked the captain if he could be served in his cabin, which got him an angry look and the response of, "We're not your fucking servants." He tried going late; he tried going early, but the two-hour windows to eat were set in stone. If he missed it, he didn't eat. Sam skipped breakfast and did his best to skip one of the other meals.

In the end, however, he couldn't avoid the faces of his fellow passengers, all of them full of hope as they fled the asteroid on a collision course with North America. Yet that very same hope had lived in the faces of all the people the moment before Sam had sentenced them to death. Sam tried to convince himself that his job before he was evacuated on the ship wasn't evil. He was simply a messenger. The Expatriation Lottery was fair, and he was simply letting people know the results.

But it *was* evil. Everyone came in with hope. But then Sam would give them the news, and they would leave with none. Emotionless, hopeless faces. Practically dead already. Their appointment with Sam was an appointment with death, despite the professionalism and sympathy.

The appointments had been every fifteen minutes. His boss had told him to act professional but sympathetic. Stick to the facts. Provide tissues if necessary. Don't be afraid to hit the panic button if the client becomes violent.

That's what he had called them: clients—the citizens who had come in, sat down or paced the room as they waited to hear their fate. Sam let them do whatever made them the most comfortable, but in the end there was no real comfort, only the extremes of fear and hope. Sam would then tell them whether they had won the Expatriation Lottery and would be sent to Europe or Africa or somewhere else. Where didn't quite matter; the winners would be free to *live*. But the others—the losers—had been told they had to stay in North America and wait for the asteroid to kill them. There just weren't enough planes or ships to take everyone.

The ones who lost: He had pulled up their results on his computer before they entered and knew that he was about to deliver the most horrific news possible. Sam had done his best, but that moment when the face went from tightly wound hope to total desperation tore a bit of his soul away each time. He would want to look away, but he couldn't; he had to be there for them, a warm and friendly face—even though he wasn't a friend; how could he ever be a friend?—in their darkest moment. It was his duty.

Thousands. There were thousands of people who had listened, their faces so full of hope as Sam said, "I'm sorry, but you have not been chosen to emigrate." But Sam himself would never have to face that moment; as a government employee, he didn't have to take part in the lottery—he had been exempt and was therefore automatically one of the lucky ones.

He had been one of the last to flee North America, with the asteroid already visible in the night sky. He and eleven others were to be squeezed onto an oil tanker with a crew of twenty-four. Thirty-six souls and one million barrels of American oil, escaping the Meyer Impact.

When the day came and he had been told it was his turn to emigrate, Sam grabbed a bottle of bourbon he had saved and did nothing but drink big gulps between anguished sobs. Eventually he was too drunk to cry or too drunk to know if he was crying. He woke not remembering the last few hours of the previous night.

Those were the best hours of his recent life.

• • •

There was only one person in the galley for dinner. The blonde woman. Sam didn't know her, but the captain called her Barbie. Sam sat down on the other side of the room with his back to her. He had just taken a bite of his hot dog when a tray slid along the table in front of him and the woman sat down.

"Hi, I'm Alex."

Sam stared at his food. "Sam," he replied.

"Nice to meet you, Sam." Alex held out a tan hand with exquisitely manicured nails. Sam shook it but didn't say anything. She had a firm grip. After a few moments of silence, she added, "Are you afraid of the ocean?"

The question seemed to come out of nowhere, and Sam almost glanced up in confusion. "What? No. Why would you think that?"

"It's just that we're already halfway across the Atlantic, and you're never out on deck with the rest of us. You just stay in your cabin."

Sam didn't reply.

Alex let out an "Oh!" then reached across the table and touched his hand. "You know, there's nothing to be afraid of. We're safe. In fact, the asteroid is close enough that you can see it clearly, and it's really not that bad."

Sam pulled his hand away.

"It's actually quite pretty now if you think of it as a celestial body that just wants to be with us on Earth." She leaned forward. "Be honest, don't you think it's pretty?"

Sam couldn't *not* glance up. "*Pretty*?"

He turned away, but it was too late. He'd seen her face. Sam closed his eyes and shook his head, but when he opened them he was back in his Expatriation Office. The blonde woman was there.

She wasn't there.

She *was* there.

They were all one.

"Yes. Do you think I'm pretty, Samuel?" The question surprised him. He had only been a Lottery Counselor for a few days and thought he had been asked every possible question, but this was new. He looked up at her. She was blonde, with a round face and bangs. She was beautiful in a girl-next-door kind of way.

"You are very pretty," Sam stammered and then stood up. "I'm sorry, but I have another appointment. Please remember that the Grief Counselor is down the hall."

The woman stood up, but rather than move toward the door, she approached Sam and fell to her knees and grabbed his legs. He considered pressing the panic button, but then she said, "Sam, would you like a blowjob?"

He stepped back and stumbled over his chair.

"Would you like me to give you a blowjob every night? I would do that for you. I would do that for you whenever you want if you just go to your computer and change my status."

Sam shuffled backward around his chair as she reached for his crotch. "Please, Sam. Just think, wouldn't it be nice to wake up with your cock in my mouth?"

Sam pressed the panic button as he maneuvered his chair between himself and the woman. (Elizabeth Mary Conroy. He would never forget the name.) "Please, Ms. Conroy. I can't help you. I can't change anything. I'm just a Counselor."

Elizabeth stood up and started unbuttoning the top of her pants. "Would you prefer to fuck me? You could fuck me, Sam. You could fuck me right now."

"I can't help you. I'm so sorry." The words came out as a whisper, but the woman heard them. Her hands fell to her side as the door slammed open and Terry, the security guard on duty, entered.

Looking over at the guard, Elizabeth finally cracked. Up until then she had been speaking in a calm, even seductive, voice, but now that fell away to raw desperation. She threw herself forward, wrapping her arms around him. "Please save me, Sam! I have twin girls. They're only three years old! Three! Don't let us die!" The words came out in sobs directly in Sam's ear as he held her up.

"Sorry, Sam," Terry said as he pulled Elizabeth off him, her hands clutching Sam's shirt and pulling him along with her. "I'll get here faster next time." Terry grabbed the woman's wrist and pulled her arm violently toward the door.

He finally untangled them, and she looked up at Sam. "My girls don't deserve to die! Please save them." Before she could say anything else, Terry pulled her out of the room. She glanced over her shoulder, and the look staggered Sam. She had reached the obscene point where she had accepted that she and her children were going to die, and all Sam could see was pure and utter loss.

Sam closed his eyes and shook his head.

He opened them to the screech of a metal chair pushing back from a table, and when Sam looked up, the blonde woman, Alex, was gone. He lowered his head and went back to his meal. Thankfully, no one else entered before he finished.

• • •

On the way back to his room after lunch he stopped by the communal bathroom to wash his hands. Thankfully it was empty. There was a large mirror above the sink, but Sam did his best to not look at it. He couldn't reconcile the face he saw in the mirror with those that surrounded him. The grief, the loss, the desperation. He saw it everywhere except in the mirror.

It wasn't right.

He dried his hands and looked up. He wasn't a bad person. He had done nothing wrong. He was a messenger. He couldn't save people, and he couldn't condemn them either. He was innocent. *I'll live because I did a difficult job that had to be done.* He forced a smile, but seeing it reminded him of a skull's grin. *I'll live, but they won't.*

Sam lowered his head and turned on the tap. When the water from the faucet was ice cold, he splashed it onto his face. He looked up at his reflection. *I'm not one of them. I'll live. I should be grateful.* Droplets slid down his cheeks. He splashed more water, hard, against his face, against his eyes. *Why am I not one of them?* He splashed hard again and again until he was slapping his face with his hands, not even bothering to make the excuse of putting water in his palms. Finally, his face was red, raw, and his hair hung down limp. It illustrated a pain that was familiar, almost comforting.

He walked back to his cabin. The asteroid was to impact North America tomorrow.

• • •

It was late the next day, and Sam had managed to ignore his hunger and remain in his room. The idea of looking at another person filled him with dread, so Sam didn't reply when there was a knock on his door.

There was a pause, and the knock was replaced by a pounding that felt like it shook the room. "Sam, everyone on deck. Captain's orders. Asteroid hits in a few hours."

"No thanks," Sam replied, not leaving his bunk.

"This isn't a request. Topside in five minutes or the captain will have me come down to drag you up."

Sam considered refusing, but the captain seemed like the type to actually send someone down to get him, so he rolled out of bed and made his way up to the deck. Everyone was gathered on the small observation area that extended over the back of the ship. He was the last to arrive, and the captain was already talking. He looked over at Sam. "Hey, slacker, I was just saying the rock hits in about four hours. If you want to watch, this is probably the best spot." Sam nodded.

The passengers were all milling about in front of the captain, who stood at the top of a short set of stairs facing the rear of the boat, his arms behind his back. The crew were off to the sides, observing from a distance. Sam turned away and gazed out toward the setting sun.

And there it was. The middle of the day, and he could see the asteroid clearly in the sky. He caught his breath and focused on the water, the giant propellers churning the sea into a violent froth that trailed off behind the ship.

"I said turn around!" Sam finally noticed the captain's raised voice. He turned and kept his head down.

"I'm sorry. I was listening," Sam replied.

There were footsteps and the captain stood in front of Sam. "Look at me. I don't think you appreciate the gravity of what we're facing here."

"I think I know better than most." Sam stared at the deck.

"Are you mocking me?" The captain reached out and pushed Sam's head up so that he had to look him in the face. "You think you know what it's like to face death?"

Sam squeezed his eyes tight and prayed that the captain would still be there when he opened them.

He wasn't.

Or was he?

They were all one.

"You sound like you're sorry, but do you know what it's like to face death?" He wasn't old, but he looked like he had lived a hard life. His skin was tan and dry. His

hair was a very dark brown, fine, and straight. It was cut short and parted on the left. He frowned, and Sam thought that he looked like a hick policeman, the kind of guy who liked to pull people over even if they weren't speeding just to ruin their day.

He slammed his fist on Sam's desk. "Do you?"

"No, sir, I'm afraid I don't, and I can't fathom how hard this is for you." The man pointed at the computer.

"Change it."

"I'm afraid I can't do that." Sam had seen enough people lose the lottery by then that he knew he didn't have to hit the panic button yet. Maybe he could get the man to calm down.

"Can't or won't?" The man leaned forward. There wasn't sadness or even desperation in his eyes. Just anger.

"I'm sorry, sir. I'm just a Counselor. I can't make any changes at all." The man didn't move. "Perhaps you should talk to the Grief Counselor. They're just down the hall." Sam stood up.

The man stood up, too. "I can't fathom how you can just sit there and lie *to me like this—" He looked down at the nameplate on the desk. "—Sam."*

"I'm not—" Before Sam could finish, the man leaned across his desk and grabbed him. Sam pressed the panic button over and over again as the man maneuvered around the desk, pulled Sam away from his chair, and slammed him against the wall. "Please—" His words were interrupted by an explosion of pain as the man's fist connected with Sam's cheek. Sam flung his arms up to block any more blows. None came. The man pulled Sam from the wall and pushed him toward the computer as the door flew open.

"Change it now, or I'll kill you!" The man screamed. The guard, a new one from the Army named Phil, wasted no time and slammed a baton across the back of the man's head. He fell onto the desk, and Sam scrambled backward against the wall. Phil pulled out his gun and shot the man three times in the back.

Phil spoke while Sam watched the man slide toward the floor off his desk. "Dammit, Sam, you need to be quicker on the trigger." The man had rolled onto his side, his eyes staring at Sam. "You have the button for a reason, you know. You can't try to calm everyone down."

The captain's mouth—wait, not the captain; did it matter?—opened a bit, and a bloody bubble formed. Sam couldn't tell when the man had died. All he could focus on were his eyes, which hadn't closed. The anger and desperation in those eyes were gone now, replaced by an emptiness. Not peace or acceptance: Emptiness.

"C'mon, Sam. Let's get you fixed up." Sam felt his cheek. He was bleeding.

He closed his eyes and took a deep breath. "I'll be okay."

"Not if you're leaning over the railing when the waves hit." Sam opened his eyes, and the Expatriation Office was gone. Phil was gone. The man was gone. Part of Sam's soul was gone. The captain tapped Sam on the forehead. "Are you with me, loner? Stop daydreaming and think! This is your life we're talking about." He looked over at everyone else. "I want everyone below decks fifteen minutes after the asteroid show ends. A ship this size has little to worry about, but I don't want to take any chances. You hear me? The waves may get nasty. So stay below decks until I give the all clear."

As the others asked more questions, Sam made his way down to his cabin. He didn't want to see the asteroid impact, and he didn't want to see any more faces.

• • •

Sam dreamed of the asteroid hitting North America as if he were watching a movie. The blast wave and impact spread fire across North Dakota and rolled across the United States. He flew backward and watched the wave obliterate buildings, cities, mountains. He felt detached from the horror. He was high up in the sky and couldn't see any people dying. It wasn't until he was watching the shockwave clear forests in Arkansas that he realized that it was catching up to him. He looked left, looked right, and tried to guide the dream to have him fly faster. But it didn't matter: The wave of force and flames closed in. He could feel the heat. He felt the edge of the power of the asteroid. The force pressed against the bottom of his shoes. He started to panic. He looked down at the charred and ruined landscape behind the line of the spreading force of the asteroid. He closed his eyes as his feet began to shake.

And he was tumbling violently, rolling over and over as the asteroid took him. Sam opened his eyes.

He had been thrown across his room in his sleep, and as he got his bearings, the room tilted in the other direction, causing him to roll back across the floor. His head hit the wall, but he was able to reach out and grab one of the bunk's metal supports, which were welded to the floor. The ship seemed to stop rolling just as the squeal of twisting metal accompanied the entire room shaking.

As if toying with him, the room tilted in an entirely new direction, sliding Sam toward the wall opposite the door. Scrambling to his feet, Sam pulled himself toward the door as the deep moan of straining metal reverberated through the metal bones of the ship. The end of the room dropped, and Sam grabbed the doorknob and opened the door. Emergency lights flickered in the hall, and iridescent water flowed down the stairs that led to the deck. The smell of oil was overwhelming.

A voice behind him yelled out, "We need to get to the lifeboats!" Sam turned as an old man approached him. He didn't know the man's name. The boat rolled again, and Sam slammed against the wall. He braced himself and moved forward.

He grasped the railing along the stairs and did his best to haul himself up, the erratic rolling of the ship tossing him in every direction. Depending on the direction that the ship rolled, the water flowed down in great enough volume that Sam found it difficult to breathe.

He reached the door to the deck, which was already open. Sam hauled himself through and supported himself against the frame as he looked outside. It was impossible: The bow of the ship was bent upward, with massive waves surrounding it on all sides. One of the waves slammed into the hull, and it took all of Sam's strength to hold onto the door and avoid being swept out to sea.

"This way!" Off to the left was a crewmember with a group of people. They pulled themselves along the tower to the lifeboats by clinging to a metal railing. The deck rose, and Sam let it propel him to the railing. As his body slammed into it, he grabbed hold. He turned back to the door; the old man was no longer there.

He looked right; the crew and passengers were making their way to the lifeboats. "Wait! There's someone else here!" One of the passengers glanced back at him, but Sam couldn't see who it was through the sudden surge of water as another wave tossed the ship. When the water and mist cleared, the people fleeing continued to move away from him.

Sam ran to the door and hurled himself at the stairs. The oily water made the railing slick, and Sam stumbled down the steps, barely keeping himself upright. Another wave of water flowed through the door and filled the hall. The old man was sitting with his back against the wall.

As Sam reached him, the man's face went wide in shock. "What are you doing here? Go! The ship is sinking!"

"I'm here to help," Sam replied, as the ship rolled again. Sam smashed against the opposite wall. He looked back at the man, who was bracing himself against the floor with his hands. His face was contorted in pain.

"I broke my leg. You can't save me. Go!" The man motioned toward the stairs with his head.

"No, I can help support you." Sam moved closer and reached for the old man's arm.

Pulling his arm away from Sam's grasp, the man looked him in the eyes. "Look, son, don't be foolish. I know I can't survive this, but you can." He grabbed Sam's arm. "Go! Save yourself." He then shoved Sam toward the staircase.

Sam didn't argue and stumbled toward the stairs. He looked back at the old man, whose face was lowered, his eyes closed. Sam paused and wiped the salty water from his eyes.

He had left enough people to face death on their own.

"What're you doing?" the old man asked as Sam slid down next to him.

"Not leaving you." Sam looked at the old man, who seemed confused and afraid, but whose face didn't remind Sam at all of any of the poor souls from the Expatriation Office.

The old man shook his head and smiled, his fear receding. "Better than being dashed against the hull, I guess." He squeezed Sam's shoulder. "Thank you." The change in the old man took Sam's breath away. There was no fear. No desperation.

Just a warm and friendly face.

The water rose, and the other faces faded. So many of them, alone as they walked out the door of his office.

Sam closed his eyes. He was finally there for someone, walking with them as they left through the door.

There was a pure and brilliant light on the other side.

AVTOMAT

Daniel H. Wilson

The animated figures stand,
Adorning every public street,
And seem to breathe in stone, or
move their marble feet.
—Pindar, 450 BC

GREAT EUROPEAN PLAIN, 1725

The five Imperial Russian infantry saunter toward us, hips rolling in their rain-spattered saddles. I raise my shashka and point the saber at the heart of the nearest guardsman. In response, the mounted dragoon smiles at me, his teeth rotting under a bushy black moustache.

Even from this distance, I can see that he is eager to fight. I lower my saber. The gesture was futile. In a few moments, these men will run us down on the empty plains.

I will have to fight. And my daughter will fight alongside me.

This morning just before dawn, Peter the Great, father of his country, founder and Emperor of the Russian Empire, true sovereign of the northern lands and king of the Mountain princes, passed from this world and left no heir. In the aftermath, those of us allied too closely with Peter lost everything. By command of Empress Catherine, newly appointed Tsarina of Russia, we have been sentenced to death.

And so today our world ends, along with the life of our sovereign.

On tall horses, the royal dragoons are confident. They trot toward us under a storm dark sky. Short wet grass rolls away from us for hundreds of miles, each blade glinting purple-green under a light rainfall.

"Stay close to me," I say to Elena.

The little girl presses her hard shoulder against my thigh and the wind pushes the tail of my kaftan over her chest. Misty rain has plastered her wig to her forehead, spreading the black ringlets like cracks over her porcelain skin. Her sculpted face is nearly lost within the hood of her cloak. My daughter is indistinct under the billowing fabric, but she moves like a small, fierce animal.

"We cannot succeed," she says, and her voice is a melody, like the singing of clockwork birds. Indeed, the mechanism that speaks for her was created from a singing wooden clock that came from the German Black Forests.

The beautiful noises signify an ugly truth.

The dragoons are trained soldiers, chosen by Peter himself from a standing force and elevated to personal Guard for the royal family. Wearing dark kaftans with red sashes crossed over their chests, the moustached men ride fearlessly with well-worn sabers hanging from their hips. Each is equipped with two saddle-mounted Muscovite wheellock pistols. The leader wears a steel cuirass over his chest and carries a long carbine. The rest carry simple Hussar lances.

Pursued by the Imperial Russian Guard, we took a risk and fled across the rolling steppes east of St. Petersburg. We hoped to disappear into the emptiness, but we knew this could happen. Our goal was never simply to survive . . . we are running to protect the secret of our existence.

A single dragoon separates from the others, gallops toward us with one hand on the pommel of his saber.

"Stay low, Elena. Survive the onslaught," I say. "After I am finished, surprise them if you can. If they take you, do not let them discover what you are."

"Yes, Peter," she says.

I shove my cloak to the side and step away from Elena, drawing my long knife. The dagger is a simple blade the length of my forearm. Long and short, both my hands now sprout fangs.

The horseman yanks the reins and his mount comes to a prancing stop fifty yards away. Steam rises from the black flanks of his horse. The others are staying back, eyes dark under their red hats, watching this sport from a distance.

Arrogant and sure, they expect us to cower. Voices drift to me on the wind as mushrooms of mist sprout from their mouths. I hear a short bark of laughter.

Eyeing my blades, the dragoon hesitates. He begins to reach for his pistols, and I lower my nearly seven-foot frame to a knee and place my long and short blades flat on the wet grass. The backs of my hands are made of leather, stained dark with the rain. I can see the brass gears moving beneath them, ridges like foothills.

The dragoon leaves the pistols holstered. As he approaches, I keep my fingers pushed into the ground. Elena stands at my side.

"Be strong, Elena," I say, without turning. "Protect Peter's legacy."

MOSCOW, 1707

Elena's face is the first thing I see—my first memory of the world—and she is the last sight I could ever forget.

I don't remember opening my eyes.

The candle-lit path of her cheek eclipses the darkness, a perfect curve, shining like the sight of a city burning from the sea. Her skin is made of hard porcelain. As she moves, the silhouette of her doll's face is a wavering blade of light. She leans over a wooden desk, clad in a girl's dress, scratching out a message with a fountain pen held in frozen ceramic fingers. Her black eyes strafe the paper without seeing.

On this first day, Elena's hand is a doll's hand. It swoops back and forth as she mindlessly writes her message in the dark. She is oblivious to the world of men, for now. A flutter of gears is lost within the folds of fine fabric that she wears and I hear a faint clicking. This is the heartbeat of my world, a rhythm that is steady and quiet and mechanical under the warm wax-smell of candles.

Another shape moves—a man, shifting between shadows that flicker like tongues on the wall. Thin and bent, he drapes long fingers in delicate patterns over me. I turn my head slightly to inspect him, blinking to focus. His taut face sharpens into detail: wrinkled bags under glittering eyes. His lips are pressed together and white within a graying beard. The man's limbs are shaking every half second as his heart beats in his narrow chest.

I will come to know this man as Fiovani. My father. Or the closest thing to it.

The man is holding his breath, watching me with wide eyes.

"*Privet,*" I say, and the old man collapses.

Without thought, I reach out and catch him by the shoulder. Eyelids fluttering, his head dips like a sail dropping to half-mast. For the first time, I see what must be my own hand. An economy of brass struts wrapped in supple leather. And now I truly begin to understand that I am also a *thing* in this world. Not like the doll who is writing a few feet away with all the mindfulness of water choosing a path downhill. Something more. But also not like this fainting man, made of soft flesh.

Somehow, I *am*. And, I tell you, I find it a strange thing, to *be*.

The idea of it settles into my mind. A world outside me, perceived through sight and hearing and other senses. And somewhere inside, I am placing the sights and sounds into a smaller, simpler idea of a world that is jarringly complex and unknowable. From within this little world in my head, I am making decisions.

Like the decision to catch my father by his shoulder.

The old man slumps, held upright by my metal fingers. His chin falls to his chest and his face is lost in strands of brown-gray hair. I have saved him from falling into a sharp patchwork of tools that lie scattered around my legs. This low room is a workshop, lit by a tilting confusion of candles placed on every surface. Splintery wooden beams stripe the ceiling, and the room stretches beyond the light and into warm darkness. A patchwork of desks and tables are arrayed in groups. Some are empty, but most are piled high with scraps of metal, twists of rope, wooden bowls filled with unknown substances, fouled spoons, and all manner of glass vials and tubes.

Somehow, the knowledge of this workshop is in me.

Half-formed body parts are sprawled among the clutter. Chunky torsos filled with fine gears, supported by whalebone ribs and riddled with India rubber veins. This place is a workshop . . . and a womb.

Sitting up, I gently lay the old man over an empty desk.

Now, I see that I am spread out on a long wooden table. Nearby, the doll-thing smiles sightlessly in the darkness, continuing to write. Her pen scratches audibly as she covers a piece of stiff paper with ink scrawls.

She and I are kin.

My shape is that of a man. Long golden legs, glowing dully as light winks from hundreds of rivets. My skin is made of bands of a beaten, gray-gold metal, fastened to a solid frame. Through narrow gaps in the tops of my thighs, I see a row of braided metal cables pulled to tension, wrapped around circular cogs.

When I move, I hear the clockwork sound again.

"Hello?" murmurs the old man. "My son?"

Gnarled fingers wrap over my golden wrist. Faintly, I can feel the heat inside his hands. I sense that he is full of warm blood, carrying energy around his body. His skin is not like mine. Nor his heart. There is no blood within me. My father and I are not alike. He is a man, and I am something else.

"Oh, you are alive," he says. "Finally, you are here."

"Who are you?" I ask, releasing him.

"I am Fiovanti Favuri Romanti Cimini, although you may call me Favo. I am last mechanician to the Tsar Peter Alexyovich. Practicioner of the ancient art of avtomata and keeper of its relics. Successor to the great alchemists who came and went before history. Knower of secrets from the past and from the future. And, if you will believe the Tsar's wife, Empress Catherine Alexeyevich . . . I am a devil."

"Last mechanician?"

"Ten years ago, the Emperor secretly visited the Netherlands, England, Germany, and Austria. He recruited hundreds of shipbuilders, artists, and mechanicians. To one group of us, he gave a special task. Given an extraordinary artifact from the past, we were told to build . . . you. But the Empress never saw the promise. And it has been so long. The rest of my group has already been sent east to exile. I am the last, toiling alone in the dark and cowering in fear from *her*."

Spittle flies from his lips in the twilight.

"But you are here now," he says, snatching a small hammer from the table. "Look at you! Talking! Can you see me? Tell me what you see!"

"A room. A man. Machines."

"Concise," he says, tapping my chest lightly and listening. "Perfect. The mixture was perfect. The old texts were right. The relic is working . . . "

The old man makes no sense. Putting my gauntlet-like hands out, I clench my fists and feel the hard metal of my fingers. Squeezing, I push to the tolerance of my strength—until I can feel the gears in my hands straining. I swing my legs off the workbench and my wooden heels scratch the floor.

I stand, the top of my head nearly brushing the low ceiling.

Favo enters the darkness. In a moment he returns, his arms wrapped around a tall golden panel. The beaten-brass mirror groans as he drags it over the dusty wooden floor. The panel seems to glow in the candlelight. He props himself against it—holding the long rectangle before me—then stops and stares.

I can feel that he is afraid.

"Look upon yourself," he whispers.

Standing at my full height, I see my movements reflected dully in the brass panel. I am tall and thin. Very tall. My face is human-like, leather that has been coated in places with some kind of rigid wax, ringed in brown curls of hair, my eyes large and dark. My lower lip is pulled to the side, slightly disfigured. I am not wearing clothes. The skin of my chest and arms is made of beaten metal banding with occasional tight swathes of leather tidily placed underneath. This body is golden and tan, strong and long-limbed. The light haunts my eyes, and I understand why Favo has fear in his heart.

"My son?" he asks.

"Yes," I reply.

"What is the first thing?" he asks.

"The first thing?"

My voice comes from somewhere deep inside my chest. I can feel some device in there, a bellows that contracts and sends wind up my throat and between my teeth. There seem to be a multitude of voices beneath my voice. I am so much bigger than this small old man standing before me.

"Yes," he whispers. "In your mind. Reach inside and tell me the first thing. The first word you ever knew. What is the Word?"

There is a hard truth to the limits of my body—to the solid press of my flesh and the clenching strength of my grip. I push into my mind to search for the answer to Favo's question, and I feel another truth—even stronger than that of my flesh. It is the truth of knowledge, of a singular purpose carved into the stone of my mind.

This is the Word that is the shape of my life.

I put my eyes onto the old man, and I feel the leather of my lips scratch as I say the Word out loud for the first time.

"Pravda," I say. "I am truth."

GREAT EUROPEAN PLAIN, 1725

Elena's hand is small on my shoulder, like a perched bird.

"Go," I tell her, and the sparrow flies.

The lead rider has closed the final distance. I do not look up from where my blades lay in the grass. The muscled forelegs of a black horse approach. It slows and stops next to me. The rider does not bother to speak. I hear the slow skim of his blade leaving its scabbard. Hear the creak of his armor as he reaches back, lifting the blade high into the gray-green air.

The dragoon raises his arm and his breath expels as he swings the blade—the motion mechanically pushing air from his diaphragm. At this moment, I roll toward his horse, snaking my long arms over the grass to grip the handles of my blades. The blow misses me. On my knees, I lift the short blade and draw a red line across the horse's belly. I fall onto my back and shove myself out of the way, watching the surprised face of the rider.

Screaming, the horse tries to rear back as a hot flood of intestines gush out of the slash in its belly. A cloud of mist billows from the cascade of bright red viscera. The rider rolls backward off his falling mount. The horse's legs buckle and it collapses screaming into its own offal.

The lightly armored horseman is already gaining his feet when I bring the hilt of my short blade down on the crown of his head. His fur-lined helmet shatters the bridge of his nose, and he bites off the tip of his tongue. I am already sliding my dagger over his throat and adding his blood to that of his steed, gauging the distance to the pounding hooves I hear approaching.

I dive over the top of both corpses as a hail of hooves spear into the mud around me. Another horse passes by and I hear the shouting of angry men now. Standing a little way off, Elena is shouting as well. Her high-pitched voice repeats the same word—almost a melody.

Poshchady! Poshchady!

Mercy, she is screaming.

MOSCOW, 1707

"They say you are my son," says Peter, taking a bite from an apple. He chews it loudly, watching me with large, intelligent eyes. I notice that his lip is disfigured, pulled to the side . . . the same as mine.

"Yes," I say, crouching, my head bowed.

"Tell me, *son,*" he says, humor in his voice. "What is pravda?"

"Truth and honor."

"Do you swear fealty to me?"

"I do," I respond.

"Rise and draw your sword," says the Tsar, walking closer to me.

Peter does not wear gaudy robes or shining armor. Instead, he has on the simple breeches of an engineer, his boots clicking on the marble floor of the study. He saunters around to my face and watches me with the appraising eye of a mechanician, takes another bite from his apple.

I am standing, eye-to-eye, with the Tsar of Russia. We are exactly the same height. I ease my blade from its wooden scabbard. I hold it by my side, the tip pointed at the ground, my hand wrapped around the hilt, arm as steady as if it were carved out of stone.

"He moves like a man," says Peter, smiling.

The Tsar leans in and snatches the hood off my head. The rawhide that covers the surface of my skull is stretched tight over cogs and gears. Brass buttons shine across the nape of my neck where the covering is fastened.

"Doesn't look much like one, though," he says.

"It follows the truth," says Favo. "As you instructed. The relic provides power and sense, but it was invoked with your exact specifications."

"Your name, avtomat?" asks the Tsar.

Nothing comes to mind.

"As you will call me," I respond.

"Strange to stand next to someone who is as tall as I am," he muses, chewing thoughtfully. "I've never done it before."

The Tsar runs a finger over my forehead.

"He is very ugly," he says.

"A result of my limited abilities, Emperor," says Favo. "Please forgive me. Over time, its appearance can be improved. Any disfigurement is the fault of my own aged hands and not the avtomat itself."

"It? You call it an it?"

"To call it otherwise would insult our Lord Christ. It is not a living thing I have made, but a bauble. Petty in comparison to God's works."

Peter laughs, a short bark that echoes.

"You fear Catherine, old man, even in private discussion. Probably smart. She does not trust in this project. Catherine feels that what has been lost to time should stay lost. She would have those artifacts of yours destroyed."

Fiovani lowers his head. "Oh no, my Tsar. I do not question the Empress, of course . . . *would* never . . . but the relics are precious. I have already found another vessel for our remaining relic. And we cannot forget . . . our enemies have their own artifacts. Other avtomat could be plotting against us even now—"

"Enough, Fiovani," says Peter. "Your studies are safe."

The Tsar turns and shoves me with both of his large hands. Sensing a test, I choose not to move. My feet are planted, hand clasped around my saber, and although the Tsar is large and he hits me hard, the force is insufficient.

"He is stronger than me," says the Tsar, face dark with exertion and a hint of anger. "Let's see how smart he is."

Peter steps a few feet away and clasps his hands behind his back.

"Avtomat," he asks. "A boyar noble demands fifty men of the Preobrazhensky regiment to protect his border. Do I accept his request?"

"No, Emperor."

"Why not?"

"Members of the Emperor's own regiment are sworn to protect their father. To send them into battle for anyone of lower rank is a dishonor."

"He is smart, too."

The Tsar takes a last bite of the apple and tosses the core across the room.

"Strike me," he says.

I do not respond.

"I am your Tsar, avtomat," he says. "I am giving you a command that you are honor bound to follow. Swing your saber and strike me."

"My Emperor," stutters Fiovani. "He is very strong. Please do not underestimate the avtomat—"

"Now," says Peter.

The impulse to obey pulls at my joints like gravity. Drawing my arm back, I let the sword tip rise. But . . . to injure the Tsar would bring dishonor. The Word blazes in my mind: Pravda.

"Do it!" shouts the Tsar.

My vision is blurring. The saber point wavers. I am compelled to obey and to disobey at the same time. The dissonance is roaring in my ears. I cannot say no and I cannot strike. I am drowning, my mind swallowing itself.

But there is a solution.

I lift the saber higher, the tip stretching toward the Tsar. Then, I rotate the flashing blade in my hands, all the way around until the point dimples the fabric of my kaftan. With both hands I tense my shoulders and I pull—

"Stop!" says the Tsar, placing a hand on my arm.

I silently return the sword to its first position.

"Welcome to Moscow . . . Peter," the Tsar says, clapping an arm around my shoulders. "A pity you can't have a drink to celebrate."

"But, my Tsar, you choose to call it Peter?" asks Favo, quietly.

"I call it by its name: Peter Alexeyevich," he says.

"I do not understand," says Favo. "Why . . . "

"Peter is my name while I am on this Earth. But with reason and patience, you have built a ruler who can someday take my place and rule the Russian Empire forever. Peter will carry my name like a banner through the ages, immune to the physical ruin of time and always faithful to pravda. An eternal Tsar."

GREAT EUROPEAN PLAIN, 1725

As blades whistle by overhead, I roll over a dying horse and fall to the wet plain. I scramble onto my hands and knees, sharp hooves flashing over me. Before I can stand, a hoof stamps my sword hand into the dirt.

Two of my fingers are left behind, severed and shining in the muddy crater.

Pulling my shattered fist tight to my chest, I stagger to my feet and raise the shashka with my other hand. The nearest dragoon makes a prancing turn and rounds on me. His thighs clenching, the rider leans in his saddle—his red belt sash snapping in the wind as he gains speed.

Silver eclipses the clouds as his saber leaves its scabbard.

I am still as the quake of hooves envelops me. The dark bulk of the warhorse grows into a blur, its breath snorting from flared nostrils as it strains to carry the armored rider to intercept me.

I turn, dropping to avoid the rider's flashing weapon.

Too late. I feel a tug between my shoulder blades. The rider's blade connects, parts my kaftan and splits the armor beneath. Broken metal ringlets scatter past my face like a shower of coins.

But my sword remains up and steady. Its single honed edge slides along the rider's unarmored thigh. As he gallops away, the leg bounces curiously and I see that it is dangling from tendons. The rider reaches for the wound, grunting at the sight of the injury. As his horse turns in place, craning to look back, the rider rolls out of the saddle. He hits the ground and now the leg does come off, coating the electric green grass with arterial blood.

The horse backs away, confused.

There is no pain in me. Only awareness. Three more riders are on the attack. My left arm is hanging uselessly now, damaged by the wide gash that has slit my back. I stumble and try to catch myself but my arms are not working correctly. I fall onto my stomach, face first into the muddy plain. Stalks of grass tickle the rough leather of my cheek. This close, I can see that the blades of grass are dancing with the vibration of hooves pounding dirt.

Arching my body, I lift up and roll onto my back.

A lance crunches into my chest, bending the metal of my frame into a deformed valley. I feel the pressure and shock of it, the tremor of the dragoon's hand on the wooden shaft. I hear my innards tearing as the horse gallops by overhead. The lance is wrenched from my chest, yanking me off the ground before dropping me sprawling onto my side.

Somewhere nearby, Elena makes a small hurt sound. She is finished shouting for mercy. There is clearly none to be had.

Though I was never born of a woman, I am in fetal position now. Wounded and cowering in the way of a mortal man. I catch sight of Elena, cringing twenty yards away, small and shapeless under her cloak.

Blood-stained hooves trample the mud all around me. The stabbing weight of a hoof snaps a strut inside my right thigh. My leg nearly comes loose from my hip socket, and I am tossed again. I land on my stomach, one brass cheekbone pushing through my leather skin and into damp earth.

Again, I am still.

A gentle rain is drumming the empty waste of the steppe. There is no more thunder. Gathered in a circle, the surviving guardsmen are speaking to each other in confused tones that sound distant and hollow.

Blood, they are saying. Blood.

They marvel that no blood is leaking from me. They are examining the blunted lance tip, noting how clean it is. What is this man made of, they wonder? What hidden armor does he wear? He is mortally wounded, yet he doesn't cry out.

Elena is running now. She is staying low, legs scissoring under her flowing cloak. This is her best chance of escape, and it is not much of a chance at all. Like predators, the dragoons spark to the movement. The three remaining soldiers move as one to surround her. Here in blood-stained mud, with wet grass caressing my face like damp tentacles, I can only pretend to be a corpse. It is not such a stretch. In most ways, I have never been alive.

It took three death blows, enough to kill three men, to fell me.

Te Deum. Thanks to God. I am still functioning.

With one eye open, helpless, I watch through a blur of rain as Elena is snatched up by her cloak and thrown over the broad, sweaty back of a warhorse. She does not shout. There is no reason for it. By her Word, Elena never acts without a reason. On the horse, her body flops loosely, about the weight of a little girl, and wearing too many clothes for the riders to think any different. For now.

Patience, Elena. Strength.

I leave my eye open and unblinking, letting it appear sightless in death. I do not even allow the lens to dilate as I observe whatever crosses my field of view. The riders circle close to each other, conferring.

Koldun, comes the whisper.

Warlock. Monster. Man with no blood. The commander wearing the shining cuirass is a superstitious one. Best not to disturb this sleeping traveler, he advises. Leave that one to his dark ways and we'll return with our prisoner.

Wise advice.

"Clean the field," orders the leader. "Leave the dead behind."

Moving quickly, a dirty-faced dragoon dismounts and loots the corpses of his two fallen comrades. Cursing, he tugs at the blood-stained saddle trapped under the disemboweled horse. He slips in the mud and falls, staining his outer jacket.

"Leave it," orders the commander. His eyes are dark and scared over a thick black moustache. His breath is visible in the moist air.

With a last wary look in my direction, the three surviving riders lead their dead comrade's horse away and gallop for the horizon. I wait until the vibrations fade before I blink. Wait until the sight of them has receded into tiny specks before I dare to stir.

I am alone in the grass with silent corpses. The sun has finished easing itself over the flat horizon. The great blue orb of the moon has appeared, jovial, its pale light sending my shadow reaching out across the plains. In the sudden chill, I can feel that I am badly broken.

Elena may still be alive. I must protect her.

The blow to my back has disabled my left arm, but I still have the right. I take a handful of grass with my thumb and two remaining fingers. With a violent yank, I drag myself an arm length forward. Part of my hip and my right leg stay in the grass behind me. My left leg is still attached but useless. I pull again, leaving a slug's trail of broken machinery glinting darkly under moonlight.

But the grass is plentiful and my grip strong.

Stars fade into view as I leave the wreck of my body behind, one arm length at a time. Hidden among the shadowed grass, I am a crooked head and part of a torso cloaked in black wool, slithering forward by virtue of one good arm. Without pause or thought, I creep onward—pushing over the footsteps of three riders who know nothing of the horror they've left for dead.

ST. PETERSBURG, 1725

My world ends in the predawn light of January 28, 1725. In one moment, the great bellows of Peter's lungs push the last breath past his lips. His massive head tilts and falls to the pillow, a relieved expression on his face for the first time I can remember.

He hid the illness. Peter hid the illness until it was too late.

Elena and I did not arrive in time. The Empress was already there. Watching her rise from Peter's bedside, I sense that she has already maneuvered into position. Outside the bedroom window, I hear the hoarse shouts of the Guards regiments echoing against the cobblestone courtyard. They have already been summoned to the capital and massed near the palace.

I put a hand protectively over Elena's shoulder. Together, we served the great man for twenty years. We fought through plague-infested cities during the war with Sweden, forged new weapons for the Guards regiments, and even served as spies in the Western countries.

Yet we never served this woman.

Catherine looks up from the corpse. She has one palm over Peter's still chest, leaning over him. Her hair is wet with tears, hanging limply over the corpse's face. Under sharp black eyebrows, her face buckles with anguish and anger.

"You . . . abominations," she says. "Did you know when he was sick? Did you say nothing?"

"No, Empress," I say, my deep voice thrumming from the black cavern of my chest. "I am the Word."

"Pravda? You are not pravda, you poor thing. You are a blasphemy. Peter was deceived into calling you an eternal Tsar. Tricked by that deformed mechanician."

I tap Elena on the shoulder and she understands immediately. *Find Favo.* The girl turns and scurries toward the door.

"Stop her!" shouts Catherine, gesturing emphatically, climbing directly over Peter's body. "Don't let either of them leave."

At the door, one of the Guard snatches Elena by the hair. Her wig comes off, and she struggles as he grabs hold of her with both hands. I cannot act outside my honor, and the Guard serve royal blood. So, I watch as the man gathers the small machine up into a bear hug and pins her thrashing against his armored chestplate.

The shouts of the Guard are growing louder outside.

"Do you hear that?" asks Catherine. She is smiling at me, her small canines flashing. "My Guards have rallied to me. Peter wished for *me* to become the next Tsar. His wife. Not you. Not a broken version of himself."

I hear a straining crack as something snaps inside Elena. Now, she is not struggling as hard. Her cloak is pulled up around her face and her thin brass legs are swinging, kicking uselessly, wooden heels scraping against the floor. I feel a twinge of anger and sadness inside my chest.

My daughter.

But there is nothing I can do until it is within pravda. For I am the Word.

"Our father is dead," shout the Guard who are mobbed outside, faint voices booming from the palace walls. "But our mother lives."

Elena's whalebone ribs are snapping. Gears inside are grinding against the intruding shards of bone and wood. She whimpers, and I know she may only have moments left before the damage is irreparable.

Pravda.

"How will you honor us?" I ask Catherine. "Will you obey Peter's wishes?"

Catherine slips a strap of her falling nightgown back over her shoulder with one thumb, climbing off of her husband's bed. She strides to me and stops only when her anger-pinched face is inches below mine. Wild dark hair stripes her forehead and her nostrils quiver with each breath.

"Honor you?" asks Catherine. "I cannot honor you. I am only sorry for you. You must be destroyed—"

A stated intention to break pravda is enough.

My right arm shoots out, and my gauntleted knuckles crunch into the face of the Guardsman who holds Elena. I feel the flimsy nose squash beneath my fist and the knock as his head impacts the wall. Elena lands scrambling on the ground as the man crumples, unconscious. I can already feel her tugging at my cloak.

"What!?" shouts Catherine. "What have you done?"

Our father is dead.

Catherine is too close to me. I could kill her with a swipe of my hand. And she knows this. The other Guardsmen watch us closely. I hear the slow grind of a blade leaving its sheath and I shake my head no. The sound stops.

But our mother still lives.

Catherine is the Tsarina. I will not harm her—*cannot* harm her—and yet to honor Peter . . . I must not allow my death or Elena's.

I take a step back, my full seven-foot height perfectly fitting the enlarged doorway to Peter's bedroom. In light mesh armor and kaftan, I look uncannily like the dead man lying across the room—as I was designed to.

"By Peter's command, we must live, Empress," I say. "We cannot accept death, but, please, for Peter's honor . . . allow us to accept exile."

GREAT EUROPEAN PLAIN, 1725

Grip the grass. Pull. Release. Reach again.

The gods who haunt the hidden angles of the constellations offer their assistance to me through clear patches of sky above. The bright eye of Mars watches as I am soaked in dew, and smiles to see the horse blood washing out of my cloak. Part of my face is caught on a serpentine root, and the leather of my cheek is torn, leaving an obscene hole in my visage.

And so it continues.

Under the gaze of a starry night, my body, made lighter by horrific damage, squirms its way over glittering waves of grass. The moon is fading on a pink horizon when I finally see the silhouettes of four horses tied to a scrubby tree.

The Guardsmen are sleeping. My Elena is a dark pile of robes next to a smoldering camp fire. Her hands and feet are tied. I slither closer through dirt, my one good arm out, head cocked to the side and my black eyes open wide to the predawn light. My broken torso drags entrails of metal, leather, and wax.

A shape stirs. I pause, arm outstretched.

Someone tosses a reindeer hide to the side. A guardsman stands, head turning warily, still clumsy with sleep. The man steps closer to where I am hidden, my body splayed out and deformed. He stops, tugs at his trousers and sprays an arc of steaming piss.

I watch him turn back and stumble toward his sleeping hides, but then he notices Elena. Quietly, he squats next to her and whispers something, even as I continue to drag myself forward. My dirt-stained armor crunches over stalks of grass as I push through the periphery of the camp. The rider is not listening for danger. He is pushing Elena silently onto her back, one hand cupped over her mouth. Untying her ankles, he roughly spreads her legs.

The man is grinning, teeth glinting red in the dawn.

I find the helmet as I pass his hide. One urgent, broken lurch at a time, I plant the metal bowl of it into the dirt and drag myself forward. The armored hat is made of steel, fur-lined underneath and peaked in the middle.

"What?" he hisses at Elena, recoiling on his knees as he finds nothing but cold metal beneath her cloak. "What are you?"

His curly black hair is rusty in the dawn light as he turns and sees me—eyes widening at the sight of my ruin, cheeks twitching in fright. I am already rearing back on the remains of my left biceps, helmet lifted high in my good hand. The dragoon is choking on a shout as I bring the helmet down.

The metal bowl glances over the bridge of his nose. His jaw snaps shut and he falls, horror and blood mingling on his face. Elena kicks with both legs, sending the rider flailing onto his back with a grunt, the air knocked from his lungs.

I bring the helmet down again.

This time it lands with a wet crunch in the middle of the rider's face. Again. A half dozen more times until I feel the skull crack and the ground is littered with teeth and blood and saliva.

I hear a gurgling scream from across the camp and see that Elena is on her feet. She has tugged a blade from the fallen rider's belt and has slit the throats of the other two riders. In moments, there are no men living.

The smoldering fire now warms only metal, wood, and leather.

"Oh Peter," says Elena. "Oh my poor Peter."

I feel Elena's arms encircle my head, cradling me on her lap. With her other hand she is patting down my body, feeling for the extent of the damage. Somewhere, a bird sings to the dawn. Faintly, I hear the trickle of blood flowing into the grass and the whinny of a nervous horse.

"You are very damaged," Elena says.

"As long as my relic is intact," I respond. "I can be repaired."

"The Empress will hunt us."

"She will," I say to Elena, my eternal daughter. "But we are not running blindly. We leave now in search of something special."

"What do we seek, Peter?"

I lock my eyes on the curve of her porcelain cheek. Elena was once a mindless doll, but now we are more than things . . . we are avtomat.

"We will find our own kind, Elena . . . even if it takes a thousand years."

DANCING WITH BATGIRL IN THE LAND OF NOD

Will McIntosh

Words were coming out of Eileen's mouth, but they didn't make sense. The voice in Ray's head, the one screaming that they had to fill the bathtub, had to stockpile more food, was making it impossible for him to understand.

He grasped Eileen's shoulders. "I don't think grocery stores are safe. Too much risk of exposure. What if I—"

"Did you hear what I just said?" Eileen asked.

She'd always reminded Ray of a cartoon ladybug, and now more than ever, with her eyes big and round, her face framed by red curls. Ray realized it was an odd thought, given the situation.

"Not really, no," he answered. "I think I may be in shock." The walls looked strange, like they were advancing and receding, advancing and receding. The virus was in Los Angeles. It was spreading like mad. They should have prepared better.

"I said I'm having an affair with Justin."

"What, what—" Ray stuttered, utterly lost. Maybe Eileen was in shock as well. "You're not making sense." He turned toward the bathroom. "We have to fill the bathtubs."

"No, Ray, listen to me." She grasped his shoulder, turned him around. "I'm having an affair with Justin."

"An affair?" They didn't have affairs. They weren't the sort of people who had affairs. They were the good guys, the couple other couples wished they could be.

Only, Eileen *was* having an affair. She'd just said so.

Ray thought he was going to vomit. "You're telling me this *now*?"

Eileen looked at her feet. "I want to face what's coming with a clear conscience. I don't want this lie between us."

It was hard for Ray to breathe, like there was something pressing on his chest.

Her eyes welled with tears. "I'm sorry."

Ray swallowed, trying to flatten the lump in his throat. He wasn't going to cry. He *wanted* to cry, but he wasn't going to. He also wanted to find Justin Schneider and smash his teeth in, but he wasn't going to do that, either.

"Do you love him?"

"With everything that's happening, I honestly don't know what I feel." Eileen looked up at Ray, blinking rapidly. "If you want me to leave right now, I'll understand."

"That would make things easier for you, wouldn't it?" said Ray. "If I kick you out, you can go to Justin with a clear conscience."

Ray had a flash of her in Justin's arms, kissing him. Ten minutes earlier that image would have struck him as absurd. Billions of people were dead, or lying paralyzed, waiting to die, and Eileen had chosen this moment to clear her conscience.

"I'll tell you what: I'll make it even easier. I'll leave." Ray spread his arms wide. "It's your house, after all. Your parents paid for most of it."

Eileen stiffened. Ray thought he saw something cross her face—hope, relief that she was fighting to mask. Suddenly he couldn't stand the sight of her. "Just go away so I can pack in peace."

She reached out. "Ray, I'm—"

He pulled away. "Just go."

There was nowhere for her to go. The virus could be anywhere. It lived on surfaces for days; one cough from someone who was infected and you were dead.

Red-eyed, Eileen looked around, and finally headed into the garage.

He had to do something to blunt the pain rising in him. There was too much of it, heaped on top of the terror. Ray staggered to the kitchen cabinet over the refrigerator—which served as their liquor cabinet—and pulled down a bottle of vodka. For the first time in his life he drank straight from the bottle.

It helped a little. Just a little.

Trying to think about nothing, Ray went upstairs. The walls in the stairway were covered with eight-by-ten photos of him and Eileen. He watched his feet, not wanting to see them.

After packing clothes and toiletries he went to the basement and brought up a brown backpack filled with survival gear they'd bought at Target two months ago, back when the possibility the nodding virus would reach Los Angeles had seemed so remote.

He had no idea where to go. Walter would take him in, but Walter and Lauren didn't need Ray sitting in their living room while they dealt with this.

When everything was packed and in the car, he couldn't bring himself to get in and drive away. Not yet, at least.

He went back inside. In the living room, newscasters updated the situation in breathless tones just shy of panic. It was in all the major U.S. cities now. It was everywhere; there were paralyzed people in a billion houses, in a million hospitals. Any minute, Ray could join them. He wouldn't know he had it until the nodding began, and by then it would be too late. It was already too late, if he had it. But they'd stayed indoors, hadn't left the house in three days. Surely he was clean.

Somewhere outside, a siren wailed.

He went to his collection room to calm himself. Being surrounded by his Batgirl memorabilia comforted him. He'd owned some of the pieces in the collection—the lunchbox, the action figure—since he was nineteen. They reminded him that he'd had a life before Eileen, and could have one after.

If he didn't catch the nodding virus.

If he did, he would sit frozen until he died of dehydration. The thought set his pounding heart racing.

He looked at his wall of autographed photos from the old *Batgirl* TV show, trying to dampen the fear threatening to swallow him, but this time they provided no solace. They were nothing but glossy paper marked with black ink.

The frame closest to the edge of the wall held nothing but a manila envelope. He'd kept it because Helen Anderson had personally written her return address in the top left corner before returning one of the photos he'd mailed to her to be autographed. The postmark was 1998; nearly twenty years ago.

Ray took the framed envelope down, studied the return address, neatly written in Anderson's beautiful, looping cursive. She was divorced, estranged from her only child. She could be alone right now, just like Ray. Her house was a thirty minute drive, in the direction of the bay, opposite the refugees fleeing the city, passing the virus between them.

Ray imagined Helen Anderson opening her door.

I'm your biggest fan, he'd say to her. *Is there anything I can do to help you?*

Right. Great plan.

But just imagining meeting Helen Anderson lifted the black cloud, the despair, if only slightly. What was the worst that could happen? She would say she was fine and thank him for his concern.

Ray already regretted his grand proclamation. He should have let Eileen pack up and leave.

He touched the glass over the spot where Helen Anderson had written her address. He knew she still lived there. He'd confirmed it on the county tax assessor website a dozen times over the years, each time he dreamed of driving over there on some pretext to meet her before talking himself out of it.

It was a crazy idea; Don Quixote on steroids. But chances were he was going to die very soon. Why not seize the day? Why not do something a little crazy?

Ray paused outside his car, considered going to the garage to say goodbye to Eileen. He might never see her again. They might both be dead in a week.

Then he remembered the look on her face, when he said he would leave. Masked joy and relief.

He climbed in, yanked the door shut.

Half a block from his house, Ray slowed.

A woman was lying on the sidewalk, twitching.

Until now it had all been on TV. This woman, lying right outside his car, made it real. Ray's every instinct screamed that he had to stop and help her. Her forehead was bleeding where she'd hit it on the pavement. Her head was jerking up and down, her eyes round with terror.

If he touched her, he would die too. The symptoms wouldn't show up for a week, but he'd be infected immediately.

Around the corner he passed a wreck—an SUV wrapped around a light pole. The driver was nodding so violently her chin was bleeding where it rubbed the airbag that pinned her to her seat. In the back, two toddlers strapped in child seats nodded in unison.

Ray's chest hitched; he raised a hand to shield his eyes from the SUV. It was too much—he didn't want to see any more pain, any more clear, terrified eyes.

He was surprised to see Walter and Lauren sitting on their front porch. He rolled down the passenger window.

Walter raised a hand in greeting. Lauren, sitting in the rocker beside him, was nodding wildly.

"Oh, shit," Ray said. He raised his voice. "Oh God, Walter, I'm so sorry."

Walter looked down at his lap. "It started an hour ago." He touched her shoulder. "I brought her outside. She'd rather see grass and sky than four walls."

"Is there anything I can do?" Ray asked.

Walter shook his head. "I'm just waiting for it to take me. I kissed Lauren on the mouth to make sure."

Ray wasn't sure how to respond. In a way he envied Walter. At least he and Lauren were going to die together.

"We've had a good life," Walter called from the porch. "Please give Eileen my love, and Lauren's love, too."

"Eileen left me," Ray blurted. "Or maybe I'm leaving her. She was having an affair."

Walter's head drooped. "I'm so sorry."

A lump rose in Ray's throat; this time he couldn't stop the tears. "Thank you. You've been a good friend." Then he remembered Lauren could see and hear everything. "You too, Lauren. I'm sorry."

Lauren went on nodding. Soon the nodding would stop, and she'd be still.

Walter raised his hand in farewell. Ray couldn't believe this was probably the last time he'd ever see Walter. No more listening to the Dodgers in Walter's backyard; no more drives to the Green Leaf for a beer. Despite being thirty years older than Ray, Walter was still his best friend—the best friend he'd ever had.

Wilshire was chaos. The sidewalks were crowded with people humping backpacks, their mouths covered by surgical masks, gas masks, scarves, scuba gear. Each minute it seemed they had more victims to step over. The road was littered with standing vehicles, their drivers frozen at the wheel, heads nodding. Ray tried not to look at them as he weaved around. There was nothing he could do, he kept reminding himself. There was no cure, no treatment, no room in hospitals.

South Doherty was completely blocked. Ray pulled onto the sidewalk and inched through the crowd until he reached the intersecting street.

The traffic lightened as he hit the winding residential roads of Beverly Hills, where mansions were set back from the road on huge shady lots. He wanted to turn the radio off, because the news made his heart hammer and turned his mouth to cotton, but he had to stay informed.

Communications were down on the East Coast. States in the Mountain West were the only ones spared the plague so far. They were shooting refugees who tried to enter.

Ray pulled onto Cardiff Drive, glanced at the envelope in the passenger seat to confirm that he was looking for eleven fifty-seven Cardiff. He slowed in front of Helen Anderson's house. It was smaller than the others, with sloping roofs and an alpine feel to it. Two big trees blocked much of the front, and the gardens and shrubbery around it were lush to the point of being overgrown. Wondering what the hell he was doing, Ray turned in and rode up the long driveway.

He took a few whooshing breaths at her front door, shifted from foot to foot. Finally he reached up and rang the doorbell.

It occurred to him that it might not be Helen Anderson who answered. As far as he knew she wasn't seeing anyone. (And if anyone would know such a thing, it was Ray, because he read everything he could find about her online.) But what if a friend, or a housekeeper answered?

A lock clattered; the door opened six inches until a chain inside snapped taut. Helen Anderson's face appeared in the crack. She was barely as tall as his shoulder. He'd known she was five-four, but somehow hadn't realized how small that was.

"Yes?" Her hair was short and unkempt. She was wearing no makeup. She was beautiful, her eyes the light gray of misty mountaintops.

"Miss Anderson, my name is Ray Parrot." His tongue clicked off the roof of his dry mouth. "I—" Suddenly the words he'd rehearsed seemed foolish. *I'm your biggest fan?* He couldn't say that. "I've come to see if you need help."

Helen Anderson tilted her head. "Do I know you?"

"No—I'm an admirer of your work."

Helen Anderson gently closed the door. Ray waited, hoping to hear the chain rattle so she could open it further. Instead, he heard receding footsteps.

He waited a few minutes, then headed down the steps, his face burning. He felt like such an idiot. Had he really thought Helen Anderson was going to swing her door open to a complete stranger, maybe invite him in for tea?

"Excuse me?"

Ray turned. Helen Anderson was on her stoop in a blue sweater and jeans.

"Yes?" He took a step toward her, paused. "I'm sorry. It was rude of me to show up on your doorstep like this."

"No, I'm the rude one. As usual. I don't need any help, but, thank you for asking. That was kind of you."

Ray nodded. "You're going to ride it out in your home?"

Helen smiled. It was not her dazzling Batgirl smile, but the saddest, most heartbreaking smile he'd ever seen. "Something like that."

"You have enough food? Water?"

She closed her eyes for a second. "More than enough."

"Well, good luck, then."

When Ray got to the end of the driveway, he put the car in park and stared at Helen Anderson's mailbox. What now? Try to get to Omaha, where his sister lived? The National Guard was shooting refugees on sight in Nebraska and the rest of the Midwest.

What had she meant by *Something like that?* It was a peculiar reply, especially paired with that sad smile. Ray wondered if she meant she was going to start drinking again. Helen Anderson was a recovered alcoholic, sober twenty years, a vocal supporter of Alcoholics Anonymous. Ray couldn't blame her for falling off the wagon at this particular juncture. If he'd ever stopped drinking he'd be leaping off the wagon.

There was something about her answer, though. Something about her whole demeanor. She hadn't been scared; she'd been *sad.*

Ray headed back up the driveway on foot.

This time when Helen opened the door, there was no chain.

Ray held up both hands, palms out. "I'm so sorry to bother you again, Miss Anderson, and feel free to slam this door in my face, but I'm worried that maybe you're not all right."

Helen raised her eyebrows. "Excuse me?"

"When we spoke a minute ago, you didn't back away from the door like you were afraid to catch the virus from me. You just seemed sad."

Helen swept a stray hair out of her face, folded her arms. "Well, Ray, I'll let you in on a little secret. I *am* sad. I've been sad for a long time."

Ray nodded slowly. "When I asked if you were going to ride this out at home, you said, 'Something like that.'"

Helen half-turned, looked off into the trees. She was fifty-eight years old. Ray could see those years in the lines under her eyes, the loose skin under her chin.

"I came back to make sure you're not going to hurt yourself."

Batgirl's eyes locked on his. "How could you possibly—" she stammered. "A complete stranger, at my door on this particular day, coming to see if I'm okay." Helen pressed her forehead. "You could have come yesterday, or tomorrow. Even two hours from now." She studied his face, shaking her head.

Finally, she swung the door open. "Come on in, Ray."

His mind reeling, Ray followed Helen Anderson into her house, through a high-ceilinged living room, into a spacious kitchen with black marble countertops.

Helen snared a bottle of tequila from the counter as she passed, took a big swig as she continued to the kitchen table, which had an army of pink pills and three prescription bottles spilled across it. Helen gestured at them. "I was just about to get started when you rang."

Movement out the window caught Ray's eye. Little birds, darting between a feeder and the safety of an orange tree. To them it was just another day.

"My wife left me today. We were married twenty-two years." It just came out.

"I'm sorry to hear that, Ray." Helen went to a cabinet and pulled down a glass, then ducked and produced a second fifth of tequila from under the sink. She set the glass on the kitchen table, twisted the cap on the fresh bottle. "Probably not a good idea to share a bottle." She poured, slid the glass in front of him, pushing some pills out of the way in the process.

Ray took a swig.

"What's your wife's name?"

"Eileen." Ray set the glass down with a *thunk* as the tequila burned its way down his throat. "She told me she's been having an affair. Justin. From work."

Helen nodded. "So, your wife walked out on you, and you got in the car and came to make sure the star of a thirty year-old TV show was all right?"

Ray shrugged. "Whenever I feel bad I watch a few episodes of *Batgirl,* and I feel better. I was feeling so bad that I figured only Batgirl herself could make me feel better."

Helen threw back her head and laughed. "Maybe if you'd turned to Eileen when you felt bad instead of a TV show, things would have turned out better."

Seeing Ray flinch, Helen clutched his forearm. "I'm sorry. That was a terrible thing to say." She reached for her bottle. "Now you know why I've had three husbands walk out on *me.*"

"They were all out of their frickin' minds."

"No," Helen said. "No. They were smart." She surveyed the pills scattered across the table, muttered, "I was always uneasy about all the higher power shit they went on about at AA, but this . . ." She shook her head. "It's like God sent you to tell me, 'Not so fast. You're not through here yet.'" She looked up at Ray and laughed. "Which makes you my guardian angel."

Ray spread his arms. "That's exactly right. That's me."

• • •

The giant TV on the living room wall was muted, which was fine with Ray, because the images were loud enough. Times Square in New York, shown from above; the streets were hopelessly clogged, drivers frozen at the wheel. People with covered faces pushed along the sidewalks, climbed through the maze of traffic, stepped over other people lying on the ground twitching, nodding, or just perfectly still. They were all trying to get out of the city, even though they were being told to stay put. The more people moved around, the more the virus spread.

Ray had always imagined that if there was an apocalypse, it would be a violent thing—people fighting, buildings burning, looting. But this was quiet. Civilized. When you're afraid to let other people breathe on you, let alone bleed on you, it made sense that things would be peaceful.

Lightning flashed outside. The sky was dark; the palm trees in Helen's back yard bent and thrashed as rain hammered the ground.

He eyed the pile of empty bottles in the corner, then looked at Helen, amazed all over again that he was there, sitting in her living room. Eileen would choke if she knew. On her good days she'd tolerated his passion for all things Batgirl with amused disdain. On her bad days she'd told him he was embarrassing himself.

Helen looked at him. "What?"

Ray shrugged. "Nothing."

"Stop staring at me all the time."

"I can't help it."

"It makes me paranoid. I feel like you're trying to catch a glimpse of Batgirl behind the bags and the wrinkles." Her words were only slightly slurred, which was impressive, given how many pulls she'd taken from the bottle since morning. "That face is gone."

Ray sprung from his seat. "Are you kidding me? Is that really what you think?"

Helen stared, glassy-eyed, into the bottle.

"I can't take my eyes off you because you *are* Batgirl. The way you move, your expressions. Since I was fifteen I've been mesmerized by you, and now you're right here, moving around this house. I can't help watching you."

She gave him a flat cynical, very un-Batgirl look. "I'm an aging has-been who had very little talent to begin with."

Ray clicked his tongue. "What a shame that you think that. So many people would give anything to be you. You should savor it."

Helen sighed heavily; she looked like she was about to cry.

The TV, the lights, flicked off. Outside, the hum of the air conditioner died.

"Damn it," Ray hissed. They'd been expecting the power to go out for days, but it was still a blow. Things were about to get harder.

Helen went to the kitchen counter and twisted open one of the prescription bottles lined up there. *"Shit."* She dumped the contents into her palm. "I only have three Xanax left." She looked around, as if searching the bookshelves for a stray bottle she might have left lying around. Her gaze settled on Ray. "I can't make it without my Xanax, Ray. I'll die."

Ray grabbed his keys off the counter, where they'd been sitting, untouched, for four days. "I'll get it."

She intercepted him as he headed for the front door, wrapped him in a warm hug. "My guardian angel. Do you want me to go with you?"

"No. Stay here."

• • •

On West Pico, Ray passed a red-haired woman wearing a surgical mask who reminded him of Eileen. Ray wondered where the real Eileen was. Home, with Justin? Lying frozen on some street corner, waiting to die? Would Justin care for her if she got the nodding virus, or just leave her? Ray had no idea, because he didn't know Justin. Eileen had cheated on him, but that didn't mean he didn't care what happened to her. He wondered if he should check on her.

The thought made him chuckle dryly. What if he showed up with Helen? Imagining it gave him a childish glee that quickly morphed into sadness. He missed her; his life felt so strange without her in it.

The parking lot of the Wal-Mart on Crenshaw Boulevard was half full, the glass doors smashed so he could step right through. Ray pulled the silicone rubber skirt of his scuba mask tighter around his ears.

Even through the mask, the stink of rot and urine hit him almost immediately. The aisles were crowded with people laying frozen—their chests rising and falling—mixed with corpses. Ray wound a path through the bodies, down the main aisle perpendicular to the registers, toward the pharmacy. Everyone who was still alive followed Ray with their eyes as soon as he stepped into view, silently pleading for help. It made his skin crawl, all of those eyes staring at him.

The store was silent, save for voices over in the supermarket section.

"Excuse me," he whispered as he stepped over a teenaged girl who stared up at him, terrified. "I'm so sorry."

A young Indian woman in a pharmacy vest lay in front of the swinging half-door that led into the pharmacy area, so Ray climbed over the counter. The shelves were almost empty, boxes scattered on the floor. The young Indian pharmacist was dead, her skin a horrible, waxy gray. Ray tried to hurry, moving up and down the shelves, a finger extended as he read the labels.

The shelf above *Xanax* was empty. The same for *Klonopin, Valium, Atavan,* and the rest of the row. Cleaned out.

"Damn it," Ray hissed.

• • •

All of the pharmacies in the area were cleaned out. In hindsight it seemed obvious that would be the case. The first person who went inside for sedatives would take them all, because who knew when there would be more? Maybe there would never be more.

The thought rattled Ray. When the Internet was still up, some had been predicting ninety percent of the world's population would die off. Some estimates were even higher. What sort of world would be left?

Helen opened the door, eyebrows raised, as Ray climbed the front steps.

He shook his head. "Cleaned out. I went to every drug store in the area."

He wasn't prepared for her reaction. She sank to the floor, covered her face with her hands, and wept. Ray squatted beside her, rubbed her shoulder.

"We'll find some. Maybe we can find a drug dealer, or a black market."

Helen shoved him away, hard. "*Where?* Where would we find a black market in the middle of *this?*" She wiped under her eyes. "I'll just have to drink more." She nodded. "I'll just have to drink more." She looked at her watch. "In fact, it's almost noon and I haven't started yet. Time to get going."

In her autobiography, Helen had described the alcoholic years after *Batgirl* was cancelled in great detail. It hadn't been pretty. "Don't do that." He thought for minute. Where could he get sedatives?

Then it hit him. He stood. "This is Beverly Hills. Every other house on this street probably has Xanax in the medicine cabinet. I'll go door to door. I'll break into the houses where no one answers."

Helen nodded, still wiping her eyes. She struggled to her feet, weaving as if they were on the deck of a ship. "God, I'm so sorry. I was such a sweet girl, before I moved to LA. Before *Batgirl*." Her gray eyes were bright with tears. "The fame does something to you. Even the little bit I had; it burned a hole right through me. All the actors I know who made it are fucked up beyond belief. None of them made it through whole."

She stepped close to Ray; he instinctively wrapped his arms around her. She pressed close, resting her cheek on his shoulder, her hands against his chest. Her breath was sour with last night's tequila, but to Ray it was the sweetest perfume. He closed his eyes, reveled in her warmth.

When her lips touched his, he was so startled he flinched.

"I'm sorry, I didn't—" Helen said.

Ray leaned in and kissed her back.

Helen turned her head aside, whispered, "Make love to me. I want to be touched. I want to feel normal for a little while."

• • •

Back in high school, when *Batgirl* was a popular prime time TV show, Ray had read *A Tale of Two Cities* in English class. Mr. Patel made a big deal out of the opening line of the novel, and that line was the only thing Ray remembered about the book. The line was: *It was the best of times, it was the worst of times.* Laying in Helen Anderson's bed, with her sleeping beside him, that line was a perfect description of how Ray felt.

He couldn't shake a tinge of guilt, as if he were cheating on Eileen. That guilt was pillowed by a soaring sense of joy; sparks of awe, magic, and wonder as he studied Helen's sleeping profile in the early morning light. That joy was wrapped in a ball of terror and dread, as the reality of what lay outside Helen's front door crept along in the back of Ray's mind. They hadn't been outside in five days, but the radio reports were enough. His terror looped right back to concern for Eileen. She'd cheated on him, she'd left him, but part of him still loved her, still worried.

Helen opened one eye. "Stop staring," she sang sleepily.

"Sorry." He lay back and stared up at the ceiling, thinking about Eileen. Odds were she had it by now. The thought rattled Ray, but in the last radio report, between seventy and eighty percent of Los Angeles residents had the disease, so yes, there was a good chance his wife was frozen, was dying. Maybe she and Justin both had it.

"What's the matter?" Helen asked.

Ray looked at her, questioning, then realized there was a tear on his cheek. He wiped it with the back of his hand. "I was just thinking about my wife. My ex-wife, I guess. I was wondering how she's doing, whether she's . . . you know."

Helen put a hand on his arm. "You're a good soul. I have a grown son in Houston, and all I'm thinking about is how to get more Xanax."

Ray reached up, took her hand in his. "You've done a lot of good in the world."

Helen laughed harshly. "Yeah. I was in a bad TV show."

"It wasn't bad, and anyway, that's not what I'm talking about. What about all the money you raised for autism research?"

Helen sighed, shook her head, but didn't argue.

"I can't stand the thought that Eileen might be like these people. All alone. Dying." He rose up on his elbow. "Would you mind if I . . ."

Helen stiffened. "You want to go to her?"

"Just to make sure she's all right."

"And what if she isn't? Will you stay with her?"

Ray hadn't thought that far ahead. "I'm staying with you. If that's what you want."

"Of course it's what I want. You're my guardian angel, remember?" She leaned over and kissed his nose. "If I was married and my husband ditched me while this hell was breaking loose, he could be bleeding to death on my doorstep and I wouldn't bring him a Band-Aid." She gave a little one-shouldered shrug. "But that's just me."

Ray wished he could feel that way; it was all Eileen deserved. But he couldn't. They'd spent twenty-two years together, and even if the in-jokes and silly banter had faded over the last five, they'd always watched out for each other. The more he thought about it, the more urgently he needed to check on her.

He turned and kissed Helen. "I'll be back in two hours. Three at the most."

"Would—" she paused. "Can I come with you?"

She was safer inside, but Ray could see this meant a lot to her. It meant they were together, not two strangers waiting out a storm together.

• • •

There were bodies everywhere. In the street, on sidewalks, on lawns, in driveways. In cars, both parked and wrecked.

Ray hit the brake as a teenaged boy lurched out from behind a delivery truck, right in front of the car. The boy's arms were raised, his head nodding, eyes wild with terror.

"I'm sorry," Ray shouted through the raised windows. "There's nothing we can do. I'm so sorry." He inched the car forward. "Please, get out of our way. Move, please." The boy set his hands on the hood of Helen's Prius, opened his mouth, trying to speak. With each jerk of his head he began to sink, his legs freezing up. Ray turned to look behind him, backed up until the boy slid to the street. He steered around him.

Helen had her hands over her eyes. "This is terrible. These poor people."

"Why are there so many in the streets?" Ray asked as he steered around a woman in a bathrobe. He was fairly sure she was still breathing, but he avoided looking at her as he passed. He didn't want to see her eyes tracking them.

"They don't want to die alone," Helen said, her voice slurred. She'd gone through half of the tequila bottle since they'd left her house. There were tears on her cheeks. "Once they start nodding, they're not afraid to catch it any longer, they're afraid to be alone, with no one to help them. So they run outside."

Head down, Helen held her hands on either side of her eyes to shield her from picking up glimpses of the accident victims in her peripheral vision as Ray inched along. He wished he could look away as well.

Helen shook two Xanax into her hand and washed them down with tequila. He'd have to locate more pills before too long.

As he turned onto Walter's street, he spotted a boy standing on a lawn, a baseball mitt on one hand. Ray slowed. The boy just stood there.

"Christ. Look at that." Helen pointed out her window at a man clutching a push lawn mower, one foot back as if he were walking. Only he wasn't walking.

On the lawn beyond, Ray spotted two older people sitting on a stoop. Across the street a man stood beside his car, a garden hose in one hand, the nozzle pointing at his truck as if he was washing it. No water came from the hose.

As they passed Walter's house, Ray expected to see Walter sitting frozen beside Lauren on their porch, but Lauren was alone.

Ray drove on. "Someone *posed* those people," he said. It was like an elaborate art exhibit, a still-life of Saturday in the neighborhood. Back when the nodding virus was nothing but an item on the evening news, one of the early reports had a doctor demonstrating how victims of the virus would stay in any position you put them in, like living mannequins. When you were infected, your muscles worked just fine; you just couldn't tell them what to do.

"This is horrible," Helen said.

"It is."

They passed a woman with short red hair kneeling over a flower bed; Ray flinched, certain for an instant it was Eileen, but they were still two blocks from their house.

Eileen's minivan was in the driveway. Ray pulled in behind it, his heart racing.

It felt strange to knock on his own door, but he did.

The door swung open. Eileen took him in, recognizing him instantly, even wearing a surgical mask. She seemed surprised, but maybe not overly-so. As she pushed the screen door open she noticed Helen, and froze. She studied Helen, her eyebrows clenched in confusion.

"What is this?" she finally asked.

Ray grasped the screen door, opened it the rest of the way. "I came to make sure you're all right."

"Is that *Batgirl?*" There was a familiar hint of disdain in her tone. "What is this?"

Helen stepped toward the doorway, stumbled, caught the door jamb to keep from falling. "No. It's not fucking Batgirl. My name is Helen Anderson."

Eileen recoiled.

"Oops," Helen said. "Seems I've had a bit too much to drink. Or not enough. Opinions vary."

Eileen looked up at Ray, wide-eyed, confused.

"Are you all right? If so, we'll leave you alone." Ray caught a glimpse into the living room. Justin was sitting on the couch, perfectly still.

"Am I all right? Let's see." Eileen looked up. "I'd have to say no. But thanks for asking. I'd invite you in, but that wouldn't be a good idea. In fact even with those masks it's probably not a good idea for you to be talking to—" She trailed off, let the breath bleed slowly out of her in a long sigh.

She was looking at Helen, surprised anew at Helen's presence, in the flesh, at her door. It did take some getting used to.

Was she bothered by Helen being here with Ray? All of Ray's petty revenge fantasies had melted away at the sight of Justin. Eileen had been exposed; unless she was one of the two or three percent of people who were naturally immune to the virus, she was going to catch it, too.

Eileen went on looking at Helen, who was clinging to the door jamb, trying to remain upright, her shoulder length golden blonde hair rising and falling with each nod of her head.

"Oh, Helen," Ray whispered. He grasped her shoulders, gently turned her to face him.

Her face was stiff, her lips pulled back in terror. "My Xanax. Keep giving me my Xanax. Please."

Ray put his arms around her. "I will. I'll take good care of you. I promise. I'm so sorry."

The last words she spoke came out garbled, but Ray understood. "Thank you. My guardian. Angel."

"Bring her in." Eileen held the screen door open.

Ray led Helen inside, put her in the big chair he'd always sat in when they watched TV. He knelt beside her for a long time, patting her knee, whispering whatever soothing words came to him as he cried.

It was ironic, that Helen had gotten sick here of all places. He would carry her to the car and take her home at some point, but for the moment his only concern was making her as comfortable as possible.

Eventually Helen's nodding slowed, then stopped, and she was still.

Ray stood, brushed her hair back into place.

He turned, and the first thing he saw was Justin on the couch, his hands in his lap.

Ray nodded to him. "Justin." He was going to leave it at that—a polite acknowledgment and nothing more, but even Justin deserved more, given the circumstances. "I'm sorry."

Eileen handed him a glass of ginger ale. "If I get it before you, I want to be outside, in the backyard. Would you do that for me?"

"Of course."

Eileen turned to look at Helen. "I'm happy for you. I was afraid you were going through this all alone. The thought of it just about killed me."

"I appreciate that." Ray was glad to be leaving things on good terms with Eileen, but offered nothing more. Helen was right there in the room, and she was in hell right now.

"Thank you for coming to check on me. You're a good man." She nodded. "You deserved better than me. And you found her, in the end."

Ray nodded. He felt uncomfortable talking about this with Eileen; he cast about the room, looking for a way to change the subject.

A wonderful idea came to him. He went to Helen, lifted her. "I want to show you something."

He carried her into his collectibles room, turned three hundred sixty degrees so she could see everything, then set her in the recliner. It was the only seat in the room, so Ray stood.

"I know you're ambivalent about *Batgirl*. I wish you weren't. I wish you could feel proud of what you did."

Ray surveyed the objects in the room, seeing children's toys. Brightly-colored junk.

"This makes me look pretty obsessive, doesn't it?" He rested a hand on Helen's shoulder, hoping it was reassuring to feel someone's touch, hoping she wasn't cringing inside. "I'm sorry. I shouldn't have shown you this."

"Let me get you some water." He went to the kitchen to get some ice water, gave Eileen, who was sitting on the couch beside Justin, what he hoped was a comforting smile as he passed.

He found straws in the back of the pantry. Then he remembered: Xanax. It was the one thing Helen had asked him to do for her. Her purse was on the front stoop, where she must have dropped it.

"Here you go." He slid a Xanax tablet onto her tongue, put the straw in her mouth. Her lips closed on it, her mouth suddenly coming alive. She drank three hard pulls, then went still again. It was a frightening reminder that she was still completely alert, able to respond, even though her nervous system wasn't allowing her to initiate any movements of her own.

What must it be like? How did it feel? A sour dread ran through Ray as he realized he might find out for himself. With every hour that ticked by, it grew a little more likely that he was one of the very lucky few, but there was no guarantee.

"Ray," Eileen screamed from the living room.

Ray flinched at the urgency in her voice. "I'll be right back."

Eileen's head was bobbing, her tight red curls bouncing. Ray hurried over, knelt and took her hand.

"My poor Eileen. I'm sorry. I'm so sorry." He kissed her hand. Justin watched him, probably jealous as Ray comforted his estranged wife.

"I'll be right back." He set Eileen's hand in her lap, and went to get Helen. It would be simpler if they were all in the same room. Ray had read about caring for victims of the nodding virus; soon he'd be changing wet and soiled clothes—even Justin's.

From her position in the recliner, the only way to lift Helen was to take her wrists and draw her forward until she fell into his arms. With her face pressed into his shoulder he carried her back to his TV chair, cradled the back of her head as he set her into it.

When she was settled, he kissed her cheek.

Straightening, he surveyed his silent charges. All of their eyes were on him. As he took a few steps, their eyes followed.

He wanted to say something, but found himself at a loss. What could he say to an audience of his ex-wife, her lover, and his newfound love? There were things he'd like to say to each of them individually, but nothing he wanted to say to all of them together.

Eileen had asked to be outside. In the week he'd spent at Helen's house, she'd spent a good deal of time in her backyard, so he guessed she would like that as well. He couldn't care less what Justin liked.

One by one, he carried them out to the padded lawn chairs on the back patio.

Justin had wet himself, so first Ray had to change him. He did his best to mask his disgust as he tugged off Justin's wet underpants.

It was a nice day, with a light breeze, the sun occasionally eclipsed by clouds. Ray sat beside Helen, trying to ignore his pounding heart, his sweaty palms. If he developed the virus there would be no one to take care of them.

"I'm not much of a cook," he said aloud, mostly because the silence made him feel terribly alone, reminded him that most everyone on Earth was either dead or dying. "I guess since all we have to eat is canned food, that doesn't matter."

He'd positioned Helen with her hands and elbows resting on the arms of her chair, as if she was about to spring into action.

For a moment, against all logic, it looked as if Helen *was* springing into action. Then Ray realized she wasn't moving—he was. His neck was.

As his heart pounded wildly, he willed himself to face this bravely. "I have it. I guess we all knew it was only a matter of time." He lifted his gaze to Eileen, struggling to keep his eyes on her as his head bobbed violently. "Eileen, we had twenty-two good years. I'm grateful for those."

Then he turned to Helen, tried to chuckle, but it came out as a gargling choke. "I've only known you for a week, Helen, but I—" He was going to say he would never forget it, but he was going to be dead in a few days. He was going to sit there until he died of thirst, but first he would have to watch Eileen and Helen die.

His chest hitched as his heart found another gear. All along, he thought he'd been facing the truth head-on, but deep down he'd always believed he'd be one of the lucky three percent.

"Shit." The words were garbled beyond recognition.

Soon the nodding slowed, and stopped, and Ray was still.

He'd made a mistake, sitting beside Helen. He couldn't look at her. Out of the corner of his eye he could see the merest shadow of her profile. That was all.

A fly landed on his hand. Its legs flitted along on his skin, and he felt it as acutely as ever, but he couldn't move his hand, not even the slightest flinch to shoo it away. His chest rose and fell, rose and fell; he couldn't speed up his breathing or slow it down, couldn't take a deeper or shallower breath.

A wave of claustrophobic terror hit him; he wanted to scream, to flail his arms, to run from this silent lawn party, but his body remained perfectly still, breathed in and out.

Eileen was watching him. He gazed back at her. What was she thinking? Did she regret her affair with Justin? Was she wishing it was just the two of them here? She looked up, maybe into the branches of the palm trees deeper in their backyard, or maybe watching a bird fly by, envying its freedom.

He looked to his left, toward Helen, straining to see as much of her as possible, but still saw only a ghostly outline. She was there, though. If he had to die in this terrible way, in his wildest dreams, he couldn't have guessed he would die beside Batgirl.

He clung to that thought—for courage, to dull the sting of dread. Helen wasn't at all the person he'd thought she was, and maybe that shouldn't have been a surprise. No one was Batgirl, after all.

• • •

The spreading, burning warmth of urine was a shock. Ray felt slightly ashamed.

It was getting dark. Soon they'd be sitting under the stars. He was afraid of what he might dream.

Eileen was looking at him again. There was something she wanted to say to him, something that had occurred to her since she became frozen and had nothing but time to think. Or maybe it was his imagination.

She looked away, over Ray's shoulder; her gaze held steady, just a bit to his right.

"Oh hell. I was hoping you made it." Walter stepped into view, stopped a few feet in front of Ray. "I'm so sorry, Ray." He wiped a tear from his cheek.

When Walter noticed Helen, his brow creased. "My God." He took a step toward Helen, studied her face. "Unbelievable. Jesus, Ray, I wish you could tell me the story." Folding his arms, he looked from Helen to Ray, then turned and looked at Eileen. "Maybe I can figure it out for myself."

Ray strained against the prison of his paralysis, willing his jaw to open.

"I guess I'm one of the 'lucky ones.'" Walter grunted. "I know I shouldn't be feeling sorry for myself. I know what you're all going through is much worse. But I'm not feeling very lucky right now. I think I'd rather be dead than see everyone I know suffer like this." He put his hand over his mouth as a sob escaped him.

"Here." He went over to Ray, slid his arms under Ray's armpits and lifted him to his feet. When Walter let go, Ray was sure he would flop back into the lawn chair, but he didn't; his leg muscles flexed and held, keeping him upright.

Walter lifted Helen from her chair, led her across the lawn toward Ray. She moved as if there was absolutely nothing wrong with her. The easy grace of her steps was astonishing.

Walter stopped Helen in front of Ray. He lifted her right hand, put it on Ray's shoulder, then took her left hand, raised it high and laced it into Ray's.

"It's all I can think to do for everybody. I'm sixty-nine years old; I can't feed and change everyone on the street forever. I'm not sure you'd all want me to, even if I could." Sobbing, his nose running, Walter put Ray's left hand on Helen's hip. "There."

Walter attended to Eileen and Justin, setting them in an identical dancing pose.

Ray looked into his Batgirl's eyes. Her face was flat, expressionless, but he could see the pain in her eyes, the fear. Her Xanax was wearing off, the tequila as well.

Music rose from the screened porch. *Tears in Heaven.* Eric Clapton. From Eileen's *Blues Love Songs* CD. The music broke the weight of the silence, and unleashed a rush of memories in Ray. They'd played the CD constantly on their vacation road trip up Route 66, in 2005. Ray had bought it for Eileen when she was in the hospital with pneumonia earlier that same year.

Over Helen's shoulder, Eileen "danced" with Justin. Her eyes met Ray's, and again, Ray couldn't help feeling that Eileen was trying to tell him something.

Did she want to tell him she'd made a mistake, that she wished she was dancing with him?

I don't want this lie between us.

The words came to Ray so clearly it was as if Eileen was speaking them. She'd said them right after her confession. Ray had been too shocked and confused to register much of what she was saying at the time, but he remembered the words now.

I don't want this lie between us, she'd said, and then, *If you want me to leave right now, I will.* That was what she'd said, wasn't it? What he'd heard was, *I want to leave you right now. I want to face this with Justin, not with you. Will you let me off the hook? Will you let me go?* But that wasn't what she'd said. The words were important. If Eileen didn't want a lie between *us,* she'd still thought there *was* an us.

She hadn't wanted him to leave; she'd wanted him to forgive her. If he'd only put his arms around her and told her that he still loved her, they'd be dancing together now, without Justin, without Helen. Helen was a kind and wonderful woman even if she didn't realize it, but she wasn't his Batgirl.

Ray tried to answer Eileen. He tried to tell her he forgave her, he loved her, that he understood it all now and wished he hadn't pushed her away. He tried to say all of this with his eyes, and could only hope it was reaching her, as night fell, and *Tears in Heaven* gave way to *I'll Take Care of You.*

BY THE HAIR OF THE MOON

Jamie Ford

May 1910

Dorothy Moy stared at the silver dime in her palm for five solid minutes. She touched the tiny inscription, the word LIBERTY, with her soiled fingertips, debating whether or not to spend her last ten cents on a taste of *yen shee,* or on a jitney cab ride to take her as far away from here as possible. Her mouth watered while she debated, as she dreamed of chewing that ball of resin, savoring the dottle scraped out of the bottom of an opium pipe. She came here to kick the gong around but hadn't been outside for more than a week. She'd barely been upright all that time and now the morning—at least she thought it was morning—seemed bleak, hopeless, even before she discovered, through a moment of sobriety, that the world was ending all around her.

"Diezen?" She asked the female attendant as she sensed the building gently rocking. Then she heard a muffled booming, like the sound of distant thunder. The Black Candle Inn was little more than a basement warren, thirty feet below the streets of Seattle's Chinatown, hidden in the center of the newly built Milwaukee Hotel.

"Not an earthquake. It's okay. Probably just the passenger Zephyr rolling by or a freight train," the attendant said as she twirled a slender punk, causing the burning joss stick to flare so she could light the pipes of patrons, nursing their flames back to life.

Dorothy could have sworn the building was rocking.

The gentle sway reminded her of her journey to the US: forty-five days in the frigid hold of a merchant airship, packed with sixty other girls. They'd fed her hard-tack, laced with pure *yapian* to suppress her appetite and ward off dirigible sickness, but even then she knew the opium was being used to build invisible chains, binding servants to their masters. But she also knew that she was one of the lucky ones. The others—the picture brides—sat motionless, their feet confined to lotus boxes. The new contraptions would break and bind the girls' feet en route, with a single turn of its iron gears each day. Dorothy remembered marveling at the acupuncturist, a man with a long gray beard who numbed the girls' pain with tiny copper needles carefully placed along their legs, arms, face, and hands. The needles were then wired to an electric generator powered by the *Lash of St. Francis,* the seasonal trade winds of the North Pacific Ocean.

Dorothy had nearly dozed off again when she heard a crashing noise. That's when she realized the tremors weren't caused by the delicious, black tar vapors wearing off. Instead, the ground was indeed shaking, lurching violently. The building began roaring, as dust fell from the ceiling in the windowless room and the smoke-stained walls erupted into a jigsaw of splintering, cracking, falling plaster. A roar, a guttural wave of subterranean sound, muffled the screaming of men and women from the gambling room upstairs—choking, gagging sounds, ivory mahjong tiles and bodies falling to the floor.

In a waning moment of opiate-induced splendor, lingering like the warmth of a goodbye kiss, Dorothy closed her eyes and tried to imagine that the rocking, swaying, was her *Nai Nai* holding her. Her grandmother, like most descendants of China's fallen Celestial Empire, had called the great comet the *Broom Star.*

The Seattle Times had renamed the astral visitor the *Sidereal Tramp.* Dorothy had also read that Edmond Halley, in a moment of colonial hubris, initially named the comet after himself, as though ship's captains hadn't been periodically led off course by that wandering light in the sky for the last four thousand years. As if planting a flag that bore a genteel name, one reflecting the teetotaling civility of Britannia could assuage the fact that the Broom Star's long tail was made of mercury cyanide and could sweep the Earth clean of all life.

Dorothy blinked as the drugs wore off. She rubbed swollen, bloodshot eyes, and saw that no one else in the dimly lit smoking parlor seemed to notice the calamity, except the attendant who had crawled beneath one of the heavy wooden bunks. The rest of the men and women—the patrons—were fast asleep, smiling euphorically as fist-sized chunks of the ceiling rained down around them. A handful lay on their sides, still amiably puffing away, even as their pates rocked back and forth on their wooden headrests.

Dorothy wanted to stay, to spend the last of her money on one more sweet breath of sugary splendor. But she was knocked to her hands and knees, then flat on her stomach. Her dime skittered away, down a rift in the floor, as the room seemed to move, jolting two feet to the north and then buckling three feet to the southwest. Dorothy covered her head as she heard the crashing of copper spittoons all around her. Tins of *Pilus Lunares,* sounding like the plucked strings of a zither as the cans bounced, pinging off the wooden floor, spilling their contents, balls of fine British opium mixed with silver nitrate, camphor and musk which pharmacists had dubbed *Hair of the Moon.* Chemists had stopped trying to turn lead into gold. It was much more lucrative to turn poppies into vaporous whiffs of Heaven, even if the potent silver turned the user's skin to an ashen shade of blue.

Dorothy struggled to sit up while the building swayed. Then her nostrils flared as the dark, fuzzy lumps of opium caught fire amid burning slicks of peanut oil. The heating lamps and bowls had shattered on the ground and the shards of manganese looked like islands of purple glass in a lake of fire. The patrons—those still nursing their long copper pipes—closed their eyes as if this were the happiest moment in all their lives; in many ways, this strange, serene dream of theirs probably was. While those who slumbered kept smiling, even as their sackcloth clothing caught fire, hair, skin, and fatty tissue burning as they succumbed to a sleep that would last from this moment until the next visitation of the comet, when no one would be left to notice the return.

I'm only sixteen. I'm too young to die! Dorothy's panicked thoughts raced, sobering her intentions. Whenever she'd imagined dying she thought about her parents who were conscripted as dredgers and now were buried somewhere beneath Mount Rainier along with four hundred other mixed-breed workers who'd struggled for tailings in a played out silver mine. Now all she had left was her Nai Nai, and an assortment of calabash cousins that she knew of but never saw, like Darwin Chinn Qi, who worked as a servant at the Sorrento Hotel. She hadn't seen him in years. Not since she'd spurned him when they were ten years old and a matchmaker's I-Ching machine predicted that they would witness an important event and then eventually wed. Dorothy thought that meant they'd get pregnant and later married. So she ran away only to be caught by British colonials. The same company that later sold her entire village to a subsidiary in the Northwest where the children had been forbidden to marry, ever, and breeding would only be allowed for the purpose of replacing themselves in the servants' lottery.

So much for predictions, Dorothy thought as she crawled over warm bodies while the earthquake subsided and spreading orange flames licked at the walls.

She struggled to her feet in the entryway where two guards were dead but their bodies still warm, the moneychanger as well, his quad-abacus shattered, beads scattered everywhere along with dirty wads of folding money. Dorothy lifted the hem of her dress and gathered her petticoats, stuffing handfuls of cash into her underwear along with a packet of opium. Then she climbed another tall set of smoke-filled stairs, sliding back the bolt and opening the heavy door. She savored a rush of semi-fresh air.

Inside the chamber she found another doorman, his face swollen, mouth twisted in a rictus of pain. There was another, a middle-aged man, finely dressed—a Caucasian, with bluish skin, probably from comet pills, the preferred drug of the rich and powerful, slumped in a chair. She recognized him as one of the club and casino owners, by the familiar cleft in his chin that was now filled with a rivulet of blood from a self-inflicted gunshot wound to the forehead.

Most had ignored the prudent warnings of the Royal Hydrographic Office. They celebrated with comet parties, she thought. *Science to the rich was like the* I Ching *to the poor—only believed when favorable. Meanwhile others surrendered to their fears.*

When Dorothy finally reached the alleyway entrance, the door was open, jammed with fallen bodies. Half-naked men in silken robes and women in skin-tight cheongsam dresses made of brushed silver lamé, patinaed in jade, were clumped together and those who'd escaped to the alley didn't travel far. Dorothy stepped over their swollen bodies scattered like leaves, arms and legs akimbo. She sniffed the cool breeze, which smelled like almonds, chloroform, and seaweed, then covered her nose and mouth with a scarf.

When she stumbled out onto South Jackson, the street was a frieze of cadaverous statuary. More men, women, and children dead on the stoops of collapsed apartment buildings, seafood restaurants, and the headquarters of the Chong Wa Benevolent Association. Others perished at the wheel of their motorcars and roadsters, steam turbines still turned, spitting jets of water vapor into the air. An electric trolley had jumped the track, crushed a jinricksha, and careened though a storefront and into the Manila Dance Hall. The passengers slumped out of their seats; others lay strewn among the broken glass and smoking rubble. Dorothy noticed a team of draft horses, still in harness, pitched on their sides. Pools of froth leaked from their nostrils. The half-dozen cloned beasts had fallen in the same direction, their markings and brands lined up perfectly, their legs jutting out as orderly as a book of matches. Scores of lifeless gulls and carrier pigeons were sprinkled among the ruin as well and feathers slowly rained like confetti. Dorothy stared at the red paper messages still tied to the legs of the many pigeons. She didn't have to read them to know they were farewells and goodbyes, frenzied words hastily sent from the dying to their loved ones, who in all likelihood, where dead as well.

As she walked, Dorothy heard the sounds of buildings settling, fires raging, and the hissing of gaslights that had been shattered, their flames extinguished, and the babbling of an old Japanese man. She found the gent with light bluish skin as he leaned against a leaking fire hydrant. His head was bleeding and he was only wearing one shoe.

"We're alive, child. *Yokatta mada Ikiteru!* We're alive! The silver saved us."

Dorothy looked away as the old man coughed and hacked. She noticed her reflection in a puddle, the Hair of the Moon had turned her skin a rich shade of porcelain blue. Her week at the Black Candle had saved her from the poisonous fumes.

Then she heard the man sobbing, moaning in agony as they both realized that he'd coughed his teeth into his hands, blood dripping from the empty sockets.

Dorothy felt the Earth move again; the buildings shook; the street signs bobbed and spun, as a storm gust sucked the air from her lungs, toppled her to the ground and pin-wheeled her halfway down the block amid garbage cans, newspapers, take-out boxes, pine cones, dead rodents—all manners of detritus. The wind subsided as it flipped her up in a sitting position in the direction of Puget Sound and the Olympic Mountains. Her dress had been shredded, her hands and elbows skinned; her knees oozed blood and puss into her cottony slip, making the fabric wet and sticky.

As she waited for the stinging pain and dizziness to subside, she reckoned that this should be early morning, but the horizon looked as though a massive sun were rising in the west—a rich, orange, sulfurous glow thrumming beneath a horizon of dark smoke that stretched the length, width, and breadth of the sky as though they were looking up at an upside down field of black cotton.

And when the Earth stopped shaking again, Dorothy took stock of other survivors, slowly emerging from the ruins—cooks and gamblers, bankers and showgirls. They acknowledged each other with glances of shock and fear and reluctance, as they shambled down the middle of a vaguely familiar street Dorothy no longer recognized. She followed along, blending into the dozen or so strangers as they passed the still-smoking mountain of trains that had derailed and piled below the King Street Station, creating a logjam of metal and brick that smoldered like a volcano. And as they passed through Pioneer Square, the many creep joints and frolic pads had become a neon carnival of the dead. There were so many broken, splintered bodies that Dorothy hardly noticed them anymore. She merely adopted the mute language of her fellow refugees, walking in silence, some in their party clothes, others nearly naked, burned and bleeding. All of them had skin in variations of blue. They were alone, together, as they migrated down Cherry Street toward Coleman Dock.

It was there, at the edge of a collapsed pier that Dorothy felt her numbered days winding down, slowing like the second hand of a broken watch. Frozen, she stared out at a deep, sprawling canyon of mudflats that had once been filled with the waters of Puget Sound. The islands of Vashon and Bainbridge now looked like green mountaintops as the vast tendrils of the Pacific Ocean had been drained away, leaving a queer, puddled moonscape of rotting seaweed, dead fish, and the wreckage of freighters, still under American, British, and Canadian flags. The ships foundered on the seabed as the water had rushed away. One large frigate had wrenched itself in two, caught fire and burned as the crew had spilled out onto the mudflats where they died of the noxious fumes, half-frozen in quicksand. Other smaller vessels slowly sank into the silt as tremors shook the landscape again and buried their hulls in fetid mudslides. To the south, on what once had been the prosperous tidal flats, a platoon of mechanized canners stood lifeless. Dorothy could see the bodies of their operators pitched forward within the metal skeletons, their long diggers extended into the sand, searching. She wondered if the clams and oysters would still be alive. Or the trees, the plants, edible crops—how long could they survive in the wake of the Broom Star?

As she turned around she noticed a wealthy couple. She could tell by the finery of their clothing, their noble, confident gait, the air of importance even as they walked around the wreckage, arm-in-arm, beneath a pair of matching silver gas masks. The woman spun her tinsel-fringed parasol and the man tipped his felt bowler hat to the blue-skinned crowd as if this were just another lovely Sunday afternoon.

Dorothy backed away when she saw the anger in the faces of the other survivors. She ran back toward Chinatown and heard screams as the crowd descended upon the couple like dogs on a sick, lame deer. Years of rage from generations of servitude had been unleashed. The affluent strollers must have emerged proudly from a generously built comet shelter, armed with the dull axe of wealth, a blunt instrument now. Their money and social standing was inert, useless at the end of the world.

When the Earth shook again, stronger than before, this time for a long minute, which stretched out like an hour, Dorothy crouched next to an overturned brewers wagon, sheltered by a copper cask the size of a bank vault. She cried into her fists, determined to see her Nai Nai one last time before the world ended. But even that familial notion seemed like a hopeless wish as she watched the Hayes & Hayes Bank building explode.

A gas main must have erupted.

When the tremors subsided, she ran away from the heat. She was four blocks away when she heard the terrifying reverberation of the Earth opening its maw as a chasm of flame swallowed what remained of the six-story building.

Ten minutes and many haggard breaths later, she arrived on the far side of the International District and the Asian Housing Zone, Dorothy found her Nai Nai where she'd last seen her—in the mixed-roots cemetery next to a potter's field.

Dorothy stared at the toppled forest of slender Buddhist headstones. The carved granite obelisks that once stood virtually shoulder-to-shoulder had all fallen, or cracked, or both. Dorothy felt bad for irreverently stepping on so many graves, but was relieved—comforted even, to find her Nai Nai's headstone in once piece. She embraced the cold grave marker and felt the vibrations of the Earth through the stone, slow and rhythmic, like a metronome.

Then the cemetery lit up as lighting flashed deep within the dark clouds rotating on the western horizon. The billowing haze spun into tornadoes that reached down with long twisted fingers, probing, searching, and wending their way across the horizon, creeping as though ready to pick the bones of the ruination of Seattle.

Dorothy watched numbly, helplessly, as a fleet of zeppelins was pulled toward the maelstrom. Their concrete anchors tore through the wrecked remains of the waterfront and the massive blimps were swallowed whole, disappearing into the spinning clouds.

"I don't have much time, Nai Nai," Dorothy cried above wind and the sporadic spotting of hailstones that were the size of the opium balls she'd been smoking, the ones that had briefly extended, if not saved, her life.

"I think I'll be seeing you soon, wherever you are." Dorothy imagined herself sucked into the sky along with her grandmother's ashes.

That's when she noticed the inscription on her grandmother's headstone—her Nai Nai's favorite quote from the *I Ching*. She touched the ornate Chinese characters.

It is only when we have the courage to face things exactly as they are, without any self-deception or illusion, that a light will develop out of events, by which the path to success may be recognized.

She heard a thick, European accent shout, "I see one!" and looked around. A block away there was a gathering of men, five or six in soiled fox hunting garb. "She's skulking in the graveyard. And she's ripe. Blue for the taking!"

"Thank Heavens," a man said, "It's only right that God favors the just."

Dorothy stood up, confounded by their words, shocked to see their mouths, their suit collars mottled with what could only be the rusty, clotted crimson of human stain. That's when she surmised that they weren't looking for stragglers to rescue. They wanted the silver in her blood. They must have been seen the blue-hued survivors and decided that drinking their cruor was the only way to stave off the effects of the comet's poison.

"Careful, you'll spook her." Another man said as the group spread out and crept toward her, "We don't have much time to find shelter from the storm."

Dorothy remembered her Nai Nai—the message on her grandmother's grave, the *I Ching* and the fateful prediction that she and her cousin would witness an event and later marry. If the *I Ching* were true, then *this* was the event, the end of the world. And she'd see Darwin again, whether she wanted to or not; her life was destined, preordained, fated. But only if she had the courage to face things exactly as they are, these men—these savages who wanted to take her blood, and make it through the storm, which was disassembling the city, block by block, sucking brick and mortar into the sky.

But she had a chance, didn't she? She had a glimmer of hope, along with a hidden packet of blue silver opium—the last *Pilus Lunares*. She'd find Darwin, alive, and she'd keep him alive. She'd save him if she could, by the hair of the moon.

TO WRESTLE NOT AGAINST FLESH AND BLOOD

Desirina Boskovich

They said the world would end on Friday. The next moment we'd all be on Planet X, which was like heaven, but in real life.

In Missouri it was supposed to happen at exactly four o'clock. We gathered 'round the living room with the shades down and the lights off, watching the TV and praying while we waited to disappear. It was me, and Jane, and Larry, and Tim. Plus Sylvie, who was crying all the time now. And Dad, of course. Mom had been enforced.

Eventually the TV turned to static as the last station went off the air. We turned it down low and waited some more.

3:55. 3:58. 3:59.

Nothing happened.

4:01. 4:02. 4:05.

Nothing at all.

Larry got up first and peeked out the blinds. That was Larry for you: always curious, always wanting to know. "There's people," he said. "Runnin' around."

Dad went to the gun cabinet and took out two double-barreled shotguns. One for him, one for me—I was fifteen, old enough to drive, and old enough to shoot, even as a girl. "Can I have one?" Jane asked, but he shook his head. She was only twelve.

At 4:25 the TV picture came back, and every channel was the President, saying: "My fellow Americans . . . We were tricked."

Apparently, like Dad, the government had had their suspicions. What if the aliens were con men, liars, cheats, and fakes? NASA, the Pentagon, the CIA—they'd reached out to others, through secret channels, the President said. They'd refused to be victims. They'd made other plans.

"We are bruised, but not beaten," he declared. "Damaged, but not defeated. Now, we must go to war against the alien invaders. We must defend not just our country, but our planet. I stand here today—and I beg you—from the bottom of my heart: Stand with me. We must—we will—*we will* stand together. God bless the United States of America!"

My father cursed and turned off the set. "Aliens," he said. "Bullshit. I knew it all along." He turned on me, sharp and harsh. "Annette. Can you *please* get your sister to stop that damn crying? I've got to make some calls."

"Okay," I said. I put down the shotgun and picked up Sylvie. "Come on, sweetie. Let's take a nap."

• • •

When I came downstairs a bunch of men were sitting around the dining room table.

I listened to them whisper. They were saying what dad had said all along: that it was a vast conspiracy, the scientists and the government and the people on the news. They wanted to impose a one-world government, install martial law, confiscate our guns. "A war on the free-minded," they called it, but actually there weren't so many free-minded left. They'd all been enforced.

Mom had been free-minded. That's why she was gone.

People kept coming to the door with stories to tell: Smashed cars scattered across the intersections. Fistfights in the streets. Gas stations run dry. City blocks aflame. Supermarkets with their windows bashed in and their shelves stark empty, three customers brawling over the last frozen ham.

And enforcers being chased down, beaten, and shot.

Jane stood behind me, listening in. She was twelve and thought she was awfully grownup, but she didn't need to hear all that. "Come help me fix supper," I said.

Supper was just sandwiches, a selection of bologna on white bread and PB&J. We were carrying the platters to the table, when someone outside started beating on the door, hammering the bell, screaming for help.

Dad looked around. "Anyone expectin' someone? 'Cause by my count that's everybody." He went to the window by the door and peeked around the shades. "It's Don."

Don went to our church, before he'd become an enforcer. No one had spoken to him since.

Jane and I set the chips and sandwiches on the table. "Go get the soda," I told her.

"You do it," she said.

Dad opened the front door a crack, the chain still up. "What do you want?" he demanded.

"Please," Don said, crying. "I heard people were meeting here. I'm begging you. Just let me in. They're going to kill me."

"Sorry," Dad said, not sorry at all.

"But what about forgiveness?" Don pleaded. It was so quiet around the table you could hear our stomachs gurgling, but outside the door sounded the roar of building chaos: yelling crowds, screaming sirens, squealing tires, and the constant crackle-pop of guns going off. "What about mercy? What about fellowship? What about turning the other cheek?"

"What about it?" Dad said, and slammed the door in Don's face.

Don shrieked and the mob howled and we heard tussling and scraping and something hard thudding against the door. A shot rang out, then another.

My brother began to move toward the curtains. "Larry," my dad said, in a dangerous voice, "Don't you *dare* look out that window." Then he returned to the table. "Now. Where were we?"

They scarfed down the sandwiches and planned a war.

Later, when no one was watching, I peeked outside the window. I saw Don, or what was left of Don—a pile of torn clothes and leaking body fluids and splattered brain matter and a lake of blood—and a broken casserole dish, tuna noodles and busted glass mixed together with all the human gore.

That night they boarded up the windows.

When bedtime came, Jane and I took the kids upstairs. Jane led the prayers, but even after she said "Amen," she continued to pray in silence, her hands folded and her eyes closed, her face turned toward the window and the night sky. I sat with her until the waxing crescent moon rose high and bright.

• • •

By the next morning the power was out, but our generator was on. Later that day the President got on TV and declared martial law, just like Dad had predicted.

Soon the army tanks were rolling down the streets, the soldiers waving, while people came out of their houses to clap and cry and wave the flag. Everyone was mad as hell; everyone was ready for war.

At our house more guys arrived all the time. Soon we had a dozen people living at our house ’round the clock and another dozen coming in and out, all hours of the day. I wanted to listen to the war plans, but I had to spend all my time cooking, doing the dishes, washing the towels and sheets. I made Larry help me, though he complained the whole time. Jane had an entire nursery going upstairs now with the motherless babies and toddlers that other widowed fathers had brought along.

I folded the laundry and watched the news. It was all overheated talk shows, playing and replaying the blurry footage of the aliens landing in Siberia or Greenland, setting up a massive camp.

“Can’t we shoot them down?” demanded one panelist. “That’s what I want to know. We have the capabilities, right? The most powerful military in the entire world. Maybe the universe, I don’t know. Is the entire Air Force asleep at the wheel?”

“Nuke them from orbit, right.”

“Annette,” my father called. “We’re all starving. Can you put something together?”

“Yes, sir,” I said.

“And turn that garbage off. You know it’s all a bunch of lies.”

“Yes, sir,” I said.

Typical: It was the end of the world and not only did I have to spend it waiting on everybody, I wasn’t even allowed to watch TV.

• • •

Everything was different with Mom gone.

It wasn’t about the practical stuff. I’d always helped with all of that. It was about the *purpose*. Because Mom always believed, and though the God of her faith was vengeful and cruel, He was always there. Her belief had gotten us through the past couple weeks when everything else began to crumble.

The schism at church happened as soon as the aliens arrived. Half the congregation believed this was false prophesy; there was no god but God, no heaven but His Kingdom, and Planet X was just another end-times distraction, sent to tempt.

The other half believed this might be God, working in His own mysterious way; He was the author of every force in the universe, and no one could understand the working of his hands. So they wanted to pray, and proselytize, and convert as many souls as they could, before the final day.

Of course, this was against alien orders; the aliens had commanded that everyone continue about their business as usual, no special preparations for the apocalypse, and certainly no last ditch efforts to save the world. They’d made one of every thousand people become an enforcer and punish violations. The punishment was instant execution. The punishment for refusing to be an enforcer was also instant execution.

Mom and Dad fought a lot that week, because he didn't want her to die. "But the Lord has called us," she patiently explained.

"Can't He call someone else? For a change?"

They enforced her on Thursday, hand in hand with other martyrs as they prayed beneath the steeple.

We used to be homeschooled, before all this started. Now, Jane wanted to continue the lessons. "I'll just start where we left off," she said, but every time I went to check on them, they were listening to radio preachers and studying the Bible.

• • •

We'd been stockpiling food for a long time, in case the end of the world happened. Then, luckily, it actually did, so all that rice and creamed corn wouldn't have to go to waste.

I expected the pantry stores to last a long time. But with the people coming in and out, making war plans and gobbling down all the stew, our food was gone in less than a week. Everyone kept saying the grocery stores were cleaned out, but somehow we'd have to find something to eat.

I went down to the basement and tried to get some help, but they were all busy and distracted, arguing over a pile of illegally encrypted two-way radios and a stack of hand-drawn maps, telling each other to shush so they could hear the news from Joplin, another rebel cell. Someone paused long enough to tell me they'd passed a ration station, just a mile down the road. So I grabbed a .22 pistol, tucked it in my purse, and set out on my own.

I hadn't been outside in a while. The whole neighborhood looked pretty bad. There were cars stranded in the street where they'd run out of gas, after thieves had come in the night to siphon it away. There was trash everywhere, battered furniture, shell casings, burned siding, broken glass.

A neighbor girl stopped me three doors down. She stood in the doorway with her baby on her hip, waving frantically and calling my name.

"Nicole," I called. "Are you okay?" My parents never let me talk to her; they said she'd be a bad influence.

"Yeah," she called back. "But we don't got no food in the house and James went out three days ago to get some and he never came back, and I'm starving and the baby won't quit crying. I'm so scared and I dunno what to do."

"You can come with me. I'm looking for food."

"Scared to come outside," she said.

"It's okay. I got a gun." I showed her the pistol in my purse, and we set out toward the corner where they said the ration station would be.

"They steal your gas?" Nicole asked, bouncing her baby a bit.

"We siphoned it off for the generator," I said, before I thought.

"Generator. So you still got lights and stuff."

"Yeah. They boarded up the windows so nobody would know."

"Smart," she said. Then she started crying. "I'm so glad you came outside," she said. "I saw what they did to that guy standing on your doorstep. And the fires, and the fights, and the soldiers came through on tanks and hauled a whole bunch of people off. Then James boarded up our windows, and he disappeared. I guess they got him, too."

"It's all right," I said, awkwardly patting her shoulder. "That guy on the steps was an enforcer. I'm sure they didn't do that to James."

"Maybe they just killed him. Because they wanted our food."

This did seem kind of likely, so I didn't know what else to say.

We reached the main road, and saw a group of people coming our way, eight or nine of them. They skipped along the yellow stripe, singing and clapping and shaking a tambourine, laughing like babies. They carried flowers and wore flowers in their hair . . . and those flowers were *all* they wore.

"What's up with that?" I asked, but Nicole didn't know.

"Hey!" I called out. "Whatcha doin'?" They didn't seem to notice. We watched as they jiggled past in the nude.

An older woman followed a few paces behind them, dressed in normal clothes. Instead of flowers she carried a large stick.

"Oh, hello," she said. "I'm Ruth. Don't I know you girls?"

She lived down the street from us, but my mother would never let any of us kids talk to her, or even walk past her yard, on account of the pentagram she had hanging in her window. I was beginning to see that the end of the world might have its perks—for the first time I could talk to anyone I pleased.

"I'm Annette," I said. "And this is Nicole. What are they so happy about?"

"Well," Ruth said. "Bless their hearts, but they're in paradise. Or at least they think they are."

"They think this is Planet X?"

"It's called seeing what you want to see. We all do it. Some more than others."

"That's fucked," Nicole said. "Fucked up. Fucked in the head."

"It's no worse than setting half the city on fire. Are you girls headed to the bread lines? Let me walk with you. I like to follow the loonies, since they're harmless. But you seem like better conversationalists."

"Okay," I said.

"We've got a gun," Nicole added.

The ration station was nothing more than a big messy row of folding tables, guarded by military and manned by city workers and volunteers. We waited in line, while the soldiers strode back and forth alongside, their heavy rifles slung across their chests.

Ruth wasn't intimidated by any of it. Straightaway she struck up a conversation with a baby-faced soldier lingering nearby: "Young man," she said, "You hardly look old enough to be in the army at all."

"I'm eighteen, ma'am," he said, half-smiling.

"My god. They get younger every year."

"I just signed up," he volunteered. He really did look young, barely older than me. He was a Midwestern boy, with blue eyes and light brown hair and a clean fresh face. "Soon's I heard the President's speech, about how there was gonna be a war. I thought we was gonna be fighting aliens, but instead they sent us to two days of basic and then up here to guard supply lines, keep the peace."

"I'm sure you'll see your aliens soon," said Ruth.

"I hope so," he said. He seemed eager to talk to us, and who wouldn't be, so young and suddenly far from home? "I heard there might be a big attack soon. Somewhere close. Like Chicago. Or St. Louis. We'll be ready! You can count on that!"

The rest of us bedraggled, half-starved people waiting for white bread and government cheese weren't so happy about the idea, and a low moan of dread ran through the line. It was bad enough with no power, and half the city a burnt-out wreck, and our kin dead and gone with no bodies to bury, but to be attacked by aliens, too? It was getting absurd.

"But you know what else?" the young soldier continued. "I heard there's rebels. People who don't even believe in aliens at all. So we got that, too. It's a war on two fronts. Don't make sense to me, though. We got an enemy, a real enemy. Like Nazis, but worse, you know? I heard they look like walking frogs."

"Okay, okay," his commander said, coming up behind him and clapping him on the shoulder. "That's enough storytelling. Let's keep it moving."

Our soldier grinned sheepishly, half-saluted at Ruth, and headed up the line.

• • •

That night there were attacks on cities in India and China and Brazil. They showed it all on the news: crumbling buildings, burning foliage, eroding skylines. Raging lakes of fire and flame. And terrified people, as they ran and cried, everything they'd loved reduced to ash. The news announcers didn't talk. They just watched with the rest of us, pale and afraid.

Nicole had followed me home, after the bread line. At first I was worried to bring her, but she was young and pretty and the rebels were mostly men, so they didn't seem to mind. Right away she handed her baby off to Jane and the men gave her a gun. Now she was leaning into their circle with a thirsty look on her face, watching the wreckage on TV.

They weren't afraid. They claimed it was all manufactured, nothing but fake. A false flag operation, they said.

"What's that mean?" Nicole demanded, and Big Doug explained.

"But aren't the dead people still dead?" I wanted to know. No one had an answer for that.

I brought dinner to Jane and the kiddies upstairs. They were all of 'em starving, because there'd been no one around to fix lunch, and nothing to fix. Timmy dove toward the plate like a hungry wolf, but quick as could be, Jane slapped him away. "*Timmy,*" she said. "We haven't had time to pray. Close your eyes, Annette," she commanded, so I did.

"For we wrestle not against flesh and blood," she said, quoting from the Bible, a verse I once knew too. "But against principalities, against powers, against the rulers of the darkness of this world, against spiritual wickedness in high places . . ."

I didn't want to listen. Eyes still closed, I slipped away.

• • •

The next day I had to go back to the ration station all over again. There were too many people at my house, eating too much food, but we had to keep it secret, or the soldiers would get suspicious. Someone else should wait in the line, but no one wanted to do that, because it was boring. It was way more fun to sit in the basement counting the hand grenades some lunatic from Rolla had brought in under cover of night. So food duty fell to me, again.

The baby-faced soldier recognized me; he came up and said hello. "Didn't I just see you yesterday?" he asked. "Did they give you enough?"

"I, um, I've got a big family," I said, which wasn't exactly a lie.

He lit up. "Oh yeah? Me too. How many you got?"

"Well, there's me, and Jane, and Larry, and Timmy, and Sylvie," I said. "And Dad. And Mom, but she got enforced."

"So did my sister Rae Ann," he said. "And my big brother Jack, and he had two kids. I like to think I'm here for him. Those people, the ones who fought back at the very beginning, they were the real heroes, don't you think? My momma says we should be grateful to them all. She'd say your momma was a hero too."

Then his commander was giving him a look, so he moved on, down the line.

On the way back I ran into Ruth. "Oh, you again," she said. "Listen, do you want to come by my house tonight? It's a full moon and seeing as how the world was supposed to end and then didn't, I figured some thanks to the goddess would probably be in order, don't you agree? Bring your friend, too. It would help complete the circle."

"I, um, okay," I said. "That sounds good. I'll see what I can do."

• • •

Nicole didn't want to go at first, because she said it sounded weird, and kinda lame, but I insisted. I'd been on my feet cooking and cleaning for days. Now the whole house reeked because we couldn't take showers anymore and the toilets were all backed up. No one was even bothering about it, because they expected the war to begin any day. Their makeshift beds were scattered all over the house, heaped with dirty clothes and damp towels they'd used to clean their privates. I just wanted to get out of the house, away from all the men with their unkempt beards and stinking feet. So I reminded Nicole that she wouldn't even be here if it wasn't for me, and finally she agreed to go.

We slipped away just after dinner when the kids had gone to bed and the men were talking by firelight to conserve the generator's fuel. They'd banned the TV completely, because we couldn't afford the power, and anyway they said it was nothing but lies.

Now that nearly all the power was gone, night was deeper than it had ever been before. Storm-heavy clouds shifted and scattered across the face of the moon. In Ruth's backyard, surrounded by overgrown hedges and the low-hanging branches of sycamore trees, it was so dark we could barely see each other. The match flared bright for a moment as Ruth lit three candles, illuminating spooky shadows across her face—for a moment she really did look like a witch.

We stood in a circle with our arms outstretched, while Ruth explained that there is only one goddess, though she goes by different names—different names for different forms. Tonight Ruth called on Hecate, the goddess in three. Hecate was ours: maiden, mother, and crone. She was the goddess of transformations, of endings and beginnings, of birth and death. Here, in this moment, as one world perished and the next came into being, she was the goddess of now.

Then Ruth prayed, though it was not like Jane's prayers. She prayed for strength, and wisdom, and harmony; she prayed for protection for women everywhere and for peace to come at the crossroads.

I could feel the heat radiating off my white candle, its warmth on my fingers and forehead.

When it ended Nicole was the first to blow out her candle without so much as an "Amen." She tossed the dripping candle into the grass and said, "So, um, that was fun? I better be getting back. Annette—you'll be along?" She slipped past the shadows and through the gate.

"And the circle is broken," Ruth said. She knelt and lodged the three candles upright in a little pile of stones and rocks, and relit Nicole's candle. She patted the grass beside her. I sat.

"I probably shouldn't tell you this," I said. "But the people at my house . . . they're planning a war. They're going to attack the army base. Or maybe just the soldiers. I'm not exactly sure."

"I thought that might be the case," Ruth said.

"I don't want anyone else to get hurt."

"I know," Ruth said. "They will, though, you know. The army is stronger. So much stronger. Your friends can never win."

"They're not my friends."

"But you still don't want them to die."

"Of course not. I don't want anyone to die." I wasn't a hero, not like my mother, not like my father. I just wanted to live.

"If you need anything, Annette, promise me you'll come to me, alright?"

I promised.

Then she told me to go home, before they started worrying.

• • •

No one had missed me. They were getting updates from Joplin; the uprising there had begun tonight. Most had been killed in the skirmishes, and the rest had fled and gone into hiding. The army base was strong as ever. The rebels had failed.

"We won't fail, though, will we?" Nicole asked. "We're stronger. We have more people. We can do this. We can win."

On the radio there was talk of new cities destroyed, demolished by alien weapons and leveled to cinders and ash. Albuquerque. Florence. Perth. Lahore. The announcers speculated on the next target. "I've heard military strategists fear an attack on the financial center of the northeast," said one. "Or perhaps a psychological strike, aimed at America's heartland."

"Omaha? St. Louis? Des Moines?"

"Tomorrow," my father said. "Dumb fucks in Joplin. Tipped our hand. Tomorrow, before they start doing block sweeps over here. Tomorrow we strike."

• • •

Jane woke me a couple hours past midnight, gripping my shoulder with her bony fingers. "Annette," she whispered. "Larry's missing. Wake up. I can't find Larry."

"What time is it?" I groaned, but then I understood and I was up like a shot.

We crept barefoot through the house, over and around the sleeping hulks of men, passed out anywhere and everywhere. We looked in the kitchen, in the backed-up bathrooms that smelled of sewage, in the abandoned backyard, and even in the basement, where a couple guys were still awake, guarding the guns. They looked us up and down as if they barely knew us. "Nope. Haven't seen the kid."

We went outside, holding hands now, more afraid than we'd admit. We should have gotten Dad, but we understood that he was no longer here for us, not like that. He'd become part of something else—he was *leading* something else—and now we were the distraction.

We found Larry standing in the middle of the street as the Paradisers had done, staring up at the brilliant full moon. The clouds had passed. Jane called his name in a quiet voice, but he didn't seem to hear.

I followed his gaze. There, soaring and zipping across the sky, I saw a spacecraft.

It was like nothing I'd ever seen before, and I knew immediately that it was completely and totally alien, not of this world. It was dimly luminescent, speedy and nimble. Along one triangular side were racing patterns of turquoise and violet light.

"Look," I said, pointing toward the sky, but Jane was occupied with Larry, and when I looked back, the spacecraft was gone.

"Is he sleepwalking?" But he seemed awake, just groggy and confused. We dragged him back to the safety of the front porch, demanding to know what was up.

"I got up to pee," he said. "Then I looked out the window and I saw an alien standing here, in the front yard. I knew it was one because it was fat and scaly like a frog. Then it waved at me. It wanted me to follow. So I did."

"But the windows are boarded up," I said. "Remember? You were dreaming. It was just a dream."

"It wasn't a dream," he insisted. "I'm awake."

"No," Jane said sharply. "Stop lying. Annette's right. The windows are boarded up. You didn't see a thing."

"I'm not lying. I saw an alien. I did."

She slapped him, hard. "There are no aliens, Larry. There's no such thing. Jesus wouldn't allow it. Now come back to bed." She grabbed him by the wrist and dragged him toward the front door.

He began to cry. "You're hurting me."

"Stop hurting him, Jane," I said. "It's okay. Everyone just go back to bed."

But I couldn't sleep for a long, long time. I lay on the floor by my siblings, remembering the way the glowing spacecraft had zigzagged across the sky. I wondered if I'd been dreaming, too.

• • •

The next morning I woke late. By the time I came downstairs, everyone was already eating breakfast. Nicole had taken over what she called "Provisions," so I didn't have to worry so much about cooking anymore.

But Nicole and Jane were telling everyone about the "witchcraft" Ruth had forced Nicole and me to do, and how it made Larry hallucinate an alien and sleepwalk down the street. All the men were cracking up at the idea of Larry following an alien because it waved at him. Embarrassed, Larry started laughing too.

Nicole and Jane were serious, though. "I'm telling you," Nicole said. "There was something real creepy about that lady. I'm not going back there. And I think Annette best not either."

"Agreed," my dad said, looking at me as if he'd just remembered I was his daughter. "We need your help around here. And no more talking to outsiders! That kind of thing could get us all killed."

I was going to tell them about the spacecraft, but then I realized they'd just laugh at me the way they'd laughed at Larry. So I didn't say a word.

I still wanted to talk to Dad, though. I pulled him into the empty pantry where we could have a moment to ourselves. "Dad. I'm afraid," I said. "I don't want you to do this. I don't want you to die. Don't you remember what you said to Mom?"

He looked like I'd hit him. "Don't you see, Annette? Your mom fought back. Now *we're* fighting back. Everyone else is a collaborator. They're followers, Annette, traitors, sheep. Not us. Not me. That's why we've all got to fight."

"But what about me and Jane and Larry and Timmy and little Sylvie? If you die, we'll be alone."

"That's just it. I'm doing this for you. So you kids can live in a future that's safe and free."

"I don't care about the future. I care about now. I just want us to be okay."

He promised that we would.

• • •

I went back to the ration station that day, hoping my soldier would still be there. I had to tell *someone* about the alien ship.

In the old days, if my parents said there were no such thing as aliens, I'd have believed them without a second thought, never mind what I thought I saw. But things were changing now. I could believe what I wanted to believe, be whatever I wanted to be.

I figured my soldier would understand. Maybe he'd even be pleased; his aliens were finally near.

Instead he bit his bottom lip and looked at me with brooding eyes. "A lot of people have been seeing things," he said. "All kinds of weird things. Things that don't always match up, don't always fit the facts. My commander says it's 'stress-induced hallucinations.' That's what he called it. Some of the boys been gettin' 'em too. Maybe sometimes we just see what we want to see."

"You don't understand," I said. "It looked so real. It felt real, too. I felt it in my skin. Like electricity. A tingle." Then I got embarrassed, talking about my tingly skin.

"Maybe it was," he said kindly, and I knew he was humoring me. "Anyway, I gotta say goodbye. I probably won't see you no more . . . I'm headed out to St. Louis tonight."

"Everyone? All the soldiers?"

"A good bit," he said. "You know, I'm sure you've heard the talk."

"Yeah," I said. "Like there could be an attack. What time you headed out?"

"Night. Maybe around oh one hundred hours," he said, like I was supposed to be impressed. "Anyway, so long. Maybe I'll run into you somewhere, after the war is over."

"Maybe," I said.

"I'd like that. You seem like a real nice girl. Good luck to your family."

"Thanks," I said. "Aren't you scared? Now that you might have to really fight?"

"I wish I'd stayed home in Oklahoma," he said. "Now go on. Get your peanut butter and powdered milk."

• • •

As soon as I got home, I went to Dad.

They'd been planning to launch the rebellion tonight, attacking lone soldiers and small patrols, raiding the ration stations, disrupting supply lines, sabotaging the movie theaters that played the propaganda reels.

But now they had my intel, they could go so much bigger.

Dad slapped me on the back. "See? I knew it. You're a fighter, just like us. I'm proud of you, hon." Then he called the rebels around. "New plan," he said, and they began arguing about whether they should set a trap with the grenades as the military caravan rolled out of town, or if they should use the rifles to pick soldiers off one by one from the side of the road, or if maybe all that would be better suited as a distraction to cause pandemonium while the rest stuck with the original plan. They weren't exactly master military strategists; the only war they'd seen was on TV.

I felt a little guilty for selling out my soldier, but he should have taken me seriously. I knew what I'd seen.

The rebels, and Nicole, set out just before midnight. Before they left, Dad gave me one of their two-way radios, so I could listen in.

The house was dark, to conserve fuel. I sat alone in the basement with a single candle, cradling one radio in my hand and listening to the other, tuned to the news. Jane sat upstairs, watching the babies while they slept, and listening to her own shows, the way she always did now. The preachers testified into the empty stretches between rural towns and lost lengths of highway; they spoke of Jesus and the devil, brimstone and blood. No wonder the kids had nightmares.

It all happened at the same time, just a little past one.

The big attack came, but it wasn't St. Louis or Chicago or Des Moines—it was Oklahoma City. I listened as they narrated the fireballs, the melting asphalt, the endless flame. It was worse, not being able to see it, just hearing the voices as they described the worst thing they'd ever seen.

The soldiers who'd been headed to St. Louis turned around and headed south, along with most of the other soldiers in town. When I sat very still I could feel the rumble and quake of their tanks headed for the highway.

Our rebels primed for battle met their force armed for war; instead of a few prowling soldiers and peacekeepers, it was half an army.

"Run away!" I screamed into the radio, hoping my dad would hear. "Go home! Hide! They're leaving! We can still be free!"

Maybe they couldn't hear me. Maybe they didn't have time to answer because they were fighting for their lives. I heard them, though; their screams and gurgles and shouts, their gasping cries for reinforcements, their pleas to fall back, their rattling breaths, just before death.

And then I understood. I was alone now, we were all of us alone, me and Jane and Larry and Sylvie and Tim. And we were fighters, too, except we were smart. Not like Mom. Not like Dad. We weren't traitors, or collaborators; we were just going to do whatever it took to survive.

I went upstairs to tell Jane what had happened. The kids were fast asleep, the radio preachers droning on, but Jane was nowhere to be found.

I came downstairs again just in time to see her slipping in the front door, wild-haired and wild-eyed, her face smudged with dirt and ash, grinning like a jack o' lantern, smelling of lighter fluid and flame. "My gosh, Jane. Where have you been?"

"I was lighting Ruth's house on fire," she said. "Ruth is a witch. This new world will be built on the ashes of the old, and in the new world there is no room for satanic practices and pagan corruption. So witches must burn."

I stared, shocked into silence.

"Come here," she beckoned, and I joined her in the open doorway, where I could see the crackling tongues of fire rising high above the roof, engulfing the ancient sycamores in flames.

"There will be no more war but holy war," she said.

Part of me wanted to throttle her. But I didn't, because she was my sister, and I knew we would need each other in the end. She was my deranged, murderous, starry-eyed sister, my mother's daughter, but blood runs thicker than water and we would hold onto our own until our fingers bled.

"Never mind about Ruth," I said. "I was just listening to the radios. I think Dad's gone."

"Not gone. Dead. I'm not a child anymore, you know, Annette."

"I know," I said. "Now go pack up whatever food is left. I'm going to drain the fuel from the generator. Then we'll wake up Larry and Timmy and Sylvie. We've got to get out of here if we want to survive."

"What about the other babies?"

"Jesus will take care of them," I said. "We've got to care for our own. Let them sleep."

Jane understood, as I knew she would.

I stood there with my sister at the crossroads, ready to call on goddesses vengeful and bloody, selfish and cruel . . . whatever it took to live. It didn't matter what name she went by; for us she was the goddess of now, and we would make her power our own.

IN THE MOUNTAIN

Hugh Howey

"Carry on," one founder would say to another. To Tracy, it had become a mantra of sorts. Igor had started it, would wave his disfigured hand and dismiss the other founders back to their work. What began as mockery of him became a talisman of strength. *Carry on. Do the job. One foot forward.* A reminder to forge ahead even when the task was gruesome, even when it seemed pointless, even when billions were about to die.

But Tracy knew some things can only be carried so far before they must be set down. Set down or dropped. Dropped and broken.

The world was one of these things. The ten founders carried what they could to Colorado. An existing hole in the mountain there was burrowed even deeper. And when they could do no more, the founders stopped. And they counted the moments as the world plummeted toward the shattering.

The rock and debris pulled from the mountain formed a sequence of hills, a ridge now dusted with snow. The heavy lifters and buses and dump trucks had been abandoned by the mounds of rubble. There was a graveyard hush across the woods, a deep quiet of despair, of a work finished. The fresh snow made no sound as it fell from heavy, gray clouds.

Tracy stood with the rest of the founders just inside the gaping steel doors of the crypt they'd built. She watched the snow gather in yesterday's muddy ruts. The crisscross patterns from the busloads of the invited would be invisible by nightfall. Humanity was not yet gone, the world not yet ruined, and already the universe was conspiring to remove all traces.

Anatoly fidgeted by her side. The heavyset physicist exhaled, and a cloud of frost billowed before his beard. On her other side, Igor reached into his heavy coat and withdrew a flash of silver. Tracy stole a glance. The gleaming watch was made more perfect in his mangled hand. Igor claimed he was a descendant and product of Chernobyl. Anatoly had told her it was a chemical burn.

Between Igor's red and fused fingers, the hours ticked down.

"Ten minutes," Igor said to the gathered. His voice was a grumble of distant thunder. Tracy watched as he formed an ugly fist and choked the life out of that watch. His pink knuckles turned the color of the snow.

Tracy turned her attention to the woods and strained one last time to hear the sound of an engine's whine—the growl of a rental car laboring up that mountain road. She waited for the crunch-crunch of hurrying boots. She scanned for the man who would appear between those gray aspens with their peeled-skin bark. But the movies had lied to her, had conditioned her to expect last-minute heroics: a man running, a weary and happy smile, snow flying in a welcome embrace, warm lips pressed to cold ones, both trembling.

"He's not coming," Tracy whispered to herself. Here was a small leak of honesty from some deep and forgotten place.

Igor heard her and checked his watch again. "Five minutes," he said quietly.

And only then, with five minutes left before they needed to get inside, before they needed to shut the doors for good, did it become absolutely certain that he wasn't coming. John had gone to Atlanta with the others, had followed orders like a good soldier, and all that she'd worked to create in Colorado—the fantasy of surviving with him by her side—had been a great delusion. Those great crypt doors would close on her and trap her in solitude. And Tracy felt in that moment that she shouldn't have built this place, that she wouldn't have wasted her time if only she'd known.

"We should get inside," Igor said. He closed the lid on that small watch of his—a click like a cocked gun—and then it disappeared into his heavy coat.

There was a sob among them. A sniff. Patrice suddenly broke from the rest of the founders and ran through the great doors, her boots clomping on concrete, and Tracy thought for a moment that Patrice would keep on running, that she'd disappear into the aspens, but she stopped just beyond the concrete deck, stooped and gathered a handful of fresh snow, and ran back inside, eating some of it from her palms.

Tracy thought of grabbing something as well. A twig. A piece of that bark. A single falling snowflake on her tongue. She scanned the woods for some sight of John as Anatoly guided her inside, deep enough that the founders by the doors could shove the behemoths closed. Four feet thick, solid steel, streaked with rust where the weather had wetted them, they made a hideous screech as they were moved. A cry like a mother wolf out in the gray woods calling for her pups.

The white world slimmed as the doors came together. The view became a column, and then a gap, and then a sliver. There was a heavy and mortal thump as the doors met, steel pressing on steel, and then a darkness bloomed that had to be blinked against to get eyes working again.

Though the doors were now closed, Tracy thought she could still hear the sound of the wolf crying—and realized it was one of the founders making that mournful noise. Tears welled up in her eyes, brought there by a partner's lament. And Tracy remembered being young once and sobbing like that. She remembered the first time a man had broken her heart. It had felt like the end of the entire fucking world.

This day was something like that.

• • •

The mountain was full of the confused. Nearly five thousand people asking questions. Their bags were not yet unpacked; their backs were still sore from the rutted, bumpy ride in the buses. And now the myriad excuses for bringing them there—the retreats, reunions, vacations, emergencies—evaporated as conflicting accounts collided.

With the doors closed, the founders set out to explain. First to family. Later, to all of the invited. Tracy had been given an equal allotment of invitations, and she had used most of them on practical people. Soldiers. Tools of retribution. When the world was clean, all she wanted was to see a bullet in the people who had done this.

Of friends, she had none. Most of her adult life had been spent in Washington or overseas. There was a doorman in Geneva who had always been kind to her. There was the guy who did her taxes. Which was to admit that there was no one. Just her meager family: her father, her sister, and her sister's husband. Three people in all the world. Maybe that was why John's decision hurt so much. He was almost all she had. All she'd *thought* she had.

At least it meant a small audience as she dispensed the horrid truth, the nightmare she'd held inside for more than a year. Tracy hesitated outside the door to her sister's small room. She raised her fist and prepared to knock. Truth waited for her on the other side, and she wasn't sure she was ready.

• • •

Her father sat on the bed and wrung his hands while Tracy spoke. Her sister April sat next to him, a look of slack confusion on her face. Remy, April's husband, had refused to sit. He stood by his wife, a hand on her shoulder, something between anger and horror in his eyes.

They were all dressed for the camping trip they'd been promised—a week of backpacking, of living in the woods. Their gear sat by the foot of the bed, would never be used. The bags and the garb were reminders of Tracy's lies. She listened as the words spilled from her mouth. She listened to herself say what she had rehearsed a hundred times: how the tiny machines used in hospitals to attack cancer—those invisible healers, the same ones that would've saved Mom if they'd been available in time—how those same machines were as capable of killing as they were of healing.

She told her family how those machines were in everyone's blood, in every human being's on Earth. And curing everyone might be possible, but it would only be temporary. Once people knew that it could be done, it was only a matter of time. A switch had been invented that could wipe out every man and woman alive. Any hacker in his basement *could* flip that switch—which meant someone *would.*

Tracy got through that part without the wailing or hysterics she'd expected, without the questions and confusion from her dad, without anyone pushing past her and banging on the door, screaming to be let out. No one asked her if she belonged to a cult or if she was on drugs or suggested she needed to take a break from whatever work she did in Washington, that she needed to see a professional.

"It was only a matter of time before someone did it," Tracy said again. "And so our government acted before someone else could. So they could control the aftermath."

Remy started to say something, but Tracy continued before he could: "We aren't a part of the group who did this," she said. She looked to her father. "We didn't do this. But we found out about it, and we realized we couldn't stop it. We realized . . . that maybe they were right. That it needed to be done. And so we did the next best thing. We created this place. We invited ourselves along. And those that we could. We'll be okay here. You all were inoculated on the way. You probably felt your ears popping on the bus ride up. Now we'll spend six months here, maybe a year—"

"Six months," Remy said.

"This can't be real." Her sister shook her head.

"It's real," Tracy told April. "I'm sorry. I never wanted to keep this from any of—"

"I don't believe it," Remy said. He glanced around the room as if seeing it for the first time. April's husband was an accountant, was used to columns of numbers in black and white. He was also a survivalist, was used to sorting out the truth on his own. He didn't learn simply by being told. Igor had warned that it would take some people weeks before they believed.

"We are positive," Tracy said. This was a lie; she had her own doubts. She wouldn't be completely sure until the countdown clock hit zero. But there was no use infecting others with her slender hopes. "I realize this is hard to hear. It's hard even for me to grasp. But the war we were bracing for isn't going to come with clouds of fire and armies marching. It's going to be swifter and far worse than that."

"Did *you* do this?" her father asked, voice shaking with age. Even with his encroaching, occasional senility, he knew that Tracy worked for bad agencies full of bad people. There were classified things she had confided to him years ago that he had been willing to shoulder for her. They would likely be the very last things his dementia claimed, little islands of disappointment left in a dark and stormy sea.

"No, Dad, I didn't do this. But I *am* the reason we have this place, a nice place to be together and wait it out."

She flashed back to that night in Milan, to the first time she'd laid eyes on the book with the word *Order* embossed on its cover. It was the same night she made John forget about his wife for a brief moment, the night when all those years of flirtations came to fruition: the bottle of wine, the dancing, that dress—the one she'd gotten in trouble for expensing to her company card. And in his room, after they made love, and hungering for more danger, she had gone to the dresser where she knew his gun would be tucked away, and she'd found that book instead.

If John had stayed in bed, she wouldn't have thought anything more of it. The book was full of the dry text that only lawyers who had become politicians could craft. Emergency procedures. An ops manual of some sort. But the way John had lurched out of bed, it was as if Tracy had let his wife into the room. She remembered the way his hands trembled against her as he asked her to put it away, to come back to bed, like she'd grabbed something far more dangerous than a gun, something cocked and loaded with something much worse than bullets.

After he'd gone to sleep, Tracy had sat on the edge of the bathtub, the book open on the toilet lid, and had turned every page with her phone set to record. Even as she scanned, she saw enough to be afraid.

Enough to *know.*

"I'm sorry," she told her father, unable to stomach the disappointment on his face.

"When—?" April asked.

Tracy turned to her sister, the schoolteacher, who knew only that Tracy worked for the government, who had no idea about all the classified blood on her hands. April was four years older, would always be older than Tracy in all the ways that didn't matter and in none of the ways that did.

"In a few hours," Tracy said. "It'll all be over in a few hours."

"And will we feel anything?" April rubbed her forearm. "What about everyone out there? Everyone we know. They'll just—?"

Remy sat beside his wife and wrapped his arms around her. The air around Tracy grew cold. Even more empty.

"*We* were supposed to be out there when it happened, too," Tracy said. "The four of us. Remember that. We'll talk more later. I have to get to a meeting—"

"A meeting?" April asked. "A *meeting?* To do what? Decide the rest of our lives? Decide who lives and who dies? What kind of meeting?"

And now Remy was no longer embracing his wife. He was restraining her.

"How dare you?" April screamed at Tracy. Their father shivered on the bed, tried to say something, to reach out to his daughters and tell them not to fight. Tracy retreated toward the door. She was wrong about the hysteria, about it not coming. There was just some delay. And as she slipped into the hall and shut the small room on her sister's screaming, she heard that she'd been wrong about the beating on the door as well.

• • •

Saving a person seemed simple. But saving them against their will was not. Tracy realized this as she navigated the corridors toward the command room, her sister's screams still with her. She could hear muffled sobs and distant shouting from other rooms as she passed—more people learning the truth. Tracy had thought that preserving a life would absolve all other sins, but the sin of not consulting with that life first was perhaps the only exception. She recalled an ancient argument she'd had with her mother when she was a teenager, remembered yelling at her mom and saying she wished she'd never been born. And she'd meant it. What right did someone else have to make that decision for her? Her mom had always expected her to be grateful simply for having been brought into the world.

Now Tracy had made the same mistake.

She left the apartment wing, those two thousand rooms dug laterally and tacked on to a complex built long ago, and she entered the wide corridors at the heart of the original bunker. The facility had been designed to house fifteen hundred people for five years. The founders had invited more than three times that number, but they wouldn't need to stay as long. The biggest job had been cleaning out and refilling the water and diesel tanks.

The entire place was a buried relic from a different time, a time capsule for a different threat, built for a different end-of-the-world scenario. The facility had been abandoned years ago. It had become a tourist attraction. And then it had fallen into disrepair. The founders chose the location after considering several options. Igor and Anatoly used their research credentials and leased the space under the auspices of searching for neutrinos, some kind of impossible-to-find subatomic particles. But it was a much different and invisible threat they actually set out to find: the machines that polluted the air and swam through every vein.

Tracy used her key to unlock the cluttered command room. A round table dominated the center of the space. A doughnut of monitors ringed the ceiling above, tangles of wires drooping from them and running off to equipment the engineers had set up. In one corner, a gleaming steel pod stood like some part of an alien ship. It had been built according to stolen plans, was thought at first to be necessary for clearing the small machines from their bloodstreams, but it ended up being some sort of cryo device, a side project the Atlanta team had undertaken. The only machine Tracy knew how to operate in that room was the coffeemaker. She started a pot and watched the countdown clock overhead tick toward Armageddon.

The other founders trickled in one at a time. Many had red eyes and chapped cheeks. There was none of the chatting, debating, and arguing that had marked their prior meetings in that room. Just the same funereal silence they'd held by the crypt doors.

A second pot was brewed. One of the engineers got the screens running, and they watched the TV feeds in silence. There was speculation among the talking heads that the presidential nomination was not quite the lock everyone had presumed. The excitement in the newsrooms was palpable and eerie. Tracy watched dead men discuss a future that did not exist.

Two minutes.

The talking heads fell silent, and the feeds switched from newsrooms to a stage outside Atlanta. The distant downtown towers gleamed in the background. On the stage, a young girl in a black dress held a microphone and took a deep breath, a little nervous as she began to sing.

The national anthem brought tears to Tracy's eyes. She reminded herself to breathe. And not for the first time, she had an awful premonition that she was wrong, that the book was just a book, that John had believed in something that would not come to pass, and that she would soon be embarrassed in that room with all the people she'd convinced to join her. She would be another in a long line of failed messiahs. Her sister would look at her like she was crazy for the rest of her life. National headlines would mock the kooks in a mountain who had thought the world was going to end. And somehow all of this felt worse than ten billion dead.

It was a guilty thought, the panic that she might be wrong.

Large red numbers on the clock counted down. No part of her wanted to be right. Either way, her world was ending. When the clock struck all zeroes, Tracy would either be an outcast or a shut-in.

On the array of televisions, the same scene was shown from half a dozen angles, all the various news stations and networks tuned to that young girl in her black dress. One of the screens cut to the obligatory jets screaming in formation overhead. Another screen showed a group of senators and congressmen, hands on their goddamn patriotic chests. Tracy searched for John, thought she might see him there near the stage with his suit jacket that showed off his handsome shoulders but also that bulge by his ribs. There were five seconds on the clock. One of the founders started counting, whispering the numbers as they fell.

Three.

Two.

One.

A line of zeroes.

And nothing happened.

"They're still breathing," someone said.

Igor cursed and fumbled for that damned watch of his.

An eternity squeezed itself into a span of three seconds. No one moved.

"Holy shit," someone said.

CNN's feed spun sickeningly to the side, the cameraman whirling, and Tracy realized it was one of the reporters who had cursed. Another screen showed a bright flash, a brief glimpse of a mushroom cloud, and then that monitor went black.

The young girl was no longer singing. She had been replaced with station identifiers and shots of stunned newscasters who stared at their feeds in disbelief. More bright flashes erupted on the last monitor running, which showed a wide vista from some great distance. Three classic and terrifying mushroom clouds rose toward the heavens, shouldering the other clouds aside. And then that last screen succumbed as well, promising impotently to "Be right back."

"Shut it off!" a reporter screamed. He waved at someone off-camera. "Shut it off—"

And then someone did. A switch flipped somewhere, in all those veins, and all the talking heads on all the screens bowed forward or tilted to the side. Blood flowed from the nose of the man who had just been waving. His jaw fell slack; his eyes focused on nothing—a quiet death.

The founders in the command room—no longer breathing—watched in silence. Hands clasped over mouths. Those who had harbored any doubts now believed. All was still. The only thing that moved on the screens was the thin red rivulets trickling from noses and ears. There was no one left alive to cut away, to change the view. And only those ten people huddled around the wire-webbed monitors were left to see.

"Kill it," someone finally said, a terrible slip of the tongue.

Tracy watched as Dmitry fumbled with the controls for the panels. He accidentally changed channels on one of the sets, away from news and into the realm of reruns. There was a sitcom playing: a family around a dinner table, a joke just missed. A bark of canned laughter spilled from the speaker, the illusion that life was still transpiring out there as it always had. But it wasn't just the laughter that was canned now. They all were. All of humanity. What little was left.

• • •

"Hey. Wake up."

Dreams. Nothing more than dreams. A black ghost clawing away at her mother, a wicked witch burying her father and her sister. Tracy sat up in bed, sweating. She felt a hand settle on her shoulder.

"We have a problem," someone said.

A heavy shadow, framed by the wan light spilling from the hallway.

"Anatoly?"

"Come," he said. He lumbered out of her small room deep in the mountain. Tracy slid across that double bunk, a bed requisitioned for two, and tugged on the same pants and shirt she'd worn the day before.

The fog of horrible dreams mixed with the even worse images from their first day in the complex. Both swirled in her sleepy brain. Slicing through these was the fear in Anatoly's voice. The normally unflappable Russian seemed petrified. Was it really only to last a single day, all their schemes to survive the end of the world? Was it a riot already? Orientation the day before had not gone well. Fights had broken out. A crowd had gathered at those four-foot-thick doors, which had been designed just as much to keep people *in* as to keep other dangers out.

Perhaps it was a leak. Air from the outside getting in. Tracy hurried down the hall barefoot, searching her lungs for some burn or itch, touching her upper lip and looking for a bleed. Her last thought as she caught up to Anatoly and they reached the command room together was that the cameras outside the crypt doors would be on, would reveal a lone man, inoculated to the sudden death but slowly dying anyway, banging feebly and begging to be let in—

"Everyone here?" Dmitry asked. The thin programmer scanned the room over his spectacles. There was no real leader among the founders. Tracy held some special status as the originator of the group, she who had found the *Order*. Anatoly was the man who had coordinated the lease and planning of the facility. But Dmitry was the brightest among them, the tinkerer, the one who had deactivated the machines in their blood. Of them all, he seemed to most enjoy the thought of being in charge. No one begrudged him that.

"What is this?" Patrice asked. She knotted her robe across her waist and crossed her arms against the chill in the room.

"The program," Dmitry said. "It . . . has changed."

Someone groaned. Tracy rubbed the sand from her eyes. The gathered braced for Dmitry's usual technobabble, which was bad enough when wide awake.

"Five hundred years," he said. He pushed his glasses up his nose and looked from face to face. "Not six months. Five hundred years."

"Until what?" Sandra asked.

"Until we can go out," Dmitry said. He pointed toward the door. "Until we can go out."

"But you said—"

"I know what I said. And it's all in the book. It says six months. But the program unspooled yesterday. It's dynamic code, a self-assembler, and now there's a clock set to run for five hundred years."

The room was quiet. The recycled air flowing through the overhead vent was the only sound.

"How are you reading this new program?" Igor asked. "Do you have those buggers in here?" He nodded toward the silver pod with all its tubes and wires.

"Of course not. The antennas we put up, I can access the mesh network the machines use to communicate. Are any of you listening to me? The program is set to run for five hundred years. This book—" He pointed to the tome sitting on the large round table. "—this isn't a guide for the entire program. It's just for one small part of it, just one shift. I think the cryopods are maybe so they can—"

"So how do we change it?" Anatoly asked. "You can tap into the network. How do we turn it all off? So we can leave right now? Or set it back to six months?"

Dmitry let out his breath and shook his head. He had that exasperated air about him that he got when any of the founders asked questions that belied fundamental flaws in their understanding of what, to him, were basic concepts. "What you're asking is impossible. Otherwise I would have done it already. I can program the test machines in my lab, but overcoming the entire network?" He shook his head.

"What does that mean for us?" Tracy asked.

"It means we have a year's worth of food," Dmitry said. "Eighteen months, maybe two years if we ration. And then we all slowly die in here. Or . . ."

"Or what?"

"Or we die quickly out there."

Sharon slapped the table and glared at Dmitry. "We've got fourteen men in the infirmary and another eight in restraints from telling everyone we'll be here for six months and that everyone they know is now dead. Now you're saying we have to tell them that we *lied?* That we brought them here to *starve to death*?"

Tracy sank into one of the chairs. She looked up at Dmitry. "Are you sure about this? You were wrong about the clock the last time. You were a few seconds off. Maybe—"

"It was tape delay," Dmitry said, rubbing his eyes beneath his glasses. "All broadcasters use a time delay. I wasn't wrong. I'm not wrong now. I can show you the code."

One of the founders groaned.

"What were you saying about the pod?"

"I think this is a manual for a single shift," Dmitry said. "And the pod is for—"

"You mean the icebox?" Patrice asked.

"Yes. The cryo unit is to allow them to stagger the shifts. To last the full five hundred years. I looked over one of the requisitions reports we intercepted, and it all makes sense—"

"Does our pod work?" Anatoly asked.

Dmitry shrugged. "Nobody wanted me to test it, remember? Listen, we have a decision to make—"

"What decision? You're telling us we're all dead."

"Not all of us," Tracy said. She rested her head in her palms, could see that witch from her dreams, shoveling soil on thousands of writhing bodies, hands clawing to get out.

"What do you mean?" Patrice asked.

"I mean we're the same as them." She looked up and pointed to the dead monitors, which had once looked out on the world, on the people with their anthems who had doomed them all. "We have the same decision to make. Our little world, our little mountain, isn't big enough for all of us. So we have a decision to make. The same decision they made. We're no better than them."

"Yes," Dmitry said. "I figure we have eighteen months' worth of food for five thousand mouths. That gives us enough for fifteen people for five hundred years."

"Fifteen people? To do what?"

"To survive," Dmitry said. But the tone of his voice said something more somber and sinister. Tracy tried to imagine all that he was implying. Someone else said it for her.

"And kill everyone else? Our families?"

"No way," someone said. Tracy watched her partners, these founders, fidget. It was the orientation all over again. A fight would break out.

"We can't live that long anyway," Tracy said, attempting to defuse the argument by showing how pointless it all was.

"Generations," Anatoly blurted out. He scratched his beard, seemed to be pondering a way to make some insane plan work. "Have to make sure there's only one birth for every death."

Tracy's eyes returned to the book on the center of the conference table. Others were looking at it as well. She remembered a passage like that inside the book. Several passages now suddenly made more sense. The answer had been there, but none of them had been willing to see it. It's how that book seemed to work.

"I won't be a part of this," Natasha said. "I won't. I'd rather have one year here, with my family, than even consider what you're suggesting."

"Will you still think that a year from now, when the last ration is consumed and we're left watching one another waste away? Either it happens now, or it happens then. Which way is cleaner?"

"We sound just like them," Tracy whispered, mostly to herself. She eyed those monitors again, saw her reflection in one of them.

"The Donner Party," Sherman said. When one of the Russians turned to stare at him, Sherman started to explain. "Settlers heading west two centuries ago. They got trapped in the mountains and had to resort to—"

"I'm familiar with the story. It's not an option."

"I didn't mean it was an *option*." Sherman turned to Natasha. "I mean, that's what we're going to start thinking a year from now. Or eighteen months. Whenever."

Natasha spun a lock of her hair. She dipped the end between her lips and remained silent.

"It would be quick," Dmitry said. "We still have canisters of the test nanos, the ones I built. Those, I can program. We would have to inoculate ourselves first—"

"This is going too fast," Tracy said. "We need to think about this."

"After thirty-six days, we'll be down to fourteen people," Dmitry said. "At the rate we'll be feeding these people, each month we delay means one spot lost. How long do you want to think about it?" He took off his glasses and wiped the condensation from them. It had grown hot in the room. "We're in a lifeboat," he said. "We are drifting to shore, but not as fast as we had hoped. There are too many of us in the boat." He returned the glasses to the bridge of his nose, looked coolly at the others.

"Every one of us should have died yesterday," Anatoly said. "Our families. Us. Every one. None of us should be here. Even this day is a bonus. A year would be a blessing."

"Is it so important that any of us make it to the other side?" Patrice asked. The others turned to her. "I mean, it won't even be us. If we were to do this.

It would be our descendants. And what kind of hell are they going to endure in here, living for dozens of generations in this hole, keeping their numbers at fifteen, brothers and sisters coupling? Is that even surviving? What's the point? What's the point if we're just trying to get someone to the other side? No matter what, the assholes in Atlanta will be our legacy now."

"That's why we have to do this," Tracy said.

Dmitry nodded. "Tracy's right. That's *precisely* why we have to do this. So they don't get away with it. Isn't that what we planned from the beginning? Isn't that why we only have enough food for a year but enough guns to slaughter an army?"

"Fifteen people is no army."

"But they'll know," Dmitry said. "They'll carry legends with them. We'll write it all down. We'll make up most of the first fifteen. We'll make sure no one ever forgets—"

"You mean make a religion out of this."

"I mean make a *cause*."

"Or a cult."

"Do we want them to have the world to themselves, the fuckers who did this?"

"We can't decide anything now," Tracy said. She rubbed her temples. "I need to sleep. I need to see my family—"

"No one can know," Anatoly told her.

Tracy shot him a look. "I'm not telling anyone. But we need a day or two before we do anything." She caught the look on Dmitry's face. "Surely we have that much time."

He nodded.

"And you won't program anything without consulting with us first."

Again, a nod.

Sherman laughed, but it was without humor. "Yes," he said. "I need sleep as well." He pointed to Dmitry. "And I want assurances that I'll wake up in the morning."

• • •

The following day, Tracy grabbed breakfast from the mess hall and found three founders at a table in the corner. She joined them. No one spoke. Between bites of bread and canned ham, she watched the bustle of strangers weaving through the tables and chairs, introducing themselves to one another, glancing around at their surroundings, and trying to cope with their imprisonment. Their salvation.

The buzz of voices and spoons clicking against porcelain was shattered for a brief moment by an awful release of laughter. Tracy searched for the offender, but it was gone as quickly as it had come. She watched Igor chew his bread, his eyes lifeless, focused beyond the mountain's walls, and knew he was thinking the same thing: They were in a room crowded with ghosts. There was no stopping what they would have to do. And for the first time, Tracy understood all that John had endured those past years. She remembered the way he would glance around in a restaurant, his eyes haunted, the color draining suddenly from his face. *Looking for an exit,* she used to think. *Looking for some way out if it all goes to shit.*

But no—he had been doing this, scanning the people, the bodies all around him. How could he search for an exit when there was none?

Tracy saw her sister and Remy emerge from the serving line, trays in hand. She started to wave them over, then caught herself. When she saw her sister among all those walking dead, she realized what she had to do. She put down her bread and left her tray behind. She needed to find Dmitry. To see if it was possible.

• • •

A new Order was required, a new book of instructions. The ten founders and the five they chose would have the rest of their lives to sort out the details, to leave precise instructions. Tracy had already decided she wouldn't go with them. If John were there, maybe it could work, but she couldn't pair off with one of the men in their group.

First she had her own orders to write, her own instructions. This included how to open the great crypt gates, in case there was no one else. She spent her days and nights in the workshop command room, helping Dmitry with the pod, pestering him with questions that he didn't know the answers to. The cryo-chamber had been designed for one person. And once they'd realized what it was, it had gone untested. Tracy squeezed inside for a dry fit while Dmitry modified the plumbing.

"Maybe one head over here and the other down there? Legs'll have to go like this."

Dmitry muttered under his breath. He wrestled a piece of tubing onto a small splitter, was having trouble making it fit.

"You need help?" Tracy asked.

"I got it," he said.

"What if . . . something happens to you all and there are no descendants? What if there's no one here to open it?"

"Already working on that," Dmitry said. "The antenna that taps into the mesh network. I can rig it up so when their timer shuts off, the pod will open. So if it's twenty years from now or twenty thousand, as long as this place has power—" He finally got the tube onto the fitting. "Don't worry," he said. "I'll take care of it. I have time."

Tracy hoped he was right. She wanted to believe him.

"So what do you think it'll feel like?" she asked. "You think it'll be . . . immediate? Like shutting your eyes at night, and then suddenly the alarm goes off in the morning? Or will it be dream after dream after dream?"

"I don't know." Dmitry shook his head. He started to say something, then turned quietly back to his work.

"What?" Tracy asked. "Is there something you aren't telling me?"

"It's . . . nothing." He set the tubing aside and crossed his arms. Then he turned to her. "Why do you think nobody is fighting for their place in there?" He nodded to the machine.

Tracy hadn't considered that. "Because I asked first?" she guessed.

"Because that thing is a coffin. People have been putting their loved ones in there for years. Nobody wakes up."

"So this is a bad idea?"

Dmitry shrugged. "I think maybe the people who do this, it isn't for the ones *inside* the box."

Tracy lay back in that steel cylinder and considered this, the selfishness of it all. Giving life without asking. Taking life to save some other. "For the last two days," she said, "all I've thought about is what a mistake all this was." She closed her eyes. "Completely pointless. All for nothing."

"That is life," Dmitry said. Tracy opened her eyes to see him waving a tool in the air and staring up at the ceiling. "We do not go out in glory. We leave no mark. What you did was right. What they did was wrong. They're the reason we're in this mess, not you."

Tracy didn't feel like arguing. What was the point? It didn't matter. Nothing mattered. And maybe that's what Dmitry was trying to tell her.

She crawled out of that coffin-within-a-crypt to check the supplies one last time, to make sure the vacuum was holding a seal. Inside the large storage trunk were her handwritten instructions, a set of maps, two handguns, clothing, all of Remy's and April's camping gear, and what extra rations would fit.

Five hundred years was a long time to plan for, almost an impossible time to consider. And then it occurred to her that she was wrong about something: She was wrong about the great doors that led into that mountain. This was not a crypt. The dead were on the *outside*. Here was but a bubble of life, trapped in the deep rock. A bubble only big enough now for fifteen people. Fifteen plus two.

• • •

Before waking her sister, Tracy stole into her father's room and kissed him quietly on the forehead. She brushed his thinning hair back and kissed him once more. One last time. Wiping tears away, she moved to the neighboring room. Igor and Anatoly were waiting outside the door. They had agreed to help her, had been unhappy with her decision, but she had traded her one spot for two others.

They stole inside quietly. The Russians had syringes ready. They hovered over Remy first. It went fast, not enough kicking to stir her sister. April was next. Tracy thought of all she was burdening them with, her sister and Remy. An accountant and a schoolteacher. They would sleep tonight, and when they woke, what would they find? Five hundred years, gone in an instant. A key around their necks. A note from her. An apology.

Igor lifted April, and Tracy helped Anatoly with Remy. They shuffled through dark corridors with their burdens. "Carry on," Tracy whispered, that mantra of theirs, the awful dismissal of all they'd done. But this time, it was with promise. With hope. "Carry on," she whispered to her sister. "Carry on for all of us."

DEAR JOHN

Robin Wasserman

Dear Neckbeard,

The fact that I'm writing this on toilet paper shouldn't make you think I don't care. This toilet paper is not symbolic, it's expedient. Writing you a letter on something I can use to wipe my ass is just a happy coincidence.

These letters are supposed to help us indulge in happier times—that's what Isaac says. Bathe in all our wonderful memories, then pull the plug and watch them circle the drain. Write out our teary *I loved you*s and *what might have been*s to all the people we've lost out there in the world, then set them on fire and say goodbye to smoke and ash. Or, in my case: Write, wipe, flush. Farewell. This, Isaac also says, will be closure. Isaac, apparently, doesn't know from mixed metaphors. And he doesn't know his flock as well as he thinks, not if he imagines wonderful memories and happy *might have been*s. That's not how you end up in a place like this.

You'd probably be surprised I ended up here, fucked up in this very specific way, but then, we haven't seen each other in a while. Things happen. Maybe I'd be surprised about where you ended up, too. I doubt it, but see me politely trying to give you the benefit of the doubt—one of those things you thought I was incapable of? Things happen; people—at least those of us who venture out of our basement every once in a while—change. Here's me, since the days of you: Austin, then LA, then back into the nation's beer belly, even if it was a little too close to home, hop-skip-jumping through crap towns on I-70, six months waiting tables for truckers feeling like I was on one of those serial killer shows waiting for my big scene as a dumpster corpse, desert then mountains then plains, and everywhere I stopped, everyone I stopped for, promised me I'd be stopping forever. Remember when I popped your cherry and you told me you were going to chain me to the bed and keep me as your prisoner until I got old and wrinkled and ready to trade in for a new model? The pillow talk got better, but the men didn't, and none of them kept me anymore than you did. Maybe people don't change so much after all. (*I've changed,* you said, but it was only because I changed you, and if that skank you tutored wanted to fuck you, it was only because I made you throw out those orange clogs and stop whispering to yourself when you thought no one was looking.) To wrap this up: I came, they came, then they left. Until I threw in with the Children of Abraham, because Father Abraham said God would never leave me—but then Father Abraham left, and the fucking world ended, on exactly the day he predicted it would—so where does that leave me?

Here, in the Ark, locked up safe and sound in a mountain compound with Abraham's kid and all of us who were fucked up enough to believe him when he and his dad said the end was nigh. The world left us, but we clued in and left it first. Followed that kid up a mountain, barricaded ourselves behind sheet metal and barbed-wire, waited for God's wrath and wondered what form it would take. No shock he took us out just like he did the dinosaurs. There's nothing much to read up here but the Bible, and I've read enough to know God likes repeating himself. He likes to smite, and very occasionally, he likes to save. I guess he must like us—the reformed hookers and crack addicts and embezzlers and sad sacks on the run from bad memories and worse husbands—because we're the ones still here. You were always so pleased with yourself about your lack of fucked-up-edness. I would say look where it's gotten you, but you wouldn't exactly hear it, would you, because that's the whole point of where it's gotten you. Out in the world with the rest of the assholes, minding your non-fucked-up business when the shit came down. Isaac says we should imagine a happy and peaceful end for all the poor souls caught unaware. An aneurysm at the moment the sky exploded. Swift, unbloodied obliteration.

I would prefer not to.

You were in the basement when it happened—that's how I prefer to imagine it. You'd been down there two days straight, fingers cramping on your joystick (and yes, I know it hasn't been called a joystick since 1988 but fuck if you're going to bully me into caring from beyond the grave), moldy pizza boxes at your feet, porn taped up to the wall because it's been so many years and so many pounds since you've lured a girl down to your dungeon that there's no point in keeping your inner perv on lockdown anymore. You were blowing shit up and giggling about it and when you heard the first explosions, you probably thought, *dude, cool sound effects, whoa,* while upstairs the sky fell down and then your roof fell down and it took another day before you thought to heave yourself off the couch and replenish the beer, and that's when you discovered the door was blocked by ten tons of rubble and the phones were out and the wi-fi was dead and too bad for you, your emergency generator ran out before your food did, so you spent your last days on Earth in the dark, unplugged, fingers twitching at the joystick like you could turn the explosions back on, then eventually switching over to your own personal joystick, huffing and rubbing while you imagined me on my knees, blowing you while you shot the crap out of some imaginary kingdom, jerking off to some sad, faint echo of my voice because you never forget the first girl to get you off, thinking about how you pinned her down on the bathroom tile when she tried to dump your ass, crying and leaking snot and begging *please baby don't leave me* while you jackhammered her into a concussion that made her foggy enough to say *okay baby if you need me I'll stay* and then she did until you got bored and left her, instead, thinking now how if you'd kept her around you might not be shivering in the dark all alone, leaking sanity at a steady pace until the food runs out, and then the beer, and you die slow and whimpering, in a pool of your own puke and cum.

Thinking of you, keep in touch!

Love,

Heather

• • •

Dear Moneybags,

Remember how you used to laugh at me for always ordering the same thing? You started ordering it for me, before I could get the words out. Wherever we went, you knew. Veal parmigiana. Pad Thai. Chicken Tikka Masala. I thought it was cute, at first, that you were pretending that it bothered you, because what kind of pretentious turd would *actually* be bothered by someone who knows what she wants and sticks with it? It's not like I was bringing peanut-butter and jelly sandwiches with me to sneak from under the table while you ate sushi, so how was I supposed to know that every time I ordered Pad Thai, or let you order it for me, I was proving to you that I was unadventurous and dull and provincial and inflexible and "unwilling to let circumstances exercise their will" on me. I was embarrassing you, somehow, in front of the waiters or your friends or maybe just some all-seeing deity who expected better from you than a girlfriend who didn't want to try veal kidney.

You wouldn't much like it here.

Here we eat beans and more beans. Canned tuna and canned peaches. We eat peanut butter when we've been especially good; we eat nothing when we've been bad. Every day is the same. Sometimes, early on, the men would suit up and go shoot something, and there would be fresh meat for a night, but then winter was too long and too cold and they say the animals are all dead. They say we don't need the outside, that's the point of our Ark. We are prepared. Months go by without a dent in our food stores. We planned well—we have enough beans to last us for years.

Years of beans and tuna and peaches and peanut butter. Can you even begin to imagine that? You, who thought it was a hardship to eat the same thing two nights in a row. Leave that kind of thing to the poors, you said, even though when I tried to leave our leftovers with an actual poor, you slapped it out of my hand and told me handouts only encouraged the weak, and left the guy to lick his veal parmigiana off the ground. That's what I get for dating a Republican, you told me that night, when you had me spread-eagled on your Sleep Number mattress, because that was your idea of dirty talk.

You didn't mind snorting the same drugs every night, I noticed. You loved the drugs; you loved that I had loser friends who could supply you with them. You loved that I looked pretty in the dresses you bought me and smiled pretty enough for your asshole buddies that they felt like shit and then went home and took it out on their ugly girlfriends; you loved that I fucked one of them when you asked me to as a special *pretty-please for me baby* favor; you loved that you could make me do that, but then you didn't love that I'd done it. Done *him*. Put him in my mouth and in my ass, and let him cum on my tits, bad enough doing it, worse that you made me tell you about it, tell you while you were inside me, tell you how he felt and that he was smaller and softer than you, that he was flabby, with bad breath and thinning hair, that he made my nipple bleed, and after I told you what you wanted to hear, you threw me out of bed and said I'd never be with you if you weren't rich, which was true, and that it made me a whore, which maybe was also. Now I think I liked your pool better than I liked you. Your pool and your stupid restaurants and your coke, even if you wouldn't have had that last without me. I liked it best when you left for the weekend and I could float on the raft in the middle of the chlorine blue, drunk and sunburned, laughing at the clouds, at the gurgle of the pool filtration system and the way my fingers wrinkled up when I stayed in too long. I pretended it was my pool, my life; I imagined your plane flying into a mountain and some silver-haired lawyer showing up at the door to cup my hands in his and tell me, gently, that you'd left it all to me.

That's a lie.

I imagined you coming back, but coming back different. Something new on your face when you looked at me, like you finally understood why you kept me around. I imagined us floating on the raft together, happy, that it would be like it was at the beginning, you bending me over the sink in gold-plated bathrooms while waiters tried not to wonder what was taking us so long, you tearing through some cheap K-Mart blouse like you were Tarzan and telling me I had a Michelangelo rack, that licking my nipples felt like desecrating priceless art, you wanting to ravish me, you wanting to My Fair Lady me, you wanting me. Instead you came back from that last trip and told me you wanted someone who better fit into your world, someone who knew enough to pick out her own sushi.

No one is rich anymore; no one is poor. There are only haves and have-nots. We, the Children of Abraham, God's favored sons and daughters, *have:* Shelter. Food. Generators. Guns. Lives.

You, the rest, have not.

I don't have to worry anymore about being left, about being wanted. For one thing, it doesn't matter what any of us want—there's nowhere to fucking go. We've got a radio here, we know what it's like out there, or we know enough to imagine. Cities obliterated; West Coast underwater; governments fallen; everywhere riots and corpses. *Tohu va vohu*—Isaac says that's how the Bible begins, in Hebrew. In the beginning, all was formless and void, all was wild and waste; so it began, he says, now so it ends. Isaac says we've all been alone long enough, that now we'll be together. Not only all of us together in the Ark, but each of us together with another soul, matched pairs, two by two by two, as it should be. Isaac will pair us. He says God tipped him off about our proper soulmates, and since that's the same God who gave him a heads-up about the end of the world and how to survive it, we have no choice but to believe him. So much easier than the old way. Isaac will pair us, then, in ten days, we'll join hands and souls in the eyes of God. We'll swear to our Lord. *Forever,* we'll swear, and that's how it will be. That's another thing that's changed from the old days. Once you know that God is willing to destroy the world when it pisses him off, you get a little more reluctant to break your word.

You said once that if I ever duped someone into marrying me, I should make sure to get a pre-nup, because that way when they left me I'd get mine. *Actually, I'd get* yours, I said, *isn't that how pre-nups work*? And you laughed. Not, you said, at the lame joke, but at the idea that *you'd* be the one marrying me.

That's when I should have known. Not because you laughed, but because of the *when.* If *you get married;* when *he leaves you.* You saw it before I did, that I was a girl to be left.

And now you've left again.

Don't worry, this time I won't make a scene.

I think you die with the rest of California when the waves come to sweep you away. You die thinking maybe you should've gotten around to learning how to swim, which wouldn't have saved you but might have let you hang on a little longer or with a little more dignity; you could've gotten to see what it looked like for LA to float, see the Hollywood sign bobbing on the waves along with all the nippled silicone implants, the Jags and the Range Rovers and the Ferraris sucked under, fish shitting on all that Italian leather, anorexic starlets with their gym-toned bodies bloating in the sun, you die and I live, even though your house was made of brick and marble and mine is made of old shipping containers. The Three Little Pigs is not a disaster survival guide, and besides, our craftsmanship is solid, all the huffing and puffing in the world won't blow our ark down. Where you live now, there is only seafood for dinner, night after night. I guess circumstances have exercised their will.

Love,

Heather

• • •

Dear John,

Remember how we used to joke about that? How I used to leave you notes that would say, "Dear John, I am not leaving you. But please pick up some milk on your way home." How we agreed that if I ever did leave you, all I had to write was, "Dear John, This time I am." You thought it was unfair, that your name was synonymous with leaving, with being left. You said, *I will never leave you. Not me. Not you.*

Is it love that makes you stupid, or is stupid just a necessary criteria for falling in love?

Feel free to think of this as the letter you never got. Feel free to think whatever you want, except that I miss you.

Onion breath. Flop sweat. Fork scraping. The tick-tock click of a pen against teeth. *Thought music,* you called it.

The kind of person who would say the words "thought music."

File it all under *Things I do not miss.*

Lying, that's another one.

I will never leave you.

I will never leave you.

I will never leave you.

The way you looked at me, all wounded puppy eyes, that I could even imagine it. The insult of the fear. Just turn it off, you told me, like you'd never been afraid.

How could I have thought that would work, a forever with a man who didn't understand fear? Here's my forever, as of this morning: black, walrus mustache and graying scruff of beard, veiny biceps and lopsided ears. Small hands, big nose. His name is Gavin, and I think, in that other life, he was rich. The kind who has a midlife crisis and when he discovers the Porsche isn't magically stripping off the years, acquires someone like me instead, sends flowers and makes promises and then signs the divorce papers and marries someone else. Except that Gavin's already left his wife, left her out there to die with the rest of the world, and now, in here, there's no one but me. Isaac says—or says that God says—we belong together. Maybe he threw darts, or picked names out of a hat. Maybe it really is God; maybe Gavin is my destiny.

I have one friend here, and she thinks this is fucked, though that's a word she would never use. Theresa Babbage, who used to babysit Isaac when he was just some kid rather than Our Savior, who told me about the time he got so freaked out by some nightmare that he wet the bed, eleven years old and swimming in piss and she swore me to secrecy because if word got out he'd know she was the one who told, and we both know what would happen then—she thinks this is fucked. She thinks Isaac's only making us marry because he outlawed fucking before marriage and too many of the single men miss it. I don't tell her that I miss it, too. She wouldn't like that. I don't tell her that the arranged marriage thing doesn't seem all that different to me than how it worked before. A man says he wants to be with you, and you stay. A man says he doesn't want to be with you anymore, and he leaves. So what if in this case, it's Isaac who says he wants me to be with someone? The only difference is that in this case, it doesn't matter whether the man wants to be with me or not.

Gavin will stay with me, and I will stay with him. That's the difference. I won't expect him to save me; I won't expect him to love me or want me. I won't expect anything, but that we will be together instead of alone.

You were the kind of guy who liked to save people, you said, and you said you'd save me. You were going to be different than the others, you said. You would be the one who stayed, who would convince me that staying was possible, that not everyone leaves. You said only the wrong people leave, that I was lucky they did, because if they hadn't, there wouldn't have been a *you*. Not all *together*s are better than being alone, you said. Only this one.

You said I didn't scare you. That no part of me would make you run away. That we would never be alone again, that instead, we would be alone together. Remember when we turned the apartment into a fort, said we would barricade ourselves away from the world forever? We would bury ourselves under blankets with an endless supply of caramels and Fresca, enough to last us through all six seasons of *The Sopranos* and every time one of Tony's henchmen killed someone, we would kiss. We were stupid then, and didn't understand forts or barricades or forever. And we never got around to finishing *The Sopranos,* which is a shame, because now there's no more Netflix and it turns out there's not as much overlap as you'd expect between premium cable viewers and doomsday cultists, so there's no one here to tell me how it ends. Even if there was, they wouldn't have acted it out in the stupid voices, the way you did when I missed an episode.

Here is what I think about sometimes: The day I figured it out, that the entitled ass who showed up every day to exchange his rental car because the seat didn't recline all the way or the gas cap jiggled or the clutch was sticky or the radio cut out at the high end of the FM band wasn't such an entitled ass after all, that you didn't give a shit about the shitty cars, you just wanted an excuse to smile at the girl behind the counter. The day I smiled back. The four days it took after that, waiting for you to make your move; the way you dimpled when I made it for you. What you said, when you dropped me off that night—the first time, before you made the U-turn in your tin can rental car because you realized taking things slow was crap—that it wasn't because you thought I was pretty, that that's not why you came back the next day. Not that you didn't think I was pretty. Of course you thought I was pretty. It's just it wasn't *because* I was pretty.

I liked it when you stammered. I liked that I could make you nervous.

It was because you didn't bother to say thank you when I handed you the keys, and I told you that wasn't very polite.

Not just a pretty girl; a pretty girl having a crap day at a job that required her to smile and be nice. A pretty girl with butterflies on her dress and a glittering stud in her nose, with army camo nail polish and a chip on her shoulder, with one assy customer too many, and something about it woke you up, you said, and you came back that first time, the next day, just to see if I had quit. You had a feeling about me, you said. Like I was some tropical bug lighting on a flower, that all it would take was a breeze to spook me away.

I liked that you remembered what I was wearing; I liked that you didn't call me a fucking butterfly.

You're right that it was different with you, I'll give you that. You're right that it was better—but in the end, it was the same, because it still ended. It doesn't matter how good something is if it doesn't last; the being better only makes it hurt more when it's over, so what's the fucking point?

It's over. That's the only *forever* for us now. We both know you're dead, and we both know how, and I don't want to talk about it.

Love,

Heather

• • •

Dear Cheating Bastard,

You die in the woods, where your smug face gets eaten off by escaped zoo bears, you chipmunk-headed fuckwit.

Love,

Heather

• • •

Dear Teach,

That was my first ever A+, and I guess I proved myself a C student through and through by being dense enough to believe in it. That when you said I had promise, you meant in life, and not in a back office, bent over your desk, skirt hiked up, both of us listening for someone coming, only one of us actually knowing what that would sound like. *You write like a writer.* That's what you scribbled on the last page. *See me after class,* and you underlined that one twice. A for effort.

I thought I was an old soul; I thought I was a portrait of the artist as a young woman. I thought you loved me for those things, and for the way I laughed like I had a secret and the way I perched on the fringe of life, expectant and ever watchful, seeing into things that most people can't see at all—because that's what you told me. Not that you loved me because I sucked you off like I'd done it a million times before or because you had some weird fetish for skinny wrists and slap bracelets, or because I was just stupid enough to believe you when you said I was smart.

I know, I know: When I whine, I sound like a child.

I'm thinking now you liked that best.

Age, you said, was just a number, which in retrospect explains why you liked fucking teenagers, because you assumed we would mistake cliché for wisdom.

A lot of things are clear in retrospect, not to mention cliché, like the things a girl will do when she grows up without a daddy and the sad vampirism of a guy in his thirties making one last lunge for his vanishing youth. I was sixteen, and you were sixteen years older—enough space for a whole other me to fit between us. Which I'm guessing you would have enjoyed.

Theresa Babbage is only nine years older than Isaac, which seems distasteful enough now, when he's only thirteen, but won't matter too much down the line, and either way, you've no room to judge. Isaac says that when he turns thirteen, he will be a man, that that's how it worked in biblical times and—look out the window—here we are again. (We have no windows here, but we all know what he means.) He says God wants him to be with a woman, and he wants that woman to be Theresa, and since age is just a number and what Isaac says goes, so be it. That's what we all tried to tell ourselves, and shrugged.

It makes sense he would pick her, not just because she's closer to his age than anyone other than the little kids, not just because she's hot, but because she was his babysitter, and that's the closest thing we've got to a teacher. (*Hot for a teacher,* there's another cliché you know pretty well.) She broke the rules for him, let him stay up after his bedtime, let him watch horror movies even after the nightmares started, the ones from God about the end of the world, and there's something intoxicating about that, breaking the rules together, sneaking around together in the dark, sharing a secret. Secrets breed.

Write dangerous, you said, when you gave us the journals, told us to write what we felt and what we feared, no sanitized shit about proms and puppies. You called them journals, not diaries, because diaries are for little girls, and you promised they would be for our eyes only. *Make the page a repository for your soul,* you told us, but when I showed you the page about how you tasted and what my heart did when you spelled words on my neck with your tongue, you told me *don't be a fucking idiot* and *never write any of this down,* and never even bothered to say if it was good.

I did what I was told. I didn't tell anyone. Even after you traded me in for that sophomore who wrote a love poem in her own menstrual blood, I didn't write any of it down. I learned my lesson about that. Never write down what actually matters. Never tell.

Even so, I still thought I might be a writer someday. If I had the time. If anything worth writing about ever happened to me. And here I am, witness to the end of the world, nothing to do but can fruit and record the fall of civilization and the mourning song of my heart or whatever, and the only thing I've bothered to write are my little collection of shitpaper letters to all you pieces of shit. There's nothing in here I want to record, and nothing out there that I can bring back by writing about it. What I want is to lie on a couch and watch TV.

You told us TV would turn us into passive consumers of other people's words and we should take a sledgehammer to the screen, impose our creative will on the world, creation via destruction, raze our brain-washed, consumerist, capitalist, shallow, pimple-popping lives to the ground and build from scorched earth; you told us no one ever died wishing they had watched more TV, but I will. I wish I'd watched more *Friends* reruns and had made a dent in the list of Boring-Sounding Shows I'm Tired of Admitting I Don't Watch. I can picture how you probably died (pierced in the jugular by exploding glass while you begged the mirror for help with your comb-over), but I'm already forgetting what the Real Housewives look like. I told you once that I thought soap operas were the most realistic form of storytelling, because they never stopped at happily ever after, they never stopped at all, and you laughed like I was making a joke, and I guess now the joke is on me because they stopped along with everything else.

There's nothing left out there now. That's what they say over the radio, although mostly, now, they don't say much of anything. Occasionally, through the static, we pick up someone crying.

There's nothing left out there and it's insane to hope that there is, and we all agree on that—except when it's time to put someone out. And then we pretend it's not a death sentence, just an alternative life choice. Anything could be out there, we say. She didn't like it in here, not enough to follow the rules and do as she was told, so maybe she'll find something she likes better.

Maybe, if Theresa Babbage preferred not to fuck a teenager, if, unlike you, that didn't turn her on, if she pretended Isaac's proposal was a question rather than a command and politely declined, then that was her choice, and maybe, after a few nights out there in the waste and wild, she won't regret it.

It's not execution, Isaac said last night, after he locked the gates behind her. Not even punishment. Simply the smart policing of a peaceful community. Go along to get along, or get out.

She said he was fucking crazy. She said what about feminism and Hilary Clinton and MTV and *how does a kid born in the twenty-first century buy any of this crap, the world hasn't worked like that for two thousand years,* and he said that the world was gone, and that a lot of things hadn't happened for two thousand years, and he didn't have to come right out and say *I am the light of the world* for us to know what he was getting at.

She probably thought her sisters would go with her, but she should have known better. She couldn't have imagined I would go with her, but she might have expected me to say goodbye. She didn't know how I feel about goodbyes.

She didn't tell me she was going to refuse him, or I would have talked her out of it. I would have told her about doing the things you need to do, about how to endure, about what it takes to be the girl who stays. I could have told her what it feels like to be left alone, but she didn't ask, and now they've pushed her out the door without warm clothes or food or any fucking idea how to take care of herself, because while the rest of us were preparing for the end by learning to shoot and make soap and forage for mushrooms, she was babysitting the future messiah, and now she's probably dead. I still have my laptop. The battery's long dead, of course, but sometimes I like to watch the blank screen, and imagine what used to be.

Even before, I liked to watch static, especially when I hurt. I liked the dead roar of it, the way you could squint into the wild and waste, almost believing that if you tried hard enough, you could resolve chaos into order, that somewhere, hiding between the squiggly lines, was a face, a voice, a world.

I want the picture back; I want it all back. I want trashy reality shows and late night infomercials and Saturday morning cartoons. I want my MTV. I want Chinese take-out and a greasy-fingered remote; I want sick days that pass in a haze of talk show rumbles and game show hosts; I want Luke and Laura to reunite and *As the World Turns* to come back from the dead; I want fat men with their skinny wives and hospitals where everyone is beautiful and dripping with sex and only boring people die; I want tornado hunters and competitive eaters and Sunday morning televangelists and even that fucking ice queen on Fox News. I want back all those afternoons that I spent with you in your car and your office and that skeezy hotel, because I could have spent them at home with a bag of Doritos and Oprah and *Boy Meets World* and now, when I lie in my bunk and pretend to sleep, breathing stale air, tuning out snores, fingering my knife and wondering if one day I'll wake up and decide to use it, I could play back all those episodes in my head, be my own laugh track, remember scripted lines and symmetrical faces, instead of you. I want oblivion, like the rest of you get to have, out there; I want not to be the one left behind when everyone else is gone.

I want. I want. I want. I'm sounding like a child again, aren't I? Like a whiny brat who thinks bad things only happen to bad people and gods play fair.

Not that I would call Isaac a whiny brat, or an ignorant kid, or delusional or pathetic, simply because he believes that we were saved because we deserved to be, that death is punishment and life reward, that we can remember what we choose to remember and forget the rest, that because he saved us once, our lives are forever in his hands. There are no teachers anymore, and even if there were, you can't teach the savior of mankind—God's chosen vessel—anything he doesn't want to know. So you see, this particular brave new world has no place for you. This is a world where children take whatever they want, and the rest of us live with what's left.

Love,

Heather

• • •

Dear John,

I said I don't miss you, and that's true enough. But I do miss fucking you. Or maybe I just miss fucking, full stop. Only one more week before Midlife Crisis and I join together in holy matrimony and connubial bliss, and you'd think I'd be more eager. He certainly is.

He tastes like fish.

Isaac keeps talking about what a joyful day it will be, but there's too much sadness in his eyes to pull it off. I can see it, even if no one else can, because I know what it looks like, the face of getting left behind.

He's got to be used to it by now. First his mother, dumping him at Father Abraham's door like one of those shitty free newspapers that always went straight into the trash. Dumping him with a father he'd never met before, a father who happened to be in the middle of a doomsday countdown with his millennial flock of fuck-ups.

Kid makes the best of that, teams up with daddy, buddies up so close to daddy's friend upstairs that he starts getting divine whispers in his own ear, turns savior, turns doomsday prepper-in-chief, teaches us to build our Ark and prepare for judgment day, and what's his prize when the sky falls down and proves him right? Dad dumps him too. Locks the kid into the promised land with the rest of us and heads down the mountain to die with the unsaved masses. Chose the world over his own kid, and said God told him to do it, which, as trump cards go, beats out *because I said so.*

Now Theresa's left him, too.

It doesn't matter that she didn't want to go; she's gone. That's how he sees it.

I couldn't help it—I felt bad for him. I said, s*he wasn't the right girl for you, Isaac,* and to his credit, he didn't pretend not to know what I mean. He didn't even try to fake a smile. *I saved her life,* he said. *Shouldn't that be enough?*

And you know what? Maybe it should. Everyone acts like love can save you, but love can't save anything. So maybe we've got it the wrong way around, maybe it's the saving that makes for love. Isaac saved us, and we should love him for it. He saved us, and so we belong to him. It's kid logic, but you've got to admit that it makes sense, and that's what I told him.

Still, I don't like the way he looks at me now.

Without Theresa, there's no one to ask about it, about whether I'm imagining things. The way his eyes follow me across the room. The way he saw me watching, and smiled.

I was just trying to be nice.

Dear John, wish you were here, that's what I'm supposed to say, I guess, since the other option is *wish you were dead*—wish you were starving or burning or being gnawed on by feral cats—but you wouldn't know what to do with yourself here. You wouldn't like being locked away, piecing things together with the static and screams and pleas on a CB radio, living in a tangle of bodies and bad breath, everywhere skin and sweat and people, all of us so pale.

I'm pale like you now, pale and thin and craving the sun. You always called me stupid for skimping on the sunscreen. Everyone's got to die sometime, I said.

I know how you died. Of course I know how you died. Why do you think I'm so good at this game? What else have I been doing since the last time you saw me but imagining how you died? I dream it, and wake up smelling disinfectant and puke, wake up tasting you, not the good you but the way you tasted at the end, like iron and rubber, like something poisonous. Sometimes I imagined I could feel it, some fluctuation in the universe, someone cutting the invisible floss that held us together, some infinitesimal weight lifting or settling—and how the fuck do any of those things actually *feel,* so it was more like I felt headaches and muscle cramps and indigestion and each time thought, just maybe, it was you.

I didn't have to be there to know how you died. Wasting away. Emaciated and skeleton skin but bloated with fluid. *Pregnant* with fluid, we might have said. High on drugs, so sky high you might have missed the headline, assumed you were easing into a nap instead of the big sleep, maybe high enough that you saw me, and smiled, because you thought you weren't alone. But you were. I know that, too.

Love,

Heather

• • •

Dear Jackass,

I guess you'll never finish that novel after all. God, the *novel,* the *novel,* always the fucking *novel.* And how could I be expected to understand such things, the bimbo who washed your filthy dishes once the fruit flies start swarming because your life of the mind precluded you from noticing such things. How could I, *bovine dumb,* so dumb I had to look up the word *bovine,* begin to process the profundities your mind was gestating, your miscarriage of literary greatness, your Solitaire games which I guess were tapping into some deep vein of emotional catharsis. If I thought there actually was a novel, I would wonder whether you'd turned me into a character, the stupid cunt who joined a cult, *can you imagine I stuck my dick in that beehive of crazy,* I can hear you saying to all your coffee shop losers, and that's why I don't feel guilty for taking your laptop when you left.

Not to be juvenile about it, or maybe *to* be juvenile about it, since according to you I'm incapable of anything else: Who's the stupid cunt now? Who's safe in the bunker with God's chosen people, and who's a rotting piece of meat waiting for someone else's cat to come by and gnaw at your intestines because you're far too busy to have one of your own?

Tell me you don't actually believe this shit, you said after those first couple meetings. *I pray to fucking non-existent god that I haven't wasted my time with someone who would fall for this.*

And I said, even at the beginning, because that's what it said in the brochure, *this is my calling* and *I need to repent before it's too late,* and I didn't tell you what Father Abraham told me, that *forgiveness is possible* and *God will never leave you* because I knew you would laugh and I wanted to believe it was true.

And eventually you said *I can't handle this shit anymore* and *the sex isn't worth the crazy,* and that was fine with me because Father Abraham's house had many rooms and plenty of empty beds, and how is that I'm never the one leaving, but I'm always the one who has to pack up my suitcase and walk out the door?

I never got around to answering your original question.

Did I believe it?

Do I believe it?

What kind of stupid cunt would I be not to believe it? A father and his son told me the world would end, and it did. They told me when it would happen, and it did. They told me how to survive it, and here I am. Abraham gathered us to his chest, Isaac built us an ark, and here we are, floating to salvation on a sea of millet and automatic rifles and kidney beans.

If I didn't believe, why did I come in the first place and why did I stay?

If I don't believe now, what more could possibly convince me?

Atheism is the only honest intellectual position, you said, and I didn't ask you what if an angel descended to Earth or a TV messiah parted the Red Seas or an eleven-year-old says God told me the world will die and the kid turns out to be right, because it was easier to let you think I wasn't listening when you talked. Maybe if you had asked me a question, I would have answered. Maybe if you asked me who I was thinking about when you were inside me, and why I would hate myself enough to let you be there, I would have told you a story.

The Holocaust, you said. *The Armenian genocide. Rwanda. What kind of a god,* etc., etc.

Everyone dies, I said. *Or do you blame Him for that, too.*

I don't know. That's the answer. I don't know if I believe in a Him, and so I don't know whether to worry about breaking a promise to Him, but the question's moot, because my soulmate-in-waiting is gone. Midlife Crisis Man slipped away in the night, mustache and all, apparently preferring certain death over an eternity bound to me.

That's assuming he left of his own accord, and obviously it wouldn't be the first time, but there's also Isaac, and the way he looked when he announced the disappearance, and the way he took my hand when he told me that I shouldn't worry about being alone for long, that God had plans for me.

Never trust anyone who says God has a plan, you told me, and that's the one thing that made sense.

I keep a knife under my pillow, in case I need it. We all have something—our own personal emergency escape plan. Some people can't handle it, losing the world. *What kind of a god,* you said, and now we have an answer, and it's one that not everyone can live with.

We've pieced it together from the radio. What happened that day, after we locked ourselves in the Ark. What it looked like when the sky fell down. On the radio, they say it was beautiful, a hailstorm of light, but that's because they're the ones who lived. I think you lived too, at least past the initial impact, and maybe you tried to write a poem about it; maybe you thought: *finally, good material.*

I think your city wasn't obliterated; your loft wasn't vaporized. You were too far from the coast to get swept away. I think you felt good about yourself, while you still had time to feel. You couldn't believe in a god that put *Fifty Shades of Grey* on the bestseller list, but a god that turned twenty million people to dust and left you still tapping ashes out of your hand-carved corncob pipe, I think that's a god you could get behind. I think it wasn't until the nukes started flying that you got in trouble, *chaos breeds chaos* you used to say, tapping on the pipe, and *it only takes one madman with a nuclear code and nothing to lose,* and I guess once you've lost the sky, what's left. I think you got a full blast of poison and your skin started falling off in patches, you heaved up everything inside of you until you were hollow, you went full zombie, scaly and moaning, radiation cannibalizing your brain along with everything else, I think you tried to kill yourself by drinking a mug of fountain pen ink because you thought it would be a poetic way to go, but you threw that up, too, and died praying to your nonexistent fucking god that the pain would stop.

Love,

Heather

• • •

Dear No Strings Attached,

It would have been a pretty big fucking string, our baby. Our un-baby, our cell grouping, our medical waste. Less a string than a cord. Or one of the ropes they use to tie up boats. Knotted, rough to the touch, stinking of fish.

The ropes they *used* to use, I guess I should say.

Hard to get used to that.

You didn't have to tell me you didn't want it. That once it was inside me, you didn't want me, either, no matter how fast I got it scraped out. You didn't have to tell me I would be a shitty mother.

These are things I already knew.

You didn't have to pay for it, either, and so you didn't. You could at least have offered.

Would I have been a shitty mother? I guess I'll have my chance to find out, if I stay here.

You like how I said that, *if* I stay? The superfluous *if,* as in, I'll meet you for coffee tomorrow, *if* the sun rises; I'll hurt when it's over, *if* it ends.

If gravity takes hold, I'll break when I hit the ground.

Be fruitful and multiply, that's the plan. Grow the compound until it's safe to leave it behind. Repopulate the Earth. Not yet, Isaac says, but soon.

He says that about the two of us, too. Soon. That we won't marry tonight with the others. We'll wait until he turns thirteen, and then we will be joined. In all ways, we will be joined.

I told him I was old enough to be his mother, though I didn't add that you don't have to be Freud to see the relevance there. I told him there was no reason for him to hurry. That he had plenty of time to become a man.

He told me not to speak to him like a child.

He told me I understood him, and we would come to love each other. God would make it so.

He told me God wants him to have a son.

It's possible that he's making this shit up, but I'm pretty sure he believes it. Which is not better.

If you don't believe in Isaac, and say it out loud, they put you out.

If you don't fulfill your responsibilities, they put you out.

If you sin against the Lord, or some big mouth accuses you of doing so because she wants those chocolate bars you're hoarding, they put you out.

If I were a mother, I would make sure my daughter knew that you do what you have to do. Even if it means letting the kid shove himself into you, enduring one scraping thrust and a whiplash jerk, the blown wad, the wilting dick, the tears.

Yes, I've thought about it. *Am* thinking about it.

But maybe, if I were a mother, when I am a mother, I'll hide the baby under my coat and steal her away from the Ark, and raise her in the world. Maybe, because she will be born into the after, she will have evolved to survive it. Or I could leave her when I go, if I went, leave her where she could be safe and tended to, if not loved, and let her accept how life is supposed to be without me there to whisper in her ear that she should want more, that once there was more.

Or maybe Isaac is right, and God will stick me with a son.

Love,

Heather

P.S. Did you think I forgot? I'd guess you died, gutshot, intestines on the ground, mouth gibbering with surprise, when you got desperate enough to take food from your neighbor and she didn't want to share. She's dead now too, I'm guessing, the one you used to spy on with binoculars when you pretended you were birdwatching, because you liked the way she bulged and jiggled when she was naked, even though you always told me I should lose weight. Not, like, in a shallow way, you said. For my health.

• • •

Dear guy in the Arcade Fire t-shirt with the stain on the collar,

You were nice. That's most of what I remember. You bought me drinks, but not too many, and didn't say anything when I bought myself a few more.

I remember you'd just gotten fired, but you had your buddy's entrance card so you could sneak into the building and smuggle out your files. You took me with you, and we didn't go to your sad, abandoned cubicle to collect what was left of your old life. You didn't want to have sex on your boss's couch or take a dump on his desk. You wanted to show me the roof, because you said it was the best view of the city and I seemed like someone who needed a good view.

I was a little afraid you were a person who needed a high place from which to jump.

I would like to remember the feel of your arms around me as we stood against the railing and watched the lights twinkle in the black, but I only remember that it felt like standing on the deck of a boat, watching fallen stars burn on a dark sea.

I thought, *maybe him.*

Maybe this.

Because that's how you think when you're the right amount of drunk, and hands and lips feel good, and someone is nice. Sometimes even when he's not.

Someone is better than no one.

That's what Isaac told me, because he doesn't want me to leave like Theresa left, doesn't want to have to *make* me leave. *Would it be so bad to be with me?* he asked, and he shouldn't have, because it made him sound so young. He told me I could have a day to think about it, before I promise myself to him. He's being generous, he says, because he likes me.

I always want to ask him whether he knows why his mother left him behind—whether he cares if she had a reason or not.

Not that having a reason is anything special. Everyone has a reason.

Would it be so bad? He won't be thirteen forever, but he would be forever mine.

I thought I loved you all—even you, even for a night—and none of you saved me. Isaac saved me, so maybe he's right that I should love him, that that's how it should work.

He chose wisely this time, chose like he could see into me.

I am the girl who stays.

I am the girl who says *yes, if you want.*

Whatever you want.

As long as you don't leave.

You didn't have time to find that out about me, and you didn't have time to test it. Or maybe you did. I can't remember.

I might have told you the truth about me, all of me; you might have told me things you'd never told anyone, the secrets that made you who you were; we might have decided this night was the beginning of all things; you might have recited poetry and I might have recited the lyrics to all the C&C Music Factory songs I know, which is three, because we wanted to impress each other, and it might have worked; we might have done nothing more up there than kiss, like people in a boring movie, deciding, because Hollywood told us it was romantic, to take it slow, that why not, we had all the time in the world; we might have shaken the Earth. I don't remember, like the next day I didn't remember your name or where the office was, which was all fine, because I gave you my number; I thought I remembered that much, but then you never called, so one way or another, I was wrong.

I think you died when it first happened, went up in a blaze of light, fused with the thing that fell from the stars. I hope they're right that it was beautiful.

Love,

the girl in the lime green miniskirt who wanted to see the sky

• • •

Dear John,

This is what I would have written, if I had written anything. *Dear John,* it's better this way. *Dear John,* it's now or later, and we're both better off if it's now. *Dear John,* you won't believe me, but I'm doing you a favor. *Dear John,* it's okay if you fucking hate me forever because I hate you too. You told me you would never leave me, and now you're leaving, so don't try to blame me for leaving first. *Dear John,* don't die, and maybe someday I'll come back.

You can see why I didn't leave a note.

Your mother took me aside. Not that first day in the hospital—there was too much crying for that, all that weeping and rending of clothes by your bedside. *It's not natural for a mother to lose a son,* she kept saying, like it isn't the most natural thing in the world, like that isn't what mothers do every day, like that isn't why she hated me, no matter what you claimed. After the first day, before the week had ended, before I went home to pack a bigger suitcase for you, because we'd moved past duffel bags, into some new category of traveler, long-term visa to the kingdom of the sick, somewhere in there, she took me aside. You can't handle this, she told me. You think you can, but you can't. She thought because her husband was dead, she knew what it took to handle things, and she thought, because you called her sometimes to bitch about me never doing the dishes, and because once, the time you thought I was sleeping with the coffee guy, you made the mistake of telling her why I didn't speak to my family anymore and why I never went to college and what I did that year in LA to pay the rent, because of everything you let her imagine, she thought she knew me.

She said you can't handle this, and if you can't handle this it's better if you go now than later. *I* can handle this, she said, and what she was actually saying was *he's mine.* You're nothing and he's mine. She probably never told you that, and so you never knew it was partly her fault. She made me weak. A witch, like I always said. She put a curse on me and it came to pass.

I am the girl who stays—except somehow, I left.

I left before you could leave me, and I did the same thing with the world, left it out there alone to die, locked myself up tight, huddled around a radio and listened to it burn.

I don't think about all the millions of people who died. I think about you, and whether your hair fell out like they said it would, and how you looked without it. What we would have done to kill time while they pumped poison into your veins, whether it would have been Scrabble or Trivial Pursuit, or if you finally would have guilted me into reading to you, even the crap poetry that you know I hate. How many more times would you have yelled at me for biting my cuticles? How many more times could I have crawled into your bed, snaked my hand around the wires and up your gown, massaged cold, veiny skin until you gasped *thank you, yes, please,* always polite, even in heat?

I will never leave you, Isaac said, and of course I've heard it before, but no one has ever meant it as much as he did. *In this life and the next. You will never have to be alone. I promise.*

He believes in his word. He believes in eternity. He won't get bored or distracted. He won't see the *tohu va vohu* at my center and realize I am a girl to be left, not loved. He will not leave. I believe he believes that, and I almost believe it's true.

I promise forever, he said. *Isn't that what you want? Isn't that what we all want?*

Love me forever if you love me at all—fairy tale love, fairy tale happily ever afters, that's what he believes in, as he should, because he's still a child.

That's what I've believed in all these years, too. That's what I've wanted, and now that a child wants me to have it, I'm thinking it may be time to grow up.

Because it turns out everybody leaves. And not all leavings are the same.

Not all endings are the same.

Not all endings come at the wrong time, and when they do, maybe it doesn't have to be anyone's fault. Maybe you leaving didn't mean I wasn't enough.

Maybe I should have waited for you to leave me, instead of leaving you first.

Sometimes I wonder, *what if.* What if there was a miracle. A remission. A cure. What if you sat up five minutes after I walked out of there, you tore the oxygen off your face, strength flooding through your veins, tumors shriveling. What if you called out my name but I was already gone.

I let myself imagine you out there somewhere, and if you got one miracle, then why not two? Why not miracles enough to survive the sky-fall and whatever came next? You could be leading a hardy band of survivors through the countryside, eating mushrooms and roasting goats, a Hollywood vision of man's triumph over god and nature, ready for your close-up. You could be the tan one now, stronger than ever, muscles bulging through tattered clothes, hair lit blond the way it always got by the end of the summer, and if you are alive, if you are a miracle, then I know that's how it would be. You wouldn't be alone; you wouldn't look for somewhere to hide, to lock yourself away and wait for the hard part to be over. You wouldn't need a knife under your pillow, you wouldn't be tempted to escape from the world. You would anchor yourself to it, raise a fist to the broken sky, shout *this is mine and you can't have it,* and then you would go looking for survivors and make the world new. Maybe you would go looking for me. Maybe you *are* looking for me.

Maybe I should go looking for you. Maybe I meant it when I said, *don't die.*

Don't die, and maybe someday I'll come back.

I could leave here. Slip away in the night. I could find you out there, huddled in the woods or in a cave or in the shelter of a decaying mall, mannequins watching over you while you forage for supplies in the camping store and gnaw at stale candy bars from a long dead CVS. That would be another miracle, but everything's a miracle in this new world. A man saw the apocalypse on the horizon; a boy listened to the word of God and built an Ark; I came to them because I thought I deserved to die, and because of that, I lived. This new world is taped together with miracles. What's one more?

I know you're dead. It's possible that if I leave this place, I'll be dead soon, too. I'll be the one chewed up by zoo animals in an overgrown forest or falling in a sinkhole and journeying to the center of the Earth, gang-raped by a merry band of anarchic survivors or shot in the back for my shoes and my canteen. But before it happens, I'll get to see the clouds again, and stomp around in the rain. I'll get to taste grass and sky, and I won't have to imagine ruined cities and rotting corpses because I'll see them for myself. I won't have to imagine and dream and wonder and wake up tasting blood and ruin, and maybe, if I return to the world, I can stop dreaming about it. Maybe I'll even find it's not as bad out there as we think. Maybe the world hasn't left us at all, not entirely, not yet, and there's still time to say goodbye, or build another miracle.

Maybe I don't have to be the girl who stays, because she's afraid of facing what's out there on her own. Maybe I don't have to say *yes, okay, whatever you want, just don't leave me alone, just don't leave.* Maybe I can be the one to leave, or the one to return, the one to decide. Maybe forever together is worse than being alone. Maybe forever is beside the point.

Love,

Heather

• • •

Dear Isaac,

I'm sorry.

If I'm still alive when the world really ends, maybe I'll come back. Sometimes people do.

Love,

Heather

ABOUT THE AUTHORS

Tananarive Due is the Cosby Chair in the Humanities at Spelman College. She also teaches in the creative writing MFA program at Antioch University Los Angeles. The American Book Award winner and NAACP Image Award recipient has authored and/or co-authored twelve novels and a civil rights memoir. In 2013, she received a Lifetime Achievement Award in the Fine Arts from the Congressional Black Caucus Foundation. In 2010, she was inducted into the Medill School of Journalism's Hall of Achievement at Northwestern University. She has also taught at the Geneva Writers Conference, the Clarion Science Fiction & Fantasy Writers' Workshop, and Voices of Our Nations Art Foundation (VONA). Due's supernatural thriller *The Living Blood* won a 2002 American Book Award. Her novella "Ghost Summer," published in the 2008 anthology *The Ancestors,* received the 2008 Kindred Award from the Carl Brandon Society, and her short fiction has appeared in best-of-the-year anthologies of science fiction and fantasy. Due is a leading voice in black speculative fiction.

Scott Sigler is the *New York Times* bestselling author of the Infected trilogy (*Infected, Contagious,* and *Pandemic*), *Ancestor,* and *Nocturnal,* hardcover thrillers from Crown Publishing; and the co-founder of Empty Set Entertainment, which publishes his Galactic Football League series (*The Rookie, The Starter, The All-Pro,* and *The MVP*). Before he was published, Scott built a large online following by giving away his self-recorded audiobooks as free, serialized podcasts. His loyal fans, who named themselves "Junkies," have downloaded over eight million individual episodes of his stories and interact daily with Scott and each other in the social media space.

Annie Bellet is the author of *The Twenty-Sided Sorceress* and the *Gryphonpike Chronicles* series. She holds a BA in English and a BA in Medieval Studies and thus can speak a smattering of useful languages such as Anglo-Saxon and Medieval Welsh. Her short fiction is available in multiple collections and anthologies. Her interests besides writing include rock climbing, reading, horseback riding, video games, comic books, table-top RPGs, and many other nerdy pursuits. She lives in the Pacific Northwest with her husband and a very demanding Bengal cat. Find her on her website at anniebellet.com.

Charlie Jane Anders' story "Six Months Three Days" won a Hugo Award and was shortlisted for the Nebula and Theodore Sturgeon Awards. Her writing has appeared in *Mother Jones, Asimov's Science Fiction, Tor.com, Tin House, ZYZZYVA, The McSweeney's Joke Book of Book Jokes,* and elsewhere. She's the managing editor of *io9.com* and runs the long-running Writers With Drinks reading series in San Francisco. More info at charliejane.net.

Seanan McGuire was born and raised in Northern California, resulting in a love of rattlesnakes and an absolute terror of weather. She shares a crumbling old farmhouse with a variety of cats, far too many books, and enough horror movies to be considered a problem. Seanan publishes about three books a year, and is widely rumored not to actually sleep. When bored, Seanan tends to wander into swamps and cornfields, which has not yet managed to get her killed (although not for lack of trying). She also writes as Mira Grant, filling the role of her own evil twin, and tends to talk about horrible diseases at the dinner table.

Sarah Langan is the author of the novels *The Keeper, This Missing,* and *Audrey's Door.* Her work has garnered three Bram Stoker Awards, a *New York Times* Editor's Pick, an ALA selection, and a *Publishers Weekly* favorite Book of the Year selection. Her short fiction has appeared in *Nightmare Magazine, Brave New Worlds, Fantasy Magazine, Lightspeed Magazine, The Magazine of Fantasy & Science Fiction*, and elsewhere. She's at work on her fourth novel, *The Clinic*, and lives in Brooklyn with her husband and two daughters. She thinks Ray Kurzweil is kind of a nut, and that, in fact, the singularity is very far away.

Nancy Kress is the author of thirty-two books, including twenty-five novels, four collections of short stories, and three books about writing. Her work has won two Hugos ("Beggars in Spain" and "The Erdmann Nexus"), five Nebulas (all for short fiction), a Sturgeon ("The Flowers of Aulit Prison"), and a John W. Campbell Memorial award (for *Probability Space*). The novels include science fiction, fantasy, and thrillers; many concern genetic engineering. Her most recent work is the Nebula-winning and Hugo-nominated *After the Fall, Before the Fall, During the Fall* (Tachyon, 2012), a long novella of eco-disaster, time travel, and human resiliency. Forthcoming is another short novel from Tachyon, *Yesterday's Kin* (Fall 2014). Intermittently,

Nancy teaches writing workshops at various venues around the country, including Clarion and Taos Toolbox (yearly, with Walter Jon Williams). A few years ago she taught at the University of Leipzig as the visiting Picador professor. She is currently working on a long, as-yet-untitled SF novel. Nancy lives in Seattle with her husband, writer Jack Skillingstead, and Cosette, the world's most spoiled toy poodle.

David Wellington is the author of the Monster Island trilogy of zombie novels, the 13 Bullets series of vampire books, and most recently the Jim Chapel thrillers *Chimera* and *The Hydra Protocol.* "Agent Unknown" *(The End is Nigh)* and "Agent Isolated" are prequels to *Positive,* his forthcoming zombie epic. He lives and works in Brooklyn, New York.

Ken Liu (http://kenliu.name) is an author and translator of speculative fiction, as well as a lawyer and programmer. A winner of the Nebula, Hugo, and World Fantasy Awards, he has been published in *The Magazine of Fantasy & Science Fiction, Asimov's, Analog, Clarkesworld, Lightspeed*, and *Strange Horizons*, among other places. Ken's debut novel, *The Grace of Kings*, the first in a silkpunk epic fantasy series, will be published by Saga Press, Simon & Schuster's new genre fiction imprint, in April 2015. A collection of his short stories will also be published by Saga in 2015.

Elizabeth Bear was born on the same day as Frodo and Bilbo Baggins, but in a different year. When coupled with a tendency to read the dictionary for fun as a child, this led her inevitably to penury, intransigence, and the writing of speculative fiction. She is the Hugo, Sturgeon, and Campbell Award-winning author of almost a hundred short stories and more than twenty-five novels, the most recent of which is *Steles of the Sky,* from Tor Books. Her dog lives in Massachusetts; her partner, writer Scott Lynch, lives in Wisconsin. She spends a lot of time on planes.

Ben H. Winters is the winner of the Edgar Award for his novel *The Last Policeman,* which was also an Amazon.com Best Book of 2012. The sequel, *Countdown City,* won the Philip K. Dick Award; the third volume in the trilogy is *World of Trouble.* Other works of fiction include the middle-grade novel *The Secret Life of Ms. Finkleman,* an Edgar Award nominee, and the parody novel *Sense and Sensibility and Sea Monsters,* a *New York Times* bestseller. Ben has written extensively for the stage and is a past fellow of the Dramatists Guild. His journalism has appeared in *Slate, The Nation, The Chicago Reader,* and many other publications. He lives in Indianapolis, Indiana and at BenHWinters.com.

Megan Arkenberg lives and writes in California. Her short stories have appeared in *Lightspeed, Asimov's, Strange Horizons,* and dozens of other places. She procrastinates by editing the fantasy e-zine *Mirror Dance.*

Jonathan Maberry is a *New York Times* bestselling author, multiple Bram Stoker Award winner, and comic book writer. He's the author of many novels including *Code Zero, Fire & Ash, The Nightsiders, Dead of Night,* and *Rot & Ruin*; and the editor of the *V-Wars* shared-world anthologies. His nonfiction books on topics ranging from martial arts to zombie pop-culture. Jonathan writes *V-Wars* and *Rot & Ruin* for IDW Comics, and *Bad Blood* for Dark Horse, as well as multiple projects for Marvel. Since 1978 he has sold more than 1200 magazine feature articles, 3000 columns, two plays, greeting cards, song lyrics, poetry, and textbooks. Jonathan continues to teach the celebrated Experimental Writing for Teens class, which he created. He founded the Writers Coffeehouse and co-founded The Liars Club; and is a frequent speaker at schools and libraries, as well as a keynote speaker and guest of honor at major writers and genre conferences. He lives in Del Mar, California. Find him online at jonathanmaberry.com.

Jake Kerr began writing short fiction in 2010 after fifteen years as a music and radio industry columnist and journalist. His first published story, "The Old Equations," appeared in *Lightspeed* and went on to be named a finalist for the Nebula Award and the Theodore Sturgeon Memorial Award. He has subsequently been published in *Fireside Magazine, Escape Pod,* and the *Unidentified Funny Objects* anthology of humorous SF. A graduate of Kenyon College with degrees in English and Psychology, Kerr studied under writer-in-residence Ursula K. Le Guin and Peruvian playwright Alonso Alegria. He lives in Dallas, Texas, with his wife and three daughters.

Daniel H. Wilson is a *New York Times* bestselling author. He earned a Ph.D. in robotics from Carnegie Mellon University in Pittsburgh, where he also received master's degrees in robotics and in machine learning. He has published over a dozen scientific papers, holds four patents, and has written eight books. Wilson has written for *Popular Science, Wired,* and *Discover,* as well as online venues such as *MSNBC.com, Gizmodo, Lightspeed,* and *Tor.com.* In 2008, Wilson hosted *The Works,* a television series on The History Channel that uncovered the science behind everyday stuff. His books include *How to Survive a Robot Uprising, A Boy and His Bot, Amped, Robopocalypse* (the film adaptation of which is slated to be directed by Steven Spielberg), and *Robogenesis.* He is also co-editor, with John Joseph Adams, of the anthologies *Robot Uprisings* and *Press Start to Play* (forthcoming). He lives and writes in Portland, Oregon. Find him on Twitter @danielwilsonPDX and at danielhwilson.com.

Will McIntosh is a Hugo award winner and Nebula finalist whose debut novel, *Soft Apocalypse,* was a finalist for a Locus Award, the John W. Campbell Memorial Award, and the Compton Crook Award. His latest novel is *Defenders* (May, 2014; Orbit Books), an alien apocalypse novel with a twist. It has been optioned by Warner Brothers for a feature film. Along with four novels, he has published dozens of short stories in venues such as *Lightspeed, Asimov's* (where he won the 2010 Reader's Award), and *The Year's Best Science Fiction & Fantasy.* Will was a psychology professor for two decades before turning to writing full-time. He lives in Williamsburg with his wife and their five year-old twins.

Jamie Ford is the great grandson of Nevada mining pioneer Min Chung, who emigrated from Kaiping, China, to San Francisco in 1865, where he adopted the western name "Ford," thus confusing countless generations. His debut novel, *Hotel on the Corner of Bitter and Sweet,* spent two years on the *New York Times* bestseller list and went on to win the 2010 Asian/Pacific American Award for Literature. His work has been translated into 32 languages. Jamie is still holding out for Klingon (because that's when you know you've made it). He can be found at www.jamieford.com blogging about his new book, *Songs of Willow Frost,* and also on Twitter @jamieford.

Desirina Boskovich's short fiction has been published in *Clarkesworld, Lightspeed, Nightmare, Kaleidotrope, Triptych Tales, PodCastle,* and more, along with anthologies such as *The Way of the Wizard* and *Aliens: Recent Encounters.* Her nonfiction pieces on music, literature, and culture have appeared in *Lightspeed, Weird Fiction Review, Wonderbook,* and *The Steampunk Bible.* She is also the editor of *It Came From the North: An Anthology of Finnish Speculative Fiction* (Cheeky Frawg, 2013), and together with Jeff VanderMeer, co-author of *The Steampunk User's Manual,* forthcoming in October of 2014. Find her online at desirinaboskovich.com.

Hugh Howey is the author of the acclaimed post-apocalyptic novel *Wool,* which became a sudden success in 2011. Originally self-published as a series of novelettes, the *Wool* omnibus is frequently the #1 bestselling book on Amazon.com and is a *New York Times* and *USA TODAY* bestseller. The book was also optioned for film by Ridley Scott, and is now available in print from major publishers all over the world. Hugh's other books include *Shift, Dust, Sand,* the Molly Fyde series, *The Hurricane, Half Way Home, The*

Plagiarist, and *I, Zombie.* Hugh lives in Jupiter, Florida with his wife Amber and his dog Bella. Find him on Twitter @hughhowey.

Robin Wasserman is the author of *The Waking Dark, The Book of Blood and Shadow,* the Cold Awakening Trilogy, *Hacking Harvard,* and the Seven Deadly Sins series, which was adapted into a popular television miniseries. Her essays and short fiction have appeared in several anthologies as well as *The Atlantic* and *The New York Times.* A former children's book editor, she is on the faculty of the low-residency MFA program at Southern New Hampshire University. She lives and writes (and frequently procrastinates) in Brooklyn, New York. Find out more about her at robinwasserman.com or follow her on Twitter @robinwasserman.

ACKNOWLEDGMENTS

Agents: John thanks his agent Seth Fishman, who supported this experiment and provided feedback and counsel whenever he needed it, and also to his former agent Joe Monti (now a book editor who he plans to sell lots of anthologies to), who was very enthusiastic about this idea when it first occurred to him, and encouraged John to pursue his idea to self-publish it. Hugh likewise thanks his agent Kristin Nelson for all of her support and for constantly playing out his leash.

Art/Design: Thanks to Julian Aguilar Faylona for providing wonderful cover art for all three volumes of The Apocalypse Triptych, and to Jason Gurley for adding in all the most excellent design elements that took the artwork from being mere images and transformed them into *books*. These volumes would not be the same without them.

Proofreaders: Thanks to Rachael Jones, Kevin McNeil, Tiffany Hughes, Mandy M. Earles, and Andy Sima.

Narrators/Producers: Thanks to Jack Kincaid for producing (and narrating some of) the audiobook version of this anthology, and to narrators Tina Connolly, Anaea Lay, Kate Baker, Mur Lafferty, Rajan Khanna, Lex Wilson, Norm Sherman, Folly Blaine, Scott Sigler, Stefan Rudnicki, Windy Bowlsby, and Stephanie Grossman for lending their vocal talents to the production.

Family: John sends thanks to his wife, Christie, his mom, Marianne, and his sister, Becky, for all their love and support, and their endless enthusiasm for all his new projects. He also wanted to thank his sister-in-law Kate and stepdaughter Grace who had to listen to him blab incessantly about this project as it was coming together, ruining many a dinner. Hugh thanks his wife Amber, who co-edits this wonderful life they have together. His chapters would be boring and lonely without her.

Readers: Thanks to all the readers and reviewers of this anthology, and also all the readers and reviewers who loved Hugh's novels and John's other anthologies, making it possible for this book to happen in the first place.

Writers: And last, but certainly not least: a big thanks to all of the authors who appear in this anthology. It has been an honor and a privilege. As fans, we look forward to whatever you come up with next.

ABOUT THE EDITORS

John Joseph Adams is the series editor of *Best American Science Fiction & Fantasy,* published by Houghton Mifflin Harcourt. He is also the bestselling editor of many other anthologies, such as *The Mad Scientist's Guide to World Domination, Armored, Brave New Worlds, Wastelands,* and *The Living Dead.* Called "the reigning king of the anthology world" by Barnes & Noble, John is a winner of the Hugo Award (for which he has been nominated eight times) and is a six-time World Fantasy Award finalist. John is also the editor and publisher of the digital magazines *Lightspeed* and *Nightmare,* and is a producer for Wired.com's *The Geek's Guide to the Galaxy* podcast. Find him on Twitter @johnjosephadams.

Hugh Howey is the author of the acclaimed post-apocalyptic novel *Wool,* which became a sudden success in 2011. Originally self-published as a series of novelettes, the *Wool* omnibus is frequently the #1 bestselling book on Amazon.com and is a *New York Times* and *USA TODAY* bestseller. The book was also optioned for film by Ridley Scott, and is now available in print from major publishers all over the world. Hugh's other books include *Shift, Dust, Sand,* the Molly Fyde series, *The Hurricane, Half Way Home, The Plagiarist,* and *I, Zombie.* Hugh lives in Jupiter, Florida with his wife Amber and his dog Bella. Find him on Twitter @hughhowey.

COPYRIGHT ACKNOWLEDGMENTS

Cover Art by Julian Aguilar Faylona.

Cover Design by Jason Gurley.

Interior Layout by Hugh Howey.

THE APOCALYPSE TRIPTYCH

We hope you've enjoyed reading *The End is Now* If so, be sure to keep an eye out for *The End Has Come* (March 2015), volume three of THE APOCALYPSE TRIPTYCH. Also, if you missed it, be sure to check out volume one, *The End is Now.*

Famine. Death. War. Pestilence. These are the harbingers of the biblical apocalypse, of the End of the World. In science fiction, the end is triggered by less figurative means: nuclear holocaust, biological warfare/pandemic, ecological disaster, or cosmological cataclysm.

But before any catastrophe, there are people who see it coming. During, there are heroes who fight against it. And after, there are the survivors who persevere and try to rebuild. THE APOCALYPSE TRIPTYCH will tell their stories.

Edited by acclaimed anthologist John Joseph Adams and bestselling author Hugh Howey, THE APOCALYPSE TRIPTYCH is a series of three anthologies of apocalyptic fiction. *The End is Nigh* focuses on life before the apocalypse. *The End is Now* turns its attention to life during the apocalypse. And *The End Has Come* focuses on life after the apocalypse.

Visit johnjosephadams.com/apocalypse-triptych to learn more about THE APOCALYPSE TRIPTYCH or to read interviews with the authors. You can also sign up for our newsletter if you would like to be reminded when the other volumes of the TRIPTYCH become available.

ALSO EDITED BY JOHN JOSEPH ADAMS

If you enjoyed this book, you might also enjoy these other anthologies and magazines edited by John Joseph Adams:

- *Armored*
- *Best American Science Fiction & Fantasy* [Forthcoming, Oct. 2015]
- *Brave New Worlds*
- *By Blood We Live*
- *Dead Man's Hand*
- *The End is Nigh*
- *The End Has Come* [Forthcoming, Mar. 2015]
- *Epic: Legends Of Fantasy*
- *Federations*
- *The Improbable Adventures Of Sherlock Holmes*
- *HELP FUND MY ROBOT ARMY!!! and Other Improbable Crowdfunding Projects*
- *Lightspeed Magazine*
- *The Living Dead*
- *The Living Dead 2*
- *The Mad Scientist's Guide To World Domination*
- *Nightmare Magazine*
- *Operation Arcana* [Forthcoming, Apr. 2015]
- *Other Worlds Than These*
- *Oz Reimagined*
- *Press Start to Play* [Forthcoming, Fall 2015]
- *Robot Uprisings*
- *Seeds of Change*
- *Under the Moons of Mars*
- *Wastelands*
- *Wastelands 2* [Forthcoming, Feb. 2015]
- *The Way Of The Wizard*

Visit johnjosephadams.com to learn more about all of the above. Each project also has a mini-site devoted to it specifically, where you'll find free fiction, interviews, and more.

45205345R00202

Made in the USA
Charleston, SC
14 August 2015